Havoc instantly pivoted and executed the *Kinteki-seashi-geri,* kicking his right instep into the Brother's testicles. The blow made Sheba grunt and drop to his knees. Havoc whipped his left hand down, his index finger extended, delivering an *Ippon-nukite* strike to the temple, his bony finger the equivalent of a blackjack.

Stunned, Sheba sagged, his hands holding his groin.

"Hold this," Havoc said, and tossed the M.A.C. 10 to Jaguarundi, who deftly caught the weapon.

"Hit the scumbag again!" Gloria urged.

Havoc reached down, gripped the Brother's chin, and snapped the man's head up so he could glare into Sheba's eyes. "No more games, asshole. I'm tired of being treated like a lightweight. This is the Force you're dealing with, you stupid son of a bitch. If you don't give me the answers I need, Jag here will do to you what he did to your friend."

DEAD ZONE STRIKE

"Look out! Here they come!"

Blade glanced at Raphaela, saw her shocked countenance fixed in the direction of the farmhouse, and spun, bringing the M60 barrel up, his gaze darting high into the air over the building. He anticipated the attack would come from a lofty elevation.

The Warrior was wrong.

Voicing twin high-pitched shrieks, a pair of inky figures swept down toward the Force, coming in low, barely skimming the roof of the farmhouse, their outlines streamlined because their wings were tucked flush with their backs for greater diving speed, their arms extended in a power dive.

Raphaela got off a dozen rounds at point-blank range, her shots smacking into the creature on the right. But whether her bullets had no effect, or whether the thing was simply moving too rapidly to be stopped by anything, an instant later she felt awesomely strong hands clamp onto her upper arms and the creature began to surge upward bearing her with it.

BLADE
DOUBLE

L.A. STRIKE/
DEAD ZONE STRIKE
DAVID ROBBINS

LEISURE BOOKS L **NEW YORK CITY**

Dedicated to...
Judy, Joshua, and Shane.
And to all the people I
inconvenienced by moving to Oregon
and back again.
Now you know what my missus puts up with
each and every day.

A LEISURE BOOK®

June 1993

Published by

Dorchester Publishing Co., Inc.
276 Fifth Avenue
New York, NY 10001

L.A. STRIKE

PROLOGUE

Damn it all!

Not now!

The shakes hit her when she was only three steps from her goal, a really bad case, and her entire body began to quiver. The need was so overwhelming that she almost cried out. If she did, she was dead. So she bit down on her lower lip, her teeth drawing blood, and clasped her arms tight about her middle. You can do it! she told herself, and leaned against the brick wall for support.

Just hang in there.

The sounds of traffic wafted up to her on the sluggish, grimy air. She inadvertently glanced down at the ground 15 stories below and almost lost her balance. Dizzy, she closed her green eyes and waited patiently for the shakes to subside.

Somewhere in the distance a siren wailed.

Gradually the trembling subsided and the gnawing hunger abated, but she knew it was only a matter of time before the need struck her again. Move, bitch! she goaded herself, and hurried to the platform at the top of the fire escape, a four-foot-wide strip of metal that swayed when she stepped upon it. Don't let me fall! She mentally pleaded. Not when she was so close.

The sooty gray door stood before her.

Her nervousness mounting, she gripped the doorknob and licked her dry lips. Please let it be open! She twisted, and to her delight the knob turned and the door creaked open an inch. Cautious now, she peeked inside at the plush corridor with its thick red carpet, ornate overhead lights, and paintings adorning the green walls.

One thing was for sure.

The bastard knew how to live in style.

She listened for sounds, dreading that he might be in his condo and not at his club, but the floor was quiet. Her skin prickling, she eased inside and hastened to his door, the only one on the right-hand side, located in the middle of the corridor. Directly across from his brown door was the red door. She looked at the red paint and barely suppressed an impulse to spit on the panel. The sight filled her with so many memories, and very few of them were pleasant.

How could she have been so stupid?

Annoyed, she shook her head to clear her thoughts, her long black hair swaying. Now was not the time for self-re-crimination. Now was the time to get her ass in gear before he returned with his spooky bodyguard.

The thought of the Claw made a tingle run along her spine.

She reached into the right front pocket on her faded jeans and withdrew the key. Her fingers quaking, she fumbled at the lock, and finally succeeded in inserting the silver key into the narrow slit. Two seconds later she stood in the condominium, her heart beating in her chest like a scared rabbit's. Swiping the bastard's key that time and having a duplicate made had been the smartest thing she'd ever done! She thought of the bodyguard again and almost changed her mind. Don't think of the Claw! Think about the crack, all that wonderful, sweet crack she would receive for her trouble!

She moved through the spacious, opulent living room to the bedroom on the east side of the condo. The door was ajar, and in three strides she was standing next to the huge water bed and glaring at the mirrors attached to all four walls. In her mind's eye she saw herself on the water bed, naked, receptive to his amorous advances, and she remembered how she'd felt when he'd traced his fingers from her breasts to her thighs. She'd given him the most precious gift she had: herself. And the prick had tossed her aside for a younger bitch!

Revenge would be hers!

Her resolve cemented, she stepped to the center mirror on the north wall, inserted her bright red fingernails into the crack between that mirror and the next one, and pulled. With deceptive ease the mirror swung out on its hidden hinges, and there, exposed to her view, was the large black safe.

She was so close!

Her left hand slid into her left pocket and extracted the slip of paper containing the combination. Taking a deep breath to compose herself, she began whirling the dial in the proper sequence: first right to one, then left to nine, then right to 50, then left to seven, and right to four.

Bingo.

A loud click signified her success, and she wrenched on the thick handle, tugging the heavy door open to reveal the three shelves. Lying on the second shelf were the four familiar blue notebooks, and she scooped them into her arms with all the passion of an ardent lover.

She had them!

Elated, she scrutinized the safe's contents, consisting of piles of miscellaneous papers, drug paraphernalia including two syringes and three baggies, and a stack of bills. She grabbed the money, her green eyes widening, estimating there must be four grand in her left hand.

Why not?

Beaming, she quickly closed the safe and swung the mirror into position, then hastened to the living room. She was half-way across when she heard the voices and her blood seemed to transform into ice.

They were back already!

For an instant she panicked, wondering if she had removed

the key and locked the door, until she touched the back of her right hand to her pocket and felt the hard outline of the key. Terrified, she darted to the sofa positioned near the south wall and moved to one side. If she recalled correctly, there was a narrow space between the back of the sofa and the wall. She knelt and squeezed into the space, scraping her shoulders, and wiggled behind the sofa, accidentally pushing it outward several inches in the process.

Would they notice?

She held her breath, scared to her core, the notebooks and the wad of money clutched to her chest. Thank goodness the bastard always left the lights on! He couldn't stand a darkened room, even when he slept. Just one of his many quirks.

The front door opened and the voices became clear.

"—know what to do when the stupid son of a bitch gets here."

The melodious voice brought a rush of memories: the night they met at Edith's party; the first time they made love; the first time they did drugs together; her eventual addiction and his loss of interest. She frowned and held herself perfectly still, thinking of the bodyguard. The Claw possessed senses like a cat.

"I know what to do, Boss."

That was him! The professional killer! She recognized his deep, raspy voice immediately. How many times had she seen his tinted shades turned in her direction and wondered what he was thinking about? Dozens, at least.

"Good. Then let's attend to business and get back to the China White. Gloria is waiting for me."

Gloria! That scuzzy buffarilla! Gloria was the one who'd stolen him away!

"I don't much like the idea of wasting the sucker here," the Claw mentioned.

Waste? Did he say *waste*? She couldn't believe her ears. What the hell was going on? She heard muffled footsteps, and then the creak of leather as someone sat down in a nearby chair. The bastard liked leather furniture. All four chairs and the sofa sported the best Corinthian leather money could buy.

"Can I get you anything, Boss?" asked the Claw.

"Not now. I need my mind sharp. Curtis won't go down easy."

The name rang a bell. Curtis Jenson, the dealer who handled a twelve-block territory on the southwest side of Los Angeles. She had talked with him a number of times, and even danced with him once at the annual New Year's bash the bastard threw for all of his people. Not poor Curtis!

"If you don't mind my asking, Boss, why are we doing him here? Why not take him down on the street?"

"My dear Claw, Curtis is no fool. He's one of the smartest dealers in my organization. We're snuffing him here because this is the last place he'd expect any grief. He'll figure I'd have to be stone crazy to kill him in my own condo."

"How do you want it done?"

"Any way you want. Just don't get any blood on the carpet. I can't abide a messy room."

The Claw laughed, a short bark devoid of genuine mirth. "Your wish is my command, Boss."

"Why don't you fix a boilermaker for Curtis? He'll be here any minute."

"One boilermaker coming up."

She heard the Claw walk to the mahogany bar situated along the north wall, and then the tinkle of a bottle pouring alcohol into a glass.

"I don't know what I would do without you, Claw. How many years have we been together now?"

"Eight, Boss."

"Eight years. We've come a long way in such a relatively short time, haven't we?"

"Sure have."

"My brains and your brawn. Together, they're an unbeatable combination."

The Claw did not respond for almost 30 seconds. When he did, his tone had softened somewhat. "Spiff tells me that Fayanne has been asking about you."

An electric shock seemed to course through her body at the mention of her name, and she came close to bumping her head against the wall in her excitement and giving herself away.

"So?"

"Just figured you should know, Boss. She told Spiff that she's trying to kick the stuff. Says she wants you to take her back."

Fayanne's eyes widened in astonishment. If she didn't know any better, she'd swear that the Claw actually cared about her. But the prospect was too ludicrous to contemplate. Or was it? The Claw had always treated her with courtesy and respect, but he treated all women in the same manner.

A snort came from the man seated in the chair. "You have a soft spot for that broad, don't you?"

"She never treated me like a freak," the Claw said.

"Fayanne is a bimbo. Always has been, always will be. I wouldn't take her back if she was the last piece of fluff on the planet. She's a loser, Claw. And I don't associate with losers."

Is that right? Fayanne wanted to yell. Well, she was going to teach that arrogant, egotistical lowlife a lesson he'd never forget.

A loud knock interrupted the conversation.

Fayanne listened as the Claw went to the door and welcomed their guest, in reality their unsuspecting victim.

"Hey, Claw. What's happening?" Curtis Jenson said as he entered. "And there's my main man himself."

"Curtis," the man in the chair said flatly.

"Mr. Bad. I'm here like you wanted."

"Decent of you to come," Mr. Bad responded, his tone dripping honey. "Why don't you pull up a chair?"

"Don't mind if I do," Curtis said.

The fool! Fayanne wanted to jump up and warn him, but to do so would be equivalent to committing suicide and she wasn't ready to go that route. Yet.

"So why the special invite?" Curtis inquired.

"We have an important issue to discuss," Mr. Bad answered, then paused. "Before we begin, would you care for a drink?"

"I'm not thirsty."

"How unfortunate. Claw has prepared a boilermaker for you."

The bodyguard must have been standing behind Curtis's chair with the drink in hand, because he promptly said, "Here you go, Curtis. Enjoy."

"Thanks, Claw."

Fayanne heard a sipping noise.

"Ahhh. That hit the spot," Curtis said. "Now then, what's this all about?"

"Loyalty," Mr. Bad stated.

"Somebody in the Brothers has turned over?"

"So I've heard."

"Who?"

"You."

A prolonged silence followed the accusation, and Fayanne tensed in expectation of a gunshot or the sound of the Claw doing what he did best.

"Are you jiving me?"

"Would I kid about such a grave matter?" Mr. Bad rejoined.

"Where did you ever hear such bullshit?"

"My source is irrelevant. The accusation is not without merit, or I wouldn't give it the slightest attention. Someone has reported to me that you are being disloyal. The claim is that you're about to turn, to go over to the Barons."

Curtis laughed.

To Fayanne, relying entirely upon her hearing to interpret the conversation, the laugh rang false. Oh, Curtis! she thought. How could you be so dumb?

"Someone has been feeding you a line, Mr. Bad," Curtis declared.

"Have they?"

"Sure. I wouldn't be so stupid as to try and double-cross you. I know what would happen if I did."

"You underrate yourself," Mr. Bad said. "You're extremely intelligent, Curtis. Too intelligent, in fact. You've taken a long look at the grass on the other side of the fence, and you've decided it's greener over there."

"No way, man. I'd never cross you," Curtis reiterated, and expelled a long breath. "Is it getting hot in here or what?"

"I'll have Claw open a window in a moment," Mr. Bad offered. "First, though, to business. Where were you one week ago at eleven P.M.?"

"I'd have to think about it. I might have been with one of the whores on Sepulveda Boulevard."

"Or you might have been with Owsley."

Curtis Jenson must have stood up because Mr. Bad suddenly snapped, "Sit down."

"Whoever told you I was with Owsley is a liar!"

"*Sit down,* Curtis." The words were razor sharp and as heavy as steel.

"I'm sitting," Curtis said. "Man is it ever hot in here."

"After all I've done for you, Curtis, I'm disappointed you would see fit to betray me. I was the one who took you in off the streets and trained you, who made you one of my trusted dealers. And now you've thrown that trust back in my face."

"I didn't, Haywood. Really I didn't."

Fayanne flinched. The bastard hated for anyone to use his real name. For some reason he despised the name his parents had bestowed on him at birth: Haywood Keif.

"Then perhaps you can explain this?" Mr. Bad inquired.

Curtis gasped.

"I'd pity you, Curtis, but I find it hard to pity someone who has demonstrated such stupidity."

"Who took this?" Curtis queried, his tone strained.

"Irrelevant."

No one said a word for a full ten seconds, and then Fayanne heard the sounds of a scuffle, a loud gasp, and the thud of a heavy blow. She figured that Curtis must be dead, but she was wrong.

"Another asinine move, Curtis. You persist in compounding your stupidity. Evidently I was mistaken about you. You're not as intelligent as I believed."

"Why am I so hot?"

"Ask Claw."

Instead, Curtis blurted out, "Oh, God! Oh, God! I don't want to die!"

"Very few ever do."

A spasm of violent coughing racked Curtis and he groaned. "You put something in my drink!"

"Arsenic," the bodyguard answered gruffly, then added, as if in explanation, "The boss doesn't want any blood on the rug."

"I'm getting out of here!" Curtis declared.

Again Fayanne listened to a scuffle, only this time the tussle was punctuated by a sharp snap, the unmistakable crack of a man's neck being neatly broken.

"Thank you," Mr. Bad said.

"Anytime, Boss."

"Let's get to the club. This pathetic wretch has delayed me long enough already. Have Dexter and Sheba dispose of the body."

"Will do."

The front door opened and closed, and silence abruptly descended on the condo.

Fayanne waited a minute to be sure they were gone, then squeezed out from behind the sofa and stood. She nearly dropped the notebooks and the money when she saw Curtis Jenson on the floor near a chair, his eyes wide, his head bent at an unnatural angle, his olive suit rumpled, the healthy sheen of his brown cheeks belying his current state. "Oh, Curtis," she said softly, then dashed to the door. A quick check verified the elevator at the north end of the corridor was almost to the ground floor. She slipped out, closed and locked the door, then ran to the fire escape.

Uh-oh.

Now what should she do?

When she had visited the condo earlier in the day and found the bastard wasn't home, she had stood in the corridor with tears trickling down her face, still unable to believe that he had cut off her credit, and she had happened to gaze at the fire escape door. Then and there the idea had occurred to her, how to get her revenge and all the crack she'd ever need, and she had impulsively unbolted the fire escape door and departed using the elevator. Now that her plan had succeeded, she was stuck with the dilemma of how to bolt the door behind her.

There was no way.

Shrugging, Fayanne decided bolting the door didn't matter. She giggled at her triumph and fled into the muggy August night.

CHAPTER ONE

The chatter of automatic gunfire attained a veritable crescendo, causing a flock of starlings roosting in an oak tree a short distance away to take flight in alarm.

His huge arms folded casually across his massive chest, the giant nodded in satisfaction as he watched the six members of the Freedom Force practice their marksmanship with M-16's. Even when he was standing at ease, the giant's bulging muscles emanated an aura of raw, unbridled power and vitality. A comma of dark hair hung above his gray eyes, which narrowed as he concentrated his attention on one of the six. A black leather vest, green fatigue pants, and combat boots served as his attire. Strapped around his slim waist were his ever-present Bowies, twin knives that had saved his life on many an occasion.

The blasting of the M-16's temporarily abated as the shooters expended the rounds in their magazines and went about inserting new ones.

His mouth curling downward, the giant saw the man on the right fumble and drop a new magazine. He uncurled his arms and snapped, "Concentrate, Lobo! You're not concentrating!"

"Says you, sucker," responded the stocky black man. He wore a black leather jacket, a blue shirt, jeans, and knee-high black boots. Only five feet, seven inches in height, he weighed in the vicinity of 190 pounds, none of it flab. He preferred to style his hair in an Afro that crowned his handsome features.

"Cease firing!" the giant commanded, and strode over to the line. "What did you say?"

"Who, me?" Lobo replied innocently.

"Do you think we're playing games here?"

"Oh, boy. Here we go again," Lobo muttered. "Here comes the speech."

The giant straightened and placed his brawny hands on the hilts of his Bowies. "I'm real tired of having you give me grief all the time, Lobo."

"Who's giving you grief, Blade? All I did was drop the lousy magazine and you jump on my case."

"If that happened in a combat situation, you'd be dead," Blade noted. "Why do you think we spend so many hours on the firing range? Why do we spend so much time on the mats practicing our hand-to-hand fighting skills? For the fun of it?"

Lobo sighed and glanced at his five companions, all of whom were regarding him critically. He faced the giant. "Look bro. We've been all through this a dozen times already. I've got the routine down."

"Do you?"

"Where's the beef, anyway? I pull my fair share of the load around here."

Blade stepped up to Lobo. "The beef, Lobo, is that I don't intend to lose another member of this team. The reason I make you practice and practice is so you'll stay alive when we're out in the field."

"I know that—" Lobo began.

"Then try harder," Blade stated sternly, "or I'll send you back to Clan with a note explaining that you have the mentality of a six-year-old."

"You wouldn't."

"Try me."

"Chill out, dude. I gave Zahner my word I'd stick this out for the whole year. If you send me back early, I won't be able to hold my head up in public."

"That's your problem," Blade said. "Shape up or I'm shipping you out."

Lobo shook his head and muttered, "Boy, what a grump."

"I heard that."

"Figures."

Turning, Blade studied the other members of the Force, wondering how many would still be alive when their tour of duty was over.

The Freedom Force had been the brainchild of one of the leaders of the seven factions comprising the Freedom Federation, factions that had banded together under a mutual defense treaty simply to ensure their self-preservation. Scattered pockets of civilization on an insane world, the Federation was devoted to maintaining a vestige of order and culture when all about them lay ruins, abandoned cities and towns, and the savage Outlands where the survival of the fittest was the unwritten law of the land, a legacy of humankind's ultimate folly.

World War Three.

One hundred and six years ago the nuclear Armageddon had finally been launched, proving that mankind's implied claim to possessing intelligence and wisdom had been a sham. By the time the war ended, after all the nuclear missiles and chemical weapons had been employed, after millions upon millions had perished and the environment had been poisoned with radioactive and chemical-warfare toxins, after the fire storms had subsided and the fallout had descended, the once-fertile and lush planet Earth had been reduced to a polluted caricature of its former self.

In the country once known as the United States of America, there were dozens of organized outposts, city-states, and territories under the rule of one group or another, but by far the major portion of the countryside consisted of the violent Outlands. The Russians controlled a belt of land in the East, the mob had taken over Nevada, the Mormons dominated Utah, the autocratic Technics governed Chicago, and there were many, many other groups, most of them intent on conquering even more land.

World War Three had not taught humanity a thing, or so it often seemed to Blade.

The Federation consisted of the more progressive, stable factions. First there was the Free State of California, the only state to retain its administrative integrity after the war. The governor of California, a man named Melnick, had first proposed forming an elite tactical force to deal with threats to the Federation as they arose. Melnick had even gone so far as to have a special facility constructed north of Los Angeles, slightly northwest of Pyramid Lake, where the Force stayed and trained while awaiting assignments. The headquarters compound consisted of 12 acres surrounded by an electrified fence topped with barbed wire and guarded by regular California Army troops. Of all the Federation factions, California perhaps most resembled the prewar society. Of its large cities, only San Diego and San Bernadino were obliterated during the war. San Francisco and Los Angeles were both intact, although both were considerably run-down in comparison to their former greatness.

The next Federation faction that came the closest to resembling prewar America was the Civilized Zone. Composed of the former states of Kansas, Nebraska, Colorado, Wyoming, Oklahoma, and New Mexico and the northern half of Texas and part of Arizona, the Civilized Zone had been created after the U.S. government evacuated hundreds of thousands of its citizens in the Midwest during the war. The region had been subsequently renamed by the dictator who took over after the U.S. government collapsed.

Of the five remaining factions, none were similar to the prewar culture.

A legion of horsemen known as the Cavalry now controlled the Dakota Territory, a throwback to the rugged pioneer days of early America where most of the men wore buckskins and the women were as hardy as their mates.

The former state of Montana was in the hands of the Flathead Indians, who had finally cast off the white man's yoke and reclaimed their land and their ancient heritage.

Another former state, Minnesota, was the home of three Federation factions. First, dwelling in a subterranean city in the north-central part of the state, were the reclusive Moles. Their city, dubbed the Mound, had started as an underground fallout shelter and gradually expanded over the years. Of all the Federation members, they were the least liked, in large measure due to their leader, a domineering egotist named Wolfe.

Also located in Minnesota, in the northwest quarter, were the refugees from the Twin Cities who had resettled in the small town of Halma and designated themselves as the Clan. They had deliberately moved to Halma to be close to the last Federation faction, the one that had helped them relocate, the one regarded as a sort of Utopia by all the rest.

The Family.

Started by a wealthy survivalist who'd constructed a 30-acre retreat on the outskirts of the former Lake Bronson State Park, the Family now numbered over one hundred members. Although they were the smallest faction in terms of sheer numbers, they wielded the most influence in Federation councils. It was the idealistic survivalist, Kurt Carpenter, who had called his followers the Family and christened their compound the Home. He'd instituted an educational and social system designed to ensure every Family member could enjoy freedom in its truest definition. The current Family Leader, Plato, was known far and wide for his sagacity and kindness.

Not all Family members enjoyed such a reputation, especially the 18 who had been chosen to be Warriors, the guardians of the Home who were responsible for defending the Family from any and all dangers. Renowned for their lethal skills, the Warriors were as celebrated in their own right as the Spartans of antiquity, and justly so. One of their number, the head Warrior, was undoubtedly the most famous man on the continent, a man who had traveled from the baking deserts of Mexico to the frigid tundra of Alaska on his missions against enemies of the Family and the Federation, a man whose reputation as a fighter was unmatched in the postwar era, whose twin Bowies were a symbol of hope for all those oppressed by despots. The man that the Russians, the mob, the Technics, and others knew by the name he had selected at his Naming ceremony on his sixteenth birthday, the man future historians would credit with being largely responsible for salvaging the world from its dark age of despair and helping to guide it toward the ultimate destiny of light and life.

Blade.

Totally unconscious of his status—although aware of the many stories told about him around many a campfire, he tended to shrug them off as idle gossip—the young giant now stood studying the Force recruits, each one a volunteer from a Federation faction, who had agreed to serve for a term of one year.

Lobo, whose given name was Leo Wood, hailed from the Clan. During his youthful days in the Twin Cities, he had been a member of a gang known as the Porns. He was street smart and as tough as they came, and his favorite weapon was a NATO, a spring-loaded knife with a four-inch blade that retracted snugly into a slot at the top of the handle.

Standing next to Lobo was Sparrow Hawk, a Flathead Indian. Five-feet-six, he had shoulder-length black hair and brown eyes. His beaded buckskins fit snugly over his powerful physique, except across his wide shoulders and down his thick arms, where the garment had deliberately been designed loosely to allow for unrestricted movement. Slung over his back by means of a brown leather cord tied to the shaft near the steel head and near the blunt end was his prized spear, a weapon that had once belonged to his father. From the left side of his handcrafted leather belt hung a large hunting knife in a beaded sheath.

After Sparrow Hawk came the volunteer from the Cavalry, a lean man dressed in a black frock coat, black pants, and black boots, all of which served to accent his white shirt.

On his head he wore a wide brimmed black hat, and on his right hip was a holstered revolver, a pearl-handled, nickel-plated Smith and Wesson Model 586 Distinguished Combat Magnum. His eyes were hazel, his hair brown. Don Madsen was his name, although everyone simply referred to him as "Dock." Prior to joining the Force, Doc had made his living as a gambler in Rapid City and other frontier towns in the Dakota Territory, where he had also acquired a feared reputation as a consummate gunman.

The fourth person on the firing line was different from all the rest by virtue of her sex and her inexperience. Raphaela was her name, and she had been sent by the Moles to be their recruit. Her still pale complexion from a life spent almost always underground contrasted sharply with her flaming red hair and her striking green eyes. At five feet eight in height, she presented the perfect picture of frailty even though she wore regulation green combat fatiques.

As did the tall man standing to her left, a broad-shouldered professional military officer endowed with the physique of a classical Greek wrestler. He stood six feet, two inches tall, and wore his blond hair clipped short in the military fashion. On his lapels were the insignia signifying his rank of captain. Mike Havoc was his name, and he was the older brother of another Force recruit who had died ten months ago. His clear blue eyes regarded the Warrior rather coldly.

Last in line, and without a doubt the most unique volunteer in the bunch, was the hybrid. Part feline, part human, the creature known as Jaguarundi had been created in a test tube by a genetic engineer. Before the war, genetic engineering had been all the rage among the scientific elite as they vied with one another to see who could produce the most superior mutation. Jaguarundi's creator, a deranged genius who had gone by the title of the Doktor, had bred an entire corps of hybrid assassins by editing the genetic instructions encoded in the chemical structure of molecules of DNA. During the course of the war between the Federation and the Doktor, which had culminated in the first Federation victory, a number of the geneticist's mutants had rebelled against their maker.

Jaguarundi had been one of them. Thin in the extreme, six feet in height, he wore just a black loincloth because clothes made him uncomfortable. And well they should, what with the coat of short reddish fur that covered his entire body from the crown of his oval head to the tips of his toes. His ears were rounded, and his slanted green eyes had vertical slits for pupils. His teeth, revealed whenever he smiled or snarled, were tapered and razor sharp. He had settled in the Civilized Zone after the Doktor was defeated, and he had volunteered to represent them on the Force.

"So are we done with the firing range for the day, or what?" Lobo queried.

The question brought Blade out of his reverie. He sighed and nodded. "For today, but we'll practice marksmanship again tomorrow and I'll expect you to be able to change magazines without dropping one."

Doc Madsen laughed.

"You find something funny, turkey?" Lobo demanded argumentatively.

"What if I do?" Doc responded, his right hand straying close to his Magnum.

"Just askin'," Lobo said.

Blade frowned. The new recruits still had a long way to go before they would mesh as a team. They had survived their first conflict, against the Mexican bandit who had called himself El Diablo, by the proverbial seat of their pants. Although all of them except for Raphaela had prior combat experience to varying degrees, as a unit they were green. He needed to cram as much training into them as he could before they were sent out on another mission.

Jaguarundi cocked his head to one side, then announced, "We have company coming." His voice was low and raspy.

A moment later Blade heard the sound too, the growl of a jeep engine approaching from the south, from the direction of the gate affording access to the Force headquarters. He turned and spied a vehicle, a roofless Army jeep containing two men, the driver and one other.

General Miles Gallagher.

"Oh, goody!" Lobo said, his gaze on the general. "This must be our lucky day. He probably has another assignment for us. I wonder who will get the chance to try and blow us away this time?"

CHAPTER TWO

The jeep sped past the three concrete bunkers situated in the center of the compound and continued to the north, to the firing range only one hundred yards farther. The driver braked, and out hopped a bulldog of a man in an immaculate dress uniform, his crew-cut brown hair and brown eyes adding to the pugnacious impression he conveyed. Initially, Gallagher had opposed the formation of the Freedom Force. An admitted isolationist, he had never believed that California needed to join the Federation. Although he'd objected strenuously, he had agreed to serve as the official liaison between Governor Melnick and the Force. Now he gave them all a brief scan and focused on the Warrior. "How are they shaping up?"

"Hello to you too, General," Blade said.

"Sorry, but you should know by now I'm not one for formality. I believe in getting straight to the point. It's my military background."

"To what do we owe this honor?"

Gallagher reached behind him and pulled a folded newspaper from his right back pocket. "Have you seen the story yet?" He unfolded the copy, the latest of the *L.A. Times.*

Blade nodded. "I read it this morning. Yes, I saw the article about our mission in Mexico." He didn't bother to mention that he still wasn't reconciled to the practice of having each Force assignment detailed in the press. Governor Melnick had instituted the practice, claiming the news reports would help present the Force in a positive image to the people of California, many of whom had entertained the same reservations about the unit as General Gallagher. Blade suspected that the stories had a twofold purpose. They boosted the Force, but they also indirectly boosted the political career of Governor Melnick. During his schooling years at the Home he had learned about the devious politicians who had frequently manipulated those they purportedly represented during the decades preceding World War Three. Not much had changed, he reflected wryly.

"What did you think of the piece?"

"It was well written," Blade said. "The style reminded me a lot of Athena's."

Gallagher did a double take. "It did?"

"Yeah," Blade stated, thinking of Athena Morris, the previous female member of the team, a journalist who had joined so she could report their escapades firsthand and advance her career in the bargain. To the amazement of everyone, including her, she had fallen in love with the former recruit from the Civilized Zone, another hybrid called Grizzly. Tragically, while under heavy sedation for an injury she sustained in Alaska, she had tried to open a hospital window and fallen to her death.

"I don't see any resemblance in style," the general said.

Blade shrugged. "What does it matter? I'm sure Governor Melnick was pleased with the article."

Gallagher's eyes narrowed. "As a matter of fact, he was."

Captain Havoc cleared his throat. "Do you have another assignment for us, sir?"

"Not this time," Gallagher said, and replaced the newspaper in his pocket. He smiled broadly. "I think you'll be happy to hear why I came."

"Bet me," Lobo mumbled.

Governor Melnick came up with the idea," Gallagher said. "In return for your outstanding performance against El Diablo, and as a token of his appreciation for bringing an end to the raids that plagued southern California for decades, he thought you would all like to have a three-day pass so you can relax in Los Angeles."

"What?" Blade said, straightening.

"You heard me," Gallagher declared, still beaming.

"Wow!" Raphaela exclaimed. "I've never been to a big city before."

"I have," Doc said. "They're nothing to rave about."

"Why not?" Raphaela asked.

"There's no varmint like a human varmint," the gunfighter commented. "And cities are full of folks who would slit your throat for the hell of it."

"Really?"

"Don't listen to the dude, Raphaela," Lobo said. "Hicks don't know squat about city life."

"And I suppose you do?" Doc queried testily.

"I was raised in a city, ding-dong. Remember?"

"You were raised in a rat-infested dung heap. No one lived in the Twin Cities except for low-life gang members. You don't know the first thing about city life."

"Oh, yeah?" Lobo countered, wishing he could come up with a wittier retort.

"That's enough," Blade directed, his gaze on the general. "We appreciate the offer, but we'll have to decline."

"Say *what*?" Lobo said.

"What's wrong with a few days off, sir?" Captain Havoc queried.

"I would like to see the City of Angels," Sparrow Hawk chimed in.

"Forget it," Blade told them.

"May I ask why?" General Gallagher interjected.

"We don't have the time to spare," Blade answered. "You persuaded me to take off for Mexico before I felt the team was ready, and we nearly lost our lives. We need to spend every spare moment in training for when the next assignment comes along."

"Surely you can spare three days," Gallagher prompted.

"No."

"Is that your final word on the subject?"

"Yes."

Lobo snorted. "What a bummer! I was lookin' forward to gettin' me some fresh wool."

Raphaela glanced at the Clansman. "What's fresh wool?"

"Uhhhh—fancy threads," Lobo blurted out.

"Threads?"

"Clothes, Momma. Clothes."

"Oh," Raphaela said. "I could use some new clothes. Will you help me find the right wool?"

Jaguarundi abruptly coughed and turned his back to them, his slim shoulders bouncing up and down.

"What's wrong, brother?" Sparrow asked.

"Listen up," Blade directed sternly. "We're not spending three days in L.A. End of discussion."

General Gallagher pursed his lips and folded his hands behind his back. "There's nothing I could say to change your mind?"

"We need to train," Blade reiterated.

"What if I gave you my word that I won't present another assignment to you for, oh, a month?"

"You can present all the assignments you want. *I* have the final say on whether we accept a mission," Blade reminded him.

"Then why not take advantage of the governor's generous offer?" Gallagher asked. "He's even arranged rooms for all of you at one of the finest hotels in the city. All the food and drinks will be on him."

"I've done died and gone to heaven!" Lobo exclaimed.

"Come on, Blade," the general continued. "Why deprive your people of an honor they deserve? Since you can reject any assignment anyway, simply refuse to go on one until you're satisfied the unit is ready. If Governor Melnick complains, remind him that taking three days off was his idea.''

"Please, Blade," Raphaela urged.

"Yeah, give us a break, Jack," Lobo remarked.

"I wouldn't mind getting in some gambling," Doc noted.

The Warrior scrutinized his team for several seconds, his resolve beginning to falter. They had performed well, despite their inexperience. If he denied them their reward, their resentment might create problems later on. At the very least, it would interfere with their training. He looked at the hybrid. "What about you, Jag?"

The mutant swung around. "I'll pass."

"You don't want to go to Los Angeles?"

"I don't like big cities. The humans are always gawking at me."

"Wonder why," Lobo said.

"How would you like your face ripped off?" Jag snapped.

"Oh, yeah? Who's going to do it?"

Jag held his hands out, displaying his inch-long fingernails. "Three guesses."

"You and what army?" Lobo demanded.

"Children! Enough!" Blade barked, glowering and taking a stride toward them.

"Who are you callin' a child?" Lobo inquired resentfully.

The Warrior walked over to the Clansman, towering above the feisty recruit. "*You.*"

Lobo gulped, then smiled. "Well, if you're going to put it that way . . ."

"What's your decision?" General Gallagher inquired.

Blade glanced at Captain Havoc. "Since we're temporarily a democracy, what's your vote?"

The officer shrugged. "Why not? I know L.A. really well, and I wouldn't mind showing the others around."

Annoyed, the Warrior looked at General Gallagher. For someone who had once despised the very idea of a Federation strike team, Gallagher of late was bending over backwards to be nice. Why? Blade wondered. The change of attitude was wonderful, and he knew he shouldn't look a gift horse in the mouth, as it were, but he felt vaguely uneasy about the general's change of heart. Somehow, it rang false.

"So do they get to go or not?" Gallagher queried.

Frowning, Blade responded, "They can go."

Lobo vented a hearty cheer. "Look out, foxes, here comes the lovin' machine!"

"The yo-yo, you mean," Jag quipped.

"Hey, kitty, I'll have you know the ladies can't get enough of me. They fall all over themselves to get a piece of my action."

"Don't call me kitty."

Raphaela stepped forward. "What about you, Blade? Will you be coming to Los Angeles with us?"

"No, thanks."

"Why not?"

"I've been there."

"What's that mean?" Raphaela asked.

"Nothing," Blade said, and nodded at the middle bunker, his HQ. "I've got a lot of paperwork to do. You go and have fun."

"But it won't be the same without you along," Raphaela said sadly, and glanced at the hybrid. "You too, Jag. We're a team, right? We should do things together."

"You have no idea what you're asking," Jaguarundi replied. "If I go to L.A. there will be trouble. Mark my words."

Raphaela looked from the giant to the mutation. "Please. I know this might sound silly, but I've never belonged to a group like this before. Heck, I've never had anyone. My parents died when I was six, and I've pretty much been on my own ever since."

"Who raised you?" Blade inquired, curious about her background. She had been remarkably tight-lipped concerning her past so far, although she had revealed enough to indicate that she had joined the Force to escape an unpleasant situation at the Mound rather than out of any patriotic sense of loyalty to the Federation.

"My aunt," Raphaela divulged, her features downcast. "But she always treated me as an outsider, not one of her own."

"Some folks ain't got no smarts," Lobo remarked.

"And you should know," Jag said.

Raphaela hardly appeared to notice their comments. Her eyes on the ground, she said, "I've never known what it would be like to be part of a regular family. This is the closest I've come, and having all of you as my friends is the greatest thing that's happened to me in ages."

Blade observed an extraordinary reaction in the four men and the hybrid. All five, even the loquacious Clansman, had been hardened by the violence and everyday rigors of the postwar era, yet each one of them seemed to soften as they listened to the Molewoman. Her words struck a responsive chord in the core of their being, and their hearts went out to the innocent waif who so transparently had gotten herself in over her head.

"We're going to be together for a whole year," Raphaela was saying. "We should try and make the most of it. And since our lives will depend on one another, we should stick together as much as possible. We should be just like a family." She paused, gazing at the hybrid. "So, please, Jag. Come with us. For me?"

"But . . ."

"For me?"

Jaguarundi closed his eyes and rubbed his right palm on his sloping forehead. "I know I'll live to regret this, but okay. For you, Raphaela, I'll go to Los Angeles."

"Terrific!" Raphaela declared, and clapped her hands together in delight. "Now what about you, Blade?"

The Warrior shook his head. "Sorry. I can't."

"Please."

"Maybe next time."

"Fuddy-duddy!" Lobo said.

"Well, if Blade can't go, he can't go," General Gallagher stated, his tone implying the giant must be stuck-up. "If the rest of you can be ready by six, I'll have two jeeps here to pick you up."

"We'll be ready, sir," Captain Havoc said.

Gallagher nodded and went to turn, then paused. "Oh. Before I forget. There are two conditions."

Blade glanced at the officer. "Conditions?"

"Yes. We want your people to enjoy themselves, but we also don't want them to attract undue attention. So everyone will wear civvies. No uniforms."

"No problem," Lobo said. "Havoc and the skirt are the only ones who like to wear those overstarched rags anyway."

"Skirt?" Raphaela retorted.

"What's the second condition?" Blade inquired.

"No weapons."

Five seconds of total silence ensued, and then several of the team all tried to talk at the same time.

"No weapons!" Lobo declared. "You must be off your rocker, Miles, baby. There ain't no way old Leo is waltzin' into L.A. without packin' a weapon."

"I don't go anywhere without my Magnum," Doc mentioned.

"And I am not accustomed to traveling unarmed," Sparrow said.

General Gallagher smiled and extended his arms, palms up. "Sorry folks. But there are laws in Los Angeles against carrying weapons. Any weapons. Decades ago, right up to the war, the city had the worst gang problem in the country. The gang members were killing each other off right and left, even mowing down citizens with automatic fire. Laws were passed to stem the tide of weapons," he explained, then added, "Not that such laws ever did any good. Criminals never obtain their weapons through legal channels because the arms are too easy to trace."

"I don't like the idea," Lobo said.

"Take it or leave it. Sorry, but the L.A. authorities take a dim view of anyone caught with a gun or knife. Even though you'll have your special I.D. cards, you could still get in hot water."

"What I.D. cards?" Blade questioned.

"Didn't I tell you? Governor Melnick has authorized the issuance of identification cards specifically for the Force so you can readily identify yourselves anywhere in California, or in any other Federation territory, for that matter."

"Whose idea was this?" the Warrior queried.

"Governor Melnick's."

"An I.D. card is no substitute for an automatic," Lobo noted.

"Those are the terms," General Gallagher said, looking at the Clansman. "What will it be, Lobo?"

"I guess I'll survive three days without my NATO," the Clansman replied reluctantly.

"Doc?"

"I reckon I can do it this once."

"Sparrow?"

"If I want to go with my brothers, I must comply."

"Excellent," Gallagher said, nodding. "Remember, the jeeps will be here for you at six."

"You're all dismissed," Blade instructed them. "Relax and enjoy the rest of the day."

The Force members began to move toward the bunker to the east, their barracks building.

"You know, I'm beginning to like this outfit," Lobo cracked. "All work and no play dampens the old wick, if you get my drift."

Doc Madsen stared at the Clansman. "Don't you *ever* quit flapping your gums?"

Lobo shook his head. "I'm not the shy, quiet type, dude. If I'm walkin', I'm talkin'."

"Tell me about it."

"There is one more thing," General Gallagher said to the Warrior.

"What?"

"I'd like to have a few words with Captain Havoc, if I may?"

"It's a free world," Blade said stiffly, and departed.

General Gallagher smirked and called out, "Captain, might I speak with you a moment?"

The junior officer, already 15 feet away, halted and turned, the corners of his mouth drooping. "Certainly, sir. What about?"

Gallagher motioned for Havoc to approach. "Over here, where we'll have some privacy."

Exhibiting the utmost reluctance, Captain Havoc slung his

M-16 over his right shoulder and walked to within a yard of the general. He stood at attention.

"You can relax, Captain."

"As you wish, sir," Havoc said, and assumed the at-ease stance, his hands clasped in the small of his back.

"Do I detect a note of hostility in your voice?"

"Of course not, sir."

"Then what's bothering you?"

"Nothing, sir."

Gallagher gazed at the retreating Force members to ensure none of them were within hearing range, then growled in a harsh, low inflection, "Don't bullshit me, mister! I know you better than that. Something is eating at you and I want to know what it is right now."

Havoc locked his flinty eyes on the general's. "If you must know, sir, I'm having serious second thoughts."

"About taking revenge for your brother's death?"

"Yes, sir."

"I see," Gallagher said, surprised by the news but not permitting his feelings to show. He pursed his lips and pretended to be interested in a plane flying along the southern horizon, stalling, searching for the right words, not wanting to antagonize Havoc and ruin his best chance ever of permanently disbanding the Force. "I was under the impression you were upset over Jimmy's needless death."

"I was," Havoc admitted, his memory taking him back to that day in October of last year when he had received word of his younger brother's demise. He'd been shocked to discover that Jimmy had perished on an unauthorized mission in Canada, that the Force had been on its way from Alaska to Los Angeles when the pilot of their jet received a distress call on a civilian frequency and Blade decided to land and investigate, even though Canada wasn't even a member of the Freedom Federation.

The Warrior's decision, Havoc believed, had indirectly caused his brother to perish. Sergeant James Havoc, the best noncom in the California military, had given his life to save one of his companions, but the sacrifice seemed senseless in light of the fact that Jimmy's death would never have occurred if Blade had stuck to procedure. If only the Force had flown to L.A. as originally scheduled, Mike Havoc reasoned, his brother would still be alive.

Bitter over the loss, Havoc had listened eagerly to General Gallagher when his superior officer outlined a scheme to get even with Blade for the Warrior's incompetence by gathering proof that the giant was unfit for command. Havoc had agreed to be the general's inside man, to report any slipups Blade made. But on their first mission against El Diablo, despite his resentment and his desire to force the Warrior to step down in disgrace, Havoc had found himself admiring Blade's leadership skills and fearless conduct. Most of all, Havoc had been genuinely moved by the sincere concern Blade displayed for every member of the team. Many times since he had asked himself the same question: Was this a man who would thoughtlessly cause another's death? And the answer that came back every time was a resounding No. He suddenly realized the general was speaking.

"I take it you intend to let Blade off the hook?"

"I don't know."

"You sound confused to me."

"I guess I am, sir."

"Why? Because the last assignment went off without a major hitch? So what? Sooner or later the unit will be out in the field again where Blade's irresponsibility will likely prove fatal for more of you. Five Force members have died already."

"I know."

General Gallagher reached out and placed his right hand on Havoc's arm. "If you don't help me close the Force down, the next death will be on your shoulders."

Havoc's lips compressed into a thin line.

"Listen to me, Captain," Gallagher said. "I've set up the three-day pass to guarantee we accomplish our goal—"

"You set it up, sir?" Havoc interrupted. "I thought you told us Governor Melnick did."

Gallagher grinned craftily. "I persuaded him to do it."

"But why?"

"Don't you see? The new recruits are undisciplined and rowdy. By sending them into L.A. before Blade has finished their training, when they're still thinking more of themselves than the unit as a whole, I'm banking on their inexperience and baser motives to get them into a world of trouble. Let's say, for the sake of argument, that they become drunk and tear up a night spot. How will that look in the press? What will the good people of California think of their precious elite team when some of its members overstep the bounds of propriety? How will Governor Melnick respond when his constituents start clamoring for Blade's head on a platter?" General Gallagher paused and laughed bitterly. "That's where you come in."

"I don't understand, sir. What can I do?"

"It should be obvious. Go along with them. Do whatever you can to turn their three-day pass into a nightmare. Get some of them drunk. Start fights. Let the fools hang themselves. Lobo and Madsen should be easy to dupe considering the short fuse they each possess," Gallagher said. "And there's always Raphaela."

Captain Havoc stood as still as stone, his eyes acquiring a steely gleam the general failed to perceive. "Raphaela, sir?"

"Sure. The bimbo is a babe in the woods. Get her drunk and who knows how big a fool she'll make of herself."

Havoc did not respond.

General Gallagher turned to leave. "Don't let me down, Captain. I'm counting on you.' He smiled, but his next words belied his friendly visage. "And remember, I don't take failure lightly."

CHAPTER THREE

"Check this out! This is my kind of city!"

"How would you know? You've never been to a city like L.A. before."

Lobo, seated across from the California Army trooper who was driving the lead jeep, twisted and looked at Doc Madsen. The Cavalryman sat directly behind him, and next to Madsen was Sparrow Hawk. Havoc, Jag, and Raphaela were riding in the second jeep. "What's with you today, Doc?" Lobo asked. "You've been getting on my case all day."

His eyes on the bright lights of the metropolis through which they were winding, Doc shrugged absently. "Have I?"

"You're mistaken, Lobo," Sparrow added.

"I am?"

The Flathead nodded. "You always seem to think that someone is picking on you, even when they're not. My people have a word for someone like you."

"What is it?" Lobo inquired, expecting to hear one of Sparrow Hawk's sixteen-syllable Indian words.

"Crazy."

Both Sparrow and Doc burst into laughter.

Sighing, Lobo turned to the driver. "See what I mean? They're always pickin' on me. Pay no attention to them. They're just jealous of my good looks and keen mind."

The trooper, a young corporal who was concentrating on the task of threading through the traffic on the Harbor Freeway, did not even bother to take his gaze from the highway. "If you say so, sir."

"Don't you believe me?"

"I don't *know* you, sir."

"What is this? A conspiracy?" Lobo asked, then added, "And stop callin' me sir."

"I can't, sir."

"Why the hell not?"

"General Gallagher's orders. Every soldier assigned to the Force facility, whether they're guards or drivers or whatever, must always address a Force member as sir," the trooper explained. "Unless, of course, it's the redhead. Her we call ma'am."

"Yeah, I guess old dog-face is a stickler for going by the book, huh?" Lobo commented.

"You don't know the half of it, sir. He's the strictest officer in California."

"Then I'm glad I'm workin' under Blade and not Gallagher," Lobo said. "Blade is a pushover."

The trooper finally glanced at the Clansman. "*Blade,* sir?"

"Yep. I've got him wrapped around my baby pinky."

"The guy who heads the Force? That Blade?"

Lobo nodded.

"The guy who is as big as a frigging mountain and who has more muscles than anyone else on the whole damn planet? *That* Blade?"

"That's the guy. Don't let this get around, soldier, but he's not as tough as he's cracked up to be. Actually, he's a bundle of insecurity."

"I've heard he's the toughest son of a bitch ever to come down the pike," the trooper said, then added, "Sir."

Lobo snorted and shook his head. "Who's been feedin' you that line of bull? Blade's squeeze? I'm tellin' you the guy is a pussycat. He can't make a decision without help. And who do you think he turns to when he's in a bind?''

"Let me guess. You, sir?"

"Damn straight. I'm the real brains behind this outfit."

The trooper shifted and cast a quick glance over his right shoulder at Sparrow Hawk. "I see what you mean, sir."

Riding in the second jeep two hundred feet to the rear, Raphaela stared through the dusty windshield at the first vehicle, then turned to her companions. "What's the matter with you guys? You've hardly spoken a word since we left."

Captain Havoc, seated behind the driver, shrugged. "Sorry. I guess I'm just not in a talkative mood."

Raphaela looked at Jaguarundi. "And what's your excuse?"

The hybrid sat slumped in the seat, his hands folded between his legs. The wind stirred his fur as he gazed morosely at her. "I should never have come along."

"Are you going to start that again?"

"You have no idea what we're in for, Raphaela. Some humans simply do not like mutations. My presence could cause all of you unnecessary aggravation."

"You let us worry about that. I'm happy you came, and I'll bet Mike is too. Aren't you, Captain Havoc?"

The officer appeared not to hear the remark. He was staring off into the distance, his mouth shut tight, his eyes almost blank. Tonight he wore a blue shirt and gray trousers.

"Mike? Did you hear me?"

Havoc blinked three times and faced the Molewoman. "Sorry, Raphaela. What did you say?"

"I said I'm happy Jag came along, and I bet you are also."

"Why wouldn't I be?"

"I should have stayed behind with Blade," Jag stated. "We're in for trouble. I can feel it in my bones."

"You're being silly," Raphaela assured him.

"Am I? You wouldn't say that if you could walk in my footsteps for a day. *You've* never been the target of hatred and bigotry. *You've* never known what it's like to have someone try to kick your face in or put a bullet in your brain simply because you happen to be different. Even in the Civilized Zone, where the people are accustomed to having hybrids in their midst, I still encountered mindless prejudice. Children would stop and stare and point at me. Women would go out of their way to avoid passing me on the street. But the men were the worst. If I were to tell you every insult I've heard, you'd blush for a month.''

Raphaela saw the torment etching his countenance and felt a twinge of guilt at convincing him to join them. ''You're among friends now. We won't let anyone give you grief.''

''What will you do? Beat the crud out of every jerk who looks at me crosswise?''

''Not me,'' Raphaela said, smiling reassuringly. ''Captain Havoc is our martial-arts expert. He holds a black belt in karate, so we'll let him beat the crud out of the jerks.''

Jag smiled, despite his misgivings. ''You'll have your work cut out for you, Havoc,'' he said to the officer.

''What?'' Havoc replied. Once again he had been gazing into the darkness.

''What's with you, buck-o?'' Jag queried. ''You're not all here tonight.''

''I have a lot on my mind.''

''Anything we can help you with?''

Havoc looked at the hybrid for several seconds, his brow furrowed, before responding. ''No, but thanks.''

''We're like a family now,'' Raphaela mentioned. ''If you have a problem, we'll help out. Any problem. You can always confide in us.''

Jag, who sensed that the officer was intensely upset about something, saw the most peculiar expression distort Havoc's features, a strange commingling of melancholy and—what? Anger? At whom? Havoc abruptly swung to the left so they couldn't see his face.

''Thanks, Raphaela.''

To change the subject, Jag leaned toward the driver. ''How much farther?''

''Not far at all, sir,'' the trooper dutifully answered. ''We'll be at the Bayside Regency in a few minutes.''

''What a nice name,'' Raphaela said. ''It sounds elegant.''

"It is, ma'am," the trooper confirmed. "You'll be staying at the best hotel in Los Angeles. The Bayside Regency was built about ten years before the war right at the edge of the Royal Palms State Beach. I've never been inside, but I hear the carpet is four inches thick and there's a gold chandelier in the lobby. Real classy joint. They're sparing no expense for you, I can tell you that."

"Wow!" Raphaela stated in amazement. "Governor Melnick and General Gallagher sure are terrific to arrange all this for us."

Jag detected movement out of the corner of his left eye, and he glanced over to see Captain Havoc staring at the Molewoman in undisguised fury. But no sooner did Jag notice than Havoc again swung away. Perplexed, Jag resolved to keep a watchful eye on the officer.

"General Gallagher is a peach," Havoc muttered.

"You've known him for a long time, haven't you?" Raphaela inquired.

"Too long."

"What?"

"Never mind."

Flashing red lights suddenly materialized up ahead. Police cars, an ambulance, and other official vehicles had blocked off the highway, creating a massive traffic jam. Passenger cars and trucks were backed up for hundreds of yards.

"Oh, great," the driver snapped. "Just what we need." He braked and pulled in behind the first jeep. "Looks like we'll be here a while."

"Do you think there was an accident?" Raphaela asked, craning her neck to glimpse the activity near the flashing lights.

"Could be, ma'am," the trooper said. "Who knows? It might be another of those gang shootings."

"Gang shootings?" Raphaela repeated quizzically.

"Yes, ma'am. The newspapers have been filled with the stories. There are two big drug gangs fighting for control of Los Angeles, and they've been killing each other off for over a month now. A lot of innocent bystanders have been killed too."

"Why would they shoot bystanders?"

The driver glanced at her. "Well, ma'am, when there's some idiot speeding down a street at sixty miles an hour and spraying lead all over the place, a lot of folks are liable to be hit."

"Why don't the police put a stop to the gang war?" Jag interjected.

"They try, sir, but there's not a whole hell of a lot they can do other than pick up the pieces. It's not as if the gang members go around advertising who they are, like they did in the old days."

"I don't follow you."

"Well, sir, most of what I'm about to tell you is ancient history, you understand, so I may not get all the facts straight, but before the war the gangs in L.A. would wear their colors to show which gang they belonged to," the soldier detailed.

"Their colors?" Raphaela said.

"Yes, ma'am. Sort of like their uniform. It might be a headband, a bandana, a jacket, or a vest, but it would always be whatever color the gang claimed as their own, or it would have the gang emblem on it."

"And they wore these . . . colors . . . right out in the open?" Raphaela inquired.

"Yes, ma'am, they used to. The gangs before the war had no fear of the law. Hell, in L.A. alone they outnumbered the police by twenty to one. So they paraded around wearing their colors, shooting one another, and dealing drugs. In the process they turned a lot of cities into war zones," the trooper said. "At least, that's what my history teacher in seventh grade taught us."

"And these gangs are still around?"

"Not the same gangs, ma'am. There was a big gang war shortly before World War Three. Two of the gangs, the Bloods and the Crips, came out on top. They wiped out almost all of the others, then went at it themselves. Neither side won, and the gang war weakened both of them. They were easy pickings when the Brothers and the Hollywood Barons came along."

"Who are they?" Raphaela questioned.

"The Brothers and the Hollywood Barons are the gangs that control L.A. today. They were just small gangs once, but they grew like hell after they rubbed out the remainder of the Bloods and the Crips," the trooper said. "Eventually, the Brothers and the Barons took over all of the city. The Brothers have the south side, the Barons the north. And now they're fighting to see which one will be the top dog."

"Do these Brothers and Barons have their own colors?"

"No, ma'am. They gave that up a long time ago. Now the gang members wear tattoos where no one can see them."

"What's a tattoo?" Raphaela queried.

"You don't know what a tattoo is, ma'am?"

"I'm a Mole, remember? We live in seclusion in the Mound. There are a lot of things I know nothing about."

"Well, ma'am, a tattoo is an indelible figure or maybe a mark that a tattooer puts on the body by sticking colored pigment under the skin."

"Sounds painful."

"I wouldn't know, ma'am. I've never had a tattoo put on me."

"What kind of tattoos do the Brothers and the Barons wear?"

"The Brothers wear a tattoo on their left thigh that shows two hands in an overhand shake, a soul grip I think they call it. The Barons wear a tattoo of a crossed dagger and a switch-blade under their right arm."

"So the police can't tell who they are unless they take off their clothes," Raphaela said.

"That's the general idea, ma'am."

"I never expected something like this," Raphaela remarked. "The Moles don't have a gang problem."

"You're lucky, ma'am. Do you have drugs at your Mound?"

"Nope. Not unless you count the natural drugs we use for healing purposes."

"There are all kinds of drugs available on the streets of Los Angeles, ma'am. Crack, bennies, acid, meth, coke, mescaline, smack, pot, you name it, the gangs have it. I have two small kids and I sure as hell hope they never become strung out on the stuff.''

Raphaela stared at the red lights and frowned. ''I never realized it before, but Los Angeles can be a dangerous place to live.''

''You've got that straight, ma'am.''

''I certainly hope I don't run into any of those horrible gang members.''

The soldier chuckled. ''I doubt you will, ma'am. There are a lot of decent people living in L.A. too. I didn't mean to get you upset. You don't have a thing to worry about.''

CHAPTER FOUR

Fayanne halted under a tree, the darkness enveloping her, and stared at the forbidding estate across the street. Her courage drained to almost nothing, and she clutched the paper bag containing the four blue notebooks to her chest and took a deep breath to steady her nerves.

Don't crap out now!

She licked her lips and scrutinized the massive wall enclosing the four-story mansion, the meticulously maintained yard, and the bright lamps set at 20-foot intervals between the huge front gate and the residence.

Arthur Owsley didn't believe in taking chances.

About to step from the curb, she froze when a match flared to life just inside the gate and a man lit a cigarette.

A guard.

Fayanne knew there would be guards. Lots of them. With the war in full swing, Owsley wasn't about to be careless. He had a reputation for being exceptionally cautious, more prudent, in any event, than Mr. Bad. But then, Owsley didn't have anyone like the Claw in his employ. None of the Hollywood Barons possessed a rep like the Claw's. For that matter, no one in the whole damn city was as universally feared as the Claw.

Muffled words arose behind the gate.

Girding herself, Fayanne strode boldly toward the estate, walking as casually as possible. It had taken her 24 hours to muster the spunk to actually deliver the goods. Here was her big chance to even the score and she wanted to relish every moment.

There were three guards stationed at the gate, and they spotted her instantly. One, a tall man in a dark blue suit, stepped up to the iron bars, the cigarette dangling from his thin, cruel lips, and regarded her with a mixture of curiosity and contempt.

"Hello," Fayanne greeted him as she halted a yard from the gate.

"Hello, yourself, foxy," the man replied, raking his eyes up and down her shapely form. "What can we do for you?"

"I'd like to see Mr. Owsley."

The request didn't seem to surprise the guard. "Uh-huh. Now why would a sweet young thing like you want to see the boss?"

"I have something for him."

Smirking, the man stared at a point between her legs and nodded. "I'll just bet you do."

Fayanne struggled to control her rising temper. "It's not what you think."

"Sure, lady," the guard responded sarcastically.

"Really, I have something important for Mr. Owsley."

He glanced at the other two guards and shook his head, then faced her. "Listen, sweet cheeks. We get broads showing up here all the time to see the boss. They all say it's important. And they're all here for the same reason. They all want to hit on the boss."

"But I don't want to hit on him. Honest," Fayanne said, her tone strained, suddenly frightened that her grand scheme might be frustrated by the moron on the other side of the gate.

The man studied her again, noting her faded green blouse and patched jeans, her worn brown shoes, the black purse suspended from her right shoulder, and the brown paper bag in her arms. "Then what do you want?"

"I need to talk to Mr. Owsley."

"Sorry. No."

"Please."

"Take a hike."

Fayanne's anger returned and she stamped her left foot. "Will you at least tell him I'm here?"

"The boss doesn't like to be disturbed unless it's for a good reason."

"Look. I don't know what I can do to convince you I'm here on serious business. Will you call somebody up at the house and have them tell Mr. Owsley that Fayanne Raymond is here? Fayanne Raymond. Got that?"

"Why does that name ring a bell?"

Fayanne stood as straight and proud as she could. "I used to be Mr. Bad's main squeeze."

Startled, the guard did a double take and took a closer scrutiny of her between the bars. "No lie?"

"No lie. And if you don't inform Mr. Oswley, and if he finds out later that I was here, he'll roast your balls over a fire."

"Don't move," the man said, starting toward the left-hand gate post. "And if you're lying to me, bitch, you'll live to regret it."

"I'm not lying."

The guard opened a small cabinet attached to the post and removed a telephone. He spoke into the mouthpiece, then apparently waited for directions from his superiors. A minute later he said a few words, nodded, and replaced the phone.

Fayanne's hopes surged.

"Okay, lady. You're going to get your wish," the man stated as he came back. "I'm to take you up to the house."

Fayanne smiled and clasped the paper bag even tighter. She'd done it! Easy street, here I come! she thought.

The guards promptly unlocked the gate and swung it open, and the tall man beckoned for her to follow him. They headed for the mansion while the other pair locked the gate once again.

"You'd better not be wasting Mr. Owsley's time," the man advised.

"Mister, I'm going to make his day."

The imposing mansion reeked of wealth and luxury. A burly Baron in a three-piece suit admitted them, then dismissed the guard and escorted Fayanne down a tastefully posh corridor to double oak doors at the very end. After rapping twice, he opened the right-hand door and motioned with his left arm. "Go on in."

Suddenly intensely nervous, Fayanne swallowed and moved tentatively past him into a spacious, elegant chamber occupied by four Barons. Three stood at various points in the room. The fourth sat behind a desk the size of a small car, his blue eyes watching her warily.

Arthur Owsley.

The current leader of the Hollywood Barons was an enormous man, as broad as he was tall, heavy but not fat, a great toad of a figure attired in an expensive ebony suit. A bald, round head perched on a squat neck, and his pale pate gleamed in the light as if it had been polished. His thick lips barely moved when he spoke, and yet his voice boomed across the chamber, a low, throaty sound rumbling from his barrel of a chest. "Good evening, Ms. Raymond. Have a seat." He nodded at one of the three chairs arranged in front of his desk.

Fayanne approached slowly, disturbed by the unblinking stare he fixed upon her. "Mr. Owsley," she said. "Thank you for seeing me."

One of the other Barons stepped over to her. "Hold it, sister. I've got to frisk you."

"I'm not packing," Fayanne responded.

Arthur Owsley leaned forward. "Just a formality, Ms. Raymond. I'm certain you understand after having lived with Haywood Keif for several years."

"Yeah, I understand," Fayanne said, extending her arms out, keeping the bag in her right hand. "Go ahead."

The Baron swiftly, expertly, ran his hands over every nook and cranny on her body, then straightened and looked at Owsley. "She's clean, boss." He faced her again. "What's in the bag?''

''A present for Mr. Oswley,'' Fayanne answered.

''Let me see it.''

Fayanne opened the bag so he could view the notebooks, and he stepped aside to permit her to take a seat.

''You have a present for me, Ms. Raymond?'' Owsley inquired, his eyes locking onto hers with an almost hypnotic effect.

''Yes, sir. And call me Fayanne, please.''

''Very well, Fayanne. You have some explaining to do. Although we have never met before, I recognized your name when the gate guard phoned the house. If my information is correct, you were Mr. Bad's lady for about three years. Correct?''

''Yes.''

''And he recently dumped you for Gloria Mundy.''

Fayanne's features clouded at the mention of the woman she hated most in the world. She frowned and looked up to find Owsley viewing her intently. ''You're very well informed.''

A slight smile creased those thick lips. ''A man in my position must stay abreast of the latest developments. For the right price, almost any information can be obtained.''

''How about the names and addresses of every Brother in the city?''

Owsley finally blinked, his brow knitting as he glanced from the woman to the bag and back again. ''That sort of information could not be obtained for any price.''

''Until now.''

''Do I understand you're here to make a deal?''

''You bet I am,'' Fayanne stated, expecting Owsley to grab the bag and inspect the contents. Instead, confusing her, he simply sat there.

''Most interesting. But anyone could offer me a list of names, claiming they're the roster of Brothers. Motives, Fayanne, speak louder than words. Why would you want to turn on Mr. Bad?''

''If you know about that bitch Mundy, you shouldn't have

to ask.''

Owsley actually smiled. "Revenge? A motive I can relate to very well." He paused and drummed the blunt fingers of his left hand on the desktop. "But you could also have another motive that would have a bearing on your credibility."

"I could?"

"Yes," Owsley said. "You're an addict, Fayanne."

The unexpected assertion caught her off guard. "You're even better informed than I thought."

"I've also heard that Mr. Bad has cut off your credit. No more crack for you unless you can come up with the bread. True?"

Fayanne nodded, amazed at the extent of his knowledge. Owsley's intelligence network of street people and low-level informants in the Brothers appeared to be more efficient than Mr. Bad's. "I know better than to try and hide anything from you, Mr. Owsley. Yeah, the son of a bitch cut off my credit. And after all we meant to each other."

Owsley scrutinized her closely. "For an addict with no source of income, you don't seem to be in need of a fix at the moment."

Fayanne grinned, thinking of the money she had taken from Mr. Bad's safe. "I came into some green recently."

"I see," Owsley said. "What's in the bag?"

"My present for you. Mr. Bad's books."

"His books?"

"He kept them in a safe in his condo. Once a month he'd take them out when the bookkeeper would come over and tally all the receipts and whatnot. Then he'd lock them up again. The bastard doesn't like to have them out of his reach. He doesn't trust anybody, except the Claw, of course."

"Of course." Owsley nodded at one of his men, who promptly brought the bag around the desk.

"You'll find everything you need in there to win your war with the Brothers," Fayanne predicted. "The names and addresses of every Brother, for starters."

Owsley removed the four notebooks and placed them on

the desk. "No one does something for nothing. What do you want in return for these books?"

"Well, I figured you'd be grateful."

"If these prove to be legitimate, I will indeed be grateful," Owsley assured her.

"They're legit, Mr. Owsley. I promise."

The head Baron spread one of the notebooks open and began reading the contents. "You still haven't told me what you want."

Fayanne cleared her throat and shifted in her chair. "Well, I was sort of hoping they'd be valuable."

"Again, if they're genuine, they're quite valuable."

Now that she was on the verge of accomplishing her goal, Fayanne abruptly felt uncomfortable and anxious, wondering if she had done the right thing after all.

"What do you want?" Owsley queried.

"I was sort of hoping you would set me up in style, you know? My own apartment somewhere, a real nice place, not like the dump I'm staying in now. And maybe a little money each month, just enough for me to get by."

Owsley looked at her. "And drugs?"

"Just a little crack now and then, whenever I'm in the need. Unlimited credit. You know," Fayanne said, then added in justification of her request, "It's a pretty fair deal, if you ask me. I'm handing you the Brothers on a silver platter. All I want is what's rightfully mine."

"I see," Owsley said, running his fingers across a page in the notebook. "I'll need to have these books checked by an expert, you understand."

"Sure. No problem."

"How did you happen to come by them?"

Fayanne laughed lightly, beginning to relax, confident of her success. "I pulled one over on that bastard. As you probably know, he keeps his main lady in the condo across from his. I was good enough to bed, but not good enough to live with," she stated spitefully.

"Keif never did have any class," Owsley agreed.

"You've got that straight. Anyway, whenever we were

in his bedroom, which was about every other night or so until he tired of me, I would always try to get a glimpse of the combination on his safe when he opened it.''

"Back up a bit. Mr. Bad has the safe in his bedroom?"

"Yep. Hidden behind one of his mirrors."

"And he would open this safe in your presence?"

"Every now and then, whenever he had money or drugs to stick in or take out.''

"He trusted you that much?"

"Not really," Fayanne admitted. "Most of the time he'd go into the safe when he thought I was asleep. But I fooled the prick!" She cackled. "I'd pretend to be asleep, then sneak a peek when he worked the combination. And every couple of months I'd get lucky and see one of the numbers clearly. After about two years I had the whole combination."

"Fascinating. But why were you trying to learn the combination when the two of you were still tight?"

Fayanne shrugged. "I don't know. I guess because I resented the fact he didn't trust me completely and wouldn't marry me like I wanted. And it was fun, you know?"

Owsley idly scratched his double chin, then nodded. "Yes, I believe I comprehend the situation fully."

"So do we have a deal?"

"First answer a question for me."

"Anything."

"What does Gloria Mundy look like?"

Surprised, Fayanne's eyes narrowed. What a strange question! What reason could he have for wanting to know about Mundy's appearance? Rather than rock the boat, she said, "The bitch is a redhead. She likes to wear classy threads. Gowns and such."

"What color are her eyes?"

"Her eyes?" Fayanne had to think for a second. "Green, I believe. Yeah. Definitely green."

"Thank you," Owsley said. "And now to the matter of these notebooks."

"Yes?" Fayanne said eagerly.

"When did you appropriate them?"

"Yesterday."

"Hmmmm," Owsley said. "So Mr. Bad has been aware of their absence for a whole day?"

"No," Fayanne replied. "Like I told you, he usually only takes the books out of the safe when his accountant enters all the receipts and stuff. Once a month, like clockwork, and the next time won't be for a couple of weeks yet."

"Perhaps he only *uses* the books once a month, but you just admitted that he goes into the safe every other night or so to deposit or take out drugs and money. Correct?"

"Yeah. But—" Fayanne began.

"Then don't insult my intelligence again," Owsley said sternly. "Do you think I was born yesterday? Mr. Bad is my worst enemy, but I'll be the first to admit he's no dummy. If he opens his safe to stash some dope, don't you think he's bound to notice a little thing like his notebooks being missing?"

"Yes," Fayanne admitted sheepishly. "But if you act fast, you can still catch the Brothers off guard."

"Perhaps. But if Mr. Bad has had twelve hours or more in which to warn them, my people will end up walking into a trap. No, I'm afraid that the time differential diminishes the value of the notebooks somewhat."

Forgetting herself, angered at the thought she might not receive as much as she had hoped, Fayanne leaned forward. "What the hell are you trying to pull, mister? A couple of minutes ago you were saying the notebooks are quite valuable."

"They are."

"Good," Fayanne said, relieved.

"But not as valuable as you hope."

"I can't believe this!" Fayanne snapped. "I risked my ass to bring those lousy books to you, and you're dumping on me!"

"My dear Ms. Raymond, had you given me fair warning the notebooks were going to be delivered, I would have arranged to meet you ten minutes after you made the snatch. That way my boys could have wiped out two-thirds of the

Brothers before those bastards knew what hit them.''

"You can still wipe them out," Fayanne stated.

"It is unlikely. The odds are that Mr. Bad has alerted his underlings by now and they will be waiting for the Barons to invade their turf."

"I've got an idea," Fayanne mentioned. "Why don't you turn the notebooks over to the police. Let the police finish them off."

"Out of the question."

"Why?" Fayanne wanted to know.

"Because the war is strictly between the Barons and the Brothers. Neither of us will involve outside parties, least of all the police."

"You're blowing a great opportunity," Fayanne commented.

Owsley's mouth compressed and he glared at her. "Don't presume to sit in judgment on me, bitch. Your minuscule mind can't possibly comprehend the factors I must take into consideration to reach a decision on a matter like this."

Afraid she had antagonized her sole hope of obtaining crack, Fayanne abruptly acquiesced. "Okay. I'm sorry. Don't get your gums in an uproar." She paused. "So what's the bottom line? Give it to me straight."

"I have no intention of setting you up for life in an apartment when you're perfectly capable of finding and paying for your own."

Fayanne slumped in her chair, dejected.

"Nor will I extend unlimited credit to you so you can indulge in an orgy of drug-taking. No one qualifies for unlimited credit."

Monumentally depressed, Fayanne stared at the floor. "No apartment. No drugs. What *do* I get? A pack of chewing gum?"

"Even if the Brothers have been forewarned, knowing all of their names is an advantage that will enable us to win this war in the end," Owsley said, folding his hands on the desk. "Therefore, I'm prepared to pay you a fair price for the notebooks and an added bonus in recognition of your service to the Barons.''

Fayanne perked up. ''How fair is fair?''

''I was thinking in the neighborhood of three hundred thousand dollars.''

For several seconds Fayanne simply sat there, stunned, speechless, her drug-benumbed mind in neutral. Finally she blinked several times and said in a whisper, ''Three hundred thousand dollars?''

''Correct. Do you agree that the figure is an equitable sum?''

''Mr. Owsley, you're the fairest man who ever lived.''

The leader of the Hollywood Barons smiled and nodded at one of his men. ''J.J. here will see to it that you receive the funds. Would you prefer cash or a certified check?''

''Cash,'' Fayanne blurted out. ''Definitely cash.''

Owsley nodded. ''Then that will be all.''

''Thank you, sir,'' Fayanne said, rising and backing toward the doors. ''Thank you, thank you, thank you.''

''Spend your riches wisely.''

''Oh, I will, Mr. Owsley. You don't have to worry about me none,'' Fayanne promised. She turned and exited as the Baron named J.J. held the door for her.

Arthur Owsley leaned back, watching her depart with a delighted grin creasing his countenance. He glanced at a nearby Baron. ''Ahhhh, the grand irony of life. Wouldn't you agree, Barney?''

''Boss?''

''To think that that miserable bitch has handed us victory on a silver platter!''

''She has?''

''Most assuredly.''

''Because now we know the names of the Brothers, huh?''

''Knowledge is only half the battle, Barney. It's how you use your knowledge that counts,'' Owsley philosophized. ''For instance, in this particular case we are going to use our knowledge to its maximum advantage.''

''How, Boss?''

''By announcing to the entire world that we have the

notebooks.''

"Huh?''

Owsley stared at his stocky lieutenant. "Give the word. I want every dealer in our organization to tell every client, every hooker, every snitch on the street that we've purchased Mr. Bad's books from Fayanne Raymond for three hundred thousand dollars.''

"Let me get this straight. You *want* everybody to know?''

"You'll never have to worry about someone accusing you of having a rapier wit,'' Owsley said dryly. "Yes, I want everybody to know.''

"But why, Boss?''

"Because once the rank and file in the Brothers discover we know their identities, they'll do some serious soul-searching. Many of them might decide to turn over, especially when they learn Mr. Bad's own ex-squeeze dumped on him.''

Barney digested the information for a minute. "But what good will it do if Mr. Bad has already warned them you have the books?''

"Hearing the news from their boss is one thing. Hearing the news bandied about on the street, with our people bragging to every mother's son about how we pulled a fast one on the Brothers, is bound to have an effect on their morale. This is the coup of the decade. The lower-rank Brothers will begin to wonder about Mr. Bad's leadership. They'll wonder if he can cut it any more. Combine the news of the books with the little surprise we have in store for Mr. Bad, and his days as head of the Brothers are numbered.''

"You're a genius, Boss,'' Barney said in appreciation.

Owsley nodded. "I know. Now start spreading the word.''

"Right away,'' Barney replied, and took several strides. A thought occurred to him and he halted and turned. "Say, Boss?''

"What is it *now*, Barney?''

"If we go spreading the news all over the street, then Mr. Bad will know who swiped his notebooks. That Raymond dame's life won't be worth a plugged nickel.''

A cackle erupted from Owsley's lips and his massive body shook and quivered. "I know," he declared. "Ain't life a bitch?"

CHAPTER FIVE

"**W**ow! Ain't this joint bitchin'?" Lobo asked in astonishment, gaping at the golden chandelier suspended 40 feet above the enormous lobby.

"It looks like the Taj Mahal," Captain Havoc commented.

Lobo glanced at the officer. "The who?"

"Never mind."

"Let's check in," Doc Madsen suggested.

The six Force members moved slowly from the entrance of the Bayside Regency toward the ornate front desk, drawing astounded stares from the patrons of the posh establishment.

"Why is everyone lookin' at us?" Lobo wondered.

"It must be my buckskins," Sparrow said. "I haven't seen one person wearing buckskins since we entered the city."

Doc reached up and tilted his wide-brimmed hat back on his head. "Beats me what the dickens they're gazing at. Some folks don't have any manners."

Jaguarundi, who was at the center of their small group, sighed. "It's me. I warned you this would happen. Most humans get all bent out of shape at the mere sight of a hybrid like me.''

They were passing a cluster of chairs where several expensively dressed men and women sat, gawking at the new arrivals. One lady, who weighed approximately 220 pounds, frowned and shook her head.

''What's your problem, fatso?'' Lobo demanded.

His remark caused the woman's mouth to go slack and she pressed her right hand to her bosom. ''Well, I never!''

''Don't come cryin' to me,'' Lobo responded. ''I wouldn't touch your fat buns with a ten-foot pole.''

The woman appeared about to have a conniption. Her mouth opened and closed repeatedly, resembling a fish out of water. ''You . . . you uncouth person!''

''Oh, yeah?'' Lobo retorted. ''I can be as couth as the next clown, sister.''

''Don't, Lobo,'' Raphaela said.

''Why not? The bimbo started it.''

''Please. We should be on our best behavior.''

''I *am* behavin' myself,'' the Clansman replied testily.

Raphaela smiled warmly at the heavyset woman, hoping to offset Lobo's crude comments with a little friendliness, but the woman only turned up her nose and averted her gaze. Oh, well. She'd tried. She looked down at her plain brown shirt and black pants, the only other set of clothes she owned besides her fatigues, and then at the beautiful dresses being worn by the clientele of the hotel, and felt self-conscious of her shabby apparel.

''Hey, Havoc?'' Lobo said as they neared the front desk.

''What is it?''

''What the hell does uncouth mean?''

The captain, who had roused himself from his moodiness in the jeep, regarded the Clansman for a moment. ''Do you ever pick your nose in public?''

''Sure. Doesn't everybody?''

''Then you're uncouth.''

''Oh. So it *ain't* an insult?''

A white-haired man in an immaculate black tuxedo watched them approach, the corners of his mouth curved downward, scrutinizing them with the air of a man inspecting a can of putrid garbage. "May I assist you people?" he asked scornfully.

"Damn straight, Jack," Lobo replied cheerily. "Where's our rooms?"

The man straightened and placed his neatly filed fingers on the top of the polished desk. "I beg your pardon?"

"Didn't you hear the man?" Doc queried. "We want our rooms."

"You people intend to stay *here*?"

Lobo snorted. "No. We just came by to ask your permission to jack off in your lobby."

"Lobo!" Raphaela stated sternly.

"This guy's a dork."

Captain Havoc stepped to the counter and smiled wanly. "Sorry about the Neanderthal. My name is Mike Havoc." He gestured at his companions. "We were sent by General Gallagher. I understand you have reservations for us."

"Havoc?" the desk clerk said, then did a double take. "*You* people are the Force?"

"That's us, chuckles," Lobo confirmed. "In the gorgeous, ever-lovin' flesh."

"Are you *sure* you're the Force?"

Doc Madsen leaned on the counter. "Was that a joke of some kind, mister?"

"No. No. Of course not," the man replied. "I've read about your exploits in the paper, but I never expected you to look . . . like . . . you do."

Lobo puffed out his chest. "Yeah. I know what you mean, dude. Wait until the babes get a load of this bod."

"What?"

"Ignore him," Havoc suggested. "What about our rooms?"

Clearing his throat, the desk clerk pivoted and extracted two keys from the cubbyholes behind the registration desk. "Rooms, sir? You have better than mere rooms. Both the Presidential Suite and the Ambassador Suite on the top floor have been reserved exclusively for all of you." He faced them and handed the keys to Havoc. "Each executive suite contains three separate bedrooms," he detailed, and smiled at Raphaela. "You will have all the privacy you require."

"Thank you," the Molewoman replied gratefully.

"Do you have any bags?" the desk clerk inquired.

"I have a paper bag I use for collecting herbs at our facility," Sparrow Hawk mentioned. "But I didn't bring it with me."

"No, sir. I meant do you have any luggage?"

"Lug what?" Lobo responded.

"No luggage," Havoc said.

For the first time the desk clerk appeared to notice Jaguarundi. "Is this . . . gentleman . . . with you?"

"He is," Havoc stated.

"Does he require any special facilities?"

"Like what, partner?" Doc rejoined.

The man studied the hybrid's fur and loincloth, then the mutant's feline features, his brow knit in perplexity. "The Bayside Regency prides itself on being able to satisfy the needs of every guest. Should we send out for some kitty litter?"

For a moment no one moved or spoke, and then Jaguarundi lunged, his tapered nails sweeping up, his mouth twisted in a snarl. "Kitty litter!"

Fortunately for the terrified desk clerk, Captain Havoc and Doc Madsen intervened, each man grabbing one of the hybrid's arms and holding tight.

"Let me at him!" Jag snarled, his indignation aroused, struggling to break free. "I'll rip him to shreds!"

"Calm down!" Havoc stated. "He didn't mean anything by it."

White as the shirt he wore, the man behind the desk had backed up against the cubbyholes, his left hand to his throat. "I'm sorry!" he blurted out. "I never intended to offend you."

"Come on, Jag," Doc urged, restraining the hybrid with difficulty. "Let it ride."

"Yeah, dude. Chill out," Lobo interjected. "How's this dummy supposed to know you've been house trained?"

Jag's enraged visage swung toward the Clansman. "*House trained!*" he bellowed, and lunged again, only this time at

Lobo, his nails coming within an inch of the Clansman's chest.

"Hey! What did I say?" Lobo snapped, retreating a good yard.

Captain Havoc glanced at the former gang member. "Nice going, rocks-for-brains."

"What the hell did I do?" Lobo demanded angrily.

The desk clerk looked at Raphaela, who had stepped to one side and was watching the proceedings in an attitude of resigned despair. "I say, miss, are your friends always so . . . temperamental?"

"No," Raphaela replied, smiling sweetly.

"Thank goodness."

"This is one of their calmer moments."

"I wish Blade was here," Sparrow Hawk commented. "This promises to be a long three days."

Jaguarundi was still trying to get at Lobo, who now added insult to injury by sticking his thumbs in his ears and waggling his fingers while sticking out his tongue. "Let go of me!" Jag cried. "He has this coming!"

Captain Havoc and Doc Madsen were holding on for dear life.

Just then, as the desk clerk was reaching for the telephone to call the police, Raphaela walked over to the hybrid and gently rested her right hand on his shoulder. "Enough, Jag," she said softly.

Jag looked at her, his features contorted in fury. "You can't be serious! Didn't you hear him?"

"Enough," Raphaela repeated quietly.

To everyone's astonishment, the hybrid slowly relaxed, his anger subsiding, and his arms dropped to his sides.

Raphaela turned to the Clansman. "Apologize, Lobo."

"Say what?"

"Apologize to Jag."

"Why should I apologize? He's the one who can't control his temper," Lobo said defensively.

"Apologize," Raphaela reiterated firmly.

Lobo muttered a few words under his breath, then glanced at the hybrid. "Sorry," he mumbled.

"Say it louder," Raphaela directed.

"What for? He heard me."

"Please."

The Clansman puckered his lips and sighed. "All right. You can't say I don't have any class. Sorry, Jag. I didn't mean to get you ticked off."

Jag averted his gaze, his head bowed, embarrassed by his rowdy display. "I'm sorry too. I'm just a bit touchy about my condition."

"A bit?" Lobo said, and snorted. "Why, if—"

"Lobo!" Raphaela stated.

"Sorry, gorgeous."

Raphaela faced the front desk. "My apologies for our behavior. I'm afraid our excitement at being in Los Angeles has all of us on edge."

The desk clerk coughed and eased tentatively to the edge of the counter, his eyes warily watching Jag. "Is this your first time to the city?"

"Yes."

"Then you'll undoubtedly be celebrating by going out on the town."

"Maybe," Raphaela answered, glancing uncertainly at her companions.

"Perhaps I could offer a suggestion?" the desk clerk said kindly.

"By all means."

"Our staff was instructed to accord you every courtesy. Anything you want is yours, and the governor's office is picking up the tab. If you plan to celebrate, you should be dressed accordingly. Right around the corner from the Regency, to the east, is an outstanding clothing store. Only the finest fashions. I know the manager well, and I would be delighted to give her a call and inform her you're coming over. What do you say?"

"I don't know," Raphaela replied. "No one told us the governor would buy us new clothes."

"I don't need new duds," Doc remarked. "These are good for another six months easy."

"And I prefer my buckskins," Sparrow said.

"Well, *I* could use some new leather," Lobo declared.

"Leather?" the desk clerk said distastefully. "I'm not quite sure if The Sophisticate sells leather clothing."

"How good can the store be if they don't sell leather, man?" Lobo responded. "Leather is bitchin'."

"Bitchin'?"

Raphaela glanced at Havoc. "What do you think? Should we buy clothes and have the governor pay for them? Will General Gallagher be mad at us?"

A peculiar smile flitted across the officer's face. "Why not?" If the governor gets upset, General Gallagher can always pay for the clothes himself."

"I guess it would be okay," Raphaela told the desk clerk.

"Wonderful. My name is Seymour, by the way. If there's anything I can do for you, you have just to say the word," he said, and gave her his most charming smile.

Lobo snickered. "Seymour? I should've known."

"Let's go up and check out our suites," Havoc suggested, jangling the keys. "Then we'll see about buying new clothes for Raphaela."

The Molewoman blinked. "Me? What about you? I'm not going to be the only one who buys clothes."

"Enjoy your stay at the Regency," Seymour said pleasantly.

"Where are the stairs?" Raphaela inquired, scanning the lobby.

"Stairs? My dear lady, the executive suites are on the twentieth floor," Seymour informed her. "You can take one of the elevators."

"What's an elevator?"

Seymour stared at her intently for several seconds, apparently trying to determine if she was serious. "If you don't mind my asking, where *are* you from?"

"Let's go," Havoc stated, and led the way toward the elevators positioned along the west wall.

"So where should we go after we got the threads?" Lobo asked of no one in particular.

"I'm not going anywhere," Jag said.

"Do you plan to spend all three days in your bedroom,

brother?'' Sparrow inquired.

''Now there's an idea.''

They reached the elevators and the officer pressed the UP button. Seconds later an elevator to their right opened with a muted hiss.

''All aboard,'' Havoc said, and gestured for them to enter.

''I've never been in an elevator before,'' Raphaela mentioned as she stepped inside. ''What does it do?''

''I don't know,'' Sparrow answered, joining her. ''I have never been in one either.''

They piled in and Havoc pushed the appropriate button for the twentieth floor.

''Thank goodness we have you along, Mike,'' Raphaela declared, and touched his arm. ''We'd be lost without you.''

Havoc glanced at her, then stared at the floor indicator. ''What are friends for?'' he replied, a bit gruffly.

''We're rising,'' Sparrow said.

Raphaela stood still, astounded by the sensation of floating skyward, her skin tingling, thrilled by the new experience. ''Elevators are neat.''

''What a bunch of chumps,'' Lobo cracked.

''I suppose you've ridden in an elevator before?'' Doc asked him.

''Well, I never exactly rode in one. But I saw 'em in the Twin Cities and an old-timer told me what they were used for,'' Lobo disclosed.

In short order the elevator arrived and the door opened to reveal a luxurious corridor.

''Everybody out,'' Havoc stated. He walked along the hall until he came to the door marked PRESIDENTIAL SUITE and inserted the key.

''Do you think these digs come with free eats?'' Lobo asked. ''I'm gettin' hungry.''

''You're always hungry,'' Doc noted.

''I'm a growin' boy.''

''At least from the neck down,'' Jag added.

Grinning, Havoc thrust the door wide open and strode into a gigantic chamber large enough to accommodate 50 people, furnished opulently, a fitting domicile for the richest of the rich. The green carpet felt spongy underfoot.

"Goodness gracious!" Raphaela declared as she gaped at the lavishly adorned suite. "This is magnificent."

"It's no big deal," Lobo said. "I'm going to have a place one day that'll make this joint look like a cave."

"Dream on," Jag said.

They fanned out, inspecting the various rooms, except for Havoc, who stood by the door watching them, grinning in amusement.

Raphaela, Sparrow, and Lobo came to the immense bathroom and gazed at the shining tiled floor and the sparkling facilities.

"Our barracks should be this clean," Lobo quipped.

Sparrow stared at the toilet, then at a strange, bowl-shaped fixture nearby that resembled the toilet in size but lacked a seat and a flush tank. "What is this?" he inquired.

"I don't know," Raphaela admitted, shaking her head. "I've never seen anything like it."

"Maybe it's a toilet they never finished," Sparrow speculated.

"Boy, are you guys dumb," Lobo said.

"Do you know what this is?" Raphaela asked.

"Of course. *Some* of us aren't from the sticks, you know."

"Then what is it?" Sparrow queried.

"It's a bathtub for babies."

CHAPTER SIX

Seymour heard their voices and pivoted, tensing at the prospect of dealing with the barbarians again, and he spied the group coming through the front doors. There was the cowboy in black and the short Indian in buckskins, the loud-mouth in the black leather jacket, and the somber, dignified blond man who appeared capable of tearing the L.A. phone book in half with his bare hands. He peered at the other two, and it took him several seconds to recognize them. "Good Lord!" he breathed in astonishment.

The redhead was stunning. She had on a form-fitting blue gown, and the fabric glistened in the light, casting her body in a shimmering aura. The bottom hem almost brushed against the carpet. Her shoulders were bare, and the snug material covering her bust accented her ample cleavage. Over her left shoulder hung a new purse. Evidently self-conscious of her appearance, she walked with her head down.

Even more surprising was the last member of the team. He wore a new black pinstriped suit and a spiffy fedora. A casual glance would not reveal anything out of the ordinary except for the brown sandals he wore instead of shoes. But closeup there would be no mistaking the fur and the feline features.

"I see you took my advice," Seymour stated as they neared the registration desk.

"Some advice," Lobo responded. "The bimbo didn't even have any leather pants. Pitiful."

"What do you think of my dress?" Raphaela inquired innocently, and spun in a circle.

"My dear, you look positively sensational," Seymour assured her. He wondered why her shoes seemed to bulge the bottom of her gown.

"We're fixin' to do some heavy partyin'," Lobo said. "Where's a really hot spot?"

"What type of entertainment do you prefer?"

"Topless broads."

"We're not taking Raphaela to a topless bar," Doc Madsen declared.

"Why not?" Lobo replied. "The broads won't have anything she hasn't seen before."

"Raphaela is a lady," Sparrow said. "To take her to such a place would be an insult."

"Why?" the Clansman asked.

"We want somewhere quiet and peaceful," Jaguarundi stated. "Somewhere we won't be noticed."

Lobo glanced at the hybrid. "No one will notice you in that getup."

Raphaela came to the counter. "Will you help us, Seymour? Mike was supposed to show us the town, but he's leaving it up to us."

"I don't know which nightclub to recommend," Seymour said. "You're such a diverse group."

"There's nothin' different about us," Lobo snapped.

Seymour brightened as an idea occurred to him. "There is one particular club that quite a few of our younger guests frequent, and the cuisine and floor shows have received favorable reviews in the press."

"What's the name of this joint?" Lobo asked.

"The China White."

"Is it far?" Raphaela inquired. "I don't want to do a lot of walking in this gown. To tell you the truth, I'm almost afraid to *sit down* in it."

Seymour grinned. "You can take a cab to the China White. The nightclub is in Long Beach, off Ocean Boulevard. Not very far at all."

"Is it expensive?" Doc queried.

"It is a high-class establishment, yes."

"Just our style," Lobo declared.

Captain Havoc tapped on the counter to get their attention, and when they all gazed at him, said, "I hate to be a spoilsport, but we'll need a lot of money to have a good time at this place. They don't pass out drinks for free. I have about seventy-five dollars. How are you fixed?"

"All I have is the money I've saved from our subsistence allowance," Raphaela said, referring to the monthly stipend paid to the Force members by the governor's office. Since their food, clothing, and shelter were already provided, they only received one hundred dollars in California currency every four weeks. "About sixty dollars."

"That should be enough," Lobo said, not bothering to mention he had eighty dollars on him. "How much can they charge for a drink at this fancy place, anyway?"

Seymour coughed. "I believe the going price is fifteen dollars."

"For one lousy drink? You've jivin' us, old-timer."

"He's serious," Havoc confirmed. "And there will be a cover charge to get in the door."

"Forty dollars per person," Seymour said.

"Forty bucks?" Lobo sputtered. "Let's forget the China White and find a place with topless chicks."

"Where did you hear about these topless women?" Doc inquired.

"From one of the California Army guards out at our headquarters," Lobo disclosed. "He told me about this bitchin' bar called the Rat's Nest where—"

"The Rat's Nest?" Doc repeated.

"Yeah. Doesn't it sound terrific?"

Sparrow leaned toward the Clansman. "No."

"Is that your final answer?" Lobo asked.

"Let me put it this way," the Flathead said. "How do you feel about being scalped?"

"I would be more than happy to call the China White and explain the situation to the management there," Seymour proposed. "I'm certain they'll permit you to ring up a tab and the governor's office will pay the bill."

"I've already spent too much money on this gown," Raphaela said. "I don't want to spend any more."

"What's the use of new threads if you can't show them off?" Lobo commented. "I vote we go check out this dive."

"For once I agree with Lobo," Doc said. "What harm can it do?"

"I have never been to a nightclub," Sparrow added. "I would like to go."

Raphaela looked at Captain Havoc. "What about you, Mike? Do you want to go?"

"If all of you are going, I wouldn't miss it for the world."

"Well, you'd better keep an eye on us," Raphaela advised. "None of us have ever been to a ritzy nightclub. We don't want to embarrass ourselves or do anything that might reflect badly on the Force, so we'll rely on you to guide us along."

Havoc stared at her for several seconds before replying. "No problem."

"Then it's settled! Let's boogie," Lobo said.

"Thank you for your help, Seymour," Raphaela remarked.

"My pleasure, madam," the desk clerk responded politely. "The doorman knows all about you. Tell him I said to hail you a cab. He'll know what to do."

"Thanks, again."

"Any time," Seymour responded, watching them walk toward the entrance and musing that during his long and illustrous career in the hotel industry he had never beheld such an outlandish group. He felt profound sympathy for the lovely redhead, thrust in as she was among such crude primitives. All except for the blond man, the officer named

Havoc. Now *he* appeared to be a perfect gentleman and the only reliable one in the bunch.

Sighing, Seymour checked in the phone book for the number of the China White and dialed. When a woman answered, he asked to speak with the manager. After a minute a gruff voice came on the line.

"Yeah? Who is it?"

"Is this the manager?"

"No, he's busy. Can I help you?"

"I was hoping to speak directly to the manager," Seymour stated. "This is very important."

"I told you he's busy."

"Very well. Will you relay a message to him for me?"

"Who are you?"

"Seymour Parkfeld, at the Bayside Regency. To whom am I speaking?"

"The name is Claw."

"My, what an unusual name."

"What's the message, man? I don't have all night."

"Well, it's like this," Seymour said, and went into full detail about the Force and their three-day pass and the unlimited credit extended by the governor's office. He concluded with, "They are on their way over to the China White right this moment. If you would be so kind, simply tally their bill at the end of the night and let me know. The governor's office will promptly issue you a check."

"Let me get this straight, man. You want me to extend credit to these Force types?"

"That's it in a nutshell."

"*You're* the one who's nuts, Seymour, baby, if you expect my boss to give credit to these turkeys. I don't know them."

"Don't you read the papers?"

"No."

"But they're the *Force*. Their credit is good."

"Not with us it ain't."

"You're being terribly rude," Seymour mentioned. "I insist on speaking to the manager."

"Insist this," the other man said, and a second later the

dial tone filled the receiver.

"My word," Seymour said to himself. He gazed out the glass doors, hoping to find the Force still there, but they were already gone. "Oh, my," he mumbled, and hung up. *Now* what should he do? The Force would show up at the China White, probably tally a huge bill, and have no way of paying their tab. He pressed his right hand to his cheek.

"Oh, *my!*"

They piled out of the taxi and stood gaping at the bright neon lights dominating the roof of the China White. The club was three stories high and painted a vivid chartreuse. Cars were constantly coming and going, and a steady stream of customers entered and departed, most laughing and engaged in lively banter.

"That'll be twelve bucks," the cab driver announced, extending his right arm toward them.

Lobo leaned down and peered in the open passage-side window. "Hey, dude, are you askin' us for money?"

"No, I'm asking for your autograph," the cabbie replied sarcastically. "Of course I want my money, you moron."

"Hey, aren't you hip to the facts, mister?"

"What facts are you talking about?"

Raphaela joined the Clansman by the window. "Didn't the doorperson tell you?"

"You mean the doorman at the Regency?"

"Yes."

"What was he supposed to tell me? That you're all dead-beats?"

"No," Raphaela said, smiling. "He was supposed to let you know that the governor is paying for all our bills."

The cabbie, a portly man in his forties, did a double take. "The governor?"

"Yes. Governor Melnick. He runs California. Have you heard of him?"

"Who hasn't, lady?"

"Good. Then all you have to do is call him and he'll make sure you get your money."

"You want me to call the *governor*?"

Raphaela nodded.

"How about if I call the cops instead?"

"The cops?"

"Yeah, lady. The L.A.P.D. They can toss you in a cell and throw away the key for all I care."

Puzzled by the cab driver's reaction, Raphaela was about to try and convince him of her sincerity when Captain Havoc materialized at her right elbow.

"How much do we owe you?" the officer inquired.

"Twelve bucks. Unless, of course, you'd like to call Santa Claus and get the money from him."

"Who is Santa Claus?" Raphaela queried. "A friend of the governor's?"

"Is she for real?" the cabbie asked Havoc.

The captain ignored the question and withdrew his wallet from his right rear pocket. He fished out twelve dollars and reached inside. "Here."

"Thanks," the cabbie said, snatching the bills as if he was afraid the fare would change his mind.

Raphaela straightened. "Well, let's go in and have some fun."

The cabbie saw them start up the cement steps to the night-club. He leaned toward the window and motioned at the blond guy, who had started to turn away.

Havoc swung around. "What is it?"

"You can level with me."

"Level?"

"Yeah. Give it to me straight. Are the people you're with from a looney bin?"

"No."

"Come on. Then they must be a theater group, right?"

"Nope."

"But that guy with all the facial hair. Where'd you dredge him up at?"

Havoc pointed at Raphaela. "He's her husband."

The cabbie glanced at the furry man in the fedora, then at the radiant redhead. "Yuck. That's gross. What does she see in an animal like him?''

Struggling to keep a straight face, Havoc looked at his teammates to ensure they were too far away to hear his next remark, then eased a little farther into the window. "Don't tell anyone," he whispered.

''Yeah? Yeah?''

''She's a nympho, and he's got a pecker fifteen inches long.''

The cab driver's mouth fell open.

Smirking, Havoc turned and caught up with the others. They were waiting for him just outside the door. All of them were staring at him expectantly, relying on him to lead them, and a twinge of guilt racked him at the thought of General Gallagher's instructions.

''What was that all about?'' Jag queried, nodding at the taxi.

''He finally realized who we are and apologized for giving Raphaela such a hard time,'' Havoc fibbed.

''What a nice man,'' the Molewoman said. She gazed at the nightclub apprehensively. ''Shall we go in?''

''Allow me,'' Havoc said, and opend the door for them. His eyes narrowed at the sight of two tall, lean men standing a few feet away. They were studying everyone who entered and left the China White. One was black, the other white, yet they wore identical brown suits and identical hairstyles. Under the left arm of each, noticeable only to a professional like Havoc, was the telltale bulge of a gun in a shoulder holster.

''Hold it,'' the black declared as they entered.

''Hey, bro! What's happenin'?'' Lobo greeted him.

''Don't bro *me*, geek. I've never seen you people here before,'' the man stated.

''This is our first time,'' Raphaela told him. ''We hear this is a hot spot.''

''Are you from out of town?''

''Yes,'' Havoc answered before any of his companions could reply. ''We're staying at the Bayside Regency and the desk clerk recommended this place.''

The black and the white looked at one another.

"The Regency, huh?" the white one said. "You have to be loaded to stay there."

"We're stayin' in the executive suites," Lobo bragged.

"Is that a fact?" the black responded. "Well, then, let me welcome you to the club. The cover charge will be added to your bill. Anything you want, you can have. Anything." He emphasized the last word meaningfully.

"Thank you," Raphaela said. "People in Los Angeles certainly are considerate."

"We aim to please, lady," the black said. "My name is Dexter. My friend here is Sheba. We're the bouncers. If anyone gives you any grief, you tell us."

"Sheba?" Lobo said, and cackled. "What a name for a guy."

The white bouncer scowled and took a half step toward the Clansman. "And what's your name, buster?"

"Lobo."

"Like you have room to talk."

Havoc saw Lobo bristle and open his mouth, and he quickly gave the Clansman a shove, sending him along the wide hallway leading to the club floor. "Don't mind him. He's had a little too much to drink."

"Make damn sure he behaves himself," Dexter advised.

"We will," Havoc responded cheerily, and gave a friendly wave as he started forward. What sort of club was this? he wondered. Why were armed guards stationed at the entrance? Did Dexter's comment about anything being available mean what he thought it meant? An uneasy feeling arose within him and he scanned his teammates. "You know, maybe coming here wasn't such a bright idea. Why don't we return to the Regency and order in some pizza?"

"We've come this far," Doc noted. "Why go back now?"

"I can hear music," Sparrow mentioned.

Jaguarundi gazed around at the dark shadows, then at the dim overhead lights. "This place isn't too bad. At least no one will notice me."

"I'd like to stay," Raphaela said.

"Suit yourselves," Havoc told them, and frowned, his inexplicable anxiety mounting by degrees with every stride he took.

"Don't worry, Mike," Raphaela said. "We'll be on our best behavior. What could go wrong?"

CHAPTER SEVEN

CHAPTER SEVEN

He'd done the wrong thing.

Blade leaned back in his chair and stared at the mountain of paperwork on the desk in front of him. When he'd accepted the offer to head the Force, he'd had no idea there would be so much pencil-pushing involved. Or pen-pushing. Whatever. It seemed as if seldom did a day go by that a report wasn't required to be filed. Personnel reports. Performance critiques. Supply requisitions. And on and on it went. A never-ending stream of paper flowing from his desk to the governor's office, by way of General Gallagher, of course.

Gallagher.

The Warrior stretched, thinking that the general had been behaving strangely of late. Why? Every time he mentioned Athena Morris, Gallagher almost laid an egg. Was the general extremely upset about her death, or was there another reason? And what was going on between Gallagher and Captain Havoc? The pair had been conducting a lot of private, almost secretive conversations recently.

Blade thought of the Force members and placed his hands

on the desktop. He'd done the wrong thing, undoubtedly. He should have gone with them to Los Angeles. They were *his* people, damn it, and they had wanted him to go along. At least, Raphaela had. After all the talks he had given them about team spirit, about loyalty to fellow Force members, and about always being there when needed by a partner, he had violated his own rules of conduct and stayed behind at the Force facility.

Why?

Because he was ticked off at General Gallagher? Because Gallagher knew the importance of the training program and had thrown a monkey wrench in the works? Although, technically speaking, he should be upset at Governor Melnick since the three-day pass had been the chief executive's brainstorm.

Or could there be another, underlying reason?

Could it be he didn't want to become *too* attached to any of the new team?

He'd socialized as much as possible with the first Force squad, had tried to be a friend to each of them as well as their leader, and had grown to care a lot for most of them. And look at what happened! Five of them had died.

So was that the real reason he hadn't gone along to L.A.?''

Subconsciously, was he afraid of cementing emotional bonds that might be prematurely severed by the death of one of the team? Did he fear losing another member so much that he was unwilling to commit himself? Had he grown soft?

He'd learned one important lesson from the wise Family leader, Plato, and from his years of experience as the head of the Warriors. A lesson he'd apparently forgotten. Leadership entailed certain responsibilities, and foremost was the supreme responsibility to the ones being led. Dedication was paramount. A loner invariably made a poor leader because a loner couldn't relate well to other people. And relating, opening up and giving of oneself to others, in this case to those who relied upon his judgment to preserve their lives, was essential.

So get off your butt and relate, dummy!

The thought made Blade smile. He grabbed the phone and

dialed the three-digit number for the guard shack at the south gate.

"Sergeant Sirak here."

"Sergeant, this is Blade."

"Yes, sir?"

"I want a jeep to pick me up in five minutes."

"Right away, sir. And may I ask where the jeep will be taking you?"

"Into L.A. I'm going to take the governor up on his offer of three days of rest and relaxation."

"I don't blame you. Party hearty, sir."

CHAPTER EIGHT

None of them, not even Captain Havoc, had ever seen anything like the China White. Jaguarundi had never been to a nightclub in his life. Doc Madsen had frequented frontier bars and saloons where he plied his gambling trade. Sparrow Hawk was accustomed to the sedate life-style of rural Montana. Lobo, for all his bragging, had never set foot in a place remotely similar. And Raphaela, raised in the cloistered confines of the Mound, where the ruler of the Moles, the arrogant Wolfe, dictated the austere parameters of their existence, was positively bewildered.

A perpetual motion machine of swirling activity, the China White throbbed with a frenetic pulsebeat in rhythm to the pounding music of the heavy metal band. Flickering strobe lights lent the dance floor and the surrounding tables and booths the aspect of another dimension. Customers were dancing and laughing and chatting, creating a clamorous undercurrent of voices as a backdrop to the driving sounds of the Dead Mastodons.

The Force members halted next to a sign that read: PLEASE WAIT TO BE SEATED. They stared at the hectic scene before them, transfixed.

"That *is* music, isn't it?" Sparrow asked. "Now I'm not so sure."

"They don't even have poker tables here," Doc said. "How can they call this a classy club?"

"Do the lights have a short?" Jag inquired.

An attractive brunette, wearing a skimpy red outfit that barely covered her waist and caused her breasts to bulge, walked toward them smiling at the men in a seductive fashion. "Hello. I'm Susie, your hostess. A party of six?"

Lobo gawked at her huge bosom and rolled his eyes. "Oh, Momma! Hurt me!"

"A party of six," Havoc confirmed.

"Follow me," Susie said, and moved to the right.

Ogling her backside as she swayed off, Lobo clutched at his chest and groaned. "I think I'm in love."

"Down, boy, down," Jag joked.

"Behave yourself, brother," Sparrow said. "Remember Raphaela is with us."

"Oh, let him act like a fool if he wants," the Molewoman stated. "We all know how playful he can be."

"Playful?" Doc said, and snorted. "Harebrained is more like it."

They trailed after the hostess as she weaved among the tables along the south side of the room.

Susie glanced over her left shoulder. "Would you prefer a table or a booth?"

"A table near those dancers," Lobo said. "I like to see the women do their moves."

"A booth," Jag said, thinking he would prefer a quiet corner in the dim recesses.

"Which will it be?" Susie queried.

"A booth," Havoc said.

Lobo sighed, his gaze glued to a big-busted woman on the dance floor who seemed about to burst the seams of her skintight dress. "Dorks!" he mumbled. "I'm surrounded by dorks.''

"What was that?'' Raphaela asked.

"Nothin'.''

The hostess escorted them to a booth in the far corner. "Your waitress will be with you in a bit,'' she stated, and left them.

"What a fox,'' Lobo breathed.

They squeezed into the booth, three to a side, with Havoc, Raphaela, and Lobo on the left. Jaguarundi took the inner seat on the right, as far from the lights as he could get. Then Sparrow Hawk and Doc Madsen sat down.

"Ain't this bitchin'?'' Lobo commented.

Sparrow leaned over the table to be heard. "This is most confusing. How can these people hear themselves think with all this noise?''

"Who wants to think?'' Lobo rejoined. "Thinkin' is for jerks. This is a place for people who want to live a little, who know how to get down and be funky.''

"Be *what*?'' Doc queried.

"Funky, bro. Funky. I wouldn't expect a corn-pone dude like you to know what it means.''

"Listen to the English expert,'' Doc cracked.

"So now what do we do?'' Raphaela asked, glancing from one to the other.

"We could order some drinks,'' Havoc suggested idly while surveying the club. He noticed there were an inordinate number of lovely women in short dresses who were circulating among the male patrons. Off to the left he spotted a man slipping a small packet of white powder into the palm of another man. "But I don't think we should stay very long.''

"Are you kiddin'?'' Lobo remarked. "I'm fixin' to spend the rest of my life here. This is heaven on earth.''

"For some,'' Havoc said, and gazed at the far side of the club where a table larger than all the rest was located to the left of the stage. This table stood out because no other tables or booths were within fifteen feet of it, and because four men in dark suits were standing near one of the chairs, their eyes constantly roving over the crowd. In that chair sat a good-looking black man attired in an immaculate white suit. On his left sat a redheaded woman in a yellow gown. And at another chair was an immense black who had somehow lost his left hand. Instead of fingers, he had a wicked-looking metal pincer at the end of his arm. He wore a gray suit. He was also bald.

"I don't mind staying as long as no one notices me," Jag mentioned.

A shapely blonde whose only garment consisted of tassels on the tips of her breasts and a lacy napkin between her legs strolled over to their booth. "Hi. I'm Arlene. Can I get you anything?"

Lobo took one look at her, then covered his face with his hands and started to whine.

"What's wrong with your friend?" Arlene inquired.

"Him? We don't know him," Doc said.

"Yeah. He just wanted to sit with us because no one else would have him," Jag added.

"Comedians, huh? Well, what would you like to drink?"

"I would like a milk, please," Sparrow informed her.

"A milk sounds nice," Raphaela agreed.

Arlene looked from one to the other. "It sounds to me like you clowns have already had too much to drink. Now what would you really like?"

"Milk," Sparrow reiterated.

"We don't serve milk."

"What about herbal tea?"

Flustered, Arlene placed her left hand on her hip and jabbed her right index finger at the Flathead. "Look, Tonto. No milk, no tea. We serve hard liquor. That's it. You can have whiskey, scotch, vodka, rum, you name it. Or maybe you'd prefer a martini or a boilermaker—"

"I'll take a boilermaker," Havoc declared, then glanced at Lobo, who was eyeing the waitress while chewing on the sleeve of his black leather jacket. "Make that a double."

"I'll have a whiskey," Doc said.

"Do you have any prune juice?" Sparrow inquired.

Arelene hissed. "No juice, mister."

"I don't know what to have," Raphaela interjected, and stared at the captain. "Are boilermakers tasty?"

"I'd recommend you try a martini. One sip of a boilermaker and you won't be feeling any pain for a month."

Sparrow Hawk's interest perked up. "Ahhh. Boilermakers must contain medicinal properties."

"You don't do much drinking, do you, Tonto?" Arlene inquired.

"Very rarely," Sparrow said. "Too much alcohol clouds the mind."

"Then what happened to you? Did a buffalo fall on your head when you were a baby?" Arlene responded, and snickered at her own witticism.

"I'll take a martini," Raphaela announced.

"Okay," Arlene acknowledged, and stared at the left corner. "And what about you there, whiskers?"

"A beer would be nice."

"What brand?"

"Surprise me."

"Fair enough," Arlene replied, then focused on the Flathead. "Have you made up your mind yet?"

"Perhaps you could suggest a suitable drink?"

"I have just the thing," Arlene assured him. "You'll love it. Goes down smooth but has the kick of a mule. It's called a flaming sucker."

"I'll try one."

"Hallelujah!" Arlene said, and went to leave.

"Hey, what about me?" Lobo cried, finally finding his voice.

"What about you?"

"Why don't you bring me a real *man's* drink?"

"You're the masculine type, huh?"

"Invite me to your place sometime and I'll show you how manly I can be," Lobo proposed, leering lecherously.

"Not unless you provide proof of your rabies vaccination," Arlene retorted. "And I'll bring you a gin gimlet. That should be about your speed." She smiled, winked, and sashayed away.

"Did you hear that?" Lobo asked excitedly. "She likes me. She's warm for my form."

"She thinks your a putz," Jag commented.

"Bull-pukey, dude. She was makin' eyes at me," Lobo insisted. He shifted so he could see Havoc. "Hey, Cap. You know this city better than the rest of us."

"Yeah, so?"

"So where can I go to get my rabies vaccination?"

To everyone's surprise, the normally staid officer put his face in his hands and started to whine.

The Claw raised his metal appendage and scratched an itch on his cleft chin. "I can't believe she'd pull a stupid stunt like that."

"I can," Mr. Bad responded angrily, his handsome features contorted in suppressed rage. "Fayanne is a bimbo. I told you that. And she's a dead bimbo once I get my hands on her."

"The boys will find her."

"To think I trusted her once!" Mr. Bad spat, and pounded his right fist on the table. "I bought her the finest clothes money can buy. She lived in the lap of luxury. And this is how she repays me?"

"She's probably getting even with you for dumping her," Gloria Mundy mentioned.

Mr. Bad glanced at his latest squeeze, his lips tightening, his eyes flinty sparks. "Figured that out all by yourself, did you, slut?"

"There's no need to talk to me like that."

Mr. Bad reached over and clamped his left hand on her right wrist, then squeezed. "I'll talk to you any damn way I want, bitch."

"You're hurting me," the woman protested, striving to jerk her arm loose.

Sneering, Mr. Bad applied more pressure, digging his blunt nails into her skin, enjoying her pained visage. "You don't seem to be aware of the facts of life, Gloria, baby. Maybe a refresher course is in order," he said, and leaned toward her. "I didn't work my way up from the streets to become one of the most powerful men in L.A. only to have a snotty whore tell me what I can and can't do. If you weren't as dumb as a brick, you'd learn a lesson from Fayanne's behavior. You'd appreciate the severity of the consequences when you cross me."

"I wouldn't cross you. Honest," Gloria promised, grimacing and feebly twisting her arm. "Please let go of me."

Mr. Bad abruptly released her wrist. "Don't ever mouth off to me again or I'll throw your sorry ass back in the gutter where you belong. And from now on, you don't set foot in my condo unless by special invite. When I'm in the mood, I'll come across the hall and visit you. Got it?"

"I got it," Gloria snapped.

Sighing, Mr. Bad leaned back in his chair and glanced at the Claw. "A man can't get any respect anymore."

Gloria stood, rubbing her sore wrist, tears moistening her green eyes.

"Where do you think you're going?"

"To the ladies' room, if you don't mind!"

"Go. Good riddance," Mr. Bad said, and waved her away with his right hand. "I hope you drown in the toilet."

Gloria stared at the head of the Brothers for a moment, her lower lip quivering, then spun and stormed off toward the rest rooms situated at the northeast end of the club.

"You were kind of rough on her, weren't you?" the Claw mentioned idly.

"What if I was? She deserved it."

"Did she? Or were you taking out your feelings about Fayanne on Gloria?"

Mr. Bad looked at his bodyguard. "What the hell are you now, a friggin' psychiatrist?"

The Claw ignored the question. Instead, he inspected the razor-sharp inner edges of his custom-designed metal pincer, patterned after the pincers on a lobster, that had been affixed to his arm nine years ago after he had lost his hand in a rumble. The pincer had cost him a bundle, and he'd had to hustle to sell a lot of coke to pay for it, but the money had been well spent. Now he had the heaviest rep in the city. Now everyone knew about the Claw.

A soft sigh issued from Mr. Bad's lips. "I'm sorry, Claw. I had no reason to talk to you like that. You're right. I'm so damn mad about this Fayanne business that I'm not thinking straight."

"It'll all work out, Boss."

"I wish I had your confidence. Now that bastard Owsley knows the identity of every Brother. He can track them down at his leisure. Some of the boys might get a little nervous."

The Claw opened and closed his pincer with a loud snap. "I can take Dexter and Sheba and finish off Owsley for good."

"Too risky. That mansion of his is too well guarded."

"You thought the condo was well guarded, remember?"

"How was I to know that bitch would unlock the fire escape door? All my boys are posted in the lobby. No one can get through them. Except for Fayanne. She talked Webster into letting her go upstairs, when he knew damn well she wasn't supposed to be allowed past the ground floor," Mr. Bad said, and scowled. "I'll take care of Webster when this business is concluded."

"Web figured no harm would be done. He was tired of her pestering him, and he knew you weren't in. He thought she'd get it out of her system and leave him alone."

"Instead she must have unlocked the fire escape and snuck back later. But where did she get a key to my place? The damn bitch!"

"You need to take your mind off her," the Claw commented. "I've got something that'll cheer you up."

"What?"

"Have you scoped out the fox in the southwest corner?"

Mr. Bad turned in his chair and focused on the redhead in the far booth. "Not bad. She's better looking than Gloria. Who is she?"

"I've never seen her in here before."

"Who are those clowns with her? And why's that blond honky crying?"

"Beats me. I've never seen them either."

Mr. Bad adjusted his tie and smoothed his jacket. "Go get her. I'd like to meet her."

"What if she doesn't want to come?"

"Be serious."

The Claw stood, his six-foot-six frame uncoiling slowly, and headed for the booth.

CHAPTER NINE

"**H**ey, check out this dude with the can opener for a hand," Lobo cracked.

Captain Havoc had already noted the big black's steady advance in their direction. He suddenly wished he wasn't seated on the inside of the booth. The guy with the pincer appeared to be staring at Raphaela. "Heads up, people," he announced. "This could be trouble."

They all reacted differently. Jaguarundi pulled the brim of his hat lower, concealing his eyes. Doc Madsen placed his right hand in his lap and twisted sideways. Sparrow Hawk dropped his left arm near his left moccasin. And Lobo stuck his right hand partway up the left sleeve of his leather jacket.

Raphaela simply stared at the bald man, who was now less than 15 feet away. "What kind of trouble? What does he want?"

"We'll know in a sec," Lobo remarked, his expression suddenly uncharacteristically hard.

"I wish General Gallagher had let us bring weapons," Havoc mentioned.

None of the others said a word, although a slight grin flitted across Lobo's face.

"Good evening," the big black announced as he reached their booth. "Are you enjoying yourselves?"

"Yes," Raphaela responded.

"We're waitin' for our drinks," Lobo added coldly.

"Can we help you?" Havoc inquired.

"The owner would like to have a word with the lady," the man addressed Raphaela.

The Molewoman blinked. "Me?"

"Yes. If you would be so kind."

"Hold the phone, turkey," Lobo said. "Who's this owner?"

"She's not going anywhere," Havoc chimed in.

The big man regarded them for several seconds, his expression inscrutable. "Are you related to the lady?"

"We're her friends," Havoc replied. "We look out for her best interest. *All* of us." He indicated the others with a sweep of his arm.

"I see," the big black said, digesting the news, glancing from one to the other. "Well, I can assure you the lady is in no danger." He smiled and pointed at the table off by itself. "The owner is right there. You can keep an eye on her the whole time."

"Eye, hell," Lobo said. "Where Raphaela goes, we go."

"Is that your name?" the man asked the Molewoman, and when she nodded in response he grinned and said, "What a lovely name. It fits such a beautiful woman."

Raphaela blushed. "Oh, I'm not beautiful," she blurted out, embarrassed by the compliment.

Captain Havoc felt an almost irresistible impulse to smash the man with the pincer in the face. He intuitively distrusted the black. Every instinct told him that the man's suave behavior was a sham, that he was as deadly as a cobra. "If the owner wants to see Raphaela, tell him to come over here."

"Can't Raphaela talk for herself?"

"Of course I can," the Molewoman said defensively. "I don't need a baby-sitter."

The big man gave a slight bow. "Then why don't you come over to the owner's table. You have my personal guarantee that you won't be harmed."

Raphaela bit her lower lip and stared at the man in the white suit, then gazed at her friends, her uncertainty transparent. "I don't want to offend anyone," she said softly.

"If you want to go, go," Havoc stated. "But take one of us with you."

"You heard the lady," the man with the pincer stated. "She doesn't need a baby-sitter."

Doc Madsen, who had not uttered one word since the conversation started, suddenly spoke, his words uttered with a steely inflection, every word clipped and precise, his hazel eyes narrowed. "No one asked you."

The black stiffened and raised his pincer to chest height. He studied the gambler closely. "You think you can do it, mister?"

"Try me."

Everyone understood the implied meaning. Each one tensed, expecting violence to erupt, and for the span of ten seconds it appeared as if the big black was about to swipe his pincer at Madsen. But then another member of the Force enunciated five words that gave the man pause.

"Can you take us all?" Jaguarundi asked.

The big man hesitated, calculating the odds, noting the chilling gaze on each of the five. They were different from most, he decided. They weren't cowed by his mere presence. If he took out the cowboy, the others would be on him before he could blink. He wasn't afraid. He knew he could take them. But if they gave him as much trouble as he believed they could, some of the other customers might be inadvertently injured or the cops might be called. And Mr. Bad was a stickler for no hassles at the club. Reluctantly, he lowered his pincer and looked at the redhead. "Will you accept the owner's invitation or not?"

"I guess," Raphaela said, hoping to avoid the possibility of bloodshed by getting the man away from the booth. She nudged Lobo. "Excuse me."

The Clansman slipped out and stood. "I'm going with you," he announced.

"I'll be okay," Raphaela stated, smoothing her gown as she straightened.

"Take him," Captain Havoc directed with an air of finality.

"Follow me," the big black said, and grinned. "You can bring your pit bull." He walked off.

"What's a pit bull?" Lobo asked testily.

"Never mind," Havoc said. "Stick with her. And Raphaela, you stay within our sight at all times. Clear?"

"I'm perfectly capable of taking care of myself," Raphaela said.

"Do it."

"Who do you think you are? Blade?"

"If Blade was here, he'd tell you the same thing," Havoc declared. The thought gave him pause. Here he was, indirectly praising the Warrior, implicitly acknowledging yet again that Blade was a competent leader who truly cared about his people. How could he even contemplate betraying the giant?

"Take Lobo along," Jag urged. "Either that or we all go with you."

Raphaela faced them and tried to adopt a stern countenance, but the happiness she felt at their concern, their caring, weakened her resolve. So she simply shook her head in silent reproof, her eyes sparkling with affection the whole while, then trailed after the big black.

"Watch out for her, Lobo," Havoc instructed.

"You've got it, man. I don't trust that big dude worth spit." The Clansman hurried after Raphaela.

"I don't like this," Jag commented.

"Neither do I," Sparrow concurred.

"Maybe we all should mosey on over there," Doc suggested.

"No," Havoc said. "Raphaela is a grown woman. We can protect her, but we can't treat her like a child. We'll sit tight and hope nothing happens."

* * *

Raphaela nervously approached the table where the owner was seated. The man with the metal pincer had already reached it and was saying something in the owner's ear. She wondered if she should have accepted the invitation, if she had made a mistake. Havoc obviously hadn't wanted her to go, and he was a better judge of others, of their true natures and motivations. She would be the first to admit her inexperience in affairs of the world. But how was she to learn to relate to others without the experience of meeting new people? She gazed at the two men and suppressed her anxiety.

"I'm right behind you," Lobo declared.

"Thanks for coming."

"You're not mad?"

"Why should I be mad? I kind of like having five goofy brothers to watch over me. I never had any real family at the Mound."

"Hey, what are friends for?" Lobo responded.

They took several more strides.

"And who are you callin' goofy?"

Raphaela mustered a smile and halted two yards from the man in the white suit. "Hello. You wanted to see me?"

"Most definitely," the owner replied, rising and motioning at the chair next to his. "Have a seat. Claw told me your name is Raphaela. I'm Mr. Bad."

"Mr. Bad?" Raphaela repeated quizzically, and heard Lobo burst into laughter.

"Are you jivin' us? What kind of idiot names himself Mr. Bad?" the Clansman queried. "And this other dork is named Claw? Prune-face would be better."

Raphaela saw both men visibly check a surge of anger. Mr. Bad glared at Lobo for an uncomfortably long time.

"Do you have any idea who I am?" the owner snapped.

"Yeah. This joint is yours. Righteous place you've got here."

"I'm a very powerful man in this city. You don't want to antagonize me."

"Should I tremble now or later?"

Mr. Bad frowned. "You're making a mistake. I won't

tolerate disrespect from anyone, least of all a nothing like you.''

Raphaela took a step forward. "If you're going to insult my friend, I'm leaving. I'm tired of all this squabbling.''

"My apologies. But you can see he provoked me," Mr. Bad replied. "Please. Have a seat. Both of you."

Raphaela sat down, and Lobo did likewise to her left. She observed that the one called Claw stayed standing although the owner took his seat again. She also noticed the four other men hovering nearby. Who were they? What had she gotten herself into now?

"You must be curious about why I invited you over," Mr. Bad mentioned, taking his seat once more.

"Yes," Raphaela admitted.

"It's because I'm a man who genuinely appreciates beauty, and you're a ravishing woman."

"Thank you," Raphaela said, confused by the flattery. She wasn't accustomed to having men compliment her so freely, and she blamed all this unusual attention on her new gown. She should never have let that saleswoman convince her to buy such a revealing evening dress.

"I'm sincere," Mr. Bad stressed, smiling warmly. He indicated the dance floor with a bob of his head. "I see lovely women in here every night of the week. Few are as stunning as you are."

Lobo yawned. Loudly.

"I would love to be able to talk to you in private," Mr. Bad proposed. "I have a condo near here. Perhaps you would be interested in going there?"

"A condo?" Raphaela said, puzzled by the reference. What the heck was a condo?

"I can have caviar and champagne brought up," Mr. Bad said. "This club is hardly the proper atmosphere in which to get to know one another."

And abruptly comprehension dawned. Raphaela felt her pulse quicken. The owner was making a pass at her! He was inviting her to his place for an intimate night together! The realization startled her. She had never viewed herself as exceptionally attractive, and with a singular exception she had never been sexually approached by any man. Of course, her aunt had had a lot to do with that. The witch had actively discouraged every suitor except one, and that one had been the source of her everlasting shame.

"Is something wrong?" Mr. Bad inquired. "Have I offended you?"

Raphaela shook her head, stunned to perceive she must have let her innermost feelings show. She had determined long ago never to tell another living soul about the horror she had undergone, not to let anyone know about her degradation. "I'm fine," she mumbled.

"Are you sure?" Lobo interjected.

Another man hastened over to the table, a skinny white man in a green suit. "Excuse me, Boss," he declared deferentially.

Mr. Bad looked up, peeved at the interruption. "Spike, this had better be important."

"I'm sorry to bother you, but Ms. Mundy has locked herself in the ladies' and she's threatening to slash her wrists with a razor."

"She's *what*?" Mr. Bad hissed, and came out of his chair with his fists clenched.

"We've tried to talk her out, Boss, but she just won't budge. There are a lot of women waiting to use the rest room. What do you want us to do?"

Mr. Bad glanced at Raphaela, maintaining his composure with a supreme effort. "Would you stay here until I return? I must deal with a trivial matter. It will only take a few minutes."

"I guess so."

"Thank you," Mr. Bad said, and stormed off to the northeast with the Claw, the man named Spike, and the four men in dark suits all in tow.

"Now what do you suppose that was all about?" Raphaela wondered aloud.

"Who cares?" Lobo responded. "I say we go back to our booth and let these jerks play with themselves."

"Why must you always be so crude?"

"Who's crude? I just call it like it is. You've got to remember, Raphy baby, that I spent almost my entire life in the toughest gang in the Twin Cities. I lived in the gutter, and I saw people for what they really are."

"Which is?"

"They're worse than animals, babe. When you get down to the nitty-gritty, most people are only lookin' out for number one. They'll screw you over every chance you get."

"That's not true. Am I trying to screw you?"

"I wish."

"What?"

"Nothin'. No, you're a decent chick."

"And what about Blade and the rest? Are they trying to screw you over?"

"No."

"They're your friends and so am I. Never forget that, Lobo."

"I'll try not to."

"I know being in the Force is rough on you. It's rough on all of us. We have to think of ourselves as one big, happy family. How else are we going to survive a whole year together?"

"Beats the hell out of me," Lobo said, and glanced toward their booth. "Look, babe, let's go back. I don't like it here."

"But I promised Mr. Bad."

Lobo sighed and tapped his fingers on the tabletop. "Raphy, I know you were raised by the Moles, and I know they're not the brightest chumps who ever waltzed down the pike, but hasn't it occurred to you that this guy isn't the kind you want to be messin' with?"

"He seems nice enough," Raphaela said defensively.

"Oh, right. Then why does everyone call him *Mr. Bad*?"

"You took the name Lobo, and you're a real peach."

The Clansman snorted and gazed off at the rest rooms. The crowd prevented him from seeing Bad and company. "What's it going to take to wake you up, girl? Life is a bitch. Everyone ain't nice and sweet like you."

Raphaela gazed around at the dancers and the throng of

patrons. "You're worried over nothing. We're in a public place. What can happen?"

As if in answer, ten men suddenly streamed through a door located in the southeast corner of the club, each man armed with a machine gun, a shotgun, or an assault rifle, and before anyone quite grasped their intention and could dive for cover, the ten opened fire.

CHAPTER TEN

Captain Havoc glimpsed a commotion out of the corner of his right eye and turned in time to see the armed men enter the nightclub. Mere seconds before the firing erupted he dove out from the booth, sliding to the floor, and yelled to his companions, "Get down!"

The next instant pandemonium erupted as the men cut loose, shooting indiscriminately into the patrons, blasting men and women alike. The blasting of the guns mingled with the shrieks and screams of the dying and the wounded, creating a raucous din, a metallic symphony of death. As the ten men fired they advanced farther into the club, their bullets mowing a path through the throng. Those customers not hit were frantically striving to make themselves scarce, and the ten gunmen found it easy to race across the previously packed dance floor toward the large table all by itself to the left of the stage.

Toward Lobo and Raphaela.

"Down, babe! Down!" the Clansman cried, rising and

hauling her from her chair. He shoved her under the table, hoping to put her out of the line of fire, then spun toward the intruders, his right hand reaching under his left sleeve. He saw four people in front of him go down, their bodies perforated and spurting blood, and his fingers were just closing on his concealed NATO when something slammed into his forehead with the force of a sledgehammer and he was hurled backwards onto the table, his senses swimming. He heard Raphaela shout his name, and his last thought before the world faded into darkness was that he hoped his friends had seen him go down and would come to her aid.

But they hadn't.

Captain Havoc looked to his left, where Sparrow, Doc, and Jag were lying prone, then at the swirling mass of confusion and bloodshed before him. His logical military mind formulated a dozen questions: Who were these men? What did they want? Why were they murdering innocent by-standers? What had the Force gotten itself into?

The majority of the patrons were fleeing in stark panic toward the corridor to the outside, some helping those who had been wounded, but most pushing and shoving one another in their frenzied eagerness to escape the spreading carnage.

Havoc took a risk. The wild crowd temporarily screened him from the gunmen, so he quickly rose and scanned the club, searching for Lobo and Raphaela. The sight he saw chilled him to the marrow. The Clansman was lying on top of the table, blood on his head, and three of the gunmen had the Molewoman in their grasp and were hauling her back in the direction they had came. Seeing her in danger shattered his customary prudence, and he started forward, bellowing, "They're taking Raphaela!" Heedless of his safety he waded into the throng, trying to break through them to the dance floor to intercept the trio ushering her out.

As yet, no one had fired a shot at the attackers.

The living wall of desperate patrons prevented Havoc from getting in the clear. Supremely frustrated, watching the three gunmen cover yards while he covered inches, he lost control and began to strike and batter the customers aside, using the karate skills he had honed to a consummate degree, never going for a death blow, only using sufficient strength to stun those who wouldn't move out of his way. He covered several yards before he realized he wasn't alone.

Doc Madsen, Sparrow Hawk, and Jaguarundi were driving a wedge into the mob, working together, standing side by side and hurling all comers from their path.

Havoc angled to assist them. He could see Raphaela and the three gunmen were already halfway across the dance floor, being covered by the seven other killers. They had ceased shooting, apparently feeling they had achieved their goal, and were slowly retreating.

Damn them!

Dozens and dozens of bodies littered the dance floor and the spaces between the tables. Even several of the band members had been slain. The drummer had pitched forward into his drums, and a guitarist had collapsed onto an amp that was spitting red and orange sparks.

Havoc realized it would take a miracle for the four of them to reach Raphaela before the gunmen made good their escape. He pushed a portly man out of the way, then barreled past two terrified women, and suddenly a narrow cleared space materialized between him and the dance floor. There stood one of the killers, an M-16 clutched in his hands.

The gunman saw the officer at the same moment and elevated the barrel to fire.

For a sinking second Havoc expected to feel slugs ripping through his torso, and he heard a gun boom but it wasn't the M-16. Instead, the shot came from his left and the killer took a bullet high in the head and stumbled several feet, then fell, the M-16 clattering on the floor. Havoc looked to the left.·

Doc Madsen had his Smith and Wesson Model 586 Distinguished Combat Magnum in his right hand. His shot had caused everyone in front of him to scatter, and he darted into the open. The trio who had captured Raphaela were almost to the door through which they had entered, and the remaining killers were backing in the same direction. Madsen never bothered to calculate the odds. He crouched and fired, three shots cracking almost as one, and three of the gunmen went down. He immediately flattened and rolled to his left, anticipating the killers would come after him.

They did.

Three more sprinted toward the Cavalryman, intent on taking revenge for their dead associates. They closed rapidly, holding their fire to ensure they wouldn't miss the still-rolling figure, and they were still advancing when a furry form hurtled out of nowhere to land among them.

Jaguarundi had lost his hat in the initial scuffle to break through the crowd. Uncomfortable in any type of clothing, his movements impaired by the restricting suit, he had halted just long enough to rip his new garments from his body, shredding the fabric with his nails, and then seen Doc slay the first killer. His steely sinews propelled him toward the gunmen in a series of vaulting leaps, and he was almost over the last of the crowd when Doc shot the three other butchers. Now he alighted among the onrushing hit men and went to work, slashing right and left, ripping his nails into the throats of two of them before the startled men could react to the shock of confronting a hybrid.

The last of the gunmen swung toward Jag and pointed a shotgun. "Die, freak!" he roared, and a millisecond later stiffened and staggered a stride, then dropped onto his knees, his eyes wide, his mouth opening and closing.

For a moment Jag didn't understand, and then he saw Sparrow appear behind the assassin and wrench a hunting knife from the man's back. The Flathead then knocked the man onto the floor. "Thanks," Jag called, and swung toward the doorway in the southeast corner.

Raphaela and the three killers were just disappearing into a hallway beyond.

Jag took off in pursuit, and as the fleetest Force member he reached the doorway before his friends. The door hung slightly ajar, and he grabbed the knob and pulled. Only his superb feline instincts saved his life, because as he opened the door a small voice in the back of his mind warned him to move and he did, ducking to the left.

A volley of automatic fire whizzed through the doorway.

Jag glanced at his teammates, but they were all right, each one flat on the floor, evidently having thrown themselves there when he took hold of the door handle. Blade's training was paying off, he thought, then peeked into the hallway.

At the far end a door was closing.

Raphaela! Her name rang shrilly in his mind as he bounded down the hall, passing a utility closet and a supply room. He came to the door and discovered that the lock and handle had been smashed when the ten killers made their entry into the club. This door, like the last, was open about an inch. He hesitated before throwing it wide, expecting to receive the same treatment as he had previously, and in the few seconds he paused he heard the distinct roar of an engine throbbing to life.

They were making their getaway!

Alarmed, he hauled on the door and sprang into the cool night, finding himself on some sort of receiving platform. There were two dead men nearby, both shot through the back. Past the platform lay a parking lot, and racing from the lot was a big limousine.

No!

Jag dashed to the edge of the platform, realizing there was no way he could catch the speeding vehicle. He watched helplessly as the limo took a left on screeching tires and sped off.

"Damn! Was that them?" a familiar voice queried anxiously to the hybrid's rear.

Frowning, Jag pivoted and nodded at Havoc. Doc and Sparrow were coming through the doorway. "What do we do now?"

"First, we check on Lobo," Havoc replied, and headed inside again.

"Why don't we steal one of these other cars and follow the limousine?" Jag asked, following.

"By the time I could hot-wire one of those cars, the limo will be long gone," Havoc said. He glanced at the Cavalryman and the Flathead as he passed them. "I thought the general told us not to bring weapons.''

"I never go anywhere without my six-gun," Doc stated. "And I reckon I don't much care what old mealy-mouth says one way or the other.''

Sparrow grinned and hefted his knife. "Do you mean this? Among my tribe a knife is considered a tool, and the general did *not* say we couldn't bring our tools.''

Havoc smiled, then increased his speed, jogging all the way to the dance floor. Most of the patrons were gone, except for a few stragglers, the moaning and groaning wounded, and the dead. He dashed to the large table, hearing the others pounding on his heels, and drew up in consternation when he saw the blood trickling from a gash in the Clansman's right temple. "No!" he exclaimed, and grabbed Lobo's right wrist to feel for a pulse.

"Is he still alive?" Jag inquired.

Havoc motioned for silence while pressing his fingertips to the Clansman's skin. Lobo was so still, his chest not even moving. But at the same second Havoc found a weak pulse, the loquacious malcontent gasped, inhaling deep into his lungs, and his eyelids fluttered. "Lobo!" Havoc exclaimed. "Can you hear me?''

"What happened?" the Clansman responded, the words barely audible. "Did Blade get tired of all my goofin' off?''

"No. Don't you remember? You were shot. Raphaela has been taken.''

Lobo's eyes snapped open. "Those bastards took her? Why?''

"We don't know yet," Havoc said. He inspected the gash and was relieved to discover it was a flesh wound, nothing more. The blood flow had already started to taper off. "We've got to bandage you and go after Raphaela.''

"Forget about me," Lobo said, and tried to rise. Dizziness swamped him and his head sagged.

"We'll lend you a hand," Doc offered, and took hold of the Clansman's left arm.

Havoc nodded, and they raised Lobo to a sitting posture.

"Sparrow, find something we can use to bandage his wound."

"On my way," the Flathead said, and departed.

"Jag, go see if you can find that bozo in the white suit or the guy with the claw. They might know what this is all about," Havoc said.

"And if they don't want to come, can I tear them into itty-bitty pieces?"

"No. We need them alive."

"Spoilsport," Jag muttered, and headed in the direction he'd seen the man in white go.

"I'll be fine," Lobo insisted. "I don't need no damn bandage. We've got to find Raphaela."

"First things first," Havoc replied. "We have to learn where those clowns are taking her, and hope they don't harm her before we get there."

"Anybody who hurts her is dog meat," Lobo vowed. He gingerly ran his fingers over the bullet crease, then stared at the blood on his hand. "I owe those suckers bad."

"We all do," Doc concurred.

"I should call Blade," Havoc mentioned, and gazed around for sign of a telephone. None were visible, and he was about to go in search of a booth when he spied Sparrow Hawk returning, a strip of white cloth in the Flathead's left hand.

"I cut this off a tablecloth," Sparrow informed them as he approached. He slowed and extended his arm. "It's the best I can do on the spur of the moment. At least it's clean."

Havoc took the cloth and proceeded to loop it around Lobo's head, binding the wound tightly, staunching the flow of blood. "Is that too tight?" he asked.

"No. Let's go find Raphaela."

"Be patient."

"We can't afford to be wastin' time, dude."

"Don't you think I know that?"

Doc Madsen suddenly straightened. "Hey. Look."

They stared toward the rest rooms. Jaguarundi was already on his way back, a skinny man wearing a green suit clasped in his iron grasp. The man was too petrified to even contemplate resisting.

"Who's this?" Havoc queried.

"His name's Spike," Jag answered. "I found him in the ladies' room, and I remembered seeing him talk to that bastard in the white suit shortly before the crap hit the fan."

"Yeah," Lobo chimed in. "He's one of Mr. Bad's men."

"Who?" Havoc asked.

"Mr. Bad. The chump in the white suit."

Havoc walked over to the hybrid and the prisoner, then seized the front of Spike's shirt and slammed him into the table, ramming the henchman's spine against the wood.

Spike cried out and clutched at his back.

"I need answers, friend," Havoc said, his voice low and gravelly. "If you don't provide them, you'll be one sorry son of a bitch."

In pain, his features livid, Spike glared at the blond man. "Go to hell."

A curious, cold grin creased the officer's mouth. "Do you see this?" Havoc remarked, and held his right hand up, his thick fingers rigid, the tips curled slightly inward.

"It's a hand. So what?" Spike said defiantly.

Havoc swept his right hand in a tight, controlled arc, driving his rock-hard fingers into the henchman's ribs, burying his hand to the knuckles.

An exquisite squeal of anguish burst from Spike's thin lips and he doubled over, wheezing and sputtering, spittle lining his mouth.

With a brutal wrench of his right hand, Havoc jerked the man erect. "You're not paying attention, asshole. Do you want me to do that again?"

"No!" Spike blubbered, shaking his head vigorously.

"Good. Then listen closely. I can break bricks and six-inch boards with my bare hands, and if you don't cooperate I'm going to do the same thing to each of your ribs. Got me?"

Spike nodded.

"What happened to Mr. Bad and that guy with the metal pincer?"

"They cut out when the shooting started, mister. They had just got Mr. Bad's old lady out of the john. Mr. Bad wanted to stay and fight, but Claw persuaded him to get the hell out of here. Claw thought the Barons might be attacking in force and he didn't want Mr. Bad to be hurt. Most of our soldiers are out on the street."

"The Barons? Do you mean this attack was gang-related?"

"Of course. Who else would be crazy enough to hit the Brothers at our own club?"

Havoc straightened. The whole incident now made sense. Except for one aspect. "Why did the Barons take our friend Raphaela?"

"How should I know?"

Suddenly Havoc remembered the other woman he had seen at Mr. Bad's table, the other *redheaded* woman, and he tensed. "What does Mr. Bad's old lady look like?"

Spike's brow knit at the unusual question. "Gloria? Oh, she's a stone fox, man. Great tits."

Havoc locked his left hand on the man's throat. "What color is her hair, moron?"

"Red!" Spike answered quickly, startled by the fire blazing from the blond man's eyes. "It's red! Honest!"

"Son of a bitch," Havoc declared bitterly, and released the Brother.

"Are you thinking what I think you're thinking?" Jag inquired.

Havoc nodded. "The Barons took Raphaela by mistake."

"And that mistake will cost them," Doc vowed.

The officer glanced at Spike. "Where would the Barons take her?"

"I don't know."

"Don't lie to me."

"I don't!" Spike whined. "They could take her anywhere."

"The Barons must have a headquarters, a base of operations," Havoc noted.

"There's Owsley's mansion."

"Who?"

"Owsley, man. The head of the Barons. He's got a mansion somewhere up in West Hollywood. I don't know exactly where."

"Who would know?"

"Well, Mr. Bad for sure, and probably Claw or Dex and Sheba, but they all took off for Mr. Bad's condo."

"And do you know where the condo is located?"

"Of course," Spike responded arrogantly. "You think I don't know where my own boss lives?" He saw the blond smile, a strangely unnerving expression, and perceived his mistake. "No! I can't!"

"You will," Havoc said.

"They'll kill me if I do."

"We'll kill you if you don't."

Spike glanced at each of them in turn, noting their hard expressions. Any one of them appeared quite capable of offing him without a second thought, but the hybrid really worried him. The thing smirked and raised its hands, then clicked its long fingernails together. Spike got the message and gulped. "All right, man. You win. I'll take you to the condo."

"Somehow I thought you would."

"But I want you to promise me something."

"What?"

"Keep that freak away from me. He gives me the creeps," Spike said anxiously.

"He'll leave you alone if you behave yourself," Havoc replied. "But if you try any tricks, anything at all, he'll gut you."

Jaguarundi beamed. "Gut, hell! I haven't tasted human gonads in ages."

Spike looked down toward his jewels, imagined those tapered teeth tearing into him, and shuddered. "You're kidding, right? You wouldn't really eat my balls, would you?''

A feral snarl issued from the hybrid and he leaned closer. ''Try me.''

CHAPTER ELEVEN

Seymour was engaged in checking the cubbyholes for a missing key to Room 1195 when a low voice addressed him from behind, surprising him because he hadn't heard anyone approach the registration desk. He almost jumped.

"Where can I find the Force?"

"Who wants to know?" Seymour responded, peering into one last slot.

"*I* do."

"And who might you—" Seymour began, rotating on his heels, his eyes becoming the size of walnuts when he saw the man standing in front of the counter, the biggest man he had ever laid eyes on, a movable mountain endowed with layer upon layer of bulging muscle, a giant with dark hair and gray eyes attired in a black leather vest and fatigue pants. There were two conspicious bulges under the vest, one above either hip. "My word!" he exclaimed.

"I'm looking for the Force," the giant reiterated, and held out his left hand. In the brawny palm rested an identification card.

Seymour took one look and almost stopped breathing. "Blade!"

"And who are you?"

"Seymour Verloc, at your service, sir. Your friends have been assigned the Presidential Suite and the Ambassador Suite on the top floor."

"Thank you," the giant said, and started to turn.

"But they're not there now," Seymour added hastily.

"Where are they?"

Seymour coughed and folded his hands on top of the counter. "They decided to go out and celebrate, and I suggested a club quite popular with our younger patrons. It's very . . . bitchin'."

The giant's eyebrows arched. "Bitchin'?"

"That's a term I picked up from Mr. Lobo," Seymour said. "He can be quite a colorful character."

"You don't know the half of it. What's the name of this club?"

"The China White."

"Where is it located?"

Seymour glanced at the entrance, through the glass doors at the waiting cabs parked outside. "I'll tell you what, sir. I'll do better than give you the address. I will personally escort you outside and get a taxi for you."

"That's very nice of you."

"Only the best for you, Mr. Blade. I know about some of your exploits, sir. I've read the accounts in the newspapers."

"They tend to exaggerate."

Seymour regarded the giant's physique for a moment. "If you ask me, sir, they don't do you justice." He hurried around the counter and motioned for the giant to follow. Every person in the lobby was staring at them, and Seymour held his head proudly, happy to be observed in such illustrious company.

The doorman had the door wide open way before they reached the entrance.

"Your friends weren't expecting you," Seymour mentioned as they reached the sidewalk. He saw three cabbies conversing near the foremost taxi and walked over to them. Two of them glanced at him, then gaped at the giant, but the third, a portly driver, was facing in the opposite direction. "Excuse me."

"What is it, bub?" the portly driver asked over his left shoulder. He was about to take a bite from a triple-decker mayo-and-corned-beef sandwich.

"Didn't one of you gentlemen take the Force to the China White?"

"You mean those weirdos? Yeah, I took them," the portly man said, the words muffled by the food crammed in his mouth. "What of it, Pops?"

"You need to take this man there right away."

"I don't *need* to do nothing," the driver snapped, and turned around. Only then did he spy the seven-foot figure standing behind the desk clerk, and he seemed to experience unexpected difficulty in talking. "H—h—him?"

"Right away," Seymour emphasized.

"Hey, whatever he wants, he gets," the driver declared. He stepped to his cab and opened the rear door. "Here you go, mister. I'll have you to that club in no time."

The giant nodded and slid into the vehicle.

In an amazing display of speed for one so out of shape, the driver darted around the taxi to his door and climbed in. He tossed the rest of his sandwich onto the front seat, twisted the ignition key, and in seconds they were on their way. "Say, aren't you the guy I've read about? The one they call Blade?" he inquired while gazing in the rear view mirror.

"That's me."

"Then those six I took to the club must be the rest of the Force!"

"Yep."

"I never would've believed it."

"Why not?"

"Well, for one thing, the newspapers never said nothing about no nympho."

CHAPTER TWELVE

"That's the place?"

"It is," Spike assured the blond guy. "Honest. I swear it. Mr. Bad's condo is on the fifteenth floor."

Havoc scrutinized the structure, debating their next move. They had ridden to within two hundred feet of the building in a battered old Ford belonging to the Brother, and now they were standing next to the parked vehicle, shrouded by the night, a cool breeze blowing from the northwest. "Does Mr. Bad own the entire high-rise?"

"Yeah."

"So there must be guards posted in the lobby?"

Spike nodded.

"How many?"

"It varies, man. Right now, with the war on and all, there must be a dozen or so."

The captain placed his hands on his hips. "You mentioned something about most of the gang members being out on the street?"

"That's right. They're out looking for Fayanne Raymond.

The bitch turned over and sold Mr. Bad's books to Owsley. Mr. Bad wants her real bad. He's offering ten grand to whoever brings her in.''

"Then that's the reason there weren't enough Brothers at the club to repulse the attack," Havoc deduced. He spied a fire escape on the south side of the structure. "Are the fire escape doors kept locked?"

"Usually."

"What are we waiting for?" Doc Madsen asked impatiently. "Let's just barge in there and get the information we need."

"We can't afford a blunder at this stage of the game, not with Raphaela's life on the line," Havoc said. "Jag, I want you to keep an eye on our friend here while I check out the lobby."

"With pleasure," the hybrid said, and stepped closer to the Brother. "You will be a good little boy, won't you?"

"Anything you say," Spike responded.

"Do you want to take my gun?" Doc offered.

"No, thanks," Havoc answered, and walked toward the building.

"But you're not armed," Sparrow pointed out.

"I have my hands and my feet."

The vehicle traffic on the adjacent avenue was moderately heavy, and there were scores of pedestrians moving in both directions. Street lamps were spaced at 50-foot intervals, affording a fair degree of illumination.

Havoc strolled casually along, his hands in his front pockets, whistling the tune to the classic song "Secret Agent Man," one of his all-time favorites. He studied the layout, seeking any weakness he could take advantage of to gain entry without having to resort to more violence. Not that he disliked violence. Quite the contrary. He had made a career out of being one of the most lethal soldiers in the California military. But without adequate firepower, the Force would be going up against nearly insurmountable odds in assaulting Mr. Bad's stronghold.

The building had been set back approximately 20 yards from the avenue. A wide walk, lined with trees, led to the entrance. A narrow strip of lawn bordered the trees on both sides.

Maintaining his air of nonchalance, Havoc turned down the walk and ambled toward a pair of glass doors. Visible inside were a half-dozen men lounging about in chairs, on a couch, and standing next to a small counter.

One of the men spied the officer and alerted his comrades.

Havoc saw more men appear, and although there were no guns in evidence, he surmised they were all armed. He plastered an inane smile on his face and walked boldly to the doors, then opened the one on the right.

"What do you want?" a burly black dressed all in black leather demanded gruffly.

"I was hoping I could use your phone," Havoc said pleasantly. "I've got a flat tire and I'd like to call a garage."

"No phone," the black said.

Havoc glanced at the counter, where a telephone rested near the wall. "Then what's that?"

Several of the Brothers converged on the officer. The spokesman walked up and poked Havoc in the chest. "You don't hear so good, sucker. I told you we don't have a phone you can use."

"Oh," Havoc said, playing the role of a typical motorist to the hilt. He counted 11 men in the lobby. "Well, if you're going to be stuffy about it, I'll find a phone elsewhere."

"You do that."

Adopting an angry expression, Havoc spun and exited. He grinned as he walked to the avenue and took a left. The others were waiting expectantly for his return.

"What did you find out?" Sparrow inquired.

"There are eleven men on the ground floor, too many for us to take on without weapons," Havoc revealed.

Spike snickered. "Then why don't you let me go and we'll forget all about this?"

"Shut your mouth," Doc snapped, and looked at Havoc. "We need to find out where those varmin took Raphaela."

"Don't you think I know that?"

"Every delay puts her life more in danger."

"I know that too."

"Then I take it you won't have any objections if I call the shots for a few minutes?" Doc commented. He walked to the driver's door and stared at the steering column to verify the keys were still in the car.

"What do you think you're doing?" Havoc queried.

"Getting us inside," the Cavalryman replied, and got into the Ford.

"How do you propose to accomplish that feat?" Havoc asked.

"Watch and learn," Doc said out the open window. He stared at the dash. "Now let's see if I can recollect those driving lessons Blade gave me."

Perplexed, Havoc stepped off the curb. "What the hell are you doing?"

The engine abruptly kicked over. Doc gave a little wave, glanced back to ensure he could merge with the traffic flow without a problem, and pulled out.

"Where's that cowboy going with my wheels, man?" Spike questioned.

Jaguarundi cackled and sprinted toward the building. "Last one there misses out on all the fun."

Sparrow Hawk took off too.

"They'll need me," Lobo said, and managed several strides before he was forced to halt by a wave of vertigo. He swayed and almost fell.

"You stay with me," Havoc stated. He took hold of Spike's arm and almost tore the limb from its socket when he hauled the Brother after him, his gaze on Doc as the gambler drove toward the stronghold, uncertain of what the Cavalryman had in mind.

Jag and Sparrow were cutting across the lawn to the front doors.

The front doors! Havoc suddenly understood and started to run, but their prisoner dug in his heels, slowing him down.

"What the hell are you assholes doing?" Spike queried angrily. "You'd better not put a dent in my wheels."

"How about if we put a dent in you?" Havoc responded, and whipped his right arm upward, delivering a *Uraken* blow to the Brother's jaw, the back of his knuckles cracking

Spike's teeth together and rocking the man's head backward. He drove his right elbow into Spike's ribs, doubling the Brother over, then rammed his right knee into Spike's face. The skinny man dropped, senseless. Instantly Havoc took off for the condo, but the delay had cost him. He was already too far away to do more than witness Madsen's gambit.

The Ford abruptly accelerated and performed a sharp turn, bumping over the curb and roaring down the wide walk as Doc floored the gas pedal. He pressed on the raucous horn and held it in.

Hearing the strident noise, the 11 men inside the lobby came to the front doors and peered out, many fingering the weapons they carried concealed under their jackets. Several of them recognized the car as Spike's, and one of them even voiced a complaint: "What the hell is that idiot doing now?" For a few precious seconds they failed to realize they were being attacked, not until one of their number cried, "Hey! That's not Spike!" Then they all broke and tried to scatter out of the path of the onrushing metallic battering ram. By then it was too late.

Doc had the car doing 58 miles an hour when it crashed into the glass doors, shattering the panes and buckling the frame in a tremendous collison, and still the vehicle kept going. The fender and the grill slammed into the packed Brothers and sent them flying, while several were ground underneath the front end, screaming as the tires crunched over them. Not until the Ford hit the wall across from the entrance did the vehicle finally stop.

Seven of the guards were out of commission, either dead or too injured to fight. The remaining four pulled their weapons and tried to fire.

The driver's door shot wide and a black form dove to the floor, a pearl-handled revolver in his right hand, and even as he executed the dive he squeezed off two shots.

A pair of Brothers went down.

A tall man armed with an Uzi trained the weapon on their attacker and was about to cut loose when something pounced on his back and drove him to his knees. Enraged, he twisted, and his fury changed to fear when he saw the bestial visage above him.

"Surprise!" Jag said, and slashed his nails twice, ripping the man's throat apart. Blood gushed forth, spattering his fur coat.

The sole guard still erect swung toward the hybrid, a SIG/SAUER P230 clenched in his right hand. A gleaming object streaked from the left and thudded into his chest, and he looked down to find a large knife imbedded to the hilt. Bewilderment flitted across his features and he pitched onto his face as his chest seemed to implode. He screamed and turned onto his side, blood spurting from his mouth, and died.

"Thanks, Geronimo," Jag quipped.

"The name is Sparrow Hawk," the Flathead reminded him, and swiftly retrieved his knife, yanking the weapon out and wiping the blade clean on his victim's clothes.

Jag snickered and advanced to the counter. "We got them all," he said, scanning the lobby, admiring their handiwork. Several of the Brothers were groaning in pain.

"Should we put them out of their misery?" Sparrow inquired.

"Forget them," Doc said rising. He began to reload the spent rounds using the cartridges he had stuffed in his pockets before departing the Force compound.

Just then the telephone started ringing.

"Want me to answer it?" Jag said.

"No," Doc replied. "It might be someone upstairs wondering what all the ruckus was about. We've got to get to the top floor."

"Where's Twinkletoes?" Jag wondered, and gazed at the entrance as Havoc and Lobo arrived. "There you are! Where have you been? Taking a leak?"

The captain entered the lobby, disregarding the barbs. He stared at the ruined car, then at the bodies, and finally at the Cavalryman. "You could have been killed."

"And what do you think will happen to Raphaela if we don't get our butts in gear?"

"Let's go," Havoc said, and made for the elevator.

The telephone was still ringing when they commenced their ascent.

"There's no answer, boss," Dexter reported, and hung up the phone.

"We've got to get out of here," the Claw declared.

"I'm through running," Mr. Bad responded harshly. "If the Barons are on their way up, let's give them a reception they'll never forget."

"We can't stay," the Claw stated. "If the Barons have snuffed Web and the other guards, then they must be attacking with every soldier they've got. We wouldn't stand a chance."

Mr. Bad glanced at his bodyguard. "I know you're not yellow, so why do you want to run?"

"If you get racked, what's left for the rest of us? The Brothers are nothing without you. Yeah, we can stay and take them on, but if they outnumber us, then they'll nail us in the end. Why not stay alive and get our revenge on Owsley?"

Hatred contorted Mr. Bad's countenance. "You've got a point. I want that son of a bitch to suffer before he dies. I want to look in his eyes and laugh in his fat face as I stick it to him."

"Then come on," the Claw urged. "We don't have that much time."

"Hey! What about me?" Gloria Mundy called out from her seat on the sofa.

"Jump off the damn roof for all I care," Mr. Bad snapped. He looked at his two lieutenants, Dexter and Sheba. "Hold them as long as you can. Then head for the warehouse."

"Will do," Sheba said.

Mr. Bad hurried into the corridor. He gazed at the elevator, surprised to notice that it had stopped on the twelfth floor, then moved to the fire escape door.

"Let me go first, boss," the Claw suggested. He threw the bolt and cautiously peeked outside. "I don't see any Barons."

"Then let's split," Mr. Bad stated. He looked back once to see his lieutenants walking toward the elevator shaft, grinned, and said, "Give the bastards hell!"

Dexter and Sheba turned. Both nodded. Both watched their employer depart. And both drew M.A.C. 10's from under their jackets. Known as "the twins" by their fellow Brothers, the pair did everything together. Worked together. Ate together. Some claimed they even showered together. Now, together, they advanced to the elevator and pointed their auto pistols at the door.

"When they open the door," Dexter said.

"We'll waste them," Sheba concluded.

The indicator light over the door rose to the thirteenth floor and continued to the fourteenth.

"Ready?" Dexter asked.

"Ready," Sheba replied.

A second later the elevator whined to a halt and the door began to hiss open.

"Now!" Dexter barked.

Both men cut loose at point-blank range.

CHAPTER THIRTEEN

"**C**ome in, my dear."

The booming voice beckoned from an immense man who was sitting behind a desk on the far side of the enormous, luxurious room, and Raphaela walked nervously forward, glancing at the half-dozen other men who were standing at various points to her right and left.

"You have nothing to be afraid of, Ms. Mundy," the man at the desk assured her. "You're a guest in my house until this unfortunate affair is concluded."

Raphaela licked her dry lips and squared her slim shoulders. The ride to the mysterious mansion had been a harrowing ordeal, what with a gun barrel pressed against her abdomen the entire trip. To compound her misery, she had seen Lobo sprawled on top of the table, and was positive that he had died while trying to protect her. Now she felt a swell of anger at these strange men who had so callously abducted her, and she focused her resentment on the huge man who appeared to be the leader of the operation. "Why does everyone keep calling me that?"

"Calling you what?" the man responded quizzically.

"Mundy."

"Because that's your name," the leader said patronizingly. "Just like mine is Arthur Owsley." He motioned at one of the chairs. "Why don't you take a seat?"

Her eyes constantly roving from man to man, Raphaela sat down and carefully deposited her hands in her lap. She was acutely conscious of the figure she must present in her skintight gown, and she wished she had never bought the thing. How could she hope to make a bid for freedom when she couldn't run very fast or even raise her leg to deliver an effective kick? She stared at her captor. "Your name may be Owsley, but mine isn't Mundy."

The leader smirked. "It's not?"

"No, it isn't."

"Your assertion is most puzzling," Owsley said. "Here you claim not to be Gloria Mundy, and yet you have red hair just like she does, green eyes just like she does, and if I may take a liberty, the same ravishing form as her." He snickered. "How, then, can you claim not to be the lady in question?"

"Easy. I'm not the woman you wanted."

"I can readily appreciate your reluctance to disclose your true identity," Owsley commented. "You undoubtedly fear for your life. Well, permit me to set your fears at rest. I know you are Mr. Bad's woman. I know you are a minor pawn in the general scheme of things. Why, you're not even an official member of the Brothers. So killing you would be a waste of my time and your beauty."

Raphaela said nothing. She hoped to learn as much as she could about the reason for her kidnapping.

"You see, my raid on the China White had a dual purpose. I hoped to catch Mr. Bad off guard while most of his men were out scouring Los Angeles for Fayanne—a ploy I masterminded, by the way. Failing to snuff him, I hoped to further embarrass the bastard by taking his woman right out from under his nose. Now I can count two coups in one week. When his people learn about your abduction, coming so soon on the heels of my triumph in obtaining his personal books, they'll desert Keif's sinking ship in droves." He smiled smugly. "There. Now that you understand, what do you think?"

"I think you're making a big mistake. When Blade learns you've taken me and killed Lobo, no one will be able to stop him."

"Blade? Who is this Blade? Why does the name sound vaguely familiar?"

"Ever heard about the Force?"

Owsley's eyes narrowed. "I've read about the Force in the paper. Blade is their leader, correct?"

"Yep."

"And what does this superman I keep reading so much about have to do with you?"

"I'm also on the Force."

Arthur Owsley and his henchmen burst into unrestrained laughter, venting their mirth for over a minute.

Raphaela waited patiently for them to stop, her cheeks crimson with indignation.

"Oh, that was priceless," Owsley stated at last, and touched the corners of his eyes. "I had no idea you possessed such a refined sense of humor."

"You won't find this situation so funny when Blade and the rest of the Force show up at your front door."

"Please, Ms. Mundy. Enough is enough. Why go to such an extreme to convince us you're a member of the Freedom Force when we both know it's patently ridiculous?"

"Don't say I didn't warn you."

Owsley leaned back and flexed his pudgy fingers. "Your stay here will be, I hope, relatively short. The Barons are looking for Mr. Bad even as we speak. His own people are scattered over south L.A., and it's only a matter of time before we nail him and end this war. Then I, Arthur Owsley, will be the reigning drug lord in L.A. My criminal empire will enable me to rule this city from behind the scenes, as it were. And who knows? From L.A. we can spread throughout the State, even establish chapters in the Civilized Zone and elsewhere."

"You're awful fond of yourself, aren't you?"

"I have every right to be," Owsley stated.

Raphaela reflected on her predicament. Now she knew her kidnappers were the Barons, one of the gangs the trooper had told her about. Somehow, she had wound up in the middle of their gang war. It must have been a simple case of being in the wrong place at the wrong time. That, and resembling the Mundy woman. It figured. Her luck was running true to form. She looked to her left as a stocky Baron stepped with obvious trepidation toward the desk.

"Uhhhh, Boss?" the Baron said.

"What is it, Barney?" Owsley asked with an air of annoyance.

"There's something I think you should know."

"First let me congratulate you on a job well done. You directed the raid on the China White admirably, even if the casualty count was higher than I anticipated would be the case."

Barney coughed lightly. "That's what I want to talk to you about."

"Elaborate."

"The boys who got racked at the club . . ." Barney began, then hesitated, his gaze averted.

"What about them?" Owsley demanded impatiently.

"Not them so much as the ones who offed our boys," Barney went on. "I've been thinking about what this dame just told us, about being on the Force and all."

Owsley laughed. "Surely even *you* don't attach any credence to her story."

Barney glanced at the redhead. "I don't know nothing about no credence, but I did read the paper about the Force outfit and what they did down in Mexico."

"So?"

"So the paper said there's a new Force. A bunch of the others got killed."

"Everyone in California knows that," Owsley stated testily. "Get to the point."

"Well, the paper said the new Force includes a redhead, an Indian, some kind of cowboy-type, a black dude, a soldier, and one of those mutation things that looks like a cat."

Owsley sighed and looked at Raphaela. "Do you see the caliber of my personnel? He beats around the bush until he's worn a rut in the ground." His hooded eyes fixed on Barney. "You have exactly ten seconds to explain the significance of your rambling."

Barney looked as if he wanted to crawl under the desk. "Well, I saw the guys who wasted our boys. One of them was a cowboy-type dressed in black, another was an Indian, and there was also some kind of cat-man."

Raphaela nearly giggled at the stupefied expression on the leader's face. He blinked a few times and gazed at her, then at the Baron called Barney.

"Why wasn't I informed of this sooner?"

Barney shrugged. "We've only been back a few minutes. And I didn't figure it was all that important. I just thought they were customers, you know?"

"Customers?" Owsley repeated softly. He abruptly rose from his chair, displaying surprising swiftness for a man with such a tremendous bulk, and glared at his lieutenant. "Customers!" he roared. "How many hybrids do you think there are in L.A.? How many Flathead Indians? How many Cavalrymen?"

"I don't know, Boss."

Owsley leaned on the desk, his visage livid. "I'll tell you, you boob! *None,* except for the members of the Force! Do you mean to tell me that the three you mentioned attacked you after you snatched this woman?"

"Yeah. And there was a big blond guy with them too, sort of a military type, if you know what I mean."

Owsley's chin sagged to his chest. "What are the odds?" he asked, apparently addressing the question to himself. "What are the *odds*?"

"Oh, yeah," Barney added. "And there was this black dude who tried to save the skirt. We offed him."

"I'm surrounded by incompetents," Owsley mumbled. His head snapped up. "You *killed* one of the Force?"

"We didn't know who he was," Barney said defensively. "We assumed he was one of the Brothers."

"You *assumed*?" Owsley bellowed, and swung toward his

prisoner. "You mentioned his name was Lobo?"

Raphaela nodded. "He was from the Clan."

"And you are—?"

"I'm a Mole. My name is Raphaela."

Owsley straightened and came slowly around the table, halting next to the stocky Baron. "Dear God, it's true! We've kidnapped one of the Force!"

"It's no big deal, Boss," Barney said. "They don't know who we are and they have no way of finding us."

Owsley's lips compressed for a moment. He glanced at another Baron. "Bennie, you're now my second-in-command."

"Bennie!" Barney exclaimed. "What about me?"

Owsley smiled, a peculiarly sinister indication of his innermost feelings. "You?" he said contemptuously. "You're history."

Raphaela was startled by the suddenness of Barney's demise. She jumped in her chair when Arthur Owsley's thick right hand, held flat and straight, swept around, up, and in, spearing into Barney's throat and crushing it.

Barney gagged and tottered backwards, clutching at his ravaged trachea, blood dribbling from the corners of his mouth. He tried to breathe, gasping loudly, and fell to his knees.

"Your incompetence has jeopardized our entire operation," Owsley said icily, advancing on the helpless Baron. "Now I must take emergency remedial measures to compensate for your stupidity." He halted, not an inch from Barney, and placed a hand on each side of Barney's head. "You've let me down, dearest Barney. Give my regards to eternity."

Raphaela saw Owsley's massive arms wrench to the right, then the left, and she distinctly heard the crackle of Barney's spine being severed. She recoiled in disgust and gripped her chair for support.

Owsley allowed the body to fall to the carpet. "Bennie, get this garbage out of my sight."

"Right away, Boss," the new second-in-command said dutifully, and gestured at two other Barons. They took hold of Barney and hoisted him into the air, then hastily exited.

"Now then," Owsley said, turning to the Molewoman, "to cases." He stepped to her left side. "You say that Blade won't rest until he has found you?"

Raphaela nodded defiantly. Although she was terrified of the psychopath, she refused to give him the satisfaction of seeing her cringe in fear. She looked him in the eye, keeping her chin firm and proud.

"And the other Force members will undoubtedly accompany him," Owsley said, more to himself than to her.

"They'll tear this place apart," Raphaela predicted.

"No, my dear. They'll try. There's a difference," Arthur Owsley said. "I have fifteen soldiers on the premises, all well-armed. They know every bush on the grounds. I'd say that the Force will be at a disadvantage should they attempt a rescue."

"You won't stop them."

"Perhaps I won't have to stop them," Owsley responded thoughtfully. He leaned against the desk and folded his arms across his chest. "What would you say to a deal?"

"A deal?"

"Yes. I'll give you your freedom in exchange for your word that you'll persuade Blade and company to refrain from coming after the Barons."

"You'll just let me walk out the front door?"

Owsley nodded.

"What's the catch?"

"There's no catch," Owsley said, and regarded her intently. "But tell me. What kind of man is this Blade? Is he everything the papers claim?"

"He's more."

"Then it doesn't matter whether you give your word or not," Owsley stated regretfully. "Such a man would never permit the death of one of his own to go unpunished. Even if we released you, he'd still hunt us down."

Raphaela did not bother to reply. Thanks to the newspaper articles, Owsley had formulated a fair estimation of the Warrior's character. If she lied, he'd know right away. "You could always turn yourself in."

"Are you serious?"

"Sure. You know what will happen if you don't. Why not surrender to the authorities and end all the bloodshed."

Owsley sighed. "If only it were that easy." He shook his head. "No, my only recourse is to prepare a lethal reception for your companions."

"What about me?"

"You'll be placed under guard in one of the upstairs bedrooms, where you should be safe."

"You're not going to kill me?" Raphaela asked, incredulous.

"Why should I? You're here by accident. You've done me no harm. Besides, I might be able to use you as a bargaining chip later," Owsley informed her, then grinned. "And who knows? If we dispose of your friends, I may just keep you for myself. It's been a while since I had a woman, and that dress of yours does wonders for your natural charms."

Raphaela tried to sink into her chair, mentally pledging never to wear a gown or dress again for as long as she lived.

"Yes, indeed," Owsley said, and licked his lips. "This could be the start of a marvelous relationship."

CHAPTER FOURTEEN

The scene at the China White resembled a madhouse. There were police cars and other official vehicles everywhere, their red lights flashing. The L.A. Police Department had established a cordon to keep out the curious. There were a half-dozen reporters already present, held at bay by two hefty officers, clamoring for answers to the questions they shouted at the man overseeing the operation, Captain Clint Callahan.

A 25-year veteran of the L.A.P.D., Callahan worked as the Chief of Detectives. He was of average height and build, with brown hair and brown eyes, and his strongest trait was his keen mind. Through long years of experience he had inured himself to the grisly sight of murder victims, or so he'd believed until he'd set foot inside the nightclub and seen the dozens of dead and dying lying in spreading pools of blood, some with their faces partly blown away, others nearly torn in half by a shotgun blast. After issuing orders, he had ventured out to the steps to inhale the cool air and collect his thoughts. He glanced distastefully at the obnoxious reporters, who he could not help but compare to a pack of braying hyenas, and was about to turn and reenter the club when he heard his name shouted and spied a patrolman hurrying toward him.

Another man accompanied the patrolman, a giant wearing a black leather vest and green fatigue pants.

Callahan studied this newcomer, and immediately detected the bulge of hidden weapons. Prudently, he kept his right hand next to the open flap of his jacket, within easy reach of his service revolver. "Yes?" he responded.

The youthful patrolman hurried up the steps and held out an identification card. "Sir, this man claims he needs to see you. I know the rule about letting civilians cross our lines, but you should take a look at his I.D."

Callahan complied, his eyes narrowing when he read the name of the man to whom it belonged and saw the governor's signature in the lower right corner. He looked at the giant, who had halted three steps below. "So you're Blade?"

The Warrior simply nodded.

"That will be all," Callahan said to the patrolman, who eagerly retraced his route. "What can I do for you?"

Blade nodded at the entrance. "I have reason to believe my team was here earlier."

"The Force? Here?" Callahan declared in surprise.

"Governor Melnick offered us three days off in L.A.," Blade explained. "My unit came here for some relaxation."

"And that's all?" Callahan asked, a tinge of suspicion to his tone.

"Why else?"

"You tell me."

Blade returned the police officer's steady gaze. "I don't know what you're talking about. I'd like to go inside, if you don't mind?"

Callahan pondered for a moment. "No, I don't mind. But be sure and tell the governor I'm such a nice guy so I can rack up some Brownie points."

"I will," Blade said, puzzled by the police officer's sarcastic tone. "Who are you?"

"Sorry. Captain Callahan, Chief of Detectives."

"Pleased to meet you," Blade remarked, and offered his right hand.

Callahan relaxed somewhat and shook, impressed by the controlled strength in the giant's grip. "So how come you weren't with your unit?"

"I had paperwork to catch up on."

"Say no more," Callahan said. "I know what you mean. I hate the damn stuff myself."

Blade glanced at the doorway. "What happened in there?"

"Come with me," Callahan directed, and led the way indoors. He surreptitiously scrutinized the giant as they walked, gauging the truthfulness of the Warrior's answers and reactions. "Do you know whose club this is?"

"No."

"Really? Well, it belongs to the Brothers. Mr. Bad runs it personally."

"Mr. Bad? The Brothers?"

"You don't know about the Brothers, one of the leading gangs in the city?"

Blade shook his head.

"Then let me enlighten you," Callahan said. "There are two gangs fighting for control of L.A. One is known as the Brothers, the other is the Hollywood Barons. They're involved in a major war right now."

"And you suspect the Barons hit this nightclub?"

"I do."

Worry lines appeared on the Warrior's face. "How many were killed?"

"We're still tallying the list," Callahan said. "So far, we have twenty-six stiffs in body bags."

"Were any of them from the Force?" Blade asked anxiously, his concerned gaze on the end of the hallway.

"Not that I'm aware of," Callahan responded. "We haven't found any with a Force I.D."

Blade expelled a breath in relief. If anything happened to them, he would hold himself accountable. He should have been with his team, not sulking at the compound. Except for Havoc, they had no idea what to expect in a big city.

"The hit doesn't make much sense, though," Callahan mentioned. "As near as we can determine, there were no Brothers killed, just innocent bystanders. It's almost as if the Barons blew away the bystanders to keep anyone from interfering with their real purpose for attacking the club."

"Which was?"

"If I knew that, I'd be a happy man."

Blade reached the club proper and paused to survey the slaughter. He had seen worse carnage, but the sight still sickened him, and the thought of so many blameless people dying at the hands of savage, amoral butchers aroused his animosity.

"Did you have any idea this place was going to be hit?" Callahan inquired.

Blade glanced at the detective in surprise. "No. How would I know?"

Callahan smiled. "Just asking."

A tall, dark-haired man wearing a brown trench coat approached, a small notepad in his left hand.

"What have we got, Harry?" Callahan inquired.

The man stopped, gave the Warrior a curious appraisal, then consulted his notes. "Just a rough sketch, so far, but from what the witnesses tell us it all started when a group of men, reports vary from seven to fifteen, came through the door in the southeast corner and began firing at random."

"The bastards," Callahan interrupted passionately.

"Yeah. Anyway, from there on out it gets real confusing. There are some reports that gunshots were exchanged, that a guy in a black cowboy outfit shot several of the attackers. We've checked for tattoos, and we've confirmed there were seven Barons killed."

"There were?"

"Yep. Someone, probably the Brothers, collected all the weapons before we arrived, so we had no way of telling if any of the dead were gang members until we verified they wore tattoos."

"I understand."

"Well, out of the seven Barons killed, four were shot, two had their throats torn to shreds, and one was knifed," Harry detailed. "Oh, yeah. And we just found a pair of dead Brothers out back."

"And they're the only dead Brothers on the premises?"

"They're all we'e found."

"Excellent. Keep me informed."

Harry hefted the notepad. "That's not all, Clint."

"What else?"

"Several of the witnesses claim that the two Barons who had their necks ripped open were attacked by a cat-man, a hybrid."

"Oh?" Callahan responded, and regarded the giant coldly.

"Yep. They also claim an Indian was involved. But here's the main item. Every witness agrees that the Brothers didn't put up much of a fight. There must not have been the usual number of Brothers at the club tonight."

"Interesting."

"And so is this. We have customers who say that the Barons kidnapped a woman."

"Any idea who she could be?"

"Not yet. The descriptions are all the same. A redheaded fox in a blue gown."

Blade's interest flared. "Redhead? Did you say redhead?"

"That's what they claim," Harry replied.

"Why is her hair color significant?" Callahan inquired.

"One of the Force is a redhead. Raphaela, the volunteer from the Moles," Blade disclosed.

"Do tell," Callahan said.

"But why would the Barons take Raphaela?" Blade wondered aloud.

"I'm hoping you can tell me," Callahan stated.

"I have no idea," Blade said softly, his emotions in turmoil. Raphaela had been captured by the Barons! His team had become embroiled in a gang war! How? Why? They had been on their own for only a few hours, and already they were up to their necks in serious trouble. He had to find them, to rescue Raphaela. "Where could I find the Barons?" he asked gruffly.

"We don't know where they have their base of operations," Callahan answered before Harry could reply.

"Who *would* know?"

"Mr. Bad might."

"And where would I find him?"

"He has a condo on Westminster Avenue. The Sorel Manor, they call the place. Seventy-five Westminster. You can't miss it."

Blade smiled at the detective. "Thanks. I owe you one." He wheeled and stalked from the nightclub.

"Did I miss something here?" Harry asked when the giant had disappeared through the doorway.

"Yep," Callahan said, and cackled.

"We know where the Barons are based," Harry noted. "It's no secret that Arthur Owsley is their head, and his mansion is at Twelve Hundred Sunset Boulevard in West Hollywood."

"I know," Callahan stated, and snickered in triumph.

"Then why did you lie to that guy?"

"Do you know who he was?"

"You didn't introduce me."

"Forgive my deplorable manners," Callahan quipped. "That was Blade."

"*The* Blade? The head honcho of the Force?"

Callahan nodded. "The one and only."

"Why would you lie to him? I thought he's a good guy."

"He lied to me so I returned the favor."

Harry scratched his head. "You've lost me, Clint."

"That cowboy and the cat-man those witnesses saw are members of the Force, just like the redhead who was abducted. I asked Blade what his team was doing here, and he had the gall to tell me they were on the town or some such bullshit. I don't buy it for a minute."

"You don't?"

"Hell, no. Here we have the Brothers and the Barons involved in a full-scale war, and the Force just *happens* to get entangled in the whole mess? Give me a break. That's too much of a coincidence for me to swallow."

"Then what's going down?"

Callahan smirked. "Our illustrious governor is pulling another of his brilliant political moves."

"Huh?"

"Haven't you noticed how Governor Melnick milks the Force for every vote he can get? Well, he's decided to sic his elite band of assassins on the Brothers and the Barons. He's aware of all the headlines since the gang war erupted. He's probably fed up with all the negative news and the repercussions for his administration. So he's sent in the Force on the sly to destroy both gangs." Callahan snickered. "The man is a wizard."

"I still don't understand why you lied to Blade," Harry remarked.

"He probably already knows all about Owsley. Even if he doesn't, I'm killing two birds with one stone. For years we've been trying to slam the lid on Owsley and Keif, but their high-priced lawyers always get them off the hook. And we're virtually helpless because we have to go by the book. We have to stick to the letter of the law," Callahan said, and nodded toward the entrance. "Blade is under no such constraints. His allegiance is to the Federation as a whole, and he has authorization to do whatever is necessary to secure the safety of any faction."

"Meaning?"

"Meaning that big son of a bitch can kick ass any way he wants, and the law be damned. He can take out both Owsley and Keif and there's not a damn thing anyone can do or say about it," Callahan said, and laughed. "That Melnick is brilliant. He's provided the Force with the perfect cover story. They can claim they were out on the town when they were attacked by one of the gangs. No one will know any different. Everyone will hail them as heroes and Governor Melnick will get the vote of everybody in L.A. for cleaning up the slime."

"Wow," Harry declared in appreciation. "You're right. Their plan is ingenious."

"Blade and the Force will take care of the Brothers and the Barons, and we don't have to lift a finger to help them."

Harry stared at his superior. "How in the world did you ever figure this all out? I never would've made the connection."

Callahan stood a little straighter. "When you've been a detective as long as I have, you develop a nose for these things."

"My compliments."

"Thanks. Now get your ass in gear."

"Beg pardon?"

"None of the higher-ups saw fit to tell us about this operation, but now that we know I'm not about to be left in the dark. I want you to follow Blade. Wherever he goes, you go. Phone in every chance you get and keep me informed on his activities."

Harry nodded and started to run for the door.

"And Harry?"

The detective paused. "Yeah?"

"Under no circumstances are you to interfere with Blade or the Force, and don't let anyone else interfere either. If anyone gives you any grief, have them call me."

"Will do," Harry said, and raced off.

Captain Callahan rubbed his hands together and beamed. This was a dream come true! The lousy Barons and Brothers wiped out in one fell swoop, and all he had to do was sit on his tush until it was all over and clean up the mess.

Christmas in August!

CHAPTER FIFTEEN

Dexter and Sheba emptied half their magazines into the elevator, their M.A.C. 10's chattering metallically, before they realized there was no one inside. They ceased firing simultaneously and glanced at one another.

"Where the hell are the Barons?" Dexter snapped.

"Maybe we were mistaken," Sheba said. "Maybe the Barons weren't attacking."

"Then what was that noise we heard that sounded like an explosion?" Dexter countered, and moved warily forward, sweeping his M.A.C. 10 from side to side.

"Mr. Bad will be ticked off if he finds out he split for no reason," Sheba predicted.

"This is fishy," Dexter said. He entered the elevator and stared at the bullet holes in the walls, then at the control panel situated to the left of the door. Elevators didn't operate by themselves. *Someone* had sent the car to the top floor. But who? And why send it up empty? If the Barons were up to no good, what purpose did it serve? It wasn't as if the sons of bitches could hide in it. Not unless they opened the maintenance panel on the roof and hid on top of the . . .

The maintenance panel!

Dexter pivoted and tried to bring his M.A.C. 10 to bear on the ceiling, but he was too late. He saw a furry form crouched in the opening, and then a thin form pounced on his chest and bore him to the floor. Claws or nails gouged into his neck and he released the M.A.C. 10 to grab his assailant.

Shocked by the abrupt assault, Sheba took several strides forward, trying to get a bead on the figure battling Dexter, but they were rolling and thrashing, turning and twisting, and he was afraid to fire for fear of hitting his companion. He glimpsed the fur and the fangs of the feline features on the creature and realized Dexter had been jumped by a mutation. So concerned was he for Dexter's safety, he failed to take into account his own.

Dexter and the hybrid rolled from the elevator, still fighting, crimson coating Dexter's neck.

"Get clear!" Sheba urged frantically, flattening against the right wall so they could pass him by. He heard a thump from the elevator and started to rotate, astonished to see an Indian springing at him, the same Indian who had shown up at the China White earlier. He swung the M.A.C. 10, but the Indian blocked it with his left palm, then delivered a stunning right to Sheba's jaw. The next instant the Indian closed in, and they grappled and fell to the red carpet.

No slouch at hand-to-hand combat, Sheba let go of the M.A.C. 10 and tried to lance his fingers into the Indian's eyes at the same moment he drove his left knee at the other man's crotch. To his consternation, both blows were deflected, and then the Indian had him in a headlock and hard knuckles were digging into the base of his throat and restricting his ability to breathe.

"Lie still or I'll break your neck!" the Indian warned.

Sheba resisted for a few more seconds, just long enough to satisfy himself he couldn't break the headlock without a supreme effort, and that in that time his adversary would undoubtedly fulfill the threat.

Footsteps pounded in the corridor.

From his position lying flat on his back with the Indian on top, Sheba looked up to behold three men appear, three more who had been to the club. He saw the cowboy, the loud-mouthed guy in the leather jacket who now sported a crude white bandage on his head, and the blond. The cowboy held a revolver, while the latter two had picked up the discarded M.A.C. 10's.

"Good job, Sparrow," the blond said.

"Thank you, Havoc," the Indian responded, and un-expectedly stood, drawing a hunting knife as he rose.

Sheba suddenly found every weapon trained on him, and he coughed and rose slowly onto his elbows. "I give up," he declared. "Don't kill me."

"Where's Mr. Bad?" Havoc asked.

"I don't know," Sheba lied. "He cut out after we heard an explosion downstairs."

"He must've gone down the fire escape," the injured guy said, and ran toward the end of the corridor.

"Be careful, Lobo," Havoc advised. "Doc, you go with him."

The cowboy in black departed.

"Can I get up?" Sheba queried.

"Be my guest," Havoc responded.

His bruised throat aching terribly, Sheba rose. "Where's Dex—?" he began, turning to the left, the word dying on his lips as he laid eyes on the blood-splattered form of his friend lying six feet away. Dexter's neck had been torn to shredded ribbons and his mouth hung open. "No!"

The furry figure crouched next to Dexter slowly unfurled to his full height and turned, his hands held near his waist, blood dripping from his nails. His slanted eyes focused on Sheba. "Do you want me to dispose of this one too?"

"Not yet, Jag," Havoc responded, scanning the corridor. Lobo and Doc were almost to the fire escape. Much closer were two doors, a closed red one and a brown door that stood ajar. "Keep an eye on him while Sparrow and I check out the condo."

"My pleasure," Jag said, and deliberately grinned to expose his pointed teeth.

Sheba flinched as if struck. "Hey, man," he said to Havoc. "You can't leave me alone with this . . . *thing*!"

"Watch me," Havoc retorted, and headed for the open door, the M.A.C. 10 gripped in both hands. He swung his back to the wall and cautiously stepped to the jamb, then quickly glanced within. There was no one in sight, but he could hear a faint noise, the clink of ice in a glass. Puzzled, he pushed the door with his right foot and leaped into the condo, staying doubled over at the waist, Sparrow on his heels. He darted forward into a living room and halted abruptly when he saw the lovely redheaded woman in a yellow gown sitting on a sofa, a large glass in her right hand.

"Hi, there, handsome," the woman said cheerily, and took a healthy swallow of her drink. She lowered the glass and giggled. "Don't mind me, honey. I'm trying to get plastered to the gills."

Mystified by her indifferent attitude to their arrival, Havoc straightened and surveyed the rest of the condo, noting there were other doors. "What's your name?"

"Mundy, handsome. Gloria Mundy," she said, and tipped her glass again.

"Is anyone else here?"

"Nope. Just little old me," Gloria replied, and giggled.

Havoc glanced at the Flathead. "Check anyway."

Nodding, Sparrow moved toward the doors.

"Don't you believe me?" Gloria queried, sounding hurt. "What is this? Dump-on-Mundy night or something?"

"I can't take any chances," Havoc told her. "This is Mr. Bad's condo, isn't it?"

"Yeah," Gloria said, her mouth curling downward. "The prick lives here."

"And what about the other one across the hall, the one with the red door?"

"That's my place, or it used to be. I've taken all the abuse I'm going to take from that son of a bitch. I plan to pack up and haul ass," Gloria stated angrily, and took yet another gulp.

"Was Mr. Bad here?"

"Yeah. He cut out a bit ago, him and that freaky bodyguard of his, the Claw.'' Gloria shuddered and drank some more, then smacked her red lips. ''I never knew straight whiskey could taste so good.''

''Do you happen to know the address of the Barons' mansion?'' Havoc inquired.

''The Barons? Nope. Sure don't,'' Gloria answered, slurring her words a tad. She tittered. ''Hey, there's an idea. Maybe I'll find out and go offer my bod to Owsley. I bet he likes a good lay as much as the next guy. And I'm a *good* lay!''

''I'll bet,'' Havoc muttered, and saw Sparrow return. ''Anything?''

''Empty.''

''Okay,'' Havoc said. He turned toward the corridor and raised his voice. ''Jag, bring that joker in here.''

Gloria Mundy winked at Sparrow Hawk. ''Hey, there, sailor.''

''I'm an Indian.''

''I can see you are, cutie-pie. I've never had an Indian before. What are you like in the sack?''

''I sometimes snore.''

''Snore?'' Gloria said, and cackled so hard she spilled a little of her drink. ''I like a man with a sense of humor. Have you ever been around the world?''

''No,'' Sparrow answered. ''California is the farthest I have been from my people.''

It took Gloria all of 15 seconds to comprehend his reply, and then she bent in half with unrestrained mirth.

Jaguarundi entered, shoving their prisoner ahead of him. ''Here's Sunshine,'' he quipped.

''Sheba!'' Gloria Mundy exclaimed. ''You look a little worse for wear, babe.''

''Get stuffed, bimbo,'' the Brother said sullenly.

Gloria tittered. ''What did I ever do to you?''

''That's enough out of both of you,'' Havoc said, and jerked his left thumb at the lean man in the brown suit. ''This guy claims he doesn't know where Mr. Bad went. What about it, Gloria?''

''He's lying.''

Sheba took a stride toward her, his fists clenched. "Shut up, you stupid bitch!"

Havoc instantly pivoted and executed the *Kinteki-seashi-geri*, kicking his right instep into the Brother's testicles. The blow made Sheba grunt and drop to his knees. Havoc whipped his left hand down, his index finger extended, delivering an *Ippon-nukite* strike to the temple, his bony finger the equivalent of a blackjack.

Stunned, Sheba sagged, his hands holding his groin.

"Hold this," Havoc said, and tossed the M.A.C. 10 to Jaguarundi, who deftly caught the weapon.

"Hit the scumbag again!" Gloria urged.

Havoc reached down, gripped the Brother's chin, and snapped the man's head up so he could glare into Sheba's eyes. "No more games, asshole. I'm tired of being treated like a lightweight. This is the Force you're dealing with, you stupid son of a bitch. If you don't give me the answers I need, Jag here will do to you what he did to your friend."

"The Force?" Sheba blurted.

"Yeah. The Freedom Force. I take it you've heard of us?"

The Brother, his eyes wide, nodded.

"Good. Then don't play around. Where did Mr. Bad and the Claw go?"

Sheba opened his mouth, then closed it.

"You asked for it, dipstick," Havoc said, straightening. "Jag, he's all yours."

The hybrid beamed and took a step forward.

"Wait!" Sheba cried, glancing nervously at the mutation. "I'll tell you what you want to know."

"I haven't got all day," Havoc snapped.

"They went to the warehouse, man."

"What warehouse?"

"Over on Warner Avenue in Santa Ana. Thirty-seven Fifty-nine Warner."

"What's there?"

"It's the warehouse where we keep our stash of weapons and where we store a lot of our big drug shipments."

"Weapons, huh?" Havoc responded thoughtfully. "One more thing. Where's the Barons' mansion located?"

"Owsley's place?"

"Do they have another mansion?"

"No. It's at Twelve Hundred Sunset Boulevard. Up in West Hollywood."

"Thank you," Havoc said politely, and snap-kicked the Brother on the jaw, causing blood to squirt from Sheba's lower lip. Without another word the man collapsed.

Jaguarundi chuckled. "I love it when you get forceful. Has anyone ever told you that you're a lot like Blade?"

The innocent query made Havoc stiffen and frown. "No," he answered testily.

"Which will we do first?" Sparrow Hawk inquired. "Go to the warehouse or go to the mansion?"

"What do you use for brains?" Jag responded. "We'll go after Raphaela first, of course."

"No, we won't," Havoc said, correcting him.

Jag did a double take. "Say again?"

"We need more weapons. Two M.A.C. 10's, the revolver, a hunting knife, and Lobo's NATO aren't enough if we're going to attack the Barons in their own stronghold. I say we go to the warehouse first and obtain the weapons we need," Havoc explained.

"Your proposal sounds wise," Sparrow said.

"I don't know," Jag said. "What about Raphaela?"

"What about her? What good would it do her for us to assault the mansion if the Barons have superior firepower? Do you think they'll be using slingshots?"

"No."

"Then we need weapons," Havoc reiterated. "And there should be all the weapons we'll require at the warehouse."

"What warehouse?" a new voice interjected, and Lobo and Doc entered the condo.

The captain turned to them. "I'll explain on the way. I don't suppose you saw any sign of Mr. Bad?"

"Nope," Lobo said. "We went all the way to the bottom. He's long gone."

"But we know where to find him," Havoc informed them.

"What about this trash?" Jag inquired, pointing at Sheba.

"Tie him up but good. We'll leave him here and phone

the police later.''

Jag walked to the right wall, picked up a lamp, and tore the electrical cord off the base with a yank of his powerful sinews.

''What about me, lover?'' Gloria Mundy spoke up.

''You can do whatever you want,'' Havoc replied.

''Goody. I think I'll help myself to a few more drinks before I take off.''

''Let's go find a cab,'' Havoc stated to the others.

''You don't need a cab,'' Gloria declared.

''We don't?''

''Nope. Look in Sheba's front pockets. You should find a key to a green Chevy parked in the lot out back.''

Havoc smiled. ''Thanks.''

''No problem,'' Gloria said. ''But there is a favor I'd like you to do.''

''What?''

''When you finally catch up with Mr. Bad, give the bum one of those fancy kicks for me.''

''It'll be my pleasure.''

CHAPTER SIXTEEN

Raphaela sat on the edge of the bed in a room on the second floor of Arthur Owsley's mansion, her expression glum, and stared at the two Barons who had been assigned to guard her. They were standing near one of the windows fronting the south side of the mansion, their arms folded, conversing in muted tones. Each man had an AK-47 slung over his left shoulder.

What should she do?

She looked down at herself, at the detestable gown, and frowned. Here was another fine mess she'd gotten herself into! And it was up to her to get herself out. She was a member of the Force, darn it all, the best combat unit on the continent. She should be able to escape without the aid of her friends.

But how?

Raphaela gazed at the closed door 12 feet to her left. There were not only guards in her room, there were Barons posted on each floor and at least a half-dozen patrolling the grounds. How could she escape when the odds were stacked against her?

"Hey, lady," one of the guards unexpectedly said. "Would you like something to drink?"

"Drink?" Raphaela repeated absently.

"Yeah. I'm going downstairs for a pop. The boss said to give you whatever you want, so do you want a drink or not?"

"A pop would be nice. Thanks."

"For a cute dish like you, anything." He smiled and left, closing the door behind him.

Raphaela studied the remaining Baron, a young man in his early twenties with sandy colored hair and blue eyes. He studiously avoided gazing in her direction. "Hi," she said.

"Hi," he mumbled while watching out the window.

"What's your name?"

"They call me Tab."

"I'm Raphaela."

"So I was told."

Raphaela scrutinized him closely, estimating they were approximately the same height and weight. His clothing particularly interested her, a beige shirt and jeans about her size. An idea occurred to her, and she decided to act before the other Baron came back. "You're not being very friendly."

"The boss told us to keep our distance or else," Tab disclosed without turning around.

"Can't you be the least bit nice? I'm scared out of my wits and I need someone to talk to."

The young Baron rotated at last and regarded her intently. "I suppose it would be okay just to talk."

Raphaela grinned and patted the bedspread beside her. "Why don't you sit over here?"

"Not on your life."

"Why not?"

"Mr. Owsley would skin me alive."

Pouting, Raphaela let her shoulders slump and bowed her head. "Oh, I understand. You don't trust me."

"It's not that," Tab said.

"Then what? You'd be doing me a favor. I'm sure Mr. Owsley wouldn't mind."

The young Baron glanced at the door, then at the bed. His eyes rested on her shoulders and the cleavage revealed by the gown. "I guess it might be okay, but just for a few minutes, until Gus gets back."

"Thank you," Raphaela said, and gave him her most radiant smile. She had never used her feminine wiles to deceive a man before, and she found the experience delightfully fascinating. Her aunt had kept her so sheltered during her teen years, a prisoner almost, that she had never dated boys her own age, never known the thrill of a romantic evening, never known the gentle touch of a man who truly cared. Her only sexual experience, if she dared call that nightmare such, hardly counted.

Tab walked over and sat down several feet from her. "What do you want to talk about?"

"Anything. How about you?"

"What about me?"

"How long have you been a Baron?"

"I don't know. Ten years maybe."

"That long?"

"Why not? I got into the gang to get the bread for my habit, and I've been going strong ever since."

"Your habit?" Raphaela questioned.

"Yeah, lady. My habit. I'm hooked on the hard stuff, you know?"

"Hard stuff?"

"Drugs, lady. Damn! Where are you from? The moon?"

Raphaela pretended to be stung by his rebuke. She averted her face and said softly, "I'm sorry I'm so ignorant. I'm from the Mound and no one there uses drugs."

Tab slid nearer. "Hey, I didn't mean anything by that remark. Really."

"That's all right. I know you're probably embarrassed talking to a dummy like me," Raphaela said sadly, her chin on her chest.

"You're not a dummy," Tab responded. "You're just upset because of everything that's happened to you." He placed his hand gently on her shoulder. "Don't worry. You'll be fine."

"I know," Raphaela stated firmly, mentally reviewing the technique Blade had taught her, hoping she could perform the move properly, tensing her right arm and holding her fingers straight and tight. Twisting, she smiled coyly at the Baron and then, when their eyes were locked, when he was totally distracted by her apparent friendliness and her physical charms, she struck. Her right arm swept out and around, her hand rigid, and she was almost as shocked as the young Baron when the edge of her hand connected with the soft flesh on his throat.

Tab gagged and tried to stand, his hands instinctively going to his neck.

Raphaela stood, brought her right arm forward, and then drove her elbow back again, planting it on the Baron's nose, breaking his nostrils and sending crimson spray shooting from his nasal passages.

Sliding frantically away from her, Tab struggled to his feet.

Raphaela spun, remembering the advice the Warrior had given her: "When in doubt, go for the gonads." She did, planting her left foot where it would do the most harm, and she was rewarded by Tab falling to his knees. He was in exquisite agony but not out yet.

Hurry! her mind shrieked.

Gus would be coming back soon!

Her anxiety mounting, Raphaela kicked him in the stomach, making him bend over. She jumped into the air and brought both her kneecaps down on the back of his head, slamming his face into the floor.

Tab went suddenly limp.

Move! Move! Move!

Squatting, Raphaela relieved the Baron of the AK-47, then began to hurriedly strip off his clothes. Fortunately he wore underwear. In less than a minute she had his jeans and shirt on the bed and was quickly removing her gown. As she peeled the garment from her like a banana skin and stood for a second in her panties and bra, she felt terribly exposed and vulnerable. Donning the jeans and the shirt took mere moments, although she had to tug to get the pants on over her combat boots.

Somewhere in the hallway a voice sounded.

Raphaela scooped up the AK-47 and moved a yard behind the door, her finger on the trigger. No sooner was she in position than the knob started to turn, and she braced herself as the door opened.

"What the hell!"

Stepping from concealment, Raphaela trained the AK-47 on Gus, who was framed in the doorway. "Quiet! Get in here!"

The Baron had a can of pop in each hand. He gawked at Tab, then glared at her. "You bitch!" he hissed.

"Quiet!" Raphaela repeated, and moved a pace closer. "Don't think I can't use this. I've been trained by the best."

His eyes pinpoints of hatred, Gus slowly elevated his arms and came into the bedroom. "And you didn't look like you could harm a flea," he muttered, watching a rivulet of blood flow from under Tab's nose.

"Never underestimate a member of the Force," Raphaela boasted. "Not put those cans and your gun on the bed. Be sure and do it very, very slowly."

Scowling, Gus obeyed her command, depositing the cans first and then carefully slipping the AK-47 from his shoulder onto the bedspread. "There, bitch. I hope you're satisfied," he snapped.

"Not quite," Raphaela responded, and moved in from the rear, her right boot lashing out and catching him behind the knee.

Taken unawares, Gus buckled.

Swinging her AK-47 in a half-circle, Raphaela slammed the Baron on the head as he went down, the heavy stock thudding against his cranium and dazing him. He landed on his left knee and attempted to right himself. "Sweet dreams," she said, and clubbed him again, then once more for good measure, and finally he pitched onto his face beside his fellow Baron.

Moving rapidly now, Raphaela went to the doorway and checked the hall, relieved to find there were no Barons in sight. She eased out and made for the stairs leading to the ground floor, hoping she could reach the front door undetected. Once outside, she could lose herself in the gardens surrounding the mansion. When only five feet from the stairs, she stopped, listening. And it was well she did.

A Baron suddenly materialized in front of her, at the top of the staircase, his head turned away from her, a shotgun in his left hand.

Raphaela reacted instantly, taking hold of the AK-47 by the barrel and swinging the weapon like a club as she charged.

The Baron heard her and tried to spin, but he was too slow.

With a pronounced thud the stock crashed into the gang member's face, full on the mouth, and the man was knocked backwards to tumble down the stairs. Raphaela stepped into the open in time to see him somersault to the bottom and wind up in a disjointed heap, apparently unconscious, the shotgun lying on the steps, about halfway down.

"What the hell was that?" someone cried.

It was now or never!

Raphaela bounded down the steps, taking three at a leap, almost losing her balance on the third one from the bottom, but she corrected her stride and came down next to the insensate Baron. The front door, if her bearings were accurate, should be to her left, and she whirled in that direction to discover a stupefied Baron not ten feet away, an M-16 cradled under his right arm.

The man tried to bring his weapon to bear.

On pure instinct, Raphaela pointed the AK-47 and squeezed the trigger, holding on tightly as the assault rifle bucked in her hands and thundered its staccato rhythm of death.

A deluge of heavy slugs tore into the Baron, perforating his torso and sending him flying. He crashed onto his back and tried feebly to rise, but couldn't.

Raphaela raced along the hall, passing the Baron and observing his eyes already beginning to glaze lifelessly. She reached the next junction, and there was the front door.

And two more Barons.

Crouching, the stock pressed against her thigh, Raphaela fired, unleashing a rain of lead that bored into the pair and drove them back against the door, blood spurting from their wounds. They started to crumple and she made for the entrance and freedom.

"Hold it!"

The bellow from her right caused her to drop and roll just as a shotgun blasted and a chunk of door exploded outward. She glanced along the right-hand corridor and spotted her foe, a skinny Baron with a ring in his nose. Before he could cut loose again, she angled the barrel and let him have a half-dozen rounds in the chest.

He screamed as he died.

There was no time to lose!

Raphaela shoved to her feet and lunged at the door, grabbing the knob and turning. Or trying to, because the front door had been locked.

NO!

She stepped back, pointing the AK-47 at the panel to blow the lock to smithereens.

"That would be naughty," said a familiar voice behind her.

Raphaela started to turn, but bands of steel seemed to enclose her body as two huge arms encircled her and held fast. She felt moist lips press against her right ear.

"Feel free to struggle, my dear. I'd enjoy that."

About to kick and thrash in an effort to bust loose, Raphaela relaxed instead, willing herself to stay calm, not to lose control. "Forget it, Owsley," she said. "I won't give you the satisfaction."

"Perhaps not now, but later you will," the head Baron predicted. "Kindly drop your weapon."

Reluctant to give up, Raphaela hesitated.

Owsley tightened his enormous arms, displaying his prodigious strength, revealing that every square inch of him was hardened muscle.

Raphaela gasped as the constriction on her chest resulted in intense pain and discomfort. Those arms of his were like pythons. She let go of the AK-47 and the gun clattered at her feet.

"How obliging of you," Owsley said. He suddenly slackened his grasp and gave her a shove, sending her sprawling into the front door. In a flash he retrieved the AK-47.

Barely catching herself in time to prevent her forehead from bashing the wooden door panel, Raphaela pivoted.

"Please don't be foolhardy," Owsley advised, his tone acidic. "I may want to trifle with you later, but that won't stop me from killing you now if you cause more trouble."

Other Barons appeared, converging from every direction.

"Gus and Tab are out cold upstairs," one of the gang members reported. "And Eddie is at the bottom of the stairs. He'll live, but his face will never be the same."

Owsley gazed at the two bodies near the door, the dead shotgun-wielder, and then at the first man she had killed farther down the hall. His lips curved downward. "Four dead and three injured. You are far more formidable than I believed." He sighed. "Very well. I shall *personally* escort you back to the bedroom and *personally* bind you so that you can't move more than your eyelids, and then we shall wait for your friends from the Force to arrive."

"They'll be here," Raphaela said defiantly.

"I hope they come soon," Owsley responded. "I can't wait to finish with them so I can repay you for all the aggravation you've caused me." He leered at her. "Three guesses what I have in mind."

CHAPTER SEVENTEEN

Gloria Mundy was having the time of her life.

She alternated her time between drinking, singing to herself, drinking, walking over to kick Sheba every now and then, drinking, and cursing Haywood Keif from the comfort of his sofa.

Right now she was taking another sip of whiskey while sneering at Sheba, who had been bent into the shape of a pretzel and bound securely and gagged by the hybrid. The Brother had regained consciousness 15 minutes ago. He was lying near the bar, facing her, glaring and uttering incomprehensible oaths through the dirty sock the hybrid had crammed into his mouth.

"What's that?" Gloria asked. "You'll have to speak up. I can't hear you." She threw back her head and laughed, rating herself as the funniest person on the planet.

Sheba voiced inarticulate growls and grunts and struggled in vain against the electrical cord binding his wrists and ankles.

Gloria leaned forward. "Did you say you have to take a

leak? Sorry, asshole. Go in your pants.''

His features beet red, Sheba bucked and heaved to no avail.

"I wish I had a camera," Gloria joked, and swallowed more whiskey. Her senses were swimming and she had difficulty focusing, but she didn't care. She was feeling no pain, and that was how she wanted to feel.

Sheba ceased his struggles and rested his forehead on the floor.

"Are you done with the temper tantrum?" Gloria queried sarcastically.

The Brother could only glower.

"How does that sock taste?" Gloria wondered. "I told that cat-guy where to find Mr. Bad's clothes hamper. Aren't I a peach?"

Sheba renewed his futile efforts to free himself.

Gloria suddenly realized her glass was empty. "Damn! How did this happen?" She stood and walked unsteadily over to the bar, pausing to give Sheba a healthy jab in the ribs with her left foot. He went insane, bouncing and rolling about like a fish out of water. "Boy, some people are real grumps," she said, and tittered.

Sheba abruptly stopped, his body aligned in the direction of the front door, his eyes almost bulging from their sockets.

"That's better," Gloria chided him. "You have pitiful manners." She grabbed the whiskey bottle and upended it into her glass, frowning when the bottle went dry after giving her only half a refill. "Will you look at this? We're running low on happy juice."

The Brother did not even bother to grunt. He seemed to be trying to sink out of sight in the carpet.

"What's the matter, honey?" Gloria asked. "Dirty sock got your tongue?" She cackled and turned to retrace her steps to the sofa.

And saw *him*.

"Dear God!" she blurted out, amazed by the gigantic figure standing not five feet away, a veritable colossus whose muscles appeared to have been sculpted from bronzed marble. She inadvertently let go of her glass and felt the whiskey splash her feet and legs. "Who the hell are you?"

"I'll ask the questions," the giant informed her.

"Whatever you say. I make it a point never to argue with a guy the size of King Kong."

"King who?"

"You know," Gloria said. "That big, hairy gorilla who goes around feeling up the broads."

The giant stared at her strangely for a few seconds, as if he couldn't decide if she was serious or not. He watched her sway from side to side and sniffed the air. "You're inebriated."

Gloria stuck her nose in the air and held her shoulders steady. "I am not, and I resent your insenu—insinula—what you said."

"Is this Mr. Bad's condo?"

"Sure is. Or was," Gloria replied, and snickered.

"He's not here?"

"Nope. Flew the coop."

Pursing his lips, the giant looked down at Sheba. "Who's this?"

"His name is Shit-for-Brains," Gloria answered.

The giant placed his hands on his hips, next to two bulges under his black leather vest. "Do you happen to know the Barons?"

"Not personally. Yet."

"Then you wouldn't know where their base of operations is located?"

"Their base?" Gloria said, perplexed, her brow furrowed. "Oh! You mean Owsley's mansion."

"Owsley?"

"Yep. Arthur Owsley. The leader of the Barons," Gloria disclosed. She glanced at Sheba. "And yeah, I do happen to know the address."

The giant loomed above her before she could take another breath, his visage a mask of strained intensity, and the next words he spoke were low and grating. "What is it?"

Gloria stared up into his piercing gray eyes and shivered. "The mansion is in West Hollywood. Twelve Hundred Sunset Boulevard."

He whirled and departed without another word, vanishing

out the front door as insubstantially as a ghost, making no sound, saying nothing more.

Blinking in bewilderment, Gloria gazed at the doorway and wondered if she had imagined the whole thing. She pondered the giant's interest in the Barons, and after a minute her sluggish mind came to a conclusion and she frowned. "Damn. So much for trying to bed Owsley." She glanced down at Sheba. "I guess the Barons can kiss their asses goodbye, huh?"

The Brother simply glared at her.

"You know something?" Gloria snapped. "You're rude." So saying, and just for the general hell of it, she kicked him in the head.

CHAPTER EIGHTEEN

"**W**e'll drive around the block one more time," Havoc proposed, and took a left at the corner, keeping his eyes on the warehouse.

Three stories in height and 50 yards in length, the exterior of the building had been painted a dull brown many years ago. The paint was now peeling, and the entire warehouse had been neglected to the point where the structure badly needed repairs. Several of the upper windows were cracked or had panes missing. The windows on the ground floor, though, were all intact and barred. On the west side a single door was located under a faded sign bearing the word OFFICE in large black letters. To the east a loading dock, bordered by a parking lot, ran almost the width of the warehouse. A towering corrugated metal door served as the entryway for the goods unloaded on the dock.

"It ain't going to be easy gettin' in there," Lobo commented.

"We've got to find a way," Doc said. "I don't like the idea of coming here while Raphaela is in the hands of those lowlifes.''

"I've already explained the reason," Havoc said.

Doc nodded. "Yep. But I still don't like it much."

The neighborhood in which the warehouse was located contained a few deserted business offices and similar storehouses. Most of the workers had departed for the day and traffic was sparse.

Captain Havoc considered the lack of pedestrians a plus. At least, he reasoned, they wouldn't have to worry about bystanders being accidentally hurt. He scrutinized the parking lot behind the warehouse, counting seven vehicles all told, six cars and a van. A frown creased his mouth. There must be other Brothers inside besides Mr. Bad and the one known as the Claw, which would make their job that much harder.

"Why are there no lights on?" Sparrow Hawk queried.

"Because they know we're after them and they're hidin' in the dark, tremblin' with fear," Lobo said, and snickered.

"They don't know we're on their trail," Doc stated.

The Clansman shrugged. "Then maybe they all went beddy-bye early. How should I know."

"I don't like it," Havoc declared. "It smells of a trap. They may not be expecting us, but they might be expecting the Barons. I wish we had more weapons." He drove into an alley to the east of the warehouse, bordering the parking lot, and braked.

"We could pull a Madsen and ram one of the doors with the car," Lobo suggested.

"No," Havoc responded. "Ramming plate-glass doors is one thing, but those on that building are probably reinforced with steel and as solid as a rock."

"Then how will we get in?" Sparrow questioned.

"We'll come up with a way," Havoc said confidently, turning off the ignition and killing the lights. He grinned. "We could always knock on the office door and claim we're selling Girl Scout cookies."

No one laughed.

"Who are the Girl Scouts?" Sparrow inquired.

"I didn't figure you California types were much good at scouting and trapping and such," Doc added.

"Are these Girl Scouts foxes?" Lobo wanted to know. "How about settin' me up on a date with one?"

Havoc sighed and climbed out, taking a M.A.C. 10 from the front seat and turning to face the warehouse and the parking lot. There were few streetlights in the industrial district. A full moon rising in the east provided pale illumination.

The others bailed out of the car.

"Want me to check out the warehouse?" Jag asked.

"We'll stick together for the time being," Havoc said, and looked at Lobo. "All except for you. You stay here with the Chevy."

"Say what?"

"You heard me."

"Why the hell should I stay here?" the Clansman replied indignantly.

"Because you were shot, remember?"

"I'm fine now," Lobo stated, and to emphasize his contention he reached up and swiftly removed the makeshift bandage.

"You're injured," Havoc reiterated. "You could become dizzy at any moment."

"He's always dizzy," Jag interjected.

"Up yours," Lobo snapped. "I'm not stayin' here and that's final."

"Yes, you are," Havoc stated.

"Oh, yeah? Who's going to make me?"

"Me."

"When did Blade die and Gallagher make you his replacement?" Lobo said angrily.

"Lighten up, Lobo," Jag commented. "Havoc is right and you know it."

"Yeah," Doc said. "We don't have time for this squabbling with Raphaela's life on the line."

The Clansman looked at each of them, then leaned against the car and folded his arms on his chest. "Fine. Be that way. If you chumps don't want me along, go by yourselves. Get wasted. See if I care."

"If we're not back in fifteen minutes, call the police,"

Havoc instructed, and ran toward the parking lot.

"Yeah. Sure," Lobo said, and watched his companions cross to the van and the six cars, then dash to the side of the loading platform where they were lost in the darkness. He grinned, waited a minute to be sure none of them would be looking back at him, and followed.

The concrete loading dock stood five feet high. Captain Havoc crouched in the inky gloom at its base and whispered instructions. "We'll split up here. Jag, you and Sparrow swing around to the right. Doc and I will take the left side. See if you can discover a way in. We'll meet out front near the office door."

"Be seeing you," Jag said, and slipped into the night with the Flathead right behind him.

"Maybe that big metal door is unlocked," Doc speculated.

"Even if it is, opening it would rouse the dead," Havoc said. "There's got to be another way." He ran along the dock until he reached the corner, then paused to scan the side of the warehouse. There was no sign of movement, no hint of light within. Where were the damn Brothers? Keeping low, he moved to the west, constantly surveying the windows for any hint of danger. When he came to the first barred-ground level window, he halted to inspect it. The bars were encased in the wall, impossible to remove without explosives or a blowtorch. He peered at the glass and discovered the reason no light was visible. Someone had spray-painted the inside of the window a dark blue or black. At the very edges a thin seam of light could be detected, but otherwise the warehouse appeared to be empty and deserted. He gazed upward, speculating on whether all the windows had been painted or just those on the ground floor.

Havoc continued westward, passing four more barred windows before he stopped at the far corner. He poked his head out and was surprised to find Jag and Sparrow had not yet arrived.

Doc eased alongside the officer. "Why don't we try that office door? It can't hurt."

Why not, indeed? Havoc sprinted to the door and pressed

his back to the wall. The hybrid and the Flathead had still not appeared. Leaning forward, he extended his left arm and gripped the doorknob lightly. At the bottom of the door faint rays of light were discernible.

"I'm ready," Doc whispered, cocking his Magnum.

Havoc began to turn the knob slowly, intending to open the door a mere hair if it wasn't locked. To his astonishment, the knob twisted easily. Too easily, as it turned out, for suddenly the door was thrown wide from within, jarring Havoc's arm and throwing him off balance. Before he could recover, an M-16 barrel was rammed into his ribs.

"Freeze or die, suckers!"

Brothers poured from the warehouse, seven of them in all, each armed with an assault rifle, each swinging his weapon to cover the officer and the Cavalryman.

Doc Madsen almost fired. He stepped away from the wall to give himself a clear shot even as the door opened, but in the instant he started to squeeze the trigger he saw the first gang member jab the M-16 into Havoc's side. He knew if he shot the Brother, the man might still get off a few rounds. If so, Havoc's life was forfeit. So superb were his reflexes, so coordinated his control of his hands, that he was able to refrain from firing, and by then it was too late to offer any resistance because the rest of the Brothers had emerged.

"Drop your guns!" the lead Brother directed. "Now!"

Reluctantly, his eyes smoldering, Doc lowered the Magnum to the ground.

Havoc eased his M.A.C. 10 downward until it rested near his feet.

"Thought you were pulling a fast one, huh, turkeys?" the spokesman said, and snorted. "We saw you jokers coming from the upstairs windows and Mr. Bad arranged this little reception."

"We're looking forward to seeing him," Havoc mentioned.

"Shut your face, honky," the Brother snapped, then glanced at another gang member. "Artie, take four guys and go find those two who were coming around the other side.

Remember, the boss wants 'em alive if possible.''

"Got it, Spooner," Artie replied. He pointed at three other Brothers and they raced to the north corner.

Artie gouged the barrel into the officer. "Inside, asshole. And don't try no funny stuff.''

His arms in the air, his features hardened in resentment of his own stupidity in being captured, Havoc stepped into the warehouse, glancing at the north corner as he did, one thought uppermost in his mind.

Where the hell were Jaguarundi and Sparrow Hawk?

"Hold it," Jag whispered when they were halfway along the north side of the structure.

"What is it, my brother?" Sparrow asked softly.

"I've got to go."

"What?"

"I have to take a leak."

"This is not the proper time for humor," the Flathead noted.

"Who's kidding?" Jag responded. "I've had to go since we left the condo, and that driving around didn't help my kidneys much." He took two strides from the wall and reached under his loincloth.

Sparrow looked both ways, then at the hybrid. "Can't you hold it in?"

"When a guy's got to go, he's got to go," Jag said, and began spraying the barren strip of land rimming the north side of the building. "Ahhhhh. Relief at last.''

Sparrow heard the urine splattering the ground and inhaled a pungent scent that reminded him of the smell of mountain lion pee. He scrunched up his nose and held his breath, waiting impatiently for the hybrid to finish. The cat-man seemed to go on forever. Sparrow was finally compelled to take a breath, and the odor almost made him cough.

"There we go," Jag whispered, and hitched at his loincloth. He headed westward again, proceeding cautiously, his keen ears alert for the slightest sound.

"Would you do me a favor?" Sparrow requested.

"What's that?"

"The next time, stand downwind."

"Smart-ass."

Jag flexed his fingers as he neared the corner. He was still six feet away when he heard a sudden commotion from the front of the building, and alarmed for the safety of Havoc and Doc, he ran to the corner and stopped. A hasty glance revealed the pair partly ringed by armed Brothers.

"What's happened?" Sparrow asked, the words barely audible.

"They've been caught," Jag replied, weighing the implications. Was it possible the Brothers had seen them approach? If so, there would be gang members after Sparrow and him within seconds. "Come on," he prompted, and jogged away from the corner, retracing their route to the nearest barred window.

"What are we doing?" Sparrow asked.

"Planning a little surprise of our own," Jag answered. The lower edge of the window came to the height of his chest, and he reached up and took hold of two bars, testing them. They would resist even his bestial strength, but he had no intention of trying to break them. "Climb," he said, and immediately did so, clambering to the top of the bars and pressing flat against the wall.

Sparrow promptly followed suit, clamping his teeth on the hilt of his knife so his hands would be free.

Seconds later the drumming of running feet heralded the appearance of four Brothers at the northwest corner. They slowed, scanning the ground, searching for the two intruders they knew to be on the property.

"Where'd they go?" one of them asked.

"Maybe they went back toward the loading dock," suggested another.

"After 'em," said the Brother in the lead.

The four gang members dashed toward the rear, hugging the wall, their attention focused on the area in front of them and the space between the warehouse and the next building to the north. None of them gave the windows more than a cursory glance because they rightly believed the bars were unbreakable and no one could gain entry on the ground level.

Jag grinned as the quartet came underneath the bars, then launched himself into the air, his fingers curled in the shape of claws, eager to tear into the Brothers, and tear into them he did, his arms in motion the moment his feet plowed into the back of the foremost gang member. He raked his nails across the face of the second Brother, ripping the skin and lacerating the man's eyes, and used the back of the collapsing leader as a springboard. He vaulted and flipped, tucking his knees into his chest, and landed between the second and third Brother.

"My eyes!" the second man shrieked, his hands clasping his face.

His motions a blur, Jag grabbed the front of the third Brother's T-shirt and lifted the man into the air, then cast him at the fourth gang member, who was in the act of bringing his assault rifle to bear.

The first Brother had already recovered. He rose to his knees and twisted, aiming at the hybrid's furry back. Out of the corner of his eye he detected movement, and then a heavy body struck him on the chest and knocked him down. Dazed, he looked up to behold, of all things, an Indian. An Indian with a knife.

Sparrow speared his hunting knife straight into the gang member's heart, hearing the thud as the hilt hit the chest, and saw the Brother stiffen and gasp. He wrenched the blade out and spun, and not a foot away stood the Brother with the torn eyes.

"Help me!" the man screeched. "I can't see!"

His right arm whipping in an upward sweep, Sparrow sank the blade into the second man's neck at the base of the throat. Warm blood cascaded over his fingers and wrist, and he yanked the knife out again.

"No!" the Brother wailed, a crimson gusher gusting from his mouth. He tottered and dropped to his knees, blubbering in anguish, then fell forward and was still.

Sparrow went to assist his friend, but the battle was over. Jaguarundi was astride the last gang member, blood and gore coating his fingers and nails. He straightened and turned. "Are you okay?"

"Yes. And you?"

"I'm just getting warmed up. Someone was bound to have heard that bozo yelling. Grab a couple of weapons and let's go."

Sparrow hastily retrieved two M-16's, slung one over his left shoulder, and moved toward the corner. The hybrid was several feet in front of him, and Sparrow noticed that Jag had not picked up a gun. "Shouldn't you have a weapon too?" he asked.

"I do," Jaguarundi responded, and wagged his hands. "Ten of them."

Lobo squatted behind the van and scrutinized the loading dock. His teammates had disappeared a short while ago, and he debated whether to follow Havoc and Doc or Jag and Sparrow. As he peered at the rear of the warehouse he noticed a window to the left of the corrugated metal door, high up near the roof.

What if the Brothers had a lookout posted there?

The idea bothered Lobo. It meant his friends would be walking into a trap unless they were very careful. But Havoc was a professional soldier. Surely the captain would have reached the same conclusion. Even so, what choice would Havoc have had except to continue the operation? They needed weapons if they were to rescue Raphaela, and the weapons they wanted were inside that warehouse.

Maybe a distraction was in order.

Lobo scratched his head, trying to devise a suitable diversion, a scheme that might draw the Brothers out or at the very least lure their attention away from Havoc and the rest.

But what?

He gazed at the parked vehicles. If he had the keys, he could drive them onto the loading dock wall or something. *That* would really grab the Brothers' attention. Only he didn't have the keys, and he didn't know how to start a vehicle without them.

So what else could he do?

Lobo thought and thought, and after a bit grinned in delight at the inspiration he received.

"Yep.

This promised to be fun!

There were seven more armed Brothers, most attired in leather clothes or jeans and torn T-shirts, waiting inside when Havoc and Doc were ushered into the warehouse.

"Here's two of the bastards," the gang member named Spooner announced. He was a heavyset black with a styled Afro.

The two remaining Brothers from the ambush detail closed the door and posted themselves on either side.

"Where's Artie and the rest?" one of the seven inquired.

"I sent them after the others," Spooner replied.

"I noticed you didn't go with them."

Spooner glared at the speaker, then prodded Havoc with his M-16. "Keep moving, honky."

The captain glanced to the right and the left, studying the layout, seeking a means of turning the tables. To his left, wide metal stairs ascended to the second floor, and partly visible through a doorway was a darkened chamber. Only the lights on the bottom floor had been turned on. To the right was a small closed office.

Directly ahead stretched an enormous expanse of concrete floor. Crates and boxes had been stacked high against each wall, reaching almost to the ceiling. Solitary bulbs positioned at 20-foot intervals sufficed for lighting. Apparently no one bothered to clean very often because dust and litter dotted the concrete. Standing 40 feet from the door, near a short column of wooden crates, were the handsome guy and the one with the pincer.

Mr. Bad and the Claw.

Havoc strolled casually toward them, his eyes roving to the crates and boxes, reading the words someone had scrawled in red magic marker on the side of each one. Many of the words made no sense to him. CRYSTAL. SNEEZE. ZIG-ZAGS. But others he definitely recognized. M-16's. GRENADE LAUNCHERS. MORTARS. There were enough crates of arms to outfit an army.

"Hey, Boss!" Spooner called out. "Got two presents for you!"

The head of the Brothers and his hulking bodyguard advanced to meet them.

At that moment a loud screech sounded outside, on the north side of the building, and a man was heard crying, "My eyes!"

"What the hell!" Spooner blurted.

Mr. Bad halted and cocked his head. Several of his men started for the door, but he stopped them with an imperious gesture.

"That was Fritzy," Spooner said. "I'm sure of it."

Seconds later the same man shouted again. "Help me! I can't see!" Then there was a terrified "No!" Then silence.

"Should we go help them, Boss?" Spooner asked.

"And be cut down before you got two yards?" Mr. Bad replied sarcastically. "No, Spooner. We stay put until I get to the bottom of this." He walked up to Havoc and studied the officer's countenance, then glanced at the Cavalryman. "Neither of you are Barons."

"What was your first clue?" Havoc joked, and immediately regretted his brashness when Mr. Bad backhanded him across the mouth. He rocked with the blow but retained his footing.

"Don't open your mouth unless I tell you to open it," Mr. Bad stated harshly, and motioned at his bodyguard.

The Claw came over and extended his left arm, his metal pincer gleaming in the light. He opened and closed the pincer with a loud snap.

"Try to be funny again and I'll have Claw crush your balls to a pulp," Mr. Bad vowed.

Havoc held himself in check with a supreme effort. He could feel blood trickling from the corner of his mouth.

"I've seen these two guys before," the Claw declared.

"You have?"

"Yeah. Don't you remember? They were with that red-headed chick at the club."

Mr. Bad stared from one to the other. "Now that you mention it, I do remember them." He leaned toward Havoc.

"Who are you? What are you doing here?"

"The name is Havoc. Captain Mike Havoc."

"Captain?" Mr. Bad said, clearly confused. "You're in the military?"

"The Freedom Force."

Mr. Bad's eyes narrowed. "This is crazy. I've heard of the Force. Why the hell would you guys be muscling in on my action?"

Havoc didn't respond.

"I won't ask you again."

"Let me make him talk, Boss," the Claw said.

Captain Havoc braced for a beating, or worse. He wasn't about to tell them about Raphaela or the fact the Force had hit Mr. Bad's condo. For that matter, he wasn't about to tell them a thing. He thought of all the innocent blood that had been shed because of the two gangs, all the people whose lives had been destroyed by the drugs the Brothers and the Barons purveyed, and he decided to go down swinging, to take as many of them with him as he could.

"Knock yourself out," Mr. Bad said to his bodyguard.

The Claw grinned and elevated his pincer to eye level. "So you're a captain, huh? You must figure you're one tough dude."

"I can take you," Havoc stated.

The assembled Brothers cackled. Mr. Bad snorted and shook his head.

"Give me a fair fight and I'll prove it," Havoc declared boldly, hoping their cocky overconfidence would prove to be their undoing. If he could engage the Claw in hand-to-hand combat, he might be able to get near enough to one of the others to grab a weapon.

The Claw gazed at the officer, his forehead furrowed. "What do you say, Boss?"

"I say snip his ears off," Mr. Bad responded.

"You heard the man," the Claw said, and opened his pincer.

Havoc tensed, about to unleash a kick, when he heard the beating of boots on the metal stairs and a voice raised in alarm.

"Mr. Bad! Mr. Bad!"

The Brothers all turned their attention to the man rushing down the steps, a Spanish gang member wearing jeans and a brown vest.

"Calm down, Mescalito," Mr. Bad advised. "What's wrong?"

Mewscalito paused near the bottom and leaned on the rail. "It's the cars. Someone is at the cars."

"How do you know? What are they doing?"

"All the lights are on, and I could see a lot of men moving around."

"Were they Barons?"

"I couldn't tell, Mr. Bad. All I saw were a lot of men running in front of the headlights."

"Damn," Mr. Bad snapped, and scowled. "If they take out our wheels, we'll be stranded." He looked at Spooner. "Take everyone with you except two men to keep these clowns covered."

"Right away, Boss," Spooner responded, and indicated two of the Brothers. "You heard the man. You stay here and cover the prisoners." He wheeled and led a general dash to the office door.

Captain Havoc almost smiled. Here was his golden opportunity. The pair of Brothers left behind were standing closer to Doc Madsen. One of them had Doc's Magnum tucked under his belt.

"I don't like this," Mr. Bad remarked. "We're getting out of here."

"What about the soldier and the cowboy?" the Claw inquired.

"They no longer interest me. Kill them."

"As you wish." The Claw grinned at Havoc. "I'll make this as painless as possible."

"Don't do me any favors."

A sudden burst of gunfire erupted outside the office door. Men screamed and cursed. A full-scale war seemed to be in progress. The chattering of assault rifles and the booming of shotguns caused Mr. Bad, his bodyguard, and the pair of guards to swing toward the door in surprise. For only a few seconds they totally ignored their prisoners.

Which was all the time Havoc needed. He leaped into the air and executed a double flying kick, his left foot connecting with Mr. Bad's nose, his right striking the Claw's chin, the force of his blows sending both men reeling backwards. With almost ballet-like grace he landed in the *Zenkutsu-tachi,* the forward stance, and instantly pressed his attack, well aware that one of the guards could send a bullet into his back at any moment. He skipped forward and delivered a devastating roundhouse kick to the side of the Claw's face, knocking the bodyguard to one knee.

Mr. Bad had recovered and was reaching under his jacket, blood flowing from his nostrils.

Havoc nearly flinched when a shot rang out, the blasting of a heavy handgun, not an M-16. He ignored the gunshot and concentrated on his task, reaching Mr. Bad in two bounds and spinning, his right leg straight and rigid, his heel catching his foe on the left knee, shattering the kneecap with a loud snap.

A cry of pain tore from Mr. Bad's lips and he went down, still game, drawing a pistol from a shoulder holster.

Havoc drove his right hand in a vicious palm-heel thrust into Mr. Bad's chin, stunning the head man. But before he could finish his adversary off with a handsword chop to the neck, a vise clamped on his right shoulder and he was hurled backwards. Something tore through the fabric of his blue shirt and bit deep into his flesh, and then he was in the clear and staring at the Claw.

The bodyguard sneered and held out his bloody pincer.

And then three events occurred almost simultaneously. Havoc saw Mr. Bad aim the pistol at his chest, and he knew he was done for because he couldn't possibly reach the man before the trigger was pulled, and he was about to make a mad, desperate lunge when Mr. Bad suddenly looked past him at something or someone, and his eyes went wide as three shots thundered, three retorts from a revolver, the familiar *bam-bam-bam* of a certain Magnum, and Mr. Bad's forehead dissolved in a shower of skin and bones and crimson a millisecond before the impact catapulted him onto his back.

"*No!*" the Claw bellowed, insane with rage, and charged. He sprang at Havoc in a frenzy, slashing and swinging in reckless abandon.

Blocking and countering one blow after another, Havoc retreated several yards, his forearms stinging from the unyielding metal pincer, reacting on sheer instinct, relying on his years of training. Unbidden thoughts of Jimmy entered his head, thoughts of why his younger brother had enlisted in the Force, of why Jimmy had given his life in the line of duty. It had nothing to do with Blade, or the Warrior's decision to land in Canada. It had everything to do with serving a higher cause, with fighting for ideals and values worth dying for if need be. It had everything to do with putting an end to human garbage like Mr. Bad and the Claw, people who ruined the lives of others for their personal pleasure or gain. All these thoughts went through his mind in a flash, and the brief distraction cost him, enabling the Claw to score a hit, to tear open his left side.

But that was the last hit the Claw ever scored.

Havoc abruptly went berserk, raining a flurry of hand and foot blows, punching and chopping and stabbing, using his rock-hard fingers to their maximum advantage, driving the Claw backwards, connecting with a *Hitosashiyubi-ippon-ken,* a forefinger fist to the ribs that staggered the bodyguard, and then landing a piercing hand thrust to the stomach that doubled the Brother in half.

A red haze seemed to shroud Havoc's eyes as he continued his onslaught, employing a handsword face chop to send the Claw stumbling to the left. He closed in, and he dimly registered the bodyguard looking at him in stark amazement, but the next instant the vision was blotted out as he lanced his right index finger into the Claw's eye.

The bodyguard jerked his head back, exposing his throat.

Havoc never missed a beat. He whipped his right hand in a sword peak jab into the Claw's neck. Once. Twice. Three times he struck, and after the third strike the Claw gurgled and collapsed. Not satisfied, Havoc adopted the cat stance, ready to fight indefinitely if necessary, staring at the form sprawled at his feet in confusion, wondering why the man was simply lying there.

"He's dead, Mike."

The softly spoken words cut through the red haze and brought Havoc back to his senses. He blinked a few times and nudged the bodyguard with his right foot.

"Mike?"

The voice belonged to Jaguarundi, and Havoc turned to find the hybrid standing next to Sparrow and Doc Madsen. All three were regarding him with peculiar expressions.

"Are you okay?" Jag asked.

"I'm fine," Havoc mumbled, finally allowing his body to relax and his arms to drop to his sides. Weariness pervaded him from head to toe.

"We took care of the rest," Jag mentioned. "Caught most of them while they were going out the door, then Doc helped us out after he took care of the few in here."

"I see," Havoc said, his tone husky. "We did well. Blade will be proud of us."

Jag, Sparrow, and Doc were shocked when they saw tears form in the captain's eyes.

"Are you sure you're okay?" Jag queried.

"Fine," Havoc responded in a whisper. "Where's Lobo?"

"You told him to stay in the car, remember?"

"Oh. Yeah." Havoc straightened and inhaled deeply, then shuffled toward the door.

A figure suddenly appeared in the doorway. "Well, *there* you bozos are!" Lobo strolled inside, grinning happily. "Did it work or did it work?"

"What are you babbling about?" Jag rejoined.

"My plan to confuse these turkeys," Lobo said. "I turned on all their car headlights and kept running around the vehicles, thinking they would figure that they were under attack. I wanted to keep their attention off you guys. Did it work?"

"It worked," Doc disclosed. "You probably saved Havoc and me from being killed."

"I did?" Lobo puffed out his chest and beamed. "See? I knew you guys couldn't manage without me. I'm the brains of this outfit. You need me to bail you out when the going gets tough. Maybe I should talk to General Gallagher about taking over from Blade. I can teach that bag of wind a—''

''Lobo?'' Havoc interrupted.

''Yeah?''

''Shut the hell up.''

The Clansman, indignant, opened his mouth to respond. He took a good look at the officer's face and abruptly changed his mind.

CHAPTER NINETEEN

Blade came over the north wall when a cloud veiled the grinning face of the moon and cast the landscape in temporary total darkness. To someone of his stature the ten-foot wall hardly qualified as an obstacle. He took a running leap and vaulted upward, his brawny hand catching on the outer edge, then hoisted himself onto his stomach. A hasty inspection revealed a half acre devoted to a lush garden replete with ferns and high trees, illuminated by the light from several posts positioned at strategic intervals. He slid off the wall, twisted, and alighted on his feet.

"Did you hear something?"

The surly voice froze the Warrior in a crouch. He estimated the speaker must be 15 or 20 feet to his right. A glance at the sky confirmed that the cloud would soon be drifting eastward and the moon would add its distant brilliance to the glow from the lamps. He was at the base of the wall, in the open, and the Barons might spot him unless he could find cover.

Not six yards away, straight ahead, rose a bushy plant,

its thin leaves rising to a height of five feet and then drooping almost to the ground, willowlike.

Blade flattened and crawled to the bush, carefully parted the leaves, and concealed himself at its base. None too soon.

"I tell you I heard something."

"You probably heard a frog fart."

The Warrior peered between the leaves and spotted a pair of armed Barons approaching from the west. One held an M-16, the other a shotgun.

"How would you know?" the shotgun wielder snapped. "You don't know nothin' about animals."

"And you do?"

"I know I didn't hear a frog fart. They sound like popcorn popping and this was different."

"You're so full of shit it's dripping out your ears."

Blade placed his hands on the hilts of his Bowies. He had removed the knives from under his fatigue pants before launching his assault on the Barons' stronghold and strapped the sheaths to his belt. After he returned to the Force compound—*if* he returned—he intended to have a long talk with General Gallagher about the policy of no weapons when in L.A. Unless the policy was changed, he'd never enter the city again.

The two Barons halted next to the wall and scanned the garden. After a minute the man carrying the M-16 sighed and said, "I don't see a thing. This is a frigging waste of our time."

"Don't let Bennie hear you say that."

"Mr. High and Mighty? Boy, the boss makes him second-in-command and he starts acting like he's God."

"Bennie can't afford to screw up. Don't forget what happened to Barney."

"Barney was a jerk."

They started to walk to the east, their vigilance slightly reduced.

Amateurs, Blade thought, and surged from under the plant, drawing his Bowies as he rose, the blades gleaming, his arms tensed to strike.

To their credit, the two Barons heard the rustle of the leaves and tried to rotate. They were only partly successful.

The Warrior reached them in two strides and speared his knives up and in, sinking each one into an exposed neck before either Baron could turn, eliciting a terrified cry from the man carrying the M-16 and a grunt from the other Baron. He quickly released the hilts, took hold of each man by the back of the head, and slammed their foreheads together to forestall further noise.

Wheezing and spitting blood, the shotgun-wielder toppled over, but the Baron with the M-16 tried to bring his weapon to bear on the giant.

Blade batted the barrel aside and swung a brutal uppercut to the man's chin, his prodigious might breaking the Baron's jaw, splintering a dozen teeth, and shattering the left cheekbone.

The Baron dropped.

Crouching, the Warrior surveyed the garden but detected no movement. Working swiftly, he pulled his Bowies out and wiped them on the pants of the shotgun-wielder, then slid them into their sheaths and took hold of the shotgun and the M-16. Now, as Lobo would say, he was ready to rock and roll. He slung the M-16 over his right shoulder and advanced in a beeline toward the mansion. After ten yards he came to a gravel-covered path winding among the plants and took it, his boots crunching lightly on the stones.

"Gage, is that you?"

Another pair of Barons appeared on the left, coming around a maple tree.

"Sure isn't," Blade replied, and shot them, working the slide action on the Mossberg Model 3000 with lightning rapidity. The two shots boomed almost as one, and both Barons were struck in the chest and sent sailing backwards, dead before they hit the ground.

All hell broke loose.

Blade raced toward the mansion, listening to the outbreak of yells and curses all around him, and wondered how many Barons were on the premises.

A stocky Baron dressed all in leather and carrying a Heckler and Koch HK-93 crashed through a row of shrubbery on the right, saw the giant, and cut loose.

The Warrior was already in motion, diving for the damp ground and rolling as the rounds from the HK-93 smacked into the earth within inches of his head. He fired as he rolled, the shotgun barrel slanted upward at the Baron, and the blast caught the gang member in the head and exploded his face outward in a shower of skin, blood, teeth, and bone.

Five down.

How many more to go?

Blade pushed to his feet and dashed to the dead Baron. Nearby lay the HK-93. He tossed the shotgun into the bushes and grabbed the HK-93 with his left hand while unslinging the M-16 with his right. He tucked both weapons against his ribs to absorb the recoil, a finger on each trigger, and resumed his attack, walking brazenly along the path. There was ample cover available, but he opted for the direct approach for two reasons. First, the Barons knew he was on the grounds and would be converging on him in force. He'd rather take the fight to them, put them on the defensive, than skulk in the bushes and try to pick them off one by one. Second, and most important, time was a crucial factor. Every moment of delay increased the likelihood that Raphaela would be harmed, if she hadn't been before he arrived.

So where are you, you bastards?

The Warrior came abreast of a flower garden, the fragrant aroma tingling his nose, and on the opposite side three Barons materialized.

"Here he is!" one of them shouted.

Blade squeezed both triggers, combining the firepower of both the M-16 and the HK-93, and swung them from side to side, sending a withering hail of lead into the trio. Only one of the Barons succeeded in getting off a few rounds, and the shots went wild and destroyed a three-foot section of flowers.

Just as the retorts of the guns died away, a piercing scream arose from the bowels of the mansion, wafting eerily on the wind, the unmistakable scream of someone the Warrior knew.

Raphaela!

Throwing caution aside, Blade plunged through the vegetation toward a sturdy oak door on the north side of the mansion. He dreaded the thought that the Barons might kill Raphaela before he could reach her, and in his haste to find her he became uncharacteristically careless.

The oak door was closed but unguarded.

Blade leaped over a rose bush and came to a narrow strip of unadorned grass. He increased his speed, his gaze riveted on the door, and when he was only six feet from his goal he detected motion out of his right eye and spun.

Too late.

A solitary Baron got off three rounds from a Ruger Mini-14 Carbine.

A scorching firebrand seared a groove in Blade's right side, racking his torso with excruciating agony, and he fell to the dank earth and stayed there, not moving a muscle, gritting his teeth to suppress the pain he felt, hoping the Baron would come close to verify the presumed kill. Stealthy footsteps sounded, drawing slowly nearer. The M-16 was pinned under his right side, but the HK-93 was still clutched in his left hand, the barrel slanted toward the ground.

The footsteps halted.

Would the man fire a few more times for good measure? Blade's skin prickled as he waited for the Baron to do something. The seconds dragged by, and then the steps were much closer and a hard object prodded the Warrior's left shoulder. Blade went with the prod, rolling onto his back and elevating the HK-93 at the startled youth standing above him. He shot at a range of less than an inch, and the heavy slugs tore through the gang member's upper chest and flung the man to the grass.

Go! Blade's mind urged.

There was no time to inspect the wound. He had to trust that his blood loss would be minimal and that he could hold out until after he found Raphaela. Grimacing from the anguish, he rose and moved to the oak door. A twist of the knob revealed it had been locked.

No problem.

The Warrior took a step backwards, then kicked, planting

his right combat boot on the panel next to the lock, cracking the wood and making a noise undoubtedly heard in every room in the mansion.

It couldn't be helped.

Blade smashed the door again with his boot, and this time the panel splintered and the door swung inward, revealing a narrow hallway.

There were no Barons in sight.

Leveling the assault rifles, Blade entered warily, his gray eyes darting from room to room as he moved deeper and deeper into the Barons' sanctum sanctorum. The complete silence was unnerving. Not even an insect stirred. But he knew the Barons were in there somewhere, ready to spring a trap.

Let them try!

He reached a junction and halted, debating which of the branches he should follow.

Another appalling scream rent the air, seeming to originate far down the hallway on the right.

Blade raced along the corridor, oblivious to the wound in his side, thinking only of Raphaela, of the naive woman he had allowed to remain on the Force against his better judgment, of the woman whose life, literally, was in his hands. He'd already lost five Force members, and he wasn't about to lose another one. He'd die first.

The corridor abruptly angled to the left and widened, and he mustered all the speed he could, his long legs flying, passing many more rooms, all of them empty. The silence had again descended and he had no way of telling if he was still going in the right direction. Just when he thought the corridor might go on forever, he came to the bottom of a flight of stairs and stopped.

Now which way?

Acting on impulse rather than a seasoned deliberation, Blade started up the stairs, taking them one at a time, his head cocked to detect any telltale squeaks or clicks or anything that would indicate a trap. The remaining Barons had to know he was now in the mansion. They also assuredly knew he would be drawn to Raphaela's cries like a moth to flame. Which meant the trap must be somewhere ahead.

It was.

Blade took two more steps and then froze when a strange *thump* sounded. Then another. And another. Perplexed, he gazed upward, his blood transforming to ice when he spied the metallic sphere bouncing down the stairs toward him.

A hand grenade!

The Warrior reverted to sheer reflexive action, dropping the M-16 and the HK-93 and gripping the railing.

Thump.

Blade vaulted over the railing, his rippling muscles propelling him in a high arc.

Thump.

The sound brought goosebumps to his flesh. He alighted on the balls of his feet, took two quick strides, and flung himself forward, his arms over his head for protection.

The hand grenade detonated with a tremendous explosion, rocking the mansion walls, blowing a gaping crater in the stairs and showering jagged pieces of wood and carpet in all directions.

Blade was almost to the floor when the concussion buffeted him, sending him tumbling end over end for a dozen yards, jarring his injured side, causing him to collide with the walls on both sides, until he came to rest on his stomach, the wind knocked out of him, engulfed in a swirling haze of smoke and tiny wood chips. His ears rang, and for several seconds he couldn't hear a sound. Then he heard words.

"—get the son of a bitch?"

"I think so."

"Teach him to mess with the Barons."

The Warrior struggled to his knees and shook his head, striving to clear the mental cobwebs. The Barons would spot him once the cloud dissipated. He stood, his legs shaky, and walked several feet.

"I can't see a damn thing!"

"Shut your mouth and keep looking."

Blade leaned on the right-hand wall for support. His strength was returning swiftly. Several yards ahead appeared an open door, and he scooted to the doorway and ducked inside, chagrinned to discover he'd slipped into a linen closet.

"Let's check the hallway."

There was no time to seek another hiding place. The Warrior stared at the shelves piled high with towels and sheets, frowning. A mouse would find it difficult to secret itself in such a small closet, so how could *he* expect to elude the Barons?

"Shoot to kill."

"You don't have to tell me twice."

The two Barons were getting very close! Blade used the only option available under the circumstances. He slid behind the closet door, pressed his back to the wall, drew his Bowies, and waited expectantly.

Would they peek behind the door?

"There's no body. We must have missed him," a Baron said softly.

"How? We had that sucker dead to rights."

The Warrior guessed the duo were within a few feet of his hiding place. He held his breath and looked through the crack between the door and the jamb. If they spotted him, he'd need to move fast.

They did.

A Baron suddenly stepped into the doorway and scanned the shelves. He was about to leave, and had even twisted and taken a half-step, when he glanced at the crack, his eyes narrowing, then widening in alarm.

Blade shoved the door, using both arms, sweeping it around and catching the Baron full in the face, the door acting like a huge club, hurling the man across the hall and into the wall. He yanked the door open, and there was the Baron, sagging on one knee and trying to bring an AK-47 to bear.

A second Baron abruptly stepped into view between the closet and the first man, apparently intending to aid his companion but instead aiding the Warrior. The Baron glanced at his companion, then at the closet.

The Warrior pounced, his powerful leg muscles driving him into the nearest Baron, and they both crashed down on the first Baron. For a moment Blade had them both pinned, and he sank his Bowie into the chest of the man under him,

stabbing for the heart and hitting his target. He swung his
left arm up and over the Baron, at the face of the man on
the bottom of the pile, and the tip lanced into the gang
member's right eye.

The Baron on the bottom screeched.

Blade straightened, drawing both bloody Bowies with him.
The Baron on top rolled off, still breathing but almost gone,
crimson spurting from his nose and mouth as he trembled
violently, uncovering his companion. The second man had
a hand pressed to his ruptured eye and was endeavoring to
rise. Blade imbedded both knives to their hilts in the Baron's
torso and held on as the man thrashed and kicked and
eventually expired.

Now to find Raphaela.

He yanked his blades out and headed for the stairs. The
grenade had blown the middle section to bits. He climbed
as far as he could, sheated his Bowies, then leaped, grabbing
the upper section of rail and gaining a foothold on a buckled
step. In a smooth motion he pulled himself onto firm footing
and sprang to the landing.

Again silence enveloped the mansion.

Blade drew his knives and moved along the corridor, his
anxiety mounting. Where were they holding Raphaela? Why
had she screamed? She might be naive, but she had impressed
him as having a certain resiliency and inner toughness that
would serve her in good stead in a crisis. What could the—

"You must be Blade."

The booming voice snapped the Warrior's attention to a
room on the right, a bedroom occupied by two people.
Standing alongside the bed, a Colt Delta Elite 10MM in his
right hand, was an immense tank of a man dressed in an
ebony suit. The gun wasn't pointed at the Warrior. It was
aimed at the figure on the bed.

Raphaela.

Blade straightened and took a step forward, his fury rising
at the sight of her tear-streaked features. She lay on her back,
her arms bound behind her, rope binding her ankles, and
cast a pleading, pitiable expression at him. The beige shirt
she wore had been torn open, partly exposing her breasts

to view, revealing red welts on her skin. He raised his Bowies, about to spring.

"If you do, this charming lady will die," the man in the suit warned. "Kindly drop those knives of yours on the floor. Now."

What choice did he have? Blade let the Bowies fall and walked calmly into the bedroom, halting just inside the doorway. "Let her go."

"What? And relinquish my trump card? You must be kidding?"

"Are you Owsley?"

"I am, sir. I'm flattered that you've heard of me."

"Until tonight I had no idea you even existed," Blade said flatly, his eyes locked on Raphaela's, trying to reassure her with his gaze.

"Really?" Owsley shrugged. "And here I thought I had acquired a modicum of fame."

Blade glanced at the head Baron. "What's this all about? Why did you kidnap Raphaela? Why did you attack the Force?"

"You won't believe me if I tell you."

"Try me."

Owsley sighed and waved the barrel of the Colt at Raphaela. "Kidnapping her was a mistake, an accident."

"An accident?" Blade repeated skeptically.

"I told you that you wouldn't believe me," Owsley said. "My men were supposed to abduct another woman named Gloria Mundy. Instead, they grabbed this luscious person by mistake."

Blade's eyebrows arched. A mistake? This whole episode had been the result of a mistake? "If it was an accident, like you say, then why didn't you simply release her?"

Owsley shook his head. "I knew you would show up eventually, and I needed a bargaining chip in case you got this far." He paused. "My compliments, sir. Every word they've written about you in the papers is true."

"I'm sorry, Blade," Raphaela interjected. "He made me scream to lure you up here. He—he . . ." She paused, tears flowing, and took a breath. "He hurt me."

Blade took a casual step closer to the leader of the Barons, doing his best to suppress his seething emotions. "You *hurt* her?"

"I gave her a little squeeze," Owsley replied, and smirked. "And I intend to give her more after I dispose of you."

"You're scum. Do you know that?"

Owsley stiffened. "There's no need to get personal." He nodded at the carpet. "Lay down with your arms extended, and no unorthodox moves or I will put a bullet in this vixen's brain."

Blade started to comply, bending forward, his arms at his sides. He planned to rush the Baron and rely on his speed to avoid a slug in the head, knowing his chance of success was extremely slim, but he suddenly received unexpected assistance from Raphaela.

The Molewoman drew her legs up to her chest and lashed out with her combat boots, striking Owsley's gun hand and swatting the Colt aside.

In a twinkling the Warrior leaped, his outstretched hands closing on Owsley's gun arm, his momentum bearing both of them to the bed. He felt Raphaela squirming under him, and then he rolled to the left, taking Owsley with him, and together they crashed onto the floor.

"Damn you!" Owsley hissed, and drove his left knee at the Warrior's groin.

Blade shifted and the knee hit him in the inner thigh, causing intense pain. He clamped his right hand on Owsley's throat and squeezed, his huge arm bulging, the veins on his temples standing out.

Mouthing an inarticulate grunt, Owsley let go of the Colt, tore his arm from the Warrior's grasp, and slugged Blade on the chin. To his surprise, his blow appeared to have no effect.

Blade felt the punch but ignored it. He focused all of his awesome might into his right hand, squeezing, ever squeezing, constricting his fingers on the Baron's neck. A blistering, irresistible rage had gripped his soul, and any semblance of self-control had been lost.

Unaccustomed to being bested in combat by any man,

Arthur Owsley gasped for air and battered the Warrior's cheek and jaw. When his punches failed to produce any result, he altered his strategy. He was lying partly under the Warrior, at an angle, and he bucked his legs and heaved, flinging his opponent from him at the same moment he wrenched on the hand strangling his throat. His maneuver worked, freeing him momentarily, and he leaped to his feet.

Blade rolled and stood, but he was a millisecond too slow. An express train seemed to ram into him, sending him tottering backwards, his arms flailing for support. His hands hooked onto the doorjamb, and for an instant he was suspended in the doorway.

Owsley charged again, his head lowered, a snorting bull intent on stomping the Warrior at all costs. His head butted into Blade's stomach as his arms looped around the giant's waist, and they both went down with Owsley on top.

Now it was Blade's turn to deliver a barrage of fists to his enemy's face, and he succeeded in forcing Owsley from him.

Both men jumped erect.

Owsley wiped a hand across his bloody mouth, and sneered. "You're the toughest mother I've ever tackled."

"And the last," Blade said.

"You think so?" Owsley responded, and assumed a boxing posture. "Why don't we do this like gentlemen?"

"Because there's only one gentleman here," Blade said, baiting him. He adopted a boxing stance of his own, glancing once over his right shoulder to ensure there were no Barons behind him.

Owsley saw and understood. "You bested all the rest. Now it's only you and me."

"Whenever you're ready."

"Then let's do it."

They clashed, exchanging a flurry of blows, jabs and hooks and crosses, blocking and ducking and clinching, both men supremely skilled, both endowed with exceptional strength and stamina. When their punches landed, they jarred the other man. Despite the Warrior's height advantage, the battle was a contest of equals.

Blade was impressed. He had fought countless foes during his action-filled lifetime, fought them armed or unarmed, fought them using wrestling, the martial arts, boxing, and other techniques, and few were the opponents who could rival Arthur Owsley. The man gave as good as he got.

Owsley aimed a right cross at the Warrior.

Parrying with an inside forearm block, Blade countered, delivering a straight right to Owsley's bulky body that rocked the Baron on his heels.

Instantly Owsley lashed out with a left jab, connecting on the Warrior's jawbone.

Dazed, Blade retaliated with a left hook, scoring a hit over the Baron's right eye, breaking the skin and starting a flow of blood.

Owsley blinked and retreated several strides, wiping his right sleeve on the cut, trying to staunch the crimson rivulet.

The Warrior pressed his advantage, closing in again, and as he passed the bedroom door he glanced in and saw Raphaela on the floor, rolling toward the doorway. Although he was puzzled and fleetingly wondered what she could possibly hope to accomplish, there was no time to ponder the matter. He traded blows with Owsley again, the two of them slugging it out with no holds barred.

For over a minute the battle continued.

Two minutes.

And then Blade gained the upper hand. Two jabs to the cut over Owsley's eye opened the wound even more, and the pouring blood restricted the Baron's field of vision.

Owsley never even saw the haymaker.

The Warrior swung his arm in a wide loop, his granite knuckles slamming into the side of the Baron's head with the force of a pile driver. Owsley tottered, his arms dropping, and Blade planted a right on the tip of the man's nose, then a left on the chin.

Grunting, Owsley staggered and sluggishly lifted his arms to defend himself. He had lost and he knew it, but he refused to quit. His lips were split, his face puffy.

Blade paused. His rage had evaporated during their fight, leaving a lingering resentment and anger. He still wanted to pound the Baron to a pulp, but his self-control had reasserted itself and he felt inclined to take the man into custody for the authorities.

At that moment the shots rang out, four of them in quick succession, and four holes blossomed in Arthur Owsley's visage, two in the sloping forehead and two near the nose. He flung his arms out and swayed, took a lurching step to the right, and toppled with a resounding crash.

Blade turned slowly.

She stood a few feet away, the Colt clenched in both hands, the tears all gone, her features hard and spiteful, her nostrils flaring. "Never again," she said softly, the two words encompassing the full gamut of human suffering and sorrow, denoting a hidden meaning in the profound tone with which they were uttered.

The Warrior lowered his arms and said nothing.

EPILOGUE

"**L**obo says you wanted to see me, sir?"

Blade placed his hands on the hilts of his Bowies, then gazed idly at the azure sky overhead. He stood outside the command bunker, savoring the peace and quiet. "Yes, I do."

"What about?" Raphaela asked. She had on fatigues, and her boots had been spit-shined until the tips gleamed.

The Warrior stared into her eyes. "How are you feeling?"

"Fine, sir."

"You haven't said very much since you shot that Baron."

Raphaela shrugged. "What's to say? He had it coming."

"I agree."

"Anything else, sir?"

"What's with all the 'sirs'?"

"As you've been trying to get through our thick skulls, this is a military unit. It's about time I behaved in a military fashion," Raphaela replied.

Blade studied her, his forehead creasing. "And you're sure everything is okay?"

"Couldn't be better."

"There's nothing you'd like to talk about?"

Raphaela's lips parted, as if she were about to reply, but she looked at the bunker and shook her head.

"Nothing at all?" Blade pressed her.

"No."

"Fair enough. But if you ever feel the need to shoot the breeze, you know where to find me."

A sincere smile curved her mouth upward and she nodded. "I'll keep that in mind, sir."

"That'll be all," Blade said, and watched her walk off to join Lobo, Doc, Sparrow, and Jag. They were all taking a brief break before they started on their unarmed combat lesson for the day. He heard footsteps and turned to find Captain Havoc hauling one of the mats they would use during the session. "I'll give you a hand," he offered.

"That's okay, sir," the officer responded. "I can manage."

"How are your injuries?"

"To tell the truth, I hardly notice them," Havoc said. He deposited the mat and knelt to unravel it on the ground.

"Do you mind if I ask you a question?"

Havoc looked up. "Certainly not, sir."

"What was that business yesterday with General Gallagher? I saw the two of you over by the VTOL hangar. He was waving a newspaper and seemed to be chewing you out."

"You know the general," Havoc answered cryptically. "He gets flustered easily."

"Was he flustered about anything I should know?"

"No, sir," Havoc answered. "He was excited over that story about us being heroes for wiping out the Brothers and the Barons."

Back to square one, Blade thought, and sighed. No, not exactly. Because now he was certain that General Gallagher was up to something. What, he had no idea. But he'd find out sooner or later, and the general had better not be up to his old tricks or there would be a reckoning.

And what about the Molewoman?

Blade stared at her without being obvious about his interest.

He'd seen the stark inner torment reflected on her face when she shot Owsley, and he suspected she harbored a deep, terrible secret that she would only reveal under duress. So now he had two members of the team he needed to watch like the proverbial hawk.

"Hey, dude!" Lobo called out. "How about if we skip the martial-arts jive today? A lean, mean, fightin' machine like me doesn't need this crap. And I could really use a nap."

Blade shook his head.

Make that three.

DEAD ZONE STRIKE

Dedicated to...
Judy, Joshua, and Shane.
And to all those who are scared of the dark;
you never know.

PROLOGUE

What was that noise?

"Whoa there, Buck!" Larry Wagner called out, bringing his plow horse to a halt. He held the traces firmly in his calloused hands and gazed skyward, cocking his head and listening intently.

He could have sworn he heard something.

Puzzled, Larry surveyed the heavens. To the west the upper rim of the sun was visible above the horizon, and brilliant hues of red, orange, and pink contended with the gathering twilight for dominance. A dozen scattered clouds were drifting lazily from the northwest to the southeast. Several hundred yards away, off to the right, a flock of starlings winged their way on an easterly bearing.

Larry wiped his sweating brow with his right forearm and scanned the essentially flat countryside. To the north, on the other side of the barbed wire fence, was his herd, 58 head of some of the best beef in the Dakota Territory. The cattle were idly munching on the cool, green grass or standing contentedly while swishing at flies with their tails.

But there was nothing nearby, nothing to account for the noise.

How strange.

Shrugging, Larry resumed the plowing. He hoped to finish the field before nightfall and he still had a 20-foot strip to turn over. In a few days he wanted to harrow, and in a week or so he intended to plant his winter wheat. He glanced to the west at the white farmhouse that had been in his family for nearly nine generations, and he speculated, for the umpteenth time, on how easy his ancestors must have had it. Imagine being able to plow or harrow or pull a hay baler or do any of the thousand and one jobs necessary to keep a large farm running smoothly using machines to do most of the work! Such a concept seemed like Utopia. He gazed over his right shoulder at the distant rusted, disintegrating remains of the last functional tractor the Wagner family had possessed, and sighed.

Ever since World War Three, 106 six years ago, the Wagners had struggled to make ends meet, to keep the soil tilled and their livestock tended. After civilization crumbled, after fuel became scarce and electricity nonexistent except in a few sections of the country, and after the factories ceased to produce spare parts for farm machinery and other contrivances, the Wagner clan had reverted to the argicultural practices of the early American pioneers, using horses and oxen for most of the heavy work and relying on reproductions of antiquated implements to accomplish in days tasks that had once taken mere hours.

Now, as Larry guided his plow horse along the row and watched the curved blades dig into the soil, he wished that he could have lived before the war, back when farmers didn't have to break their backs just to get their winter wheat into the ground.

Then again, maybe his ancestors hadn't had it so easy, after all. Farming was *never* easy. A farmer's livelihood depended on the capricious fluctuations of fickle nature and supremely hard toil the likes of which few men were willing to tolerate. Anyone who believed farming and indolence went hand in hand possessed rocks for brains.

A faint swishing sound wafted from overhead.

Larry stared upward. There it was again. But other than a low cloud directly overhead, there wasn't anything close enough to account for the swishing. And clouds certainly didn't make noise. He looked every which way, mystified, wondering if he should take the time to travel all the way to Rapid City so he could have his hearing checked by the doctor. This was the second evening in a row he'd heard the odd sound.

Oh, well.

He'd discuss the matter with Elvy later.

His wife always gave him sage advice.

Larry concentrated on the plowing, urging Buck to go faster, beginning to doubt whether he'd complete the field before it was too dark to see the plow. A full moon would help, would enable him to finish, but the next full moon would take place in nine days, during the last week of September.

Fat lot of good that did him.

Buck came to the end of the field and turned well clear of the barbed wire, his ponderous hooves thudding on the earth, his mighty frame pulling the heavy plow with deceptive ease. Four years of experience had turned the horse into the perfect plow animal. Buck knew when and how to turn and seldom made a mistake.

"Let's go, boy," Larry said softly. In one respect horses were a lot like dogs. Gentle words of encouragement did wonders for their disposition and performance. As a man who'd spent all of his life around animals, he knew how to elicit the response he wanted.

Buck completed his swing and started in the opposite direction.

Yawning, Larry gazed at the house and saw the windows brighten as Elvy went from room to room lighting the lanterns. He thought of the precious new life she carried in her womb, and anticipated with pride the blessed event that would transpire in six months. Their first child! He prayed the infant would emerge healthy and normal.

Nowadays there was no telling.

Not with all the radioactive and chemical substances contaminating the environment.

Larry recalled the harrowing ordeal of the Tamberlines, Kirk and Susan. Kirk was his best friend, and he'd been present at their home the night the baby was delivered. He vividly remembered the shocked expression on Kirk's face upon hearing from the midwife that the baby had been born with three legs, one arm, and no eyes. Susan had just about gone over the deep end.

What if the same thing happened to them?

What if their child turned out genetically disfigured, or worse?

He shook his head, trying to clear his mind, unable to blot out the memory of how the Tamberlines had tried, really tried, for over ten months, how they had lavished love on their offspring to no avail, how the child had eventually died and they had vowed never to have another.

How would Elvy react if their baby was deformed?

Larry absently stared at Buck, feeling depressed. He'd heard of babies coming into the world minus arms and legs or having extra limbs. He'd heard of infants with oversized heads and even two heads. Once, incredibly, a child had been born endowed with rudimentary wings, if his cousin was to be believed. But the Tamberline baby had been the first instance he knew of where there weren't any eyes.

A sudden chill breeze blew from the west.

Involuntarily shuddering, Larry glanced at the western horizon and realized the sun had set. Darkness encroached on the landscape. He'd be able to finish the row, then have to call it quits until morning. All he'd need would be an hour tomorrow and the field would finally be done.

The swishing sounded again, only somewhat louder.

Larry tilted his head and saw stars dotting the firmament. The noise persisted for a full ten seconds before stopping. Perplexed, he scratched his head. More than anything else, the swishing resembled the sound someone would make when rubbing a hand up and down on rough fabric, like when he brushed dust and dirt from his pants after working in the fields.

It made no sense.

"We'll wrap this up, Buck," Larry stated. His stomach growled, reminding him of how hungry he was and of the piping-hot stew Elvy would have waiting for him. His mouth began to water.

Perhaps he should have stopped earlier.

From the south, from at least a quarter of a mile away, arose the familiar yipping howl of a coyote.

Larry smiled. Why was he dwelling on morbid subjects when he had so much to be thankful for? He'd been honored with the sincere love of a beautiful woman. He owned a 200-acre farm in one of the lushest areas in the Dakota Territory. And most of all, unlike the majority of the people living in the ruins of America a century after the holocaust to end all holocausts, he belonged to one of the truly free organized factions currently in existence, the Cavalry.

Composed of the descendants of those ranchers, farmers, Indians, and others who had refused to be evacuated by the U.S. government during the war, the Cavalry controlled most of the former states of North and South Dakota. After World War Three, when there were hordes of scavengers and raiders roaming the countryside, a prominent South Dakota rancher had organized his neighbors into a vigilante group he'd dubbed the Cavalry. Soon other residents had joined, and before long they had driven out the scavengers and taken to governing themselves. For a hundred years the Cavalry had existed on its own, acquiring a reputation as being tough and independent, renowned far and wide for its members' superb horsemanship.

Every citizen in the Territory was required to own a horse and be ready at a moment's notice to respond to a request for assistance in case of an invasion. A standing unit of 200 horsemen was maintained in battle readiness at all times.

They were billeted in Pierre, where the present leader of the Cavalry resided, a man by the name of Kilrane who was the most wildly respected Cavalryman of all. Larry had seen the man on two occasions, when Kilrane came to Rapid City to give a talk on the issues and problems the Cavalry would need to confront in the years ahead, and each time Larry had been very favorably impressed.

Kilrane was a born leader, an exceptional horseman.

Larry stared at the inky silhouette of the barn, barely visible to the right of the farmhouse, thinking of his other two horses, the roan and the mare. While Buck served as his work animal, the others were exclusively reserved for riding. Champ, the roan, was easily the equal of any horse in the—

What was that?

He glanced at the sky once again, listening to a new outbreak of swishing, only this time the noise was much louder and more distinct. The longer he listened, the louder it became, until the swishing resembled a distinct sort of . . . flapping.

Flapping?

As in wings?

Larry pursed his lips, reflecting on whether an owl might be responsible. Some owls, like the great horned owl, were quite large and their heavy flapping could be heard from several dozen yards away when there was no other noise. Crows too could sometimes be heard, but they didn't fly at night.

So what was up there?

Larry surveyed the heavens as he walked along. Not attaching much important to the random beating of wings in the night, he didn't totally focus his attention, and almost missed spotting the missing stars.

What in the world?

His brow knit in confusion at the sight of an irregular black blotch in the heavens, an area where there should be stars but there weren't, an area almost directly overhead. He stared at the bizarre blotch, watching its dimensions shift and fluctuate, astounded, at a loss to explain the celestial spectacle.

Then the obvious hit him.

The blotch wasn't caused by something off in space somewhere. The stars were still there, the heavens still intact.

No.

The black shape was caused by something *in* the air, something interposed between the stars and the earth, something huge, hovering in the cool night and flapping its enormous wings.

Dear God!

It couldn't be!

Larry abruptly released the traces and sprinted toward the farmhouse, going for the Winchester he kept in a gun cabinet in the living room. He had 40 yards to cover. If his supposition was right, he'd never make it. Please let me be wrong! he mentally pleaded. Please! He pumped his legs for all he was worth.

The flapping grew in volume, coming closer.

There could only be one reason.

The thing was after him!

His heart pounding in his chest, Larry breathed heavily. After an entire day of plowing his leg muscles were fatigued and sluggish, and he couldn't seem to attain his top speed no matter how hard he tried.

The flapping continued to grow louder.

Larry covered the 20 feet to the west edge of the field and paused for just a second, scanning the gloom for the gate. He spied the dull glint of the metal posts and dashed forward, trying to recollect if he left the gate open or closed.

A breeze gusted at him from above.

Swallowing hard, Larry reached the gate, found it closed, and shoved. In an instant he was through and racing toward the farmhouse, but he only managed to travel a few yards before a tremendous blow to the center of his back sent him sprawling forward onto his hands and knees. Pain racked his spine. His senses swam for a moment.

The thing hissed.

Larry shivered, incipient fear gnawing at his mind, and shoved to his feet, resisting an urge to glance over his shoulder at the horror lurking in the darkness. He ran, ran as he had never run before, and opened his mouth to shout for Elvy to grab the rifle.

What was he doing?

If she came outside, the thing might go after her.

Or there might be more than one.

Larry closed his mouth and sped onward. He wouldn't endanger his wife under any circumstances.

An eerie cry rent the night, resembling the piercing shriek of a bird of prey.

The front door unexpectedly opened and Elvy stood framed in the doorway, wearing her gray slacks and green blouse, a lantern in her left hand. She peered to the east. "Larry?"

"Go back!" Larry shouted, terror welling within him. "Get inside!"

Instead, she took three steps into the yard. "Larry! What's wrong?"

Before Larry could answer, before he could scream at her to hasten to safety, something smashed into his right temple with the force of a mule's kick. He stumbled, tripped, and fell to his knees, dazed. Frantically striving to recover, shaking his head vigorously, he placed his hands on the grass, about to rise.

The flapping abruptly emanated from directly behind him.

Larry felt steely hands slip under his arms and loop around his chest, and in the blink of an eye he was airborne, being conveyed into the night at a startling rate. He struggled to break free, watching the earth recede underneath him, seeing Elvy's upturned, terrified visage, and then he was sailing over the house, over the shingles on the roof, and in seconds he was hundreds of feet up in the atmosphere.

From far below came Elvy's plaintive wail. "Larry!"

He ceased resisting, knowing he'd be dashed to pieces if he fell from such a height. The air became colder, the wind stronger. Stunned, his arms limp at his sides, he stared in disbelief at the receding ground.

The thing holding him made a rumbling noise deep in its chest.

Larry licked his dry lips and twisted his head, trying to get a glimpse of his captor, but all he could distinguish was a vague, inky form. He placed his hands on the arms encircling his torso and felt hair under his palms. Goose bumps erupted all over his flesh. He gazed forlornly at an expanse of forest below, and despair flooded his soul as he realized he might never see his beloved wife again.

The creature flapped onward under the star-filled heavens.

CHAPTER ONE

Which one should it be?

The giant leaned back in the office chair and thoughtfully studied the six manila folders on his desk, reading the name printed on each one, trying to come to a decision. As he read off a name he mentally catalogued strengths and weaknesses, weighing the pros and cons of each team member. He wanted to appoint one of them as his second-in-command.

But which was most deserving of the honor?

More to the point, which could perform the job satisfactorily?

Should he select Captain Mike Havoc? As a professional military man with Special Forces training, not to mention graduation from Officers Training School, Havoc, at first glance, appeared to be the most qualified. At six feet two, weighing in the neighborhood of 210 pounds, the blond-haired, blue-eyed Havoc, with his superbly conditioned physique, possessed the physical prerequisites for the post. In addition, Havoc held a black belt in karate and had earned a marksmanship ribbon. A perfect candidate.

Almost.

Frowning, the giant stood, rising to his full height of seven feet, and stretched, his bulging muscles rippling, his black leather vest and green fatigue pants threatening to burst at the seams. He idly glanced to his right and happened to see a reflection of himself in the small mirror attached to the west wall, scarcely noticing the comma of dark hair that hung above his troubled gray eyes.

How could he appoint Havoc to the post when he entertained grave reservations about the officer? Havoc was up to something. What, he didn't know. But the officer had been acting suspiciously ever since joining the Force. And to top it all off, Havoc had been spending a lot of time in the company of General Miles Gallagher. After the fight with the drug lords in Los Angeles, General Gallagher had chewed Havoc out but good. He'd seen them both with his own eyes. Yet both had acted evasive when he later questioned them. Why?

He sat down again and looked at the second folder.

Sparrow Hawk. The volunteer from the Flathead Indians, who now ruled the region once known as the state of Montana. A skilled tracker and hunter, Sparrow Hawk lacked any tactical experience whatsoever. Powerfully built, only five feet six, with shoulder-length black hair and brown eyes, the Flathead possessed remarkable endurance and could wield a spear and a knife exceptionally well. But none of his skills qualified him to be second-in-command.

The giant's eyes strayed to the third folder.

Don Madsen. Alias Doc. The lanky gunfighter and gambler hailed from the Cavalry. Appropriately, he dressed almost excusively in black: a wide-brimmed black hat, a black frock coat, black pants, and black boots. He was also partial to white shirts. Of all of them, the giant knew the least about Doc's personal life prior to joining the Freedom Force. Like any good gambler, Doc kept his cards close to his chest. A hair under six feet, Doc had cold hazel eyes and clipped brown hair that tended to contribute to the image he projected of being a man better left alone. A loner. Hardly the type to lead a fighting unit, even if he was a wizard with his Smith and Wesson Model 586 Distinguished Combat Magnum.

So who was next?

Raphaela. No last name. Simply Raphaela. A stunning red-head with striking green eyes, she'd been sent by the Moles to be their reprsentative cn the team. Typically, she'd had no combat experience at all when she arrived in California. She tried hard, but she definitely didn't qualify.

The giant gazed at the next folder.

Jaguarundi. Now there was a possibility. Lean, intelligent, and endowed with extraordinary strength thanks to his hybrid heritage, the mutation possessed the proper mix of personality traits and temperament. As a cross between a human and a feline, the cat-man could bring a unique perspective to the position. But although Jaguarundi didn't hate humans as many hybrids did, he still adopted a superior air periodically, as if being unique made him automatically better than his human counterparts. Still, Jag was a possibility.

The last name caught the giant's attention and he laughed.

Leo Wood. Otherwise known by the name he used during his gang days in the Twin Cities, the monicker he preferred: Lobo. If ever there was a misnomer, Lobo was it. A rampaging rabbit conveyed a meaner impression than the volunteer from the Clan. Lobo stood five feet nine, weighed 190 pounds, and often appeared to be all mouth. The man could talk rings around a petrified tree. He tried to look formidable, what with his Afro, black leather jacket, and skin-tight jeans, but once he started to flap his gums his true character ruined the image.

Nope.

Lobo couldn't lead a kindergarten class, let along a unit composed of seven elite fighters.

Well, somewhat elite.

The giant propped his elbows on the desk top and rested his chin in his hands. This wasn't going to be easy. But selecting someone to serve in his stead was essential. If he should be injured or slain while the Force was out in the field, they'd need someone to take over the reins, someone who could get them back safely, someone who could instill discipline on a bunch of individualistic noncomformists.

Bringing him back to square one.

Which one should it be?

He stared at the south wall, reflecting, dwelling on his responsibility as the leader of the strike force organized to deal with any and all menaces to the security of the Freedom Federation. Ironic, wasn't it, that six years ago the Federation hadn't even existed, and now the alliance of seven disparate factions promised to be the salvation of civilization if they all could survive long enough.

And talk about an unusual merger!

The Free State of California most resembled the prewar society in its level of industrial and technological development. It had been the leader of California, Governor Melnick, who had initially proposed forming the tactical team to deal with all threats and graciously offered to house the unit at a special facility located north of Los Angeles, near Pyramid Lake. Captain Havoc was their latest volunteer, replacing his younger brother, who had been slain during an earlier mission.

The second member of the Federation, the faction from which Jaguarundi hailed, was known as the Civilized Zone. During World War Three the government of the United States had relocated in Denver, Colorado, and forcibly evacuated hundreds of thousands of its citizens into an area embracing the states of Kansas, Nebraska, Wyoming, Colorado, New Mexico, and Oklahoma, and portions of Arizona and Texas. Renamed after the collapse of the United States, the Civilized Zone almost rivaled California in its cultural attainments. Recently the Civilized Zone had reinstituted public schooling, and hoped to be able to supply electricity to all its rural areas within the next decade.

The remaining factions were as different as night from day.

The Flathead Indians now lived as their ancestors did before the arrival of the white man on the continent, hunting and fishing and trapping to supply their food and clothing. They were fiercely determined to remain a free people, and they were honored to belong to the Federation. They'd sent the best candidate in the Flathead Nation, Sparrow Hawk, to serve on the Force for the required period of one year.

By contrast, the Moles had sent the least qualified. Their leader, Wolfe, knew the importance of the unit, knew that each faction was supposed to send a representative skilled in the arts of combat. So what had Wolfe done? Sent Raphaela. There seemed to be no rhyme nor reason to the Moles' behavior. They resided in an underground city located in north-central Minnesota, and they tended to keep to themselves.

The Cavalry, thankfully, was vastly more dependable. The rugged horsemen of the plains enjoyed a lifestyle very similar to that of the early American pioneers in the Old West. Most made their living by ranching or farming. They owned few mechanical contrivances and generally shunned the use of cars and trucks, although both California and the Civilized Zone had offered both types of vehicles in trade. They were a hardy lot, proud and independent. Doc Madsen was typical of their breed.

Straightening, the giant thought about the last two factions.

First there was the Clan, refugees from the ravaged Twin Cities of Minneapolis and St. Paul who had relocated to the small town of Halma in northwest Minnesota. Composed of former warring gangs, the Clan had united and received a new lease on life due to the efforts of the giant's own faction.

The Family. Descendants of a survivalist and his followers, they dwelt in a 30-acre compound on the outskirts of Lake Bronson State Park. They were the smallest numerically, but the most influential in Federation councils. Renowned for their wise leadership and fearless fighting class, the Warriors, the Family was the heart and soul of the Federation. Eighteen Warriors safeguarded the Home, as their compound had been dubbed, and the giant held the distinction of being the head Warrior, the best of the best, as it were.

Some distinction! he thought wryly. His expertise had earned him the dubious reward of being asked to lead the Freedom Force, of being responsible for molding six persons who couldn't eat a meal together without squabbling into a cohesive fighting unit.

Talk about impossible tasks!

The giant rested his brawny hands on the pair of Bowies strapped around his lean waist, pondering his selection of candidates for the position of second-in-command, then stiffened when he heard footsteps pounding on the stairs leading down to his office from the outside.

A moment later the office door flew open and in rushed the recruit from the Flatheads, attired as usual in beaded buckskins and carrying a spear in his right hand, the spear that had once belonged to his father, the same spear he had used to kill the mutation responsible for his father's death. "Blade, you must come quickly!" Sparrow Hawk declared.

"What's the problem now?"

"They're at it again."

Blade sighed and rose. "Lobo and Jag?"

"Yes."

"What happened?" Blade inquired, moving around his desk and heading for the stairs.

Sparrow fell in behind the giant. "Captain Havoc was conducting our daily class in the martial arts. He paired off Lobo and Jaguarundi to spar together."

"Let me guess. They got carried away and now they're at each other's throats."

"You must be clairvoyant," Sparrow said, and grinned.

Blade exited his office, took a left, and hurried up the stairs to the outer door. As he stepped into the brilliant morning sunshine he squinted and paused, allowing his eyes to adjust to the glare.

In front of the Warrior, spread out on the ground in the shape of a square, were the four large gray mats used during hand-to-hand combat sessions. Standing in the middle of the mats and glaring spitefully at one another were the two Force members in question.

On the left stood Lobo, his fists clenched, sweat caking his ebony skin, his nostrils flaring. "Oh, yeah?" he snapped. "Mess with me, sucker, and you'll be sorry you were ever born!"

The object of the Clansman's anger hissed and raised his fur-covered arms, extending his tapered nails. "Rub it in, you scuzzbag!"

Lobo blinked a few times. "Rub in what?"

"The fact that I was created in a test-tube!" Jaguarundi stated harshly in his low, raspy voice.

Uh-oh. Blade took a stride forward and rested his hands on the hilts of his Bowies. He well knew how touchy the hybrid could be concerning the Genetic Research Division. The thought sparked a torrent of memories.

Years ago a nefarious scientist, a genetic engineer who went by the title of the Doktor, had created a corps of hybrid assassins in the laboratory. By improving on the techniques developed by geneticists prior to the war, and by skillfully manipulating the hereditary factors incorporated into the chemical structure of molecules of DNA, the Doktor had mixed and matched genetic traits as he desired. His personal army of mutations had included beast-men and animal-women of every combination conceivable. There had been lion-men, tiger-women, monkey-men, and snake-women. Frog hybrids, dog hybrids, ox hybrids, and leopard hybrids. To preclude their breeding without his authorization, the Doktor had never created two mutations exactly alike. Each of his genetically engineered mutants in the G.R.D. had been unique.

Jaguarundi was a case in point. There wasn't another being like him on the face of the planet. Six feet tall, 175 pounds, Jag possessed a lean, muscular build. A reddish coat of short hair covered his body from the top of his head to his toenails. His sturdy, sharp fingernails were an inch long, and he could rip an opponent open with a single swipe. Like the animal he was named for, Jag's head was small, his ears rounded.

Easily the most unnerving aspect of his face were his slanted green eyes, their vertical slits lending him an almost alien mien. A black loincloth was his sole article of clothing.

"What's going on here?" Blade demanded.

Lobo and Jag both glanced at the giant.

"He started it!" the Clansman said.

"Did not!" Jag responded. "This moron started it."

"Who are you callin' a moron?" Lobo asked.

"Do you see any other Cro-Magnons around here?"

"Takes one to know one!" Lobo retorted.

Blade moved onto the mats. "Enough! Stand at attention, both of you!"

The hybrid scowled but promptly obeyed.

Lobo sneered at the mutation. "You're lucky the Big Guy showed up when he did or you'd be history. I don't have a heavy rep as a lean, mean fightin' machine for nothing, you know."

"If you don't stand at attention right this second, you'll acquire a reputation for being the only man in California who walks around with his left arm shoved clear up his nose," Blade stated sternly.

Doing a double take, Lobo snapped to attention.

"That's better," Blade said. "Now I want to know what's going on. One at a time. Jag, you first."

"We were sparring and I got this turkey in a headlock," the hybrid explained. "That's when he insulted me, and when I requested an apology from him, he refused."

"Requested my ass," Lobo muttered. "He told me to apologize or he'd tear my face off."

"Did you insult him?" Blade inquired.

"Not really," Lobo answered.

"What did you say?"

"I can't remember now."

Blade leaned toward the Clansman and locked his flinty eyes on Lobo's. "I trust your amnesia will be as short-lived as my patience with your childishness. That is, if you *like* having two legs."

Lobo gulped. "Hey. Guess what? I think it's comin' back to me."

"I sort of figured it might."

"Well, it was like this," Lobo said. "We were sparrin' and Jag cheated—"

"He cheated?" Blade said interrupting.

"Yeah. He jumped me when I wasn't lookin'."

"Do you make it a habit of turning your back on your sparring partners?"

"No way, dude. You know me. I'm as tough as they come. Anyway, he got lucky and got his arm around my head. That's when I made an innocent little comment, and the next thing I knew he was gettin' all bent out of shape and tryin' to tear my head from my shoulders."

"What was the comment?"

"Huh?"

"What did you say to him?"

"Nothing much."

Blade reached out and tapped the Clansman's blue T-shirt. "I want to know your exact words."

"They're not important."

"I'll be the judge of that."

"Boy, some people got out on the wrong side of the bed this morning, didn't they?"

"*What did you say?*" Blade asked, almost shouting the words.

Lobo cleared his throat. "I made this teensy-weensy crack about him needin' a bath."

The Warrior glanced at the hybrid. "Is that true?"

"Not quite."

"Then tell me what he said."

Jaguarundi frowned. "When I had him in the headlock, he sniffed my armpit and made a snide reference to B.O. in alley cats."

Lobo snickered.

"Were those your words?" Blade asked.

"Kind of."

"And you think they're funny?"

"Don't you, dude?"

"Not half as funny as you jogging five miles."

"Say *what*?"

Blade motioned to the west. "Five miles. Right now. On the double."

"You're kiddin' me, right?"

"Do I look like I'm kidding?"

"But it's hot out. Do you know what five miles in this heat will do to my complexion?"

Blade smiled sweetly. "I'll requisition Supply for a case of cosmetics."

"I must've been nuts to join this chicken-doo-doo outfit." Lobo said, and jogged off. "If I get heat stroke, it'll be your fault."

"I'll try to live with the guilt."

Mumbling under his breath, the Clansman kept going.

"Thanks, Blade," Jaguarundi said.

"Don't bother thanking me."

"Why not?"

"Because *you're* doing ten miles."

"I am?"

"Yep."

"May I ask why?"

"The reason is simple. You're more mature than Lobo."

The hybrid regarded the Warrior quizzically. "I don't quite follow you."

Blade hooked his thumbs in his belt. "Lobo is always sticking his foot in his mouth because he doesn't know any better. He has the emotional maturity of a four-year-old." He paused. "Make that a two-year-old. You, on the other hand, are an intelligent, mature adult. You do know better. But you have a short fuse when it comes to comments concerning your creation. You're touchy about being a mutation endowed with human and animal traits. I expect you to be able to control your sensitivity. As the leader of the Force, I can't allow anyone to disrupt the effective functioning of this unit with their personal shortcomings. Lobo has to learn to keep a lid on his mouth, and you've got to learn to restrain your anger.''

''I try.''

''I know. Just try harder.''

''I'm sorry I let him get to me.''

''He gets to everybody.''

Jaguarundi pivoted and sprinted after the Clansman.

Another petty problem resolved, Blade reflected. He went to turn toward the door when a female voice stopped him in his tracks.

''How could you? That was mean.''

The Warrior rotated to the east.

Twelve feet away, past the edge of the mats, were the three remaining members of the Force. On the left, wearing his customary black frock coat, his hat pulled down to his eyebrows, was Doc Madsen. In the center, his arms folded across his wide chest, wearing camouflage fatigues, was Captain Mike Havoc. And on the right, also wearing camouflage fatigues, stood the Molewoman.

''What was mean?'' Blade queried.

''You know darn well,'' Raphaela said. ''You had no call to punish Jaguarundi when Lobo was to blame.''

''Jag should have controlled his temper.''

''I wouldn't have punished him.''

''You're not in charge,'' Blade reminded her, and saw the corners of her mouth curl downward. ''As I explained to all of you on the day you arrived at this facility, I expect each of you to behave in a professional manner and to abide by the rules I lay down. In our line of work discipline is essential. One slipup in the field and we could all wind up dead, which is why I can't tolerate any serious breach of our training regimen.''

Doc Madsen nodded. ''If you ask me, partner, they both had it coming.''

Blade glanced at the officer. ''What about you? Any comments?''

Captain Havoc's blue eyes darted to Sparrow Hawk, who was standing near the doorway to the command bunker, then back to the Warrior. "I could have kept them in line, sir. There was no need for anyone to go get you."

"Don't criticize Sparrow Hawk for doing his duty," Blade responded curtly. "If I hadn't intervened, Lobo and Jag might have gone at it. We're supposed to be a team, remember? We're supposed to function as a unit both on and off duty. First and foremost we must be loyal to one another. And that means we don't try to pound each other into a pulp at the slightest provocation. Or carp when someone does the right thing. Understand?"

"Yes, sir," Havoc stated, an edge to his tone.

"Is something else bothering you?"

Havoc's arms dropped to his side and he straightened. "Sir?"

"I get the impression that something else is bothering you," Blade reiterated. "What is it?"

"Nothing, sir."

"You're sure?"

"Positive, sir."

The Warrior sighed and gazed at a white cloud floating over the southern portion of the Force compound. Encompassing 12 acres, the entire facility was enclosed within an electrified fence and patrolled by regular California Army troopers. To the south was the concrete pad, 50 yards square, on which sat one of the Hurricanes utilized to ferry the Force to any hot spot in the country. The second VTOL was parked in the hangar to the east of the pad. In the middle of the compound were the three concrete bunkers, arranged in a row from west to east: the supply bunker, the command bunker, and the barracks bunker. The northern third of the compound was preserved in its natural state and used for training exercises.

"Should we continue with the hand-to-hand sessions?" Havoc inquired.

Blade looked at the officer. "No. Roll up the mats and

store them in the supply bunker. When Jag and Lobo have completed their laps, let me know. We'll work on our marksmanship this afternoon.''

''Yes, sir.''

''We may need to postpone the shooting practice,'' Doc Madsen interjected.

''Why?'' Blade asked.

Doc nodded to the south. ''Guess who's paying us a visit?''

The Warrior knew what he would see before he pivoted. Coming through the gate in the south fence was a topless jeep bearing two men, the driver and General Miles Gallagher. Which proved the old adage to be right once again.

When it rained, it poured.

CHAPTER TWO

"**S**o how's the training proceeding?"

Blade sat down in the chair behind his desk and gestured for the general to take one of the pair on the other side. "As well as can be expected."

Gallagher took a seat and grinned. A bulldog of a man with brown eyes and crew-cut brown hair, he served as the personal liaison between the Force and Governor Melnick. Whenever a leader of one of the Federation factions required the assistance of the Force, the leader would send a letter to Melnick by way of the routine shuttle runs on which the VTOLs were dispatched on a regular basis. Once Governor Melnick received the word, he would have Gallagher bear the tidings to Blade.

"What's so amusing?" the Warrior inquired.

"I saw Lobo and Jaguarundi jogging along the south fence on my way in," Gallagher mentioned. "They passed right by the jeep and Lobo asked me for a lift."

"He did, did he?"

"I doubt if you'll ever make a team player out of him," the general stated. "If he'd been under my command I would have given him the boot long ago."

"Lobo shows promise."

"Who are you fooling? He promises to be a royal pain in the butt for as long as he stays on the Force, and that's about it."

Blade's eyes narrowed. "Is this a social visit or are you here for a specific reason?"

"As a matter of fact, I'm here on official business. Let me ask you a question. Are your people ready for another mission?"

Blade leaned back and regarded the general coldly. "Why this sudden concern for our readiness? You were the one who rushed us into the Diablo affair, remember? And you didn't give a damn when I objected to interrupting my training schedule so the Force could take time off and spend three days in L.A."

"I'm not sure if I like what you're implying."

A smirk curled the Warrior's lips. "I'm not implying anything. I'm stating flat out that you haven't displayed much concern for our welfare in the past. Why start now?"

Gallagher's features hardened and for a moment he appeared ready to explode in indignant fury. Then, in a sudden transformation, he softened and smiled. "I apologize if I've given you the wrong impression. And I take issue with your assertion that I don't care about your unit. Yes, I persuaded you to take the Force after El Diablo, but the assignment entailed tracking the bastard to his lair and reporting back to me. You weren't supposed to become embroiled in a full-scale battle. You attacked his base on your own initiative."

"We had no choice."

"And need I point out that you have the final authority for accepting or rejecting Force assignments? You didn't have to go."

Blade said nothing.

"Now as far as L.A. is concerned, Governor Melnick offered the Force the three-day pass, not me. How can you blame me for interrupting your training schedule when the idea wasn't even mine?''

"I suppose I can't," Blade said.

General Gallagher grinned, presenting an image of unsullied innocence. "Now that we've disposed of that little matter, let's get down to cases. I need to know if your team is ready for a mission because we've received a request for assistance."

"From whom?"

"Kilrane, the head of the Cavalry."

Blade knew Kilrane well and admired the man highly. They had met on a number of occasions and he considered the top Cavalryman a friend. "I'm surprised. The Cavalry can hold their own against anybody. What kind of problem could they be having that requires our help?"

"Their people have been disappearing."

"I seem to recall Governor Melnick mentioning that in Anaheim."

Gallagher nodded. "During the past decade alone, over two hundred men and women have up and vanished without a trace."

"Two hundred!"

"Kilrane wrote a detailed letter to Governor Melnick," General Gallagher said, and patted the right side of his uniform jacket. "I have it right here for you to read. The pertinent point is that the Cavalry has been trying to discover the reason for the strange disappearances ever since they started, and until recently there wasn't a clue."

"Then what happened?"

"The Cavalry lucked out. They finally have a witness, a woman who saw her husband disappear right before her eyes."

Blade thought of his darling Jenny and imagined how he would feel if something should ever happen to her. The very idea disturbed him immensely, and he felt sympathy for the unfortunate Cavalrywoman. "Who is she?"

"Just a second," Gallagher said. He took Kilrane's letter from an inner pocket and unfolded the sheet of paper. "Let's see. Here it is. Elvy Wagner.''

"Go on.''

"Her hubby, Larry, was out plowing a field. The sun had set and she was preparing their supper when she heard an unusual cry. Naturally she stepped outside and called out Larry's name. He yelled at her to go back inside, and the next thing she knew he sailed over her head, clear over their house, and faded into thin air.''

Blade sat up. "Let me get this straight. He flew over their house?''

"She thinks something was carrying him. She heard a flapping sound and saw a large form, but it was too dark for her to note details.''

"So an unknown creature is the culprit.''

"That's Kilrane's guess. But the thing has never left any tracks, never left so much as a hair at the scene of the abductions.''

"Does Kilrane happen to mention whether any of his people disappeared in broad daylight?''

"According to the information he's gathered, all of the victims vanished at night.''

"Which means the creature is nocturnal.''

"So it would seem," Gallagher concurred.

The Warrior debated whether to accept the assignment. He still didn't believe his team was ready to go up against another enemy like El Diablo. They required more time to hone their skills before they'd be able to handle a bloodthirsty army of raiders. Although each of them, with the exception of Raphaela, was extremely deadly in his own right, as a team they had a lot to learn. He wouldn't take them on any mission unless he believed they had at least a fifty-fifty chance of surviving. The last thing he wanted was a repeat of the tragedy that had decimated the first Force. He wouldn't go through that ordeal again if he could help it.

Losing five members of the unit had been sheer torment to his soul.

Their names came unbidden to Blade's mind. Spader.

Kraft. Athena Morris. Thunder-Rolling-in-the-Mountain. Sergeant James Havoc. They'd all died in combat except for Athena. Her death had been meaningless, an almost incomprehensible travesty of justice, a supreme absurdity in the stream of human events.

She'd fallen from a window!

Athena Morris, the enterprising journalist who had worked so diligently at joining the Force, who had gone so far as to take Special Forces training so she would qualify, who had honestly related every Force assignment in her syndicated column in the newspapers, who had done more to convince the citizens of California that the Freedom Force was critical to the future of the Federation than anyone else, had died when, while heavily sedated, she'd tried to open the window of her seventh-floor hospital room and fallen to the pavement below.

What a horrible way to go.

Her death had been all the more tragic because she had finally come to terms with her love for another Force member, a hybrid by the name of Grizzly. So far as was known, no human woman had ever chosen a mutation as her mate. It had taken considerable courage on her part to confess her affection, and equal courage on Grizzly's part to acknowledge her feelings and reciprocate.

Poor Grizzly!

Blade recalled the tortured expression of the hybrid at the funeral. Grizzly had been inconsolable, and instead of returning to the Civilized Zone, where he had lived prior to joining the Force, Grizzly had ventured into the savage Outlands, those vast areas of the country beyond the boundaries of the few organized factions. In the Outlands might made right. There were no laws, no rules of conduct. Anything went. The weak were invariable exterminated by the strong and the brutal. Blade had tried to talk Grizzly out of going, but the hybrid had been insistent. Where was Grizzly now? he wondered.

The Warrior suddenly became aware that Gallagher was

speaking to him.

"—take this assignment or not? I'll need to send a reply to Kilrane right away if you're not going."

"We'll go on the mission."

"You will?" Gallagher queried, sounding surprised.

"We need the experience. I can't quite understand why Kilrane sent for us when he has trackers every bit as skilled as Sparrow Hawk, but we'll do the best we can."

"Kilrane doesn't have a mutant at his disposal. Maybe he thinks Jaguarundi can succeed where his own men have failed."

Blade stared at the oficer. "You know that Jag prefers to be called a hybrid."

"Hybrid, mutant, what's the big difference?"

Blade didn't bother to waste his breath arguing. The general knew the differences as well as he did.

Three types of mutations were currently in existence, two of them as a direct consequence of the war. Ordinary mutations were those babies and animals born with their genetic codes scrambled. The massive amount of radiation saturating the environment was the cause, and thousands upon thousands of deformed embryos had been born since human-kind had tried to wipe itself out in the ultimate folly. Hapless infants and animals emerging from the womb with extra limbs or an extra head were doomed to a miserable existence of alienation if they lived long enough.

Chemical weapons, specifically the regenerating chemical clouds, were responsible for the second type of mutation, those vile creatures known as mutates. If mammals, repitiles, or amphibians should be caught in one of the green clouds, they underwent a repulsive metamorphosis, transforming into deranged monstrosities endowed with insatiable appetites. Pus-filled sores would cover their bodies, and they would roam the countryside slaying every living thing they encountered. Of all the mutations, the mutates were the most feared.

The third category embraced the hybrids, those beings

who, like Jaguarundi, were the product of genetic engineering. They were the smallest numerically, and many normal humans wished they could be eliminated entirely. As was so typical of the human species whenever diverse races mingled, prejudice and bigotry had reared their ugly heads. Countless humans despised the hybrids for no other reason than they were different.

"When will you be leaving?" General Gallagher inquired.

"Tomorrow morning."

"Excellent. I'll instruct Captain Laslo and Captain Franklyn to be ready to fly your team out at nine A.M."

"Fine," Blade said absently. "We'll have our gear at the pad by eight."

"Governor Melnick will be pleased to hear you're going," Gallagher stated. Then he went on in an offhand manner. "He was a bit upset to learn you'd objected to the Force spending time in L.A."

"You told him?" Blade questioned in surprise.

"Sure. Why not?"

Blade kept silent, suppressing his annoyance, peeved at the general's lack of tact. Why would the officer inform Melnick unless Gallagher wanted the Force in hot water?

"Will you need any special equipment on this mission?"

"Yeah. I'd like an infrared scope and a parabolic mike."

"No problem. I'll issue you one of the new Nite-Vision systems and our Penetrator sound detector. They're both state-of-the-art. Anything else?"

"A high-powered rifle."

Gallagher blinked a few times. "What's wrong with the standard M-16's?"

"Nothing. The others will take M-16s. The rifle is for me."

"I thought you were partial to the M60?"

"I'm taking both."

"Both?" The general studied the Warrior for a moment, then grinned. "Do you know something I don't?"

"The M60 is a heavy-caliber machine gun, and like most

machine guns it's not noted for pinpoint accuracy. Sure, it can spray lead all over the landscape and it can hit a given target with reasonable consistency, but I want a gun that can hit the head on a nail ten times out of ten.''

''Do you have a specific rifle in mind?''

''A Weatherby Mark Five.''

''A Weatherby!'' Gallagher exclaimed. ''Do you have any idea how hard they are to come by? They're very rare.''

''There must be one you can dig up. We have several in the armory at the Home.''

''I'll try,'' Gallagher said, ''but I'm not making any promises. They were the cream of the crop back in their day, and anyone who owns one now won't part with it easily.'' He paused. ''Why not take a Winchester or a Marlin? We have plenty of them.''

''A Weatherby,'' Blade insisted. ''A 460 Weatherby Magnum.''

Gallagher came out of his chair. ''A 460 Magnum! Are you sure you don't want it gold-plated?''

''Can you locate one by tomorrow?''

''Who knows? Keep your fingers crossed. If I do, it'll qualify as a damn miracle.''

''Keep me posted.''

''Okay,'' General Gallagher said, and sighed. He placed the letter on the desk. ''Here. I'd better get my butt back to my office. I'll probably be on the phone all day.''

The drumming of boots on the stairs heralded the arrival of Captain Havoc, who stepped into the office bearing a newspaper in his left hand. He saluted smartly and looked at Blade. ''Sorry to disturb you, sir. This was just delivered.''

''Give it here.''

''Yes, sir.'' Havoc walked toward the desk.

Blade surreptitiously glanced at the general as he leaned forward and extended his right arm.

Gallagher's brown eyes darted to the rolled newspaper and he unconsciously licked his thick lips. He glanced at Havoc, at the paper again, then seemed to wrestle with his emotions for a second before turning a calm face toward the desk.

"Thank you, Captain," Blade said as he grasped the newspaper.

Havoc saluted and stuck his right foot behind his left, about to do an about-face.

"Hold up," Blade directed.

The captain paused and gazed uncertainly at the Warrior. "Sir?"

"I have an announcement to make that concerns you," Blade told him. "I might as well do it while General Gallagher is here, just in case he has any objections."

"Objections to what?" Gallagher inquired.

"To my appointing Captain Havoc as my second-in-command," Blade informed them, studying their reactions.

The normally stoic Havoc did a double take. His features shifted into a peculiar expression, a commingled astonishment and—something else.

General Gallagher's mouth dropped open. He recovered his composure an instant later and grinned slyly, as if amused by a joke only he knew.

"Me, sir?" Captain Havoc declared.

"You."

"You didn't tell us you were planning to pick a second-in-command, sir," Havoc said. He seemed to be thinking intently.

"Surprise, surprise."

"But why me, sir? What about Doc or Sparrow or Jag? Any one of them can handle the job."

Gallagher glanced at the junior officer. "If he wants you, Captain, why object? Consider your appointment an honor."

"Yes, sir," Havoc responded, devoid of enthusiasm.

Blade smiled at the captain. "My decision is final. I want you. Break the news to the others."

"What if they don't like the news, sir?"

"Tough."

"I'll tell them, sir," Havoc said unhappily. He saluted once more and departed.

General Gallagher beamed expansively, suddenly in exceptional spirits. "My compliments. You've selected an excellent man for the post."

"I figured you would approve of my decision."

"Havoc is a competent man. He won't let you down."

"I hope not."

The general moved toward the door. "Well, I'll be seeing you. I've got to get to work on locating a Weatherby."

"Good luck," Blade said, and spread the newspaper open on the desk. "I wonder if there are any articles today about the Force?"

Gallagher halted and looked at the paper. "I believe there is one. I read the *Times* earlier while eating breakfast."

Blade idly scanned the front page, then turned to the next. "There have been quite a few stories about us lately," he mentioned casually.

"No more than usual."

"Oh, I don't know. I can understand the story they printed about our battle with El Diablo and with the gangs, but yesterday I saw a piece on our favorite weapons." He paused. "Strange."

General Gallagher tensed perceptibly. "What is?"

"I don't recall being interviewed by a *Times* reporter about our weaponry. And I don't believe a reporter spoke to any of the others. I wonder how the newspaper found out?"

The officer shrugged. "You know news reporters. They have their sources."

Blade flipped another page. There, in the upper right corner, was an article entitled FREEDOM'S PRICE: THE FORCE IS NEEDED. "Ahhhh. Here it is. Heavy stuff."

"It's a good article."

Blade glanced up and noted the air of nervousness the general radiated. "Shouldn't you be trying to find me a Weatherby?"

"Yeah. On my way." Gallagher stared at the paper one last time, then left.

The Warrior grinned and leaned back. Got them! He'd

deliberately made the announcement of his new second-in-command in their presence to test them, to gauge their response, and his ruse had been a success. If there had been any lingering, subconscious doubts concerning their duplicity, those doubts were now dashed on the rocks of hard evidence. Their expressions had indicted them to his satisfaction, and combined with their previous secretive behavior, had aroused his suspicions to a feverish pitch.

They were definitely up to something.

But *what?*

And why did General Gallagher almost have a coronary every time he picked up a newspaper? Of what significance were the articles about the Force?

Blade rested his forearms on the desk and quickly read the piece in the *Times*. The writer went on at length about the necessity of preserving the vestiges of true freedom embodied in the various Federation factions, and tried to emphasize the point that the Force served as the first line of defense against the savage denizens of the Outlands and the power-hungry petty dictators who frequently arose.

So what was the big deal?

Blade sighed and stared thoughtfully at the south wall. The article was about average for those he'd seen on the Force. Athena Morris had written several articles in the same vein. In fact, the crisp, precise writing style reminded him very strongly of Athena's own style. He looked at the piece again, rereading the opening paragraph.

And then it hit him.

As if struck by lightning, Blade jerked erect, stark astonishment etching his countenance, and for several seconds he was too stunned to move or speak. Finally he stared at the newspaper, then at the doorway, and breathed three words: "It can't be!"

CHAPTER THREE

Rapid City, Dakota Territory. Once one of the major cities in South Dakota with a population of 55,000 before the war. Now it was a frontier town with a population of only 8,000. Many of the buildings had been abandoned and neglected and the streets were in a state of severe deterioration. Once it had been the leading wholesale center for the Black Hills; now ranchers and farmers from hundreds of miles around came in to sell or trade their cows, steers, vegetables, and grain. Where once apparel of every type and color adorned the populace, now buckskins and woolen garments were prevalent. And where once primarily only law-enforcement officers wore firearms, now almost every man and most of the women carried a gun.

Blade mentally noted all these facts as the Hurricane flashed down out of the sparkling blue sky toward a field on the northwest outskirts of the town. Its mighty engines whining, the jet slowed rapidly. He twisted and gazed out the rear of the cockpit at the second jet, likewise on its descent approach to Rapid City.

The two Hurricanes were the pride of the California military establishment. Possessing vertical-takeoff-or-landing capability, they combined some of the characteristics of a helicopter with the power of a conventional jet. Both had been modified to carry extra fuel tanks and could transport up to five passengers at a time. And each was outfitted with 10,000 pounds of blistering firepower that included rockets, bombs, Sidewinder missiles, and machine guns.

Blade glanced at the other occupants of the leading jet. Captain Havoc sat on his right. Behind them were Doc Madsen and Sparrow Hawk. The rest of the team—Raphaela, Lobo, and Jaguarundi—were all in the second jet along with their gear.

Havoc noticed the Warrior's glance and returned it. "I want to thank you again for appointing me as your second-in-command."

"I appreciate your gratitude, but you've already thanked me at least ten times. Enough is enough," Blade said, and grinned.

The captain stared out his side of the cockpit at the ground below. "You never stop surprising me, sir."

"Is that good or bad?"

"Good, I guess."

"You *guess*?"

Sparrow Hawk leaned toward them. "I, for one, am satisfied with your decision," he told the giant. "Captain Havoc did an outstanding job of leading us when we fought the gangs in Los Angeles."

"I'm glad you agree," Blade said, and looked at the Cavalryman. "What about you, Doc?"

Madsen had been sitting with his head bowed, his hazel eyes unfocused, apparently deep in reflection. At the sound of his name he roused himself and glanced at the Warrior. "Sorry. I didn't quite catch that. What did you say?"

"How do you feel about Havoc being second-in-command?" Blade inquired.

"Don't make no never mind to me," Doc replied. "I'll take orders from whoever is in charge. I signed up with this outfit to go around killing folks for a year, and I aim to uphold my end of the bargain.''

Captain Havoc shifted in his seat. ''There's more to being on the Force than killing.''

''Like what?'' Doc asked.

''Like defending the Federation at all costs.''

''And how do we defend the Federation?'' Doc said. ''We do it by killing the Federation's enemies.''

''That's a rather narrow-minded outlook,'' Havoc commented.

Doc snorted. ''You're a fine one to talk, partner. You're a professional soldier, and the last I heard soldiers don't plant daisies for a living. You kill. That's your job.''

''At least I kill in the line of duty.''

Madsen straightened. ''What's that crack supposed to mean?''

''We all know you made your living as a gambler before you volunteered for the Force. The word is that you also had a reputation as a gunfighter. One of the best in the Dakota Territory.''

The Cavalryman looked at the Warrior. ''Someone's got a big mouth.''

''Don't blame Blade,'' Havoc said, correcting him. ''I heard it from General Gallagher.''

''Then I reckon I'll have a talk with that hombre after we get back.''

''If you decide to punch his lights out, hit him once for me,'' Havoc stated with a bitter, vehement intensity.

Blade pretended to be interested in watching the pilot to cover his surprise at the captain's stinging remark. If he didn't know better, he'd swear Havoc hated Gallagher's guts. But if that was the case, why did the two spend so much time conversing in hushed tones?

''You must be excited at the prospect of going home,'' Sparrow said to the gunman.

''I'm tickled pink,'' Doc declared testily.

''Don't you want to visit your friends and family?''

''I joined the Force to get away from the Dakota Territory

for a spell,'' Doc answered. ''The last thing I wanted was to come back so soon.''

''I don't understand,'' Sparrow said.

''And you never will.''

Blade folded his hands in his lap. As if he didn't already have enough to worry about with Havoc and Gallagher acting like criminals, now Doc was acting up. ''You should have told me how you felt,'' he mentioned. ''If your reason was valid, I might have permitted you to stay behind.''

''I'm part of this outfit. Where you guys go, I go,'' Doc asserted.

''Suit yourself,'' Blade said.

The pilot, Captain Peter Laslo, abruptly interrupted their conversation. ''Check your seat restraints, gentlemen. I'm taking this baby down.''

''Try to keep my kidneys in one piece,'' Blade joked.

''Philistine,'' Laslo quipped, and concentrated on his task. Banking sharply to the right, he dove the aircraft straight at the field. ''There's our designated landing spot. And there's a reception committee waiting for us.''

Blade peered downward and spotted two rows of horsemen on the east side of the field. Kilrane and company. The Cavalry leader's letter had stated he would await the arrival of the Force in Rapid City rather than Pierre. Kilrane had given the Force three days to respond to his request; otherwise, as he related in his letter, he intended to hunt for the creature or creatures himself. Blade had to smile as he remembered reading that comment. Kilrane never had been one to sit idly by when trouble brewed.

Displaying consummate skill, Captain Laslo brought the Hurricane down to within 300 feet of the field, then engaged the Hover Mode. Slowly, its engines roaring, the VTOL settled to the ground near the waiting horsemen. The grass underneath was flattened by the 22,000 pounds of thrust and dust billowed into the air, obscuring the riders.

''Here we are,'' Captain Laslo said while busily flicking switches. ''Dakota International Airport. I thank you for flying No Frills Express.''

The engines abruptly ceased roaring and the strident whine gradually tapered off. The second jet came down 40 yards to the west.

Blade unfastened his seat belt. ''Thanks, Pete. Next time, though, why can't you provide one of those stewardesses like they have on the civilian flights?''

''You want a stewardess? I bet your wife would find that interesting.''

''Forget I mentioned it.''

''Coward.'' Laslo pressed a toggle switch on the control panel and a hatch on the right side of the canopy swung outward. Although the canopy itself could be opened, the pilots were under standing orders to use the hatch unless they knew the landing area was one-hundred-percent secure. The Hurricanes had been designed to carry commandos and other specialized tactical units into combat zones, and the hatch served as their means of exiting the craft while the canopy remained closed to protect the pilot from possible sniper fire.

Blade glanced at Captain Havoc. ''I'll leave it up to you to assemble the team on the east side of the field. I want to talk to Kilrane.'' He slipped from his seat and eased to the hatch. ''And don't forget to bring my M60 and the Weatherby.''

''Yes, sir,'' Havoc responded.

The Warrior unfurled a green rope ladder lying next to the opening, then turned around and slid his legs onto a rung. He observed a frown on Madsen's face, then nodded at the others and rapidly climbed to the ground.

''Blade!''

At the familiar, friendly bellow, Blade pivoted and smiled. ''Kilrane!''

The leader of the Cavalry had dismounted and was walking briskly toward the giant. A big man in his own right, Kilrane wore fringed buckskins that complemented his rugged good looks. His eyes were blue, his long hair brown tinged with gray streaks. On his right hip hung an ivory-handled Mitchell

Single Action revolver, and his proficiency with that weapon had earned him the notoriety of being rated one of the fastest Cavalrymen who ever lived. Only a few others were considered to be in his class when it came to gun-handling. One of them, a man named Boone, had been the previous representative of the Cavalry on the Force. Another one was the gunfighter-gambler known as Doc.

Blade hastened to meet his friend. He extended his right hand and scrutinized Kilrane from head to toe. "It's great to see you again."

"Same here," Kilrane acknowledged, and shook vigorously.

"You have a few more gray hairs," the Warrior noted.

"I'm amazed you don't have any."

"Clean living keeps me young."

Kilrane laughed and gave the giant a playful slap on the shoulder. "How are Jenny and Gabe?"

"They're fine. Gabe is growing like a weed."

"And Hickok and Geronimo?"

"They're as crazy as ever. Hickok has two kids now."

"Two?"

"Yep. He adopted a little girl we rescued in Atlanta."

"Hickok did? That man has to be the most unpredictable son of a gun on the face of the planet."

Blade looked at the two rows of Cavalrymen. "I notice you brought an army along."

"Just a hundred men."

"Is Boone with them?" Blade inquired eagerly, scanning the nearest row.

"Nope. Sorry. He sends his regards. But I had to leave somone reliable to hold down the fort in Pierre and he's one of the few men I trust completely."

"Too bad," Blade said. "The next time you see him, be sure to relay a hello from me."

"Will do."

"So fill me in. What can you tell me about the disappearances that you didn't mention in your letter?"

A frown curled Kilrane's mouth and his handsome features softened, mirroring his acute sadness. "To tell you the truth, Blade, I'm at my wit's end. I've tried everything I can think of and I'm no closer to solving the problem than I was when it first began." He looked into the Warrior's eyes. "That's why I sent for you. If anyone can get to the bottom of the mystery, you can."

"Thanks. But you might be overrating my ability."

"Am I? Who was it who defeated the Doktor and that scum of a dictator, Samuel the Second?"

"I had a lot of help."

"And who was it who beat the Technics, the Superiors, the Gild, the Dragons, the . . ." Kilrane paused and smiled. "Well, you get my drift. You've licked everyone who's taken on the Federation. Not to mention all the lowlifes you wasted who were stupid enough to go up against the Family."

"Again, I had a lot of help. Don't forget the other Warriors. We're all trained to perform our job competently and professionally."

"Yeah. But some of the Warriors are deadlier than others. Hickok, for instance, is walking death. Yama and Rikki are the same. But you're in a league all your own."

Blade made a show of staring down at his feet. "Boy, it's a good thing I'm wearing these combat boots. It's starting to get deep around here."

"You can argue all you want to, but every living soul in the Federation knows you're the man to call to get the job done. Any job. And I'm hoping you can succeed where we've failed. The disappearances must stop!"

"Your letter indicated they began about a decade ago."

Kilrane nodded. "At first no one paid much attention to a few measly disappearances. What with all the wild animals and mutations roaming the countryside, everyone generally assumed the people who vanished were attacked by a mutate or some such and eaten. It didn't help matters that all of the disappearances took place at night. A rancher would be out late riding his range and never come home. Someone would go walking along a country road after dark and never be seen again. And the incidents were scattered over hundreds of square miles. News spreads slowly out here. There are only a few newspapers in the whole Territory. So it's perfectly understandable how someone could vanish in, say, White Owl one week and Kadoka a week later and no one would make the connection.''

"When did you begin to put the pieces together?''

"Not until three years ago. I appointed one of my lieutenants to keep track of all disappearances in the Territory and to plot them on a map. Within six months of starting the project a definite pattern had emerged and he brought it to my attention.''

"What type of pattern?''

"We discovered that eighty percent of the disappearances occurred within two hundred miles of the extreme southwest corner of our Territory,'' Kilrane said, and frowned. "Within two hundred miles of the Hot Springs Dead Zone.''

"The what?''

"A Dead Zone, an area that was hit by a nuclear weapon during the war. We have several within our boundaries. Geronimo once told me that the Family refers to these regions as Hot Spots.''

"Yes. Now I remember. He ended up in one of your Dead Zones during his first visit to your Territory and nearly lost his life.''

"I know. I was with him,'' Kilrane remarked. "You have to see these areas to appreciate how eerie they are. Nothing grows in a Dead Zone. Not so much as a single blade of grass. We used to believe the Dead Zones were totally devoid of life, but now we know better. Now we know the radiation has produced some truly monstrous mutations.''

"I was in a Hot Spot in California once. I know all about them. Do you think these creatures come from the Hot Springs Dead Zone?''

"Yep.''

"Why was Hot Springs hit? Was there a military base

nearby?''

Kilrane shrugged. ''Beats me. No, there wasn't a base. Hot Springs was a town of about seven thousand when the war broke out. Made a lot of money off the tourists, what with being located almost smack dab between the Black Hills National Forest, the Buffalo Gap National Grassland, the Badlands National Park, and the Custer State Park. Plus there were all those caves in the region.''

''Caves?''

''The Jewel Cave National Monument, the Wind Cave National Park, the Ice Cave, and others. Some of them were huge caverns,'' Kilrane related. ''There's no logical reason why Hot Springs should have been hit. As near as we can figure, the other side must have aimed one of their nuclear missiles at Ellsworth Air Force Base, and missed.''

''It's possible,'' Blade said slowly. From the information the Family had gathered over the decades, including the intelligence they had learned from their allies in the Federation, there were apparently over a score of such Hot Spots or Dead Zones scattered about the country once known as the United States of America. And some of the locations of the Dead Zones made no sense from a military perspective. Evidently the incoming missiles hadn't been as accurate as the enemy had claimed. Then again, when a person considered that the missiles had flown thousands and thousands of miles in some instances, it was easy to comprehend how the slightest deviation in the trajectory could result in missing the target by hundreds of miles.

''I figured we would spend the night in Rapid City and cut out at first light for the Dead Zone,'' Kilrane stated. ''If it's all right with you?''

''Fine by me. Is the Dead Zone still hot?''

''We have teams of experts who monitor the Zones regularly, measuring the radioactivity with Geiger counters and whatnot. After a century, the radiation level is only slightly elevated, not enough to pose a danger to us.''

"Have you any idea what type of creature we're looking for?"

"We reckon a mutation is to blame, maybe an overgrown bird of some sort. All we have to go on is the eyewitness testimony of Elvy Wagner. She saw whatever it was carrying her husband off, but she didn't get a good look at the creature. She did hear the swishing and beating of its wings."

"Swishing?"

"That's how she described the sound."

Blade stared at the ground, his memory piqued. Swishing sound. He vaguely recalled hearing a strange swishing sound once, years ago, and he attempted to remember exactly when. It had been during the war against Samuel the Second and the Doktor, back when the duo had ruled the Civilized Zone with an iron fist, before the Civilized Zone joined the Federation. And it had something to do with the night, if he was right.

Suddenly he remembered.

The episode had transpired during the war. He and other Warriors had been en route to Catlow, Wyoming, and they had jumped a jeep patrol one night. One of the troopers had fled into the darkness, and before the Warriors could overtake him there had terrified shriek and they'd heard a distinct swishing as *something* carried the young soldier away.

"What's wrong?" Kilrane inquired, studying the giant's face.

"I may have had a run-in with one of the creatures in northern Wyoming about six years ago, but at the time I had no idea what it was."

Kilrane abruptly slapped his right palm against his forehead. "Damn! Why didn't I think of that? Odds are those things have been taking folks from the northeast corner of the Civilized Zone too. I should get together with President Toland down in Denver and compare notes."

"And you estimate the things have abducted two hundred of your people?"

"More or less. It's hard to tell since we don't know their range."

"Even so," Blade said, and the dawning realization horrified him, "if the creatures have been grabbing people from the Civilized Zone and elsewhere at the same rate as here in the Dakota Territory, then we're looking at four or five hundred victims within the last ten years."

Kilrane nodded grimly. "And they're snatching more and more folks each and every year. At the rate it's going, no one will be able to step outside at night within another year or two."

The gravity of the situation staggered the Warrior. A few isolated abductions had blossomed into the systematic extermination of the human populace in the region. If the beings responsible weren't stopped now, they might spread their reign of terror farther and farther afield until the Midwest became completely under their sway, became their private hunting preserve, as it were.

Kilrane summed up the situation succinctly. "Either we find these things and wipe them or we're in a world of hurt."

"We'll find them."

"I like a man with confidence," Kilrane commented, and gazed past the Warrior. "So those are your new recruits?"

Blade shifted and discovered the six members of his team lined up at attention 15 yards away, each with an M-16 over a shoulder and a backpack strapped to his or her back. Captain Havoc held the M60, two ammo belts, and the Weatherby. "That's my new team."

"How's Doc doing?"

"He follows orders and he doesn't give me any grief, which is more than I can say for some of the others."

"It really shocked my shorts when he volunteered to replace Boone. He was the last person I would've expected to want the job," Kilrane said. "Which reminds me. Is there any chance you could order him to spend the night sleeping in one of those jets?"

Blade glanced at the frontiersman. "Why in the world would I want to do that?"

"Because if you don't, by tomorrow morning he could be dead."

CHAPTER FOUR

The saloon and bar owners of Rapid City were seeing dollar signs in front of their eyes. They usually enjoyed a thriving business after the sun went down anyway, but now they were doubly fortunate to have the 100 riders comprising Kilrane's personal detachment as customers and the presence of the Freedom Force members to draw in patrons from the surrounding countryside. With the notable exception of Doc Madsen, the new Force members were unknown to the Cavalry populace at large and therefore generated intense curiosity. As if that weren't enough, Blade was in town, the most famous man in the entire Federation, the giant reputed to have slain hundreds of foes, the Warrior renowned for his heroic exploits.

Farmers, ranchers, and other residents flocked in from miles around.

At eight o'clock that night Blade and Kilrane entered The Rushmore, one of the premier gambling establishments in all of the Dakota Territory. Named after the famous monument located south of the town, The Rushmore sported plush red carpet and genuine crystal chandeliers. Gaming tables of every type filled the ground floor, while private card games were conducted in the rooms upstairs. And card games weren't the only activities taking place in those rooms. Attractive women in skimpy dresses mingled among the players and spectators, and many a man was escorted upstairs by a young lovely.

Kilrane led Blade through the crowd and up to the mahogany bar. The press of customers parted readily to permit their passage, and a number of patrons openly gawked at the giant. "How does it feel to be so famous?" Kilrane inquired, and motioned to the bartender.

"It can be a pain at times."

A stocky man attired in checkered trousers, a white shirt, and red suspenders hurried down the bar. "Good evening, gents. What will be your pleasure?"

"Whiskey," Kilrane said.

The bartender looked at the Warrior. "And you, sir?"

"Milk."

Utter astonishment lined the bartender's countenance. "Milk, sir?"

Blade nodded.

"Uhhh, begging your pardon, sir, but this establishment doesn't serve milk."

"How about juice then?"

The bartender looked as if he wanted to crawl into the woodwork. "All we serve are distilled spirits."

Blade frowned and placed his hands on the counter. "Can I get a glass of water?"

"Yes, sir," the man responded enthusiastically, relieved at being off the hook. "One large water on the rocks coming right up."

"I'd prefer some ice if you have any."

The bartender did an exaggerated double take, and seemed about to burst into laughter until his gaze roved over the giant's bulging physique. "Water with ice, sir." He moved off to fill their order.

"You never drink liquor, do you?" Kilrane inquired.

"Never. None of the Warriors do. We'll have some wine

now and then, but that's about it."

"What do you have against liquor?"

"We're taught to avoid it from childhood. Our parents and our teachers are fond of pointing out that liquor ruined countless lives in the prewar society. So did drugs. We want nothing to do with either."

Kilrane surveyed the gambling tables. "How do you feel about dens of iniquity?"

Blade laughed and turned his back to the bar. "You've visited the Home. You know about the exalted ideals we strive to attain."

"Yeah," Kilrane said, a tinge of melancholy in his tone. "If you ask me, your Family sets its sights too high."

"Why?"

"Look at yourselves. You try to live in peace and harmony. You all try to be guided by the Spirit in everything you do. And you believe in ideals of brotherly love and striving for perfection."

"What's wrong with that?"

"You're trying to forge a piece of heaven on earth, and it just can't be done. You know better than most what this world is really like. It's dog-eat-dog and only the strongest survive. You can't be spiritual and last very long nowadays."

"Our Family has lasted for a hundred and six years, and if I have anything to say about it the Family will last for a hundred more. Yes, we know what the world is like. We know all about the perverse violence so rampant everywhere, and we recognize there are those who would crush us underfoot without mercy," Blade said. "Why do you think our Founder created the Warrior class? Specifically to deal with the degenerates and the psychopaths who would harm the Family. We believe in higher ideals, true, but we also believe in taking whatever steps are necessary to preserve those ideals."

Kilrane had listened attentively. He saw the bartender deposit their drinks and raised the whiskey glass to his lips. "Let's drink to higher ideals."

Blade picked up the water. "Fair enough."

They clinked glasses and drank.

Kilrane glanced toward the entrance and nodded. "Here comes one of yours."

The Warrior looked up and spotted Doc Madsen entering the establishment. After Madsen came Sparrow Hawk. The others were probably making the rounds. They had been thrilled at the prospect of having the night off to do as they pleased so long as they stayed out of trouble. "Any sign of those four men you told me about?"

"Not yet."

Blade sipped the water, watching Doc and Sparrow walk to a blackjack table, and reflected on the story Kilrane had confided in him earlier. A tale that explained a lot.

No one knew Doc Madsen intimately. He was the sort of man who kept to himself and who had erected an impenetrable reserve around his innermost thoughts. But certain facts were widely known. He had been born on a farm near Lake Oahe, and until the age of 14 or 15 he had worked diligently with his father in the fields. The family had been on exceptionally friendly terms with the Cheyenne Indians who dwelt in the region west of the lake where before the war they had been confined to a reservation.

Rumor had it that the youthful Madsen had fallen in love with the daughter of a prominent rancher who lived not far from Seneca. The girl's father, however, objected, and his objections grew stronger the longer the budding romance continued. Instead of simply flatly refusing his daughter permission to see Madsen, the rancher applied pressure on the boy's father. The elder Madsen refused to interfere in his son's affairs.

According to Kilrane, who had learned most of the information from a close friend of the rancher's, the ill will between the rancher, Brett Quist, and Frank Madsen intensified. Frank told Quist to leave his son alone and stay off his property. Quist retaliated by sending some of his men to harass the Madsens. Fences were torn down in the night, livestock killed, crops trampled. Frank Madsen took all he could take. Then one day he confronted Quist on the main street in Seneca. Witnesses to what happened next gave conflicting reports. Most claimed that eight of Quist's hands heard the argument and came to the aid of their employer. They beat Frank Madsen and goaded him into going for his gun. One of the hired hands, a brutal man named Harvey Kiernan, a man with a minor reputation as a gun-hand, outdrew Madsen and shot him dead. An investigation was held, but the investigators were clearly partial to Quist and their subsequent report concluded the shooting had been a case of justifiable self-defense.

Everyone in the community expected more trouble, expected the younger Madsen to avenge his father's death. But Don Madsen stayed on the farm and worked the fields for almost a year, and then his mother died. Some said she succumbed because of grief over her husband, that she allowed herself to merely waste away. In any event, Don Madsen put down the plow and picked up a gun. For three months he practiced from dawn to dusk, day in and day out. He went into town and purchased a new wardrobe, trading in his flannel shirt and jeans for a black frock coat, black pants, and a black wide-brimmed hat. He also bought a new revolver, a pearl-handled Smith and Wesson.

Days later one of Madsen's neighbors noticed smoke billowing above the farm. The fire brigade was called out, but when the volunteers arrived at the scene they found the house, barn, and outbuildings all blazing to the ground, and Don Madsen standing idly nearby observing the conflagration. He warned them to let the place burn down, then mounted his horse and rode into Seneca.

In a few days Brett Quist and four of his riders came into town. They had no sooner dismounted than Don Madsen walked out to the middle of the street and started calling Quist every dirty name in the book, purposely insulting the rancher, prodding Quist and his men. Ultimately one of the riders snapped and went for his gun.

They never stood a chance.

Displaying the speed and uncanny accuracy for which he would become famous, Don Madsen killed all five men, each with a single shot to the head. He coolly reloaded, remarked sarcastically that someone should fetch a doc, and rode off. From that day forth he became known as Doc Madsen.

In the months that followed, Doc confronted other Quist hands, always in public, and he always made sure they went for their guns first. Eight more were killed. The rest fled for parts unknown, and one of them was Harvey Kiernan, who had concocted excuse upon excuse to explain his reluctance to venture off the Quist spread. Quist's widow and daughter were left to run the sprawling ranch alone. The daughter, Virginia, sent word through a friend that she would like to meet with Doc.

Inexplicably, Madsen left the area, heading south to Pierre, where he took up gambling. His reputation preceded him, and before long gunmen who wanted to enhance their reputations were calling him out. Nineteen men died in two years. As his fame grew, there were fewer and fewer challenges. He drifted from town to town, playing cards, a rootless loner whom no man dared mess with. Everywhere he went he asked about Harvey Kiernan.

One day, in Sioux Falls, he barely survived being shot in the back by three toughs who crept through the rear door of a saloon and aimed their rifles at his back while he sat at a table engrossed in poker. Another man saved his life, a man who cut loose with a pair of .44 Magnum Hombres and downed the bushwhacking trio before they could squeeze off a shot, a man named Boone.

The pair developed an unusual friendship. Boone was well-liked by everyone and mingled freely; Doc was shunned by everyone and inspired fear wherever he went. Through Boone, Doc met Kilrane, and it was only natural for the Cavalry leader to casually mention some months back that he would need a replacement for Boone on the Force when Boone's enlistment was up.

Doc Madsen had astounded Kilrane by asking for the job.

Why? Blade wondered as he finished his water and set the glass on the counter. He adjusted the ammo belts slanted across his broad chest and rested his right hand on the strap to the M60 slung over his right shoulder. Why would a man like Madsen want to join an elite combat unit? The man had been a loner all of his adult life, yet now he wanted to be part of a team. It just didn't add up.

"If the information I received is correct, if Harvey Kiernan and three of his cronies are in Rapid City, they just might try to gun Doc down," Kilrane commented, and swirled the whiskey in his glass.

"Even after all these years? You'd think Kiernan would have the common sense to leave well enough alone."

"From what I can gather, Kiernan's not the brightest guy around. He must have been in town and read the story in the paper about the letter I sent to you and the fact the Force was expected to arrive here soon."

"What if I'd refused the mission? You'd be left holding the bag."

Kilrane smiled. "I knew you wouldn't let me down."

"How could you be so certain?"

"A man with your high ideals would never desert a friend in need."

Blade chuckled. "I had no idea you were a student of psychology."

"Psychology, hell. I know my friends."

Blade saw Doc seated at the blackjack table. "I think I'll watch a card game," he stated, and walked toward the gunfighter.

"I've got nothing better to do," Kilrane said, joining the Warrior.

They strolled over to the table and stood on Doc's right, near Sparrow. The Flathead glanced up and grinned.

"Doc is teaching me how to play cards."

"Where are the others?" Blade inquired.

"Jag wanted to stay in his hotel room. He said he was tired of everyone gawking at him."

Blade frowned.

"Captain Havoc, Raphaela, and Lobo are at a place three doors down called The Beef and Brew. They're eating a steak dinner."

"I'm surprised Lobo didn't come with you," Blade mentioned, observing the dealer slide two cards in front of Doc.

"He wanted to tag along but Havoc lost the bet."

"What bet?"

"Doc and Mike flipped a coin to see who would have the honor of Lobo's company for the night. Doc won the toss."

"Wasn't Lobo upset?"

"Quite. He was looking forward to, in his words, teaching these cowboys chumps how to party hearty," Sparrow replied. His forehead creased. "Sometimes his words are most perplexing."

"Don't bother trying to understand him," Blade advised.

"No?"

"No. If Lobo ever starts making sense to you, let me know and I'll give you an extended vacation."

Sparrow Hawk threw back his head and laughed. "I'll keep it in mind."

The Warrior stepped closer to Doc Madsen and leaned down. "I need to talk to you."

"Hit me," the Cavalryman said to the dealer, then looked at the giant. "Right this minute? I'm in the middle of a card game."

"It's important," Blade stated.

"I thought we have the night off to do as we want."

"It's really important," Blade stressed.

"Is it about Harvey Kiernan?"

Blade's eyebrows arched. "You already know?"

Madsen nodded and picked up the new card he'd been dealt. "The desk clerk at our hotel told me. And I only had to pay him ten dollars in California silver coins.''

"What do you plan to do?"

"Sit here and play cards all night."

"But you're a sitting duck here."

"Sparrow is watching my back for me," Doc said. "I'll be fine." He gazed at the entranceway.

"I don't like it," Blade said. "I can't afford to lose another member of the unit. Give me your word you won't go looking for trouble."

"I don't have to."

"Why not?"

Doc motioned toward the glass doors at the front. "Because trouble has come looking for me."

The Warrior straightened, his hands dropping to his Bowies at the sight of four gunmen who had spread out just inside the entrance, their hands hovering near their revolvers. All four wore typical Western attire.

One of them, the scruffiest of the quartet, a big man whose greasy black hair was plastered to his skull, suddenly barked out, "Madsen! Your killing days are over!"

CHAPTER FIVE

Every patron in The Rushmore swung toward the front doors and an abrupt hush gripped the room. Those customers who were standing between the entrance and the blackjack table suddenly evinced a desire to be somewhere else, and in seconds a clear stretch of floor materialized, affording the foursome an unobstructed view of the table, Doc Madsen, and the three men beside him.

The big man with the greasy hair advanced slowly, his dark eyes darting from the calm gunfighter in black to the giant, the Indian, and Kilrane. He halted 20 feet from them and jabbed his right forefinger at the leader of the Cavalry. "This doesn't concern you, Kilrane! We have no beef with you."

"You must be Harvey Kiernan," Kilrane said flatly. "I don't believe we've ever met."

"But I know who you are," Kiernan stated, and looked at the giant. "And I know about you too, mister. We don't want any grief from you either. Our business is with Madsen."

"Doc is a member of my team," Blade said icily. "If you threaten him, you threaten me."

Kiernan's eyes narrowed. He glared at his nemesis and sneered. "Is that right, Madsen? Do you let others do your fighting for you, killer?"

Doc, who hadn't moved a muscle since the quartet entered, slowly laid down his cards. "No one will interfere."

"Then what are you waiting for? Why are you just sitting there like a bump on a log?" Kiernan snapped. "Do you know how long I've waited for this day?"

"You could have found me any time you wanted," Doc said, pushing his chair back and standing. "It took you all these years to get up your nerve."

Kiernan bristled and took a step forward. "And you could have found me whenever you wanted. Why didn't you? Why did you keep me waiting in suspense? For nine years I've been looking over my shoulders, never knowing when you'd show up. For nine years I've been jumping at every shadow and every sound."

"Good," Doc said, and smiled.

"Good?" Kiernan repeated quizzically, then hissed. "You son of a bitch! You planned it that way! You wanted me to suffer!"

Doc stepped lightly to the left, away from the table and his friends. "You're smarter than I gave you credit for, Harvey." His eyes flicked over the other three gunmen. "Who are your buddies?"

"I was hoping you'd ask," Kiernan spat. He pointed at a lean man on the far right. "That's Ike Millnick. Maybe you've heard of him?"

"They say he's right handy with an iron."

"Damn straight he is," Kiernan declared, and grinned. He indicated the nearest man on his left, a hefty gunman packing a pair of revolvers around his stout waist. "That's Ted Hulcy."

The hefty gunman nodded.

"And the last gent is Forrest Lockaby. Bet you've heard of him too."

"All those names ring a bell."

Kiernan laughed, a bitter, brittle, scornful derision, an insult in itself. "Ain't feeling so damn high and mighty now, are you?"

"I'm a bit puzzled," Doc said.

"About what?" Kiernan asked suspiciously.

"About why three hombres like Millnick, Hulcy, and Lockaby have hooked up with you?"

"Why do you think?" Kiernan rejoined caustically.

Doc calmly scrutinized the three gunmen. "They can't be in this for the money because you couldn't afford to hire a penniless tramp. So what brings three top gun-hands together to work with scum like you?"

Kiernan made a hissing noise.

"As far as I can figure it, the only reason that makes any sense is they came all this way to add to their rep," Doc stated, contempt lacing his tone. "Is that right, Hulcy?" he said to the hefty gunman.

The man named Hulcy shrugged. "You know how it is, Madsen. When you're at the top, you've got to expect that there will be someone who wants to take your place."

"And the three of you reckon you can do the job?"

"There's three of us and only one of you," Hulcy said, emphasizing the obvious.

"Hey, don't forget about me," Kiernan interjected.

Doc Madsen smiled and carefully lifted the right flap of his frock coat aside, exposing the pearl handles on his nickel-plated Distinguished Combat Magnum. Then he did a strange thing under the circumstances. He smiled contentedly and surveyed the quartet. "You're all overlooking one little point."

Kiernan licked his lips, his fingers fidgeting nervously. "What's that?"

"There may be four of you, but there's five bullets in my gun."

All conversation ceased.

Blade stared at Doc, debating whether to interfere. He could unsling the M60 and compel Kiernan and the gunmen to leave, but that would only delay the inevitable. He could side with Doc, but he knew Madsen wanted to handle this alone. Can I blame him? Blade asked himself. This confrontation was the culmination of a decade of hatred on Kiernan's part and the attainment of vengeance for Doc, if he survived. He tried to put himself in Madsen's shoes. How would he have felt if his father had been gunned down?

Who was he kidding?

He knew *exactly* how Doc felt. His own dad had been ripped apart by a deadly mutate, and ever since then he'd depised all such mutations. And he still savored the sensation of elation he'd felt when he terminated the mutate responsible for his dad's death. No, he certainly couldn't fault Doc for wanting revenge. And he decided he wasn't about to interfere.

At that precise moment someone else did.

Boots pounded just outside the glass doors, and the next moment in rushed Lobo, moving at full speed. He came through the doors so quickly no one had time to react, and before he could stop himself he collided with Harvey Kiernan, slamming into the Cavalryman from behind and sending the scruffy gunman sprawling onto the floor. "Oops! Sorry, dude!" Lobo exclaimed. "Didn't see you there."

Kiernan, initially startled, recovered and pushed to his knees, his face contorted in fury. "You dumbass nigger!" he roared, and went for his gun.

The irate Cavalryman never cleared leather.

Lobo's right hand streaked to his coat pocket and out again, and everyone within ten feet heard the distinctive click as the blade on his favorite weapon popped out, the tip a hairsbreadth from Kiernan's right eye. Years ago Lobo had found an automatic, a knife with a spring-loaded blade that slid out a slot at the top at the slightest press of the release switch. On its black handle were imprinted the words NATO MILITARY. He could wield the weapon with dazzling expertise.

Kiernan's eyes widened and he flinched as the gleaming

four-inch blade almost skewered his right eyeball. His right hand froze in the act of gripping his revolver.

"*What* did you call me, honky bastard!" Lobo snapped.

Harvey Kiernan's mouth opened, but he couldn't seem to find his voice.

"I asked you a question," Lobo stated harshly, leaning down, his features steel hard.

"I—I didn't mean nothing," Kiernan blurted out. "Honest!"

"*Nobody* calls me that and lives to talk about it," Lobo said.

"Look, it slipped out, all right?" Kiernan stated. "You caught me off guard."

"You don't fool me, sucker," Lobo said. "I think I'll do the world a favor and cut your throat."

"No!" someone yelled.

The sharply shouted word rent the air like a shot. Lobo glanced up in surprise and saw Doc Madsen walking toward them. "What's with you?"

"Don't kill him."

"Give me one good reason why I shouldn't?" Lobo replied testily.

"He's mine."

"Wait your turn."

Doc halted. His next words were barely audible. "He killed my father."

Lobo looked at the man kneeling at his feet, then at the gunfighter. "I didn't know. No problem, dude. You want this scumbag, he's yours." He slowly straightened and wagged the NATO in front of Kiernan's eyes. "Now take your hand off your hardware before I change my mind."

"Don't do nothing hasty," Kiernan said, and held both arms out from his sides.

The hefty gunman unexpectedly stepped forward and gazed at Kiernan in evident disdain. "You can count me out of this, Harvey."

"What? Why?"

"I agreed to help gun Madsen because you claimed you had a legitimate grudge," Hulcy said. "Sure, I wanted to add to my rep. But I've never gunned down anyone who didn't deserve it, and as near as I can tell Madsen doesn't deserve it." He paused. "Plus there's another reason."

"What?" Kiernan asked.

"You're yellow."

Harvey Kiernan rose, his countenance livid. "Nobody calls me a coward!"

"What do you aim to do about it?" Hulcy responded with a sneer, his hands held close to his revolvers.

Kiernan wanted to draw. Everyone in the room could tell he was on the verge. But he suddenly deflated like a punctured balloon and mustered a wan grin. "I'm not about to slap leather on a pard."

"I was never your friend," Hulcy stated, and swung toward the man in black. "My mistake, Madsen. No hard feelings?"

"No," Doc said.

Hulcy reached up and touched the brim of his brown hat. "Buy you a drink sometime." He began to leave, but stopped and glanced at Millnick and Lockaby. "If you guys are smart, you'll bow out of this scrape. You're in the wrong, and you can't win when you're on the wrong end."

"That's superstitious bunk," Millnick said.

"Have it your way," Hulcy remarked, and departed.

Blade came around the blackjack table. "Lobo, what are you doing here?"

The Clansman blinked. "What a dork! I almost forgot!" He stepped forward, looking from the Warrior to Kilrane. "Another person has up and vanished."

"How do you know?" Blade asked.

"There's some dude down at The Beef and Brew. He's all bent out of shape. Seems something snatched his squeeze. He heard Kilrane was in town and came here lookin' for him. Found us first. Havoc is tryin' to calm the guy down. I was sent to bring you."

Kilrane and Sparrow Hawk joined the Warrior and the Clansman.

"When did the abduction take place?" the Cavalry leader inquired.

"Not long ago," Lobo said. "The guy lives about five miles south of Rapid City. He about rode his horse into the ground gettin' here."

"Let's go," Blade directed, and gestured at the glass doors. "Every minute counts." He twisted to stare at Doc, who hadn't budged. "You too."

"I'm not done here."

"For now you are."

Doc's eyes were locked on Harvey Kiernan. "I have unfinished business."

"Don't you think I know that? But your business will have to wait until we get back."

Doc looked at the giant. "Can't you handle this without me?"

"No. You're part of the Force, like it or not. And we're a team, remember? You can tend to your personal business on your own time. As of this second you're on duty, so let's go," Blade commanded.

"Yeah, run out while you've got the chance," Kiernan declared, and laughed.

Blade almost shot the man himself. He hastened outside and found Kilrane, Lobo, and Sparrow waiting for him.

"Where's Doc?" the Flathead queried.

"He's coming," Blade said, and gazed at the glass doors, waiting expectantly, not knowing if he would see Madsen emerge or hear the blasting of gunfire. He began to count to ten, intending to go back in when he finished, and he was on nine when the doors swung out and the gunfighter stepped from The Rushmore.

From inside arose mocking laughter.

Doc swung the doors shut behind him and frowned. He looked at the Warrior. "Don't ever ask me to do something like that again."

"Duty comes first."

Kilrane took off at a run to the east. "This way."

Pedestrians scattered out of the path of the five men, some venting exclamations, a few oaths. Most merely gaped at the titan beside Kilrane.

Blade unslung the big M60 as he ran, his mind racing with the implications of this new information. If the creatures had struck just a while ago, the Force might be able to arrive at the scene before the clues, if there were any, were obliterated. He eagerly stayed abreast of Kilrane, passing two buildings in a row, and slowed when they reached the wooden door affording entry to The Beef and Brew.

The Cavalry leader went in first.

Quickly Blade followed, and immediately he spotted Captain Havoc and Raphaela. They were seated at a round table with an elderly man whose gray hair was disheveled and whose expression showed a profound inner turmoil.

"What's happened?" Kilrane demanded, hurrying to the table. He stared at the gray-haired man for a moment, his eyes roving over the man's flannel shirt and overalls. "I know you from somewhere."

"Valesh, sir. Alan Valesh. We met once at a rodeo in Sioux Falls. You were putting on a shooting exhibition and I brought my nephew up to you so he could get an autograph."

"You live near here?"

"Yes, sir. We were in Sioux City that time visiting my son. But Martha and me live five miles south of Rapid City," Valesh said, and his lower lip quivered. "Poor Martha!"

Kilrane moved to the man's side and placed his right hand on Valesh's shoulder. "There, there. Tell me about it."

"Well, like I told these nice young folks, about an hour ago I was putting the stock up for the night in the barn," Valesh explained. "I have a farm, you see. Anyway, we were running late and it was getting quite dark, so Martha went into the house for a lantern." He stopped and swallowed, his throat bobbing.

"Then what happened?" Kilrane prodded gently.

"I heard this god-awful scream and ran out of the barn. And there was Martha forty feet up in the air! I couldn't believe it. Something had a hold of her. She pleaded for help. I could hear this funny noise, like the flapping of an owl or something, and I ran to the house for my rifle." Valesh inhaled loudly and tears moistened his agonized eyes.

"Take your time," Kilrane suggested.

"I'm okay, sir." Valesh sniffled, and continued. "I got my gun and ran out again, but she was gone. Martha was gone!" He bowed his head. "I called out for her again and again, even walked out into the field shouting her name. The full moon lit up the sky fairly decent, but I still couldn't see her anywhere. After a spell I remembered about you being here tonight and I saddled my horse and cut out. Here I am," he concluded wearily.

"Are you up to taking us to your spread?"

"You bet. I want to save Martha."

Kilrane nodded and smiled. "We'll do our best, Alan." He turned to the Warrior. "What do you say?"

"Need you ask? I'll round up Jag and collect our gear. We'll be ready to go in ten minutes."

"Make it twenty. I gave half my team the night off, and it'll take me at least ten minutes just to get the word passed out along the street for them to regroup."

"Twenty minutes, then."

Kilrane dashed out the door.

"You can come with us," Blade told the farmer.

"We'll take care of you," Raphaela added.

"You folks sure are nice," Valesh said, rising. "I pray you can find my Martha before it's too late."

"Did you see the thing that grabbed her?" Blade inquired.

"All I saw was a big dark thing, kind of like a raven."

"Do you have any idea which direction it went?"

"Nope. Sorry."

"You have nothing to apologize for. You did all any man could have done."

"I didn't save poor Martha."

"That's our department," Blade said, and made for the door. "Let's get our tails in gear."

"Here we go again," Lobo said, and groaned.

"What's the matter with you?" Captain Havoc queried.

"I don't know if I can take any more horse-ridin'. I'm not used to bouncing around on top of a smelly animal that takes a dump every fifty feet."

"You did okay when we rode into town," Havoc pointed out.

"Are you kiddin'? I think I damaged the family jewels."

"The what?" Raphaela interjected.

"Never mind," Havoc advised her. "Believe me, you *don't* want to know."

"Well, at least I should look at the bright side," Lobo mentioned as he headed for the entrance.

"What's that?" Havoc asked.

"We're finally going to kick some butt."

CHAPTER SIX

Led by Alan Valesh, the Force and Kilrane's Cavalry detachment rode out of Rapid City 30 minutes later. They headed to the south, paralleling U.S. Highway 16, and thanks to the full moon they were able to maintain a brisk pace. The night was warm, the temperature in the low fifties, and a sluggish breeze wafted from the northwest. Stars sparkled overhead.

Blade rode a big black gelding, a tractable animal that responded superbly to the reins and the pressure of his legs. The M60 hung over his left shoulder and swung from side to side with the motion of the horse. The Weatherby rested in a scabbard on the gelding's right side. He gazed at Kilrane and Valesh, riding ten feet in front.

The countryside consisted of low, rolling hills generally covered with trees, interspersed with plains of high grass.

"What happened back there with Doc, sir?"

Blade glanced to his left at the question from his new second-in-command, then looked over his shoulder to see Madsen, Raphaela, Lobo, and Sparrow 15 feet away. Behind them were the 100 Cavalry riders. The drumming of so many hoofs resembled the beating of countless drums. "He ran into an old enemy.''

"So Lobo was telling us," Captain Havoc said. "Doc hasn't spoken a word since we were at The Beef and Brew."

"He has a lot on his mind."

"Will he need our help?"

"Yes and no."

"I don't follow you, sir."

"Yes, he could use our help, but no, he won't ask for it. He wants to handle the problem alone and we'll respect his wishes," Blade said. "And you can stop calling me sir."

"Old habits are hard to break, si—" Havoc said, and caught himself.

"I know you've devoted your life to the military and you're accustomed to doing things the military way," Blade stated. "But I'd much prefer to be called by my name."

"It's hard for me to call a superior officer by his name."

"How about if I make the request a direct order?"

Havoc grinned. "That might do the trick. Blade." He stared straight ahead, thinking of how much he had grown to like the Warrior in the past few months, and he felt a twinge of guilt at the deception he was practicing. How could he betray a man he respected so highly? The giant had turned out to be a decent, conscientious leader devoted to the people under him.

The captain sighed. Why couldn't Blade be a heartless bastard? It would make the job of ruining him that much easier. He thought of his younger brother, Jimmy, and about how Blade had to shoulder the blame for Jimmy's death. If the Warrior hadn't made an unauthorized stop in Canada when the Force was en route from Alaska to California, Sergeant James Havoc would still be alive.

How he missed Jimmy! Havoc averted his face from the giant and frowned. He'd been especially close to his adventuresome sibling. Out of the five Havoc children, they'd been the closest. Their childhood had been spent playing and hiking and hunting together. They'd encouraged one another to enter the service, and been mutually supportive of their career decisions. Perhaps the fact they were only eleven months apart in age accounted for their enduring brotherly affection.

And that affection had made Jimmy's loss all the harder to bear. Havoc scowled and stared at the heavens. The idea of his brother being slain by murderous pirate riffraff had been difficult enough to accept without the added realization that Jimmy wouldn't have died if Blade had adhered to orders and flown directly to California.

Was it any wonder he had initially despised the Warrior? Could he be blamed for siding with General Gallagher in the general's clever, clandestine scheme to discredit Blade and cause the Force to disband? Would the heavy finger of censure point at him later when the job was done? After all, the general himself believed California had no business being part of the Federation and subsidizing the Freedom Force.

The damn general!

The unmilitary reflection startled Havoc. He'd never entertained a remotely rebellious notion in his entire service career, and doing so now jolted his finely honed perception of loyalty and unquestioning obedience. But he had to admit his feelings to himself, and he felt intense resentment at the general for not being permitted to drop his vendetta.

Who would have figured he'd up and change his mind? After working with Blade for over two months, after getting to know the Warrior and discovering that no one cared for the team members more than Blade, Havoc had changed his mind about destroying the Force from within. General Gallagher, however, wasn't about to let him off the hook. Gallagher insisted on carrying through with their plan, which explained the good general's elation at Havoc's new position as second-in-command. Gallagher believed the job would be easier as a consequence, and just prior to the departure of the Force for the Dakota Territory, while the others were stowing the gear, the general had taken Havoc aside and stressed the need to destroy the Force at all costs.

Captain Havoc suddenly became aware the giant was

speaking.

"—happy about your promotion."

Havoc glanced at the Warrior. "I'm sorry. What was that?"

"I couldn't help but notice General Gallagher was extremely happy about your promotion," Blade said, repeating his observation.

"Yes, he was," Havoc responded flatly, his forehead creasing. Why had the Warrior made such a comment? Did Blade suspect?

"At least I'll have some help keeping Lobo in line," Blade quipped.

"I'll do what I can, but I'm not a miracle worker," Havoc responded in kind.

Blade smiled, then tensed when he saw Kilrane rein up and signal for the column to halt. He goaded the gelding forward and stopped on the right side of the Cavalry leader's Palamino. "What is it?"

"Your hybrid," Kilrane said, and pointed to the south.

Blade spotted Jaguarundi a moment later, sprinting toward them at a deceptively easy long-legged pace. He had sent the mutation on ahead for three reasons. First, horses reacted skittishly to Jag's mere presence, and for Jag to be able to mount and ride one was next to impossible. Second, Jag could cover ground just as fast as any horse; years ago the notorious Doktor had clocked Jaguarundi's top speed at 52 miles an hour. Third, Jag had asked to scout the terrain and Blade had seen no reason to refuse. He had insisted that Jag take an M-16.

"We shouldn't have very far to go," Kilrane commented as they waited for the mutation to reach them.

"Less than a mile," Valesh confirmed.

"Did you alert your neighbors before you rode into Rapid City?" Blade thought to inquire.

"Just my neighbor to the east," Valesh answered. "Gary Norman. I swung by his place on the way into town."

"Had he seen anything unusual?"

"Nope. He offered to ride to my spread and stay there until I got back."

"Nice neighbor."

Valesh nodded. "Out here folks know how to pull together. It's not like the towns and cities where every mother's son is out to stab you in the back."

Blade glanced at the hybrid, who was now only 30 feet distant. He adjusted the M60 and leaned forward. "Anything?"

"I found the farm—a two-story farmhouse and a big red barn," Jag replied as he slowed. "There wasn't any sign of anyone."

"Nothing at all?"

"Except for a white horse hitched to a post in front of the house," Jag said, amending his statement.

"That would be Gary Norman's horse," Valesh disclosed. "He must be there somewhere."

"Maybe he was in the house or the barn," Blade speculated, his gaze on Jag. "Did you go in?"

"Nope. Just looked around a little and came on back."

"Okay. Lead the way. Don't get more than thirty feet in front of us, and holler if you see or hear anything unusual."

"You've got it," Jag said, and pivoted. He jogged into the darkness, his supple form outlined in a pale glow by the full moon.

"Strange critter," Valesh remarked. "I've never seen his like before."

"And you won't again," Blade mentioned. "He's unique, a one-of-a-kind hybrid."

Valesh stared skyward. "Kilrane told me a mutation might have taken my Martha." He paused. "I'm not too fond of mutants at the moment."

"Head out," Kilrane directed, and motioned with his right arm.

Blade rode southward, wondering why Kilrane bothered with the hand motion when most of the Cavalrymen wouldn't be able to see the gesture in the gloom. Force of habit, he figured, and concentrated on the plain ahead.

A minute elapsed. Then two.

Buildings materialized up ahead, a house and a barn, both illuminated from within by lanterns that cast their radiance through the windows of the home and the open barn doors

"That's odd," Valesh said.

"What is?" Kilrane asked.

"I didn't light all those lanterns. Gary must have done it."

The column started across a field bordering the structures Crickets chirped on all sides.

"From what I can see, you have a nice spread," Kilrane stated tactfully.

"Thanks," Valesh replied absently, his gaze riveted to the farmhouse and the barn. "But it won't mean a thing to me without Martha at my side."

Blade saw Jag standing between both buildings, awaiting them. He looked over his left shoulder at the members of his team. "Stay frosty, people."

"Do you think the creature might still be around?" Raphaela inquired.

"I doubt it, but you never know."

"Can we take a break from all this ridin'?" Lobo wanted to know. "I've about bounced my buns down to nothing."

"I've observed your riding technique," Sparrow said. "My sympathy lies with your horse."

"Was that a cut?" Lobo snapped.

"No."

"Good."

"I'd never insult a horse."

Blade noticed that Jag was staring at the stars, and he looked up and discovered a number of clouds floating tranquilly in the air over the buildings. There was nothing out of the ordinary. Fifteen seconds later Blade reined up six feet from the hybrid and slid to the ground, relieved to be on the ground again. He hadn't ridden in a while and his inner thigh muscles were aching from the strain.

"I heard something," Jag bluntly announced.

"What?" Blade asked.

"Something in the sky. A swishing noise, sort of."

Kilrane stayed in the saddle and scanned the firmament. "How high up?"

"Hard to determine."

The Cavalry leader twisted and barked out instructions. "Armitage, take half the men and scour the fields for a mile in every direction. Treon, take the other half and form a perimeter around these buildings. Keep your eyes on the sky."

"Yes, sir."

"On our way."

Displaying practiced precision, the two lieutenants led their contingents off. The horses raised clouds of dust as they filed to their appointed duties.

"Excuse me for asking, sir," Captain Havoc stated, speaking to Kilrane. "But is it wise to divide your force? We don't know the enemy's strength."

"There has never been more than one of the creatures reported at any given time," Kilrane responded. "Even if there are several, we have enough firepower to take them down. Plus, for once they won't have the element of surprise working in their favor."

Blade unslung the M60. "Captain Havoc, I want you and the others to stand guard right here while Kilrane and I inspect the house and the barn."

"Yes sir."

"I'll go with you," Valesh offered.

The Warrior walked toward the farmhouse, passing the tethered white horse.

"Yep. This is definitely Gary Norman's animal," Valesh confirmed.

"Where could he be?" Kilrane queried, dismounting with a Winchester in his right hand.

"Probably in the house," Valesh suggested.

Blade took the lead and moved along a narrow cement walk to a wooden porch. Both the screen door and the inner door were ajar, and he paused, feeling vaguely uneasy. There were heavy drapes over both front windows, backlit by the lanterns within but concealing the interior from view.

"I know I didn't leave the doors open," Valesh observed. "That Gary can be a forgetful cuss." He made for the door.

"Let me," Kilrane proposed quickly, and slid past the farmer to reach the doors first.

Valesh halted abruptly. "You don't reckon there's something in my house?"

"You never know," Kilrane said, and pried the screen door wide with his left boot. He glanced at the Warrior. "You coming?"

"I thought I'd stay out here and enjoy the fresh air."

"You're getting as bad as Lobo."

"There's no need to be insulting," Blade cracked, and stepped to the right of the door. "Ready when you are."

Kilrane nodded, kicked the inner door open, and ducked into the house.

His nerves on edge, Blade did likewise. He bore to the left once he was in, scarcely paying attention to the immaculate floors and walls or the quaint furniture, searching for signs of life.

The two friends went down a hall, past stairs, a moderately spacious living room, a sewing room, and a closet, and ultimately found themselves in a tidy kitchen where the delectable scents of delicious meals past lingered in the air.

"Nothing," Kilrane said.

They retraced their route to the stairs located to the left of the entrance.

"Me first this time," Blade stated, and bounded up the steps three at a time, frowning at the loud creaking noises accompanying his ascent. At the top he crouched and scanned another corridor, narrower than the hall below, with two doors on either side. "I'll take the right," he said.

"Just scream if you need me," Kilrane quipped.

Blade sidled to the nearest door, which hung partly open, and shoved with the M60. Within was a bedroom, decently furnished and as neat as the proverbial pin. But no monsters. So far.

Beginning to relax, and attributing his jittery condition to a case of nerves, Blade strode to the second door and pushed. He discovered yet another bedroom, as spotless and homey as the rest of the house, the king-sized bed covered with a thick blue quilt. "All clear here," he announced.

"Nothing on this side," Kilrane stated, and sighed. "Those things must be long gone."

As if to contradict the Cavalry leader's statement, gunfire erupted outside, the brittle chatter of an automatic weapon.

Blade instantly took off, racing down the hall and descending the stairs four at a bound. He slammed the screen door aside and dashed across the porch to the yard, the M60 pressed tight against his right side, ready for the worst.

All of the Force members were gazing skyward, all with their M-16's pointed upward.

Blade ran toward them. He saw Lobo berating Raphaela.

"—don't ever do that again, Red! Damn! You scared me out of ten years of growth!"

"Clam up, Lobo," Captain Havoc barked.

The Warrior reached the end of the walk. "What was all that firing about?"

"It was this crazy Molewoman!" Lobo replied before anyone else could. "She's jumpy as hell. Damn near took my head off with her first shot."

"I did not," Raphaela retorted defensively.

"What were you firing at?" Blade inquired, striding over to them, his gray eyes probing the heavens.

"I saw something," Raphaela stated.

"What?"

"I don't know. I looked up and there was this big shadowy form diving right at us. I just fired automatically," Raphaela explained. "And I came nowhere near Lobo," she added.

"Says you, woman."

Blade glanced at the captain. "Did you see anything?"

"No, sir," Havoc said with evident reluctance.

"Don't ask me, dude," Lobo interjected. "I was too busy dodgin' bullets."

The Warrior faced the Clansman. "Do you remember what Captain Havoc just told you?"

"Of course. If you ask me, he's lettin' this second-in-command business go to his head."

"When he gives you an order you're to obey his commands just as if I'd given them to you," Blade stated sternly. "If you don't, you'll answer to me."

"Geez. Doesn't anyone in this outfit know how to chill out?"

"Consider yourself on report."

Lobo blinked in surprise. "Say what?"

"And if you open your mouth again, if you so much as burp, I'm shipping you back to the Clan."

"You wouldn't!"

"Try me."

Lobo's mouth widened, then abruptly closed.

"That's better," Blade said, and surveyed the others. "Did anyone else see the thing Raphaela shot at? Doc? Sparrow?"

The gunfighter and the Flathead both shook their heads.

"What about you, Jag?" Blade questioned.

"I heard something," the hybrid answered, his puzzled face upturned.

"What?"

Jag shook his head. "I'm not sure. A whistling."

The Warrior studied the stars and the few clouds drifting overhead. "Whistling?"

A bob of Jag's chin accented his comment. "A strange sort of whistling, almost like the noise the Hurricane makes when it's in a power dive, only this sound was almost inaudible."

Blade looked at Raphaela. "Did you hit it?"

"I don't know. It swooped back up again so fast I almost thought I'd imagined the whole incident."

The Warrior smiled at her. "You did good."

"I did?"

"One of us would be missing right now, snatched from our very midst, if you hadn't fired."

Raphaela beamed proudly. "It's nice to know I'm appreciated."

Blade turned to Havoc. "I believe you tied the cases containing the scope and the mike on Sparrow's horse. Get them."

"You've got it," the officer promptly replied, and gestured at Sparrow. "Give me a hand."

They walked over to the horses.

"I'd like to check my barn for Gary," Valesh mentioned.

"I'll go with you," Kilrane spoke up.

The Warrior glanced at the enormous barn, troubled at Gary Norman's prolonged absence. The man had to have heard Raphaela's shots. So where was he? "Lobo, tag along with them," he instructed.

For once the Clansman didn't argue.

Blade watched the three men move toward the open barn doors. Since Raphaela, Doc, and Jag were all scrutinizing the sky, he didn't bother lifting his own head to the heavens. Consequently, he had no idea they were in immediate danger until the Molewoman uttered a strident cry.

"Look out! Here they come!"

CHAPTER SEVEN

Blade glanced at Raphaela, saw her shocked countenance fixed in the direction of the farmhouse, and spun, bringing the M60 barrel up, his gaze darting high into the air over the building. He anticipated the attack would come from a lofty elevation.

The Warrior was wrong.

Voicing twin high-pitched shrieks, a pair of inky figures swept down toward the Force, coming in low, barely skimming the roof of the farmhouse, their outlines streamlined because their wings were tucked flush with their backs for greater diving speed, their arms extended in a power dive.

Blade glimpsed the uncanny duo when they crested the front porch and sped straight at his team. He snapped off a burst, hurrying his shots in his anxiety for his people, and his first rounds missed the creatures and tore into the farmhouse.

Cleaving the night air like huge birds of prey, the two grotesqueries were upon the humans in the blink of an eye.

It all happened so incredibly fast that Havoc and Sparrow, who were standing next to the horses, and Kilrane and Lobo, who were near the barn, had to hold their fire for fear of hitting their companions.

Raphaela got off a dozen rounds at point-blank range, her shots smacking into the creature on the right. But whether her bullets had no effect, or whether the thing was simply moving too rapidly to be stopped by anything, an instant later she felt awesomely strong hands clamp onto her upper arms and the creature began to surge upward bearing her with it.

"No!" Jag bellowed, and reverted to his feline nature. He dropped the useless M-16 and leaped at the thing holding Raphaela, intending to land on its back and rip his nails into its flesh.

Reacting too swiftly for the eye to follow, the second creature swerved and delivered a stunning blow with both clenched fists on the hybrid's temple, dropping him like a stone.

Forgetting her training and her resolve to persevere no matter what transpired, Raphaela, whose nostrils were tingled by an alien, musty odor, and who saw hair and teeth and feral eyes all in a rush, screamed.

No one could fire without striking her.

With a notable exception.

Not even bothering to employ the M-16 slung over his left arm, Doc Madsen took three strides, his Magnum flashing from its holster, and angling the barrel, planted two shots apiece into the back of the creature holding the Molewoman, aiming high on the monstrosity's shoulder, well above Raphaela's head.

The thing screeched, its mighty wings flapping, and suddenly gained a wobbly momentum, arcing into the night with its victim clasped in an iron embrace. Right on its heels came the second being.

"Raphaela!" Lobo shouted.

Blade was seething. He ran a few yards after the things, distinguishing their flapping forms at least 60 feet overhead, until the futility of the pursuit occurred to him. "Damn!" he fumed, and spun. "Havoc! The scope and mike! On the double, man!"

Hooves thundered from every direction as the Cavalrymen

assigned to guard the perimeter rode in to investigate the din.

Kilrane ran up to the Warrior. "What do you want me to do? Send some of my men after them?"

"Your men couldn't keep up with them in the dark," Blade responded harshly, furious at himself for allowing Raphaela to be taken. He pivoted impatiently and found Havoc and Sparrow running toward him, the captain bearing the scope, the Flathead holding the mike. "Hurry it up!" he snapped.

Doc Madsen was helping Jaguarundi to rise.

Blade looked at the somberly sinister sky, and off to the south he detected motion, perhaps the continued flapping of heavy wings, which meant the fiends were already hundreds of yards distant.

In confirmation came a plaintive appeal from that direction. "Blade! Mike! Someone help me!"

Rarely had Blade felt as intensely frustrated as at that moment. He gripped the M60 until his knuckles hurt.

"Here you go, sir," Captain Havoc declared, halting on the giant's right.

Blade slung the M60 over his brawny left shoulder and grabbed the Nite-Vision device. He pressed the eyepiece to his right eye and stabbed the proper button to activate the system.

Painted a nonreflective black, the military's infrared wonder consisted of two short, squat, circular tubes placed one on top of the other, with a padded support extending from underneath the bottom tube to be used as a brace on the shoulder. The top tube contained the infrared light source; the lower tube housed the viewing lenses, which in this case included a special zoom lens capable of pinpointing the head on a nail at 500 yards with the clarity of atmospheric light at twilight.

"Any sign of her?" Havoc inquired apprehensively.

"Not yet," Blade said, sweeping the Nite-Vision back and forth across the southern sky. Seconds later the device picked up Raphaela and the two creatures at the extreme limit of its range. Their forms were ambiguous shapes and he could discern few details. He noticed that the thing bearing the Molewoman appeared to be having difficulty keeping up with its comrade. Doc's shots must have had an effect, he deduced, and a horrendous thought hit him.

What if the creature dropped her?

"Give me the mike," Blade directed, handing the Nite-Vision scope back to the captain.

"Here you go," Sparrow said, extending the device.

The Penetrator sound detector was also painted black to minimize glare during night use. It was comprised of a hand-held tube about 12 inches in length and four inches in diameter, which housed the sophisticated battery-powered electronic circuitry, and included a miniature super-sensitive microphone attached to the center of the small parabolic dish affixed to the end of the tube. A single knob on top served the dual purpose of on switch and volume control. At the inner end of the tube was a tiny speaker and an input jack to be used with headphones.

Blade didn't bother with the headphones. He snatched the sound detector, twisted the knob, and pointed the parabolic dish in the general direction of the departing creatures. From the speakers issued the unmistakable flapping of huge wings.

"What is the range on that?" Sparrow Hawk inquired.

"About a mile," Blade disclosed, and glanced over his left shoulder. "Jag!"

The hybrid came over, rubbing his sore left temple. "What do you need?"

"I want you to take off after those things," Blade ordered. "Stay as close to them as you can, but don't let them know they're being followed. With this you can stay a half mile or more behind them and have a margin to spare." He handed the detector to the mutation.

"No problem," Jag said. He aimed the dish to the south and detected the beating wings. "Don't worry, I won't lose them. I owe those creeps. And if it' all the same to you I'd like to leave my M-16 here. It would only slow me down.''

"Leave it," Blade said. "We'll be hard on your heels. Mark the trail as best you can. Use stones or tree limbs or whatever.''

Jaguarundi started on his quest, accelerating speedily.

"Remember," Captain Havoc called out, "if you lose them, we lose Raphaela.''

"You think I don't know that?" Jag said in parting, without looking around, and sprinted out of sight within 30 seconds.

"God, that poor woman," Havoc commented with uncharacteristic emotion.

Blade stared at the officer for a second, mulling the possible implication, then turned to Kilrane. "Can we be ready to leave in five minutes?''

"You've got it," the frontiersman responded, and moved toward a cluster of Cavalrymen.

"What about me?" Alan Valesh inquired, approaching the giant. "What about Martha and Gary?''

"I don't know about your neighbor," Blade said. "The things may have grabbed him. You keep searching your property. In the meantime, we'll track the creatures to their lair and rescue your wife and Raphaela.''

"I'll pack some grub and go with you.''

"No.''

"But it's my wife we're talking about," Valesh protested. "I have a right to go along.''

"Ordinarily I would agree, but we'll be riding hard night and day if necessary. You might not be able to keep up.''

The farmer snorted. "I could ride before you were born, mister. I'll keep up. Don't you worry.''

"I'm afraid the issue isn't open to discussion," Blade informed him politely. "If I say you're not going, you're not going.''

Valesh arched his spine. "And just who the hell do you think you are to be giving me orders? I'm not one of your Force people.''

"The authority was vested in me by the Federation leaders.

Kilrane agreed to the provision. We're working together on this mission, and I know he'll back me up. If you don't believe me, ask him."

"I sure as hell will!" Valesh declared, and marched stiffly in Kilrane's direction.

"He's ticked off, and I can't say as how I blame him," Captain Havoc said.

"It can't be helped," Blade said, and nodded at the scope. "Put that back in its case and strap the case on Sparrow's horse."

"You don't want it on yours?"

"No. You did right the first time. The equipment is too valuable to risk losing it in an accident," Blade said, and looked at the Flathead. "You're one of our best horsemen so you get to carry the gear."

"Doc is a better rider than I am," Sparrow noted.

"True, but Doc is too preoccupied right now to think straight," Blade remarked.

Havoc and Sparrow started for the Flathead's horse.

"Captain, you can take Jag's M-16 with you," Blade directed.

"Yes, sir."

Satisfied with the arrangements but chafing with impatience to be off after Raphaela, Blade rotated to gaze southward.

And there stood Doc Madsen.

The Warrior recovered from the embarrassment quickly. "You heard?"

Doc nodded. "Don't feel bad. You were right on the money. I am preoccupied. If I wasn't, I would have nailed those creatures sooner." He paused. "It's partly my fault they grabbed Raphaela."

"Your shots didn't faze that one very much. I doubt whether the outcome would have been any different even if you had been fully alert."

"Maybe," Doc said without conviction.

Blade studied the gunfighter's features. "We haven't had a chance to talk about what happened in town, and I can't spare any time now, but I will let you know that none of us will interfere unless you want our help.''

"Thanks."

"I take it Harvey Kiernan isn't long for this world?"

"Need you ask? You, better than all the others, should understand. A man does what he has to do.''

"Don't I know it," Blade said, and frowned. "Okay. When we get back you're on your own. Let's mount up."

Doc's thin lips cracked in a friendly smile and he made for his animal.

"What about me, dude?"

Blade faced the Clansman. "What about you?"

"Maybe I should stay here and guard the old geezer."

"No."

"But what if those things come back, man? He wouldn't stand a snowball's chance in hell against those mutants and you know it.''

"If Valesh stays indoors he should be safe," Blade stated. "And like it or not, you're part of this team. You're coming with us.''

"No big deal. I'm hoping to waste some of those flyin' chumps myself.''

"Mount up," Blade ordered, and watched the Clansman hurry to his horse. Now what was *that* all about? Why would Lobo volunteer to stay behind when Raphaela's life was in danger. He thought they were close friends. What if his estimation of Lobo's character was way off base? What if the Clansman only cared about number one? He shook his head to dispel those thoughts for the moment, and out of the corner of his left eye spied Alan Valesh returning.

An irate Alan Valesh.

"I hope you're satisfied, Mister High-and-Mighty!" the angry farmer declared. "Kilrane says if you don't want me to go, I can't go.''

"It's for the best," Blade said, trying to console him.

"Best my ass! I bet if it was your wife who had been

captured by flying freaks that you wouldn't stay home twiddling your thumbs while someone else went after her.''

"We're experts at this sort of job, Alan. If anyone can save Martha, we can.''

"You avoided the issue. Would you stay home if it was your wife?''

Blade looked the farmer in the eyes. "Nice try, but you're staying put and that's final.''

"What's this world coming to when one man can tell another what to do and what not to do?'' Valesh said bitterly. He walked toward the farmhouse. "The Dakota Territory is turning into a damned dictatorship.''

"Keep your doors locked,'' Blade suggested.

"You know where you can shove the doors.''

The Warrior sighed and hastened to the black gelding. He mounted, careful to avoid banging the M60 against the horse, and shifted to stare at his team. "Everyone set?''

"We're ready, sir,'' Captain Havoc answered for the group.

"Our primary priority has been changed,'' Blade told them. "We still need to locate the lair these creatures are using and eradicate them, but first and foremost we've got to save Raphaela. Martha Valesh is important. And so is Gary Norman, if they have him. But Raphaela is one of our own. We don't come back without her.''

"Now you're talkin', dude,'' Lobo commented.

"Don't worry, sir,'' Havoc said. "We've taken your teachings to heart. None of us will rest until she's found.''

Blade nodded and turned just as Kilrane rode up.

"I've sent word to Armitage. The other half of my men should be here shortly.''

"Good.''

Kilrane stared at the heavens. "Did you happen to see those things?''

"All I got was a glimpse. They were moving too fast.''

"Did you notice they were covered with hair?''

Blade nodded.

"Which means they aren't birds," Kilrane said. "They're animals of some kind."

"That'd be my guess."

Kilrane rested his hands on the pommel of his brown saddle. "This is the first time more than one of the things have been involved."

"So far as you know."

"Yeah," Kilrane said flatly. "It's so damn frustrating. We're completely in the dark. We have no idea what we're fighting."

"We're not totally in the dark," Blade amended.

"How do you figure?"

"Like you pointed out, we now know the things are mammals. Since they've been abducting humans for decades, and maybe longer, they must have a viable population for reproducing. There could be dozens of the creatures."

"There could be hundreds," Kilrane remarked, his countenance indicating he found the likelihood unpleasant.

"Could be," Blade agreed. "It's also probable they're strictly nocturnal, and nocturnal mammals usually have certain traits in common. They hole up during the day, their eyes don't adjust well to bright light, and their hearing is invariably sharp because they have to rely more on their ears than animals who go abroad during daylight hours. So we know a little."

"There's one additional likely fact you've overlooked," Kilrane said.

"Which is?"

"They're probably meat-eaters."

The arrival of Armitage and the rest of the Cavalry detachment served as the catalyst for action. Kilrane organized his men into a column behind the Force, with two Cavalrymen riding abreast all the way down the line. He placed Armitage and the other lieutenant, Treon, at the head of the column, then joined Blade at the forefront. In minutes they were under way.

Blade pushed the gelding hard, engrossed in reflection, dreading the idea of harm befalling Raphaela. Once again he stood an excellent chance of losing one of his team, and once again his emotions were torn ragged by the strain of uncertainty. Yet another mission had gone awry. A simple assignment to track down and slay a mutation had apparently escalated into open warfare between the human race and only the Spirit knew what.

It figured.

He held the reins loosely in his left hand and surveyed the rolling terrain, keeping his eyes close to the ground ahead, searching for the signs Jaguarundi would leave. After a while they came to a series of high hills covered with dense forest, and at the edge of the woods, at the very base of the first hill where the trees and the grasses met, the trunk of a dead tree and several branches had been arranged in the shape of a gigantic arrow 15 feet in length.

The arrow pointed to the southwest.

Blade barely slowed. So the creatures had changed direction slightly! He angled the gelding on the course indicated, grateful for the bright moonlight, well aware trailing Jaguarundi would be impossible without it.

Animal sounds arose in the forest: howls and snarls and yips, mingling in a bestial chorus, the cries of the predators and their prey.

With over a hundred mounted men at his back, Blade wasn't particularly concerned about the column being attacked by a wild beast or a mutation. Most wildlife would naturally avoid such a sizeable group of humans. Mutates would pose a problem, but they were becoming scarcer every year because the number of regenerating chemical clouds was dwindling.

Still, Blade kept his eyes and ears open as he rode into the hills, bearing in a generally southwesterly direction, hoping he wouldn't accidentally miss the next marker.

Fifteen minutes went by. A half hour. The night air became cooler, the breeze stronger.

Blade began to wonder if the rolling landscape would ever end. At least now he understood why the region had been named the Black *Hills*. He recalled reading during his schooling years at the Home that the Indians of long ago, back in the days of of the early American frontier, had viewed the Black Hills as sacred. Those Indians, the Sioux, had been "given" the Black Hills in a treaty. Later, after gold was discovered, the Black Hills were wrested from the Indians and "taken" by the white man.

Was it sheer concidence that now creatures spawned in the aftermath of the nuclear Armegeddon could well end up "taking" the Black Hills for their own?

Blade smiled, remembering a saying popular in California. What goes around, comes around.

How true.

Twenty minutes later the trees began to thin out and the hills gave way to flat land.

"We're almost to the Dead Zone," Kilrane disclosed.

The Warrior frowned. Terrific. Just what he wanted to hear. The last time he'd been foolhardy enough to venture into a Dead Zone, he'd been lucky to emerge with his skin intact. He saw a sapling lying on the ground in front of him and started to skirt it. Only when he glanced down did he realize the thin tree was another marker deposited by Jag, and he reined up. "Look at this," he said.

The lower branches had been stripped off the sapling, and the bottom end of the tree had been aligned to point to the southwest.

"There's no doubt about it. We definitely know where they're headed," Kilrane remarked.

"If only we knew where they are," Blade stated absently.

A second later he found out when the swishing of countless wings filled the air, mixed with dozens of raucous shrieks, and heavy forms plummeted in droves onto the Force and the Cavalry.

CHAPTER EIGHT

Jaguarundi loped at a steady pace, his lean limbs pumping rhythmically, the parabolic microphone clutched in his right hand, his loincloth brushing his thighs as he ran. Two hundred yards from the Valesh house he glanced over his right shoulder for a parting glimpse of his friends.

Did he say friends?

The thought gave him food for contemplation as he faced to the south and pressed alone into the murky land of shadows and malevolent whispers. He truly did regard his teammates as friends, even that lame-brained Lobo, which in itself was quite remarkable. There had been a time, years ago, when he'd firmly believed hybrids and humans could never experience genuine friendship.

Back in the good old days.

The ironic phrase brought a twisted grin to his mouth. How could anyone in their right mind label those days spent under the Doktor's paternal, eternally vigilant watch as good? The Doktor had been the vilest son of a bitch ever to put on pants, human or otherwise. When future historians got around to compiling a catalogue of the worst bastards in the history of the planet Earth, the Doktor would rank right up there with Jack the Ripper and Adolf Hitler. Come to think of it, the Doktor had been a curious combination of those two notorious gentlemen, combining all of their wickedest traits into a single demented personality.

Yes, sir.

A regular butcher.

But try as he might, Jag couldn't bring himself to hate the Doktor as much as he felt he should. How could he totally loathe the man who had brought him into existence, even if that man qualified as Depravity Incarnate? If not for the pioneering genetic work of the Doktor's, if not for that evil man's undeniable genius, Jag would never have known life, never have breathed in the crisp air on a radiant morning, never have known the thrill of feeling his blood pumping through his veins when he exerted himself.

How could a person despise his own creator?

The hoot of an owl brought Jag back to reality and he paused in surprise at his carelessness. With Raphaela's life at stake, now was hardly the time to indulge in musing. He raised the dish and checked the southern sky, and within seconds the beating of leathery wings came distinctly from the small speaker.

They were still out there, still bearing Raphaela to the south.

Jag switched the control knob off to conserve the battery power and resumed his pursuit. He partly blamed himself for Raphaela's predicament. If he hadn't been looking the other way when the creatures swept over the farmhouse, if he'd had time to react, he might have intercepted them before Raphaela was snatched and prevented them from taking her. Then again, he might not have made a difference. He gingerly touched his left temple, reliving being struck, vividly remembering the sheer power behind that blow.

Whatever they were, they were strong.

He also recalled the unfamiliar scent he'd detected. Once before his sensitive nostrils had registered such a tangy odor, but he couldn't isolate exactly when. Had it been during his years at the Doktor's Citadel in Cheyenne, Wyoming? Or elsewhere perhaps?

And what about that face!

Jag mentally reviewed the unsettling vision of the creature's bestial face sweeping toward him. He'd seen a gaping mouth rimmed with tapered teeth, a sloping forehead, and fantastically huge triangular ears. The thing's dark eyes, in particular, had arrested him with their malevolent intensity.

What were they?

He felt he should know their identity, and his failure to peg them annoyed him. If anyone should know about the various kinds of mutations, about all the genetic permutations to which normal species were susceptible, he should be the one. He'd spent the better part of a decade working in the damn Citadel; he'd witnessed the Doktor at work countless times and listened to the madman discourse about genetic engineering and the effects of radiation on the biosphere.

Something snorted.

The unexpected noise caused Jag to stop short, listening to the night sounds of the wildlife. He wondered if a predator had picked up his scent. The last thing he needed was to be delayed by an animal intent on consuming him for din-din.

The animal snorted again.

This time Jag determined the direction. Due west. He peered at a stand of trees 20 yards distant and perceived a dim, inky bulk moving against the backdrop of vegetation. It was the size of a cow, and since, by his estimation, he must still be on the Valesh farm, he assumed the animal actually was a cow.

Cows weren't anything to be worried about.

Grinning, Jag continued southward, and he had taken several loping strides when he heard the thumping of powerful hoofs hitting the earth, and it abruptly occurred to him there were other large farm animals that snorted on occasion.

Horses, for one.

Bulls for another.

A bull!

Jag glanced over his right shoulder and the fine hairs at the nape of his neck tingled as he laid eyes on a charging brown bull, over half a ton of throbbing muscle and sinew, and saw its curved horns revealed in the glow of the moon.

Not now!

Scowling, Jag took off to the south, running fast but not at his top speed, fleetingly furious at Valesh for not mentioning a bull was kept in the nearby fields. His fury dissipated with the realization that Valesh had been preoccupied with more important matters. He looked back, confident he could outrun his bovine pursuer, and he felt genuine surprise at seeing the bull gaining.

Damn!

What did Valesh feed the thing?

And why wasn't the brute fenced?

Jag pumped his arms and legs, holding tightly to the parabolic microphone, and scanned the terrain ahead. The field terminated les than 40 yards away at the base of a grass-covered hill.

Perfect.

He'd lose the sucker on the opposite side of the hill.

Not unduly concerned, Jag checked on the bull again, and the second he turned his head he tripped. His left foot caught in a rut and he went down hard onto his knees, arching his back, the Detector clasped to his chest to avoid damaging the device. He got his left foot on the hard ground, then heard an enraged snort and the thundering of hoofs from only a few yards to the north.

There was no time to look, no time for anything but instinctive action.

Jag threw himself to the right, onto his right shoulder, and he felt something brush his side. Clumps of dirt struck his fur. He rolled on his shoulder and pranced lightly erect.

The horned patriarch of the pasture had lumbered for 15 yards before realizing it had missed. Displaying amazing alacrity for such a massive beast, the bull wheeled, snorted, pawed the turf, and charged once more.

Jag was ready. He ran straight at the bull, the microphone tucked safely into his left elbow, grinning at the challenge. One good charge deserved another, he reasoned, and extended his right arm.

The bull was oblivious to everything except its intended victim. Its brutish mind entertained a single imperative, to destroy the violator of his territory. It fixed its blazing eyes on the cat-man and drove its mighty legs forward.

Jaguarundi tensed his leg muscles, gauging the distance between them critically, steeling himself not to panic as the bull drew nearer and nearer, forcing himself to stay calm, concentrating on the maneuver. He'd spent many an hour in the gym at the Citadel, honing his acrobatic skills, and now all that practice paid off a healthy dividend.

Ten feet separated them.

Six.

Four.

Jag leaped in a high arc, bringing his slim body horizontal to the ground, his right arm still outstretched, timing his tactic superbly. The bull passed underneath him a millisecond later, and in that instant he thrust his right palm against the bulging hump between the bull's front shoulders and shoved off, using his arm as a fulcrum to gain added momentum, even as he executed a flip and sailed up and over the beast.

The rampaging bull kept going.

As if he possessed the mass of a mere feather, Jag alighted on the grass with etheral grace and promptly raced toward the hill, smiling cockily. Once again hybrid superiority had prevailed! He looked back and saw the bull standing still, belligerently sniffing the air and gazing to the right and the left, clearly confounded by the loss of its quarry.

What a dummy!

Jag would have laughed if not for the fact he didn't want the brute after him again. He came to the hill and sprinted to the crest, glad the parabolic device had survived the encounter unscathed. Thinking of the detector brought

Raphaela to mind and he halted, anxious to verify whether he was still bearing in the right direction. He switched on the microphone and pointed the dish to the south. Sure enough, from the speaker fluttered the flapping of those mysterious creatures.

Right on target.

Jag rotated and aimed the device at the open range below. The mike detected the raspy breathing of the irate bull, but not as strongly as he anticipated. Puzzled, he moved the dish back and forth to pinpoint the animal's exact location. The sound increased dramatically as he moved the detector to the right, which indicated the bull was moving to the east.

Heading off to trample some innocent raccoon, no doubt.

Chuckling, Jag turned off the sole link between the Force and Raphaela and resumed his interrupted journey. In a mile the rolling plain gave way to high hills blanketed with trees. He ascended the first hill and employed the parabolic microphone again. His mouth curled downward when he discovered the things had changed their course.

The creatures were now flying to the southwest.

Peeved, Jag retraced his path to the bottom of the hill. He'd need to leave a marker informing Blade of the change. Something big. A downed tree, long since toppled by lightning, was ideal for the purpose. He hauled the trunk to the edge of the plain, then collected a few branches and constructed an enormous arrow.

That should do it.

Concerned about the loss of precious time, Jag proceeded on his tireless trek, plunging into the dank forest and bearing in the new direction. He felt as if he'd submerged himself in an ocean of wildlife. The woods teemed with bestial cries and challenges. To his nostrils wafted the scents of rabbits, deer, and bear, as well as an occasional scent belonging to none of the known species. He wasn't the only mutation abroad.

Just so nothing else tried to stop him.

The hills seemed to go on forever. Twice he stopped and

used the parabolic microphone, and each time he confirmed the creatures were maintaining their southwesterly heading. Eventually the forest became thinner and he reached another plain.

Time for another marker.

Jag placed the device on the ground and scoured the vicinity for an object he could utilize. He decided on a thin sapling, which he pulled from the ground with considerable effort. After stripping off the bottom limbs he aligned the tree to point to the southwest.

Blade was bound to notice it.

Satisfied with his handiwork, Jag retrieved the detector and stuck with the chase. The plain underwent a remarkable transition less than a mile later. It was as if he'd stepped onto an alien landscape. He entered a desert realm where not so much as a single blade of grass grew, where the air was warmer than the surrounding countryside because the parched, barren earth soaked up the heat during the day and released extra warmth at night.

He'd entered the Dead Zone.

Jaguarundi tried to recall everything Blade had taught him about such regions. The soil underfoot possessed the grandular consistency of sand. Where before he could hardly hear himself think for all the animal noises, now the silence of the tomb enshrouded him. The patter of his footfalls was the only sound at all. He gazed at the expanse of emptiness in front of him and experienced a riveting premonition of palpable evil.

Something was out there.

The creatures.

Kilrane had been right.

He advanced cautiously, trusting in his reflexes and his lightning speed to see him through any difficulty that might arise. The knowledge there were other mutations abroad in the Dead Zone didn't deter him one bit. After all, he was a hybrid, a genetically superior specimen, not some run-of-the-mill radiation-spawned abberation. He was better.

Somewhere a bird chittered.

Jag stared idly at a cloud off to his right, his mind drifting. All those years of being viewed as different by humans, of being labelled as freaks, had left their mark on his soul. He knew that most human regarded themselves as vastly superior to every mutation in existence, whether the mutation had been the product of a contaminated environment or created to order in a test tube. So he derived some solace from knowing he was stronger and faster than every human alive, with a notable exception.

Another bird chittered.

That exception was a remarkable human called Blade, one of the very few who had never evinced the slightest bigotry toward him. Oh, Havoc and the others were polite in his presence. He doubted they were prejudiced, but he suspected he made them nervous simply by his very nature.

More birds joined the chorus.

Jag took three more strides and the incongruity slammed into his consciousness like a physical blow.

Birds?

At night?

He glanced skyward, his gut constricting, and his breath caught in his throat as he beheld the tangible apparitions swooping down upon him.

The creatures were everywhere!

Jag cut and ran, bearing to the east, then slanting to the south, running a zigzag pattern. Now that he knew they were there, the things began voicing a perplexing commingling of sounds, barks and growls and yelps, almost as if they were communicating. High-pitched shrieks punctuated the racket. He felt something tug at his head and he jerked free and darted to the right.

A flapping form descended directly in front of him.

Snarling, Jag twisted aside and raked the creature with his nails as he passed, across its furry chest and neck, and a strident screech of pain was his reward. He ducked to the left and raced all out.

The atmosphere seemed alive with beating wings and hovering figures, some of which were silhouetted by the full moon.

A talon or nail ripped into Jag's right shoulder. He gritted his teeth and angled to the right, only to find several of the mutations barring his escape, hovering just above the ground, their wings beating-beating-beating.

Supremely frustrated, Jag bore to the left, but there were more of them. He realized there were too many, way too many, and they had him at their mercy. But they wouldn't take him without a fight! He paused to get his bearings and in doing so made a mistake. From every direction they poured down on top of him, burying him under an avalanche of fur and wings. He fought back, releasing the detector to slash and tear, and he succeeded in maiming two or three before a succession of bony fists showered upon his head and he was swept away in a monsoon of agony that eclipsed his consciousness.

CHAPTER NINE

The battle was sheer bedlam.

Blade felt a heavy body smash into his back between the shoulder blades, and the impact sent him flying from the black horse. He came down hard on his left side and flipped onto his back just as one of the creatures pounced on his chest. The thing seized his wrists and pushed into the air, apparently intending to get airborne. But it misjudged both his size and his strength. He wrenched on his arms and managed to loosen the creature's hold for an instant, long enough for him to twist his forearms and seize his attacker just above the wrists. Pulling sharply downward, he hauled the creature off balance, causing it to bend forward at the waist, bringing its midriff within range of his boots. He lashed out with his right combat boot, planting the heel in the thing's abdomen, and suddenly the mutation tore from his grasp and flapped heavenward.

Close by a man screamed.

The Warrior surged erect, his ears assailed by a veritable din. Gunshots blasted. Men shouted and cursed and fought with noble ferocity. Horses whinnied in terror. And packing the air were scores of flying mutations, ready to assist their fellows who had dropped onto the humans.

They'd waltzed into a ambush!

Blade unslung the M60 and aimed at the flapping monstrosities overhead. He cut loose, the big machine gun blasting and bucking, and he was gratified to see the rounds rip through a half-dozen mutations in the space of five seconds, rupturing their torsos repeatedly.

Four of the creatures plummeted to the earth.

Blade stepped aside as one of the things thudded to the earth within inches of the spot where he was standing. He glanced down and saw it clearly, noting its features, raking it from head to toe in a twinkling.

The mutation exhibited the biform traits of a bat and a human. It was impossible to determine if the thing was a gigantic bat possessing a humanoid form or a human endowed with the countenance, wings, and fur of a bat. In any event, the radiation or chemical toxins had transformed its ancestors into an entirely new species. Six and a half feet in height and rather stockily built for beings adapted to flight, the bat-man was covered with dark brown fur over every square inch of his body. The wings were darker than the body and leathery, their pointed tips extending a full six inches above the creature's head. While the body more distinctly resembled a human form, the face was decidedly batlike. A sloping forehead and enormous ears lent a sinister aspect to its visage. The fingers and toes, stunted in comparison to human digits, were tipped with black talons.

All this Blade registered in a moment's time. He looked up again, and there was one of the bat-men diving straight at him, its mouth wide, its pointed teeth exposed in a snarl of defiance. "Eat this, turkey!" he exclaimed, and fired.

The slugs caught the bat-man in the face and crumpled its forehead. Without uttering a sound the thing fell.

Blade surveyed the conflict. The Force and the Cavalry were holding their own. He saw Sparrow, still mounted, thrust that deadly spear through a hovering mutation. Doc was keeping the things at bay with his Magnum. On the ground nearby were Captain Havoc and Lobo, both grappling with the same creature.

A bat-man suddenly rose from the melee, a struggling Cavalryman clutched in its hands. The intended victim was putting up such a fight that the mutation couldn't gain altitude.

Blade ran to his horse, which seemed rooted with fear a few yards away, slingng the M60 over his left arm. He couldn't chance using the machine gun when the Cavalryman and the bat-man were so close together. But the Weatherby was another story. He slipped the rifle from its scabbard, worked the fluted bolt, and pressed the gun to his right shoulder.

The bat-man and the Cavalryman were still struggling.

Blade sighted on the creature's head, held his breath, and squeezed the trigger. The Weatherby thundered like a cannon.

The high-velocity bullet nearly took the mutation's head off. The force tore the thing from the Cavalryman, who dropped to the ground, and caused the bat-man to catapult end over end before crashing down in a heap.

Blade heard someone shout his name and turned to find Doc Madsen pointing the Smith and Wesson directly at him. The sight prompted immediate action, and Blade ducked down.

The Magnum cracked.

Blade glanced over his left shoulder and saw one of the creatures clutching its head and striving to get higher. He swung around, injecting a fresh round into the chamber, and fired the Weatherby from the hip.

The bullet drilled through the bat-man's chest, and it sank like the proverbial rock.

Suddenly a succession of earsplitting whistles split the night, and on cue the bat-men flapped en masse hundreds of feet into the atmosphere, then bore swiftly to the southwest. Dozens carried captive Cavalrymen who were yelling for help and endeavoring to break free even though a fall from such a height would undoubtedly prove fatal.

Kilrane materialized on the Warrior's right, the Mitchell Single Action revolver in his right hand, a nasty gash marring his brow. He glared at the retreating bat-men and shook his left fist at them in unchecked rage. "Damn them! They're dead! If it's the last thing I ever do, I'm going to wipe out every last one of those monsters!"

"You won't be doing it alone," Blade vowed.

"I'm going to see how many of my men are missing or dead," Kilrane stated, and ran off.

Blade turned, worried about his own people. Sparrow still sat on the horse, his gore-covered spear held in both hands. Doc was reloading the Magnum while watching the mutations.

"Hey, dude! Got a present for you."

The Warrior pivoted, surprise lining his face.

Lobo and Captain Havoc had caught one of the things. They had it pinned under them, flat on its back, each man holding a furry arm, their bodies slanted across the creature's chest and thighs. The mutation hissed and snapped at them, all the while attempting to buck them off.

"Tough mother," Lobo commented, holding on with all of his might.

"Do you want us to kill it, sir?" Captain Havoc inquired.

"Not yet," Blade said. He glanced at the bat-men to ensure they were continuing to fly into the distance, his skin crawling at the sight of the great, dark, flittering mass of mutations. There must be over a hundred, at the least. He hadn't expected so *many*!

"Do you reckon they have Jag?" Doc asked.

"I don't know," Blade said slowly. "If anyone could evade them, it would be him."

"They have an army," Sparrow mentioned. "If we don't stop them . . ." He left the sentence unfinished.

"We'll stop them," Blade declared. He walked to his horse and slid the Weatherby into the scabbard, then returned to Lobo and Havoc.

The captured creature growled at the giant, but it ceased

resisting.

"Can it talk?" Blade asked.

"It hasn't yet," Havoc responded. "I doubt it can. They're more animal than human."

"Look at those teeth," Lobo said, gazing at the mutation's open mouth. "They could bite through a two-by-four."

Blade nodded. "Now you know how Little Red Riding Hood felt."

"Who?"

The Warrior grinned. "Never mind. You'd need to have kids to understand that one."

"Whatever you say, dude."

Doc Madsen stepped over to study the bat-man. "We were lucky," he remarked.

Lobo laughed contemptuously. "Lucky? How do you figure, cowboy? Those things came close to cartin' us all away."

"That's just it," Doc said. "They were mainly interested in carrying us off, not in killing us. It could have been a lot worse."

"I've heard of lookin' at the bright side, but you take the cake."

"Doc is right," Blade stated, and turned to the north.

The Cavalry riders were trying to get organized. Kilrane walked among them, barking orders. Injured frontiersmen were being tended by their fellows. Dozens of riderless horses milled on the plain, and a roundup detail was in the act of bringing them together.

Blade's gray eyes scoured the ground. He counted 19 dead bat-men, and the tally pleased him. The creatures had paid a dear price for the attack; they would pay even more dearly before he was done with them.

"We should follow those devils before they're out of sight," Sparrow Hawk noted.

The Warrior glanced at the receding cloud of mutations. Sparrow had a point. "Go get Kilrane," he instructed the Flathead.

Sparrow nodded, wheeled his animal, and rode off.

"You're not thinkin' what I think you're thinkin', are you?" Lobo inquired.

Blade nodded.

"You're crazy. We'll wind up caught ourselves."

"Are you forgetting Raphaela?"

"No. Of course not," Lobo said defensively. "But committin' suicide doesn't strike me as the smartest way of savin' her."

Doc Madsen began to walk away. "I'll collect all of our horses," he volunteered.

"Thanks," Blade replied absently, deep in thought. With so many bat-men abroad, venturing into the interior of the Dead Zone did seem like a foolish idea. If he waited until daylight, and if the bat-men truly were nocturnal, the Force conceivably could locate their lair unchallenged. But the delay could prove costly to Raphaela and the captured Cavalrymen—not to mention Jag if the hybrid had fallen into the clutches of those flying deviates.

If.

If.

Sometimes he despised that word.

"I don't get how there can be so many of these freaks," Lobo commented while staring into the bat-man's hate-filled eyes.

"They've had a century or so to breed," Blade speculated. "They've kept to themselves, flourshing in secrecy, increasing their population to the point where now they don't seem to care whether humans know they exist or not. Their overconfidence will prove to be their undoing."

"You hope," Lobo muttered.

Blade gazed to the southwest. The bat-men were getting farther and farther away by the second. Unless he hurried, he'd lose them.

"Can we tie this hairy sucker up?" Lobo requested. "Its breath is enough to gag a maggot."

"No."

"Why not, dude?"

"Because I said so."

"That's good enough for me."

The Warrior focused on the mutation, which appeared to find him intensely interesting. Their eyes met and locked and the creature's thin lips curved in a wicked grin. A glimmer of intelligence flickered in the thing's eyes.

"Ugly, ain't it?" Lobo said.

"I've seen uglier," Captain Havoc remarked.

"You have?" Lobo responded. "Where?"

"In the bunk across from mine every morning when I wake up," the officer stated.

Lobo's forehead creased for a moment. "Hey! I'm in the bunk across from you."

"Really?" Havoc said innocently.

Smiling, Blade pivoted to the north and saw Sparrow heading back. Kilane was riding double with the Flathead, riding as if he was in the saddle instead of behind it. "Hold onto our friend for another minute, Captain," he stated.

"Yes, sir."

Kilrane's glowering countenance served as an accurate barometer of his frame of mind. He slid to the ground the moment Sparrow reined up and took a stride toward the captured mutation. "I should plug this son of a bitch!"

"Don't," Blade urged, stepping between them. "We need it."

The Cavalry leader's right hand drifted near his revolver, his fingers twitching. He came close to slapping leather, but he controlled himself with a visible effort and slowly relaxed. "All right. I'll let the rotten thing live."

"How bad is it?" Blade asked.

"Four dead, seven wounded, and twenty-six missing," Kilrane answered harshly. "Those vultures have twenty-six of my men!"

"How soon will you be ready to ride?"

"I don't know. We have to catch the rest of our horses,

and the wounded are being bandaged. Maybe twenty minutes.''

"That's what I figured," Blade said. "We're taking off now."

"By yourselves?"

"I don't have any choice. There's a chance the creatures may have Jag. My best bet is to follow them to wherever they hole up. Every minute we delay could cost us more lives."

Kilrane stared at the southern horizon, where the bat-men were faintly discernible. "You'd best skeddadle or you'll lose them."

"I have a better idea," Blade said, and moved over to the prisoner. He drew his right Bowie. "Let it go."

"Do what?" Lobo blurted.

"Release it," Blade reiterated.

"Are you out of your tree?"

"Now," the Warrior snapped.

"You heard the man," Captain Havoc said, and rolled to the right.

Startled at finding himself suddenly holding the mutation alone, Lobo let go and scrambled to the side.

Snarling viciously, the bat-man placed its palms on the earth and started to launch itself into the air. But it only managed to rise to one knee, its wings beating sluggishly, when the muscular colossus armed with the knife struck.

Blade's left hand whipped out and he seized the mutation by the throat. The creature screeched like a tomcat and grabbed his wrist, even as it snaked its talons at Blade's eyes. Blade dodged his head to the right, avoiding those wicked nails, then rammed his Bowie to the hilt in the thing's stomach.

The bat-man grunted and sagged.

Blade's teeth ground together as he methodically sliced the Bowie upward, the razor-sharp blade cleaving the creature's tough flesh as readily as slicing through a loaf of bread. He made a six-inch slash, exactly six inches, then pulled the Bowie out and stood back.

Gasping, the mutation pressed its hands over the breached abdominal wall and staggered backwards two feet. It gurgled, flung its head back, and took off, flapping unsteadily upward. Intestinal fluids gushed from the wound, over its fingers, and spattered onto the ground below.

"Why didn't you waste the sucker?" Lobo asked, rising.

"Watch," Blade said. He wiped the knife clean on his pants and replaced the Bowie in its sheath.

With evident effort, the bat-man attained a height of only 50 feet and flew at a snail's pace to the southwest.

"I get it!" Lobo exclaimed. "We're going to follow that crud back to their roost."

"Mount up," Blade commanded, and looked at Kilrane. "We'll find some way to let you know which way we're heading. Just stay on a southwesterly bearing until you find our sign."

"Are you sure you can't wait twenty more minutes?"

"If I could, I would," Blade responded. He walked to the black gelding and swung into the saddle. "Ride as hard as you can to catch up. We won't make a move on their lair, if we can help it, until you arrive."

"Take care," Kilrane advised.

Blade nodded, scanned his team to confirm they were all astride their horses, and rode out, his gaze on the injured bat-man, heading for the heart of the Dead Zone, riding willingly into the very heart of darkness.

CHAPTER TEN

Stark terror seized her very soul.

Raphaela stared at the surface of the earth hundreds of feet below and couldn't repress a shudder. She envisioned what would happen if the creature should let her slip, or if the thing should abruptly go into a sickening spin and carry her down to certain destruction, and she bit her lower lip to stifle a groan in her throat. She didn't want the mutation to know how truly scared she was by the ordeal; she refused to give it the satisfaction.

The creature suddenly coughed violently and lost 20 feet in altitude before it recovered and flew onward, its wings beating barely fast enough to keep it airborne.

Raphaela gulped and tightened her hold on the M-16, which was trapped between her body and the creature's. She wished the thing had grabbed her from behind instead of from the front. Her head was pressed against the mutation's chest, her left cheek flush with its fur. A pungent odor assailed her nostrils every time she inhaled, and it made her want to sneeze.

Then there was the blood.

She could feel a damp, sticky sensation on her cheek, and

she knew the creature had been gravely wounded. Either her shots or Doc's had almost bagged the brute. From its constant coughing and wheezing, from the irregular, weak beating of its wings, and from the evidence of the blood, she surmised the thing was staying in the air through sheer willpower.

The other creature seemed to be offering support to its injured companion. Uttering soft cries of encouragement, the second mutation flew in circles around the first, apparently ready to move in if the wounded one collapsed.

Raphaela still hadn't been able to get a good look at their facial features, but from the features she detected on the circling mutation, combined with the impression of the leathery wings and the short fur, she believed they were batlike beings.

Where were they taking her?

What did they intend to do to her once they arrived at their destination?

Even more importantly, how in the world was she going to get out of this mess?

She knew Blade and the others would come after her. Her confidence in them was unbounded, especially in the giant. He would never let his people down, never desert them while breath remained in his body. But how would Blade know where to find her? The bat-things weren't leaving a trail, and even Jag couldn't track an enemy through thin air.

The terrain below changed several times. Cast in the pale light of the moon, the landscape presented a ghostly aspect. They flew over plains and hills, and eventually came to a desert, or a region very much resembling a desert. There was no sign of vegetation, just a limitless tract of sandy ground.

Could that be the Dead Zone Kilrane had mentioned on the ride into Rapid City from the landing field?

Raphaela squirmed, trying to ease the painful cramps in her shoulders and upper arms, and the creature holding her hissed in annoyance. She resigned herself to enduring the terrible strain on her body and her emotions for as long as necessary. If there was one lesson she had learned from the titan with the Bowies, it was to never give up hope.

Never give up.

Hadn't she told herself the very same thing over a year ago when the first unspeakable indignity had occurred? Hadn't she endured, despite the repeated violations, and eventually salvaged the vestige of her self-respect by volunteering for the Force? After the living hell she'd suffered, after experiencing the ultimate degradation any woman could know, being captured by hairy bat-men paled into insignificance.

The thought made her laugh bitterly.

Sometimes she was tempted to think that her entire life qualified as a continuous nightmare intermittently punctuated by rare and all too brief moments of happiness. Well, that wasn't completely true. Until the tender age of six her life had been reasonably happy, so far as she knew.

And then her parents had died.

She could recall vividly the day her mom and dad had dropped her off at her aunt's chambers in the underground city known as the Mound. Her parents had wanted an afternoon to themselves, and they'd ventured to the surface to enjoy a picnic and some fishing. How were they to know a band of murderous scavengers was in the area? The lake near the Mound was a favorite haunt of the Moles, and many others were there that fateful June day casting for fish, boating, or swimming when the scavengers struck. Seventeen Moles had been killed before a security detail from the Mound routed the vile scavengers, and among the fatalities had been Raphaela's parents.

She never had been able to comprehend how God could allow such a tragedy to befall her. From the age of six until her twelfth year she had subscribed to the childish idea that she must have committed a grievous sin, else why would the compassionate Father of the Universe have inflicted so staggering a blow to one so tender of age? Later she'd come to the conclusion she couldn't lay the blame on God. Certain events simply transpired without the guiding hand of the Supreme Being behind them. Still, one question bothered her. Even if God didn't deliberately inflict punishment, how could a loving Deity permit rampant suffering to exist?

She still didn't know the answer to that one.

Distressing memories of her years with her aunt filled her mind. The first 18 months hadn't been too bad because Aunt Gitana had been single and seemed to appreciate having Raphaela around. But then Gitana had married a lieutenant in the security forces, the handsome Zelig, and Raphaela's life was transformed into a living hell. Because underneath that dashing exterior lurked a devil of a man who drank way too much and who took out every petty frustration on his wife and children. Perhaps, Raphela had often reasoned, his motivation for having so many kids lay in his unconscious desire to make as many people miserable as he possibly could in the span of one sodden life.

If there was one accomplishment at which Zelig excelled, other than drinking more liquor in a day than most men consumed in a month, it lay in producing offspring. In seven years he sired seven children, four boys and three girls, and the birth of each child only added to the misery in the household. Gitana became increasingly withdrawn and spiteful. Instead of her maternal instincts being aroused by the births, they atrophied. She expended the least amount of effort possible in her daily tasks, and she often ignored the children and left them to fend for themselves.

By virtue of being the oldest, Raphaela was the one the others looked up to, the one they relied on to fill the void their parents refused to acknowledge even existed. Raphaela mediated disputes, bandaged them when they cut themselves, and frequently prepared their meals when their mother couldn't be bothered.

Dear Lord, what a life!

Work, work, and more work.

She might not have minded so much if her mother hadn't turned her brothers and sisters against her later. Raphaela had been bewildered and stung to her core when Gitana began making snide references to the fact that she had been adopted, continually stressing Raphaela wasn't really part of the family. To Raphaela's dismay, after a year or two of such treatment, her brothers and sisters started treating her coldly and behaving in the same way as Gitana.

Tears moistened her eyes.

How happy she'd finally been two years ago after taking an apartment of her own and acquiring a position on the kitchen staff of the imperial residence. If only she'd known! If only she'd foreseen the torment she would have to endure after he'd spotted her!

The worst part had been not being able to confide in anyone, to beg for help. He would have had her and whoever she told killed. There had been nowhere she could flee, short of leaving the Mound and entering the dreaded Outlands. So she'd borne the horror until, incredibly, he'd tired of her and moved on to another victim. Her shame, however, had lingered and intensified. Every time she saw him, every time she passed him in the corridor, she'd wanted to curl up and die.

When the official announcement requesting volunteers for the Freedom Force was posted, she'd signed the list more as an outlet for her frustration than anything else. She'd never really expected him to send her, and she still wondered why he did. Maybe he couldn't stand the sight of her, or, more likely knowing him, he was hoping she would meet the same fate as the previous recruit from the Moles: an early death.

All of those thoughts whirled through Raphaela's mind as the wouunded bat-man conveyed her deeper and deeper into the Dead Zone. She lost all track of time and the distance covered, and it wasn't until a lofty escarpment appeared ahead that she blinked and took stock of her surroundings.

What was that?

After so many miles of flat, barren land, the escarpment presented a welcome, if singular, change of scenery. It was at least 500 feet high, and the pale lunar radiance revealed the northern face of the cliff to be pockmarked with the entrances to scores of caves. And moving about those entrances, either on foot or flying to and from the escarpment, was a legion of winged demons.

It was their lair!

The realization caused Raphaela to shiver as a chill ran along her spine. There were so many! Her mind boggled. She suspected there were even more within the caves, and a minute later she got to confirm her supposition when the bat-man bearing her dove at a sharp angle toward one of the openings situated in the middle of the rocky escarpment.

Mesmerized by the eerie tableau, feeling as if she had been bodily transported to another realm, another planet, Raphaela belatedly reacted to the wind streaming past her face and the frantic flapping of her captor's wings. With a start she perceived they were descending too fast; indeed, the speed took her breath away.

They were going to crash!

Raphaela braced for the collision, certain she would be crushed against the sheer rock wall or sent hurtling to her death at the base of the escarpment. She saw other creatures standing idly in the mouth of the cave toward which they plummeted, and she would have shouted at them to do something if she thought her prompting would do any good.

The cliff loomed closer and closer.

Just when she was certain of impending doom and she inadvertently opened her mouth to voice her death cry, the mutation unexpectedly checked its swift descent, its wings beating madly. The floor of the cave, which extended over 20 feet beyond the edge of the ceiling, had rushed up to meet them, but suddenly they were settling gently to the ground.

Gasping, the bat-man released her.

The injured mutation sank to its knees and cradled its head in its hands.

Elation filled Raphaela. She was alive and she still had the M-16! Despite the overwhelming odds, she might be able to find a hiding place in the caves and escape later. She leaped to her feet and started to run.

A furry covered arm came from behind her, gripped the barrel of the assault rifle, and tore the weapon from her grasp as easily as she would pluck a toy from an infant.

Furious, she completed the turn and froze.

A huge mutation reared above her, the largest bat-man she had yet seen, almost seven feet tall and endowed with layers of prominent muscles. His wings flared above his broad shoulders like the uplifted cowl of a majestic cape. A head twice the size of any other creature's fit the contours of his form perfectly.

Raphaela gaped. Her intuition told her that here stood the leader of these mutations. His tremendous size alone would have marked him for leadership under any circumstance, but he possessed an additional attribute, the uncanny gleam of malevolent intellect in his feral eyes, that distinguished him even more.

The towering figure uttered a sharp bark. Immediately four bat-men materialized at his side. He motioned at the Molewoman, and two of the creatures stepped forward to take her by the arms.

Resentment and revulsion flared in Raphaela's breast and she futilely resisted, tugging and twisting heedless of the consequences. "Let go of me!" she exclaimed angrily.

A chittering noise issued from the leader. He leaned down and inspected her minutely, sniffing loudly as he ran his left hand through her hair.

"Don't touch me!" Raphaela snapped, jerking her head back.

Ominously, the bat-man smiled, a leering sort of expression every bit as sinister as the lecherous countenance of the worst kind of human pervert.

Raphaela trembled. She had seen such an expression before, many times, on the face of the man who had forced her to endure unspeakable debasement. All too vividly she

relived the pressure of his lips on her body and the probing
of his hands where they had no business being.

The leader chattered at the pair holding her.

A feeling of weakness seeped into Raphaela's limbs and
she shook her head, fighting the sensation. Now was hardly
the time to buckle under! She must be strong or perish. Even
if Blade and the other Force members were coming to her
rescue, they wouldn't arrive for hours. She was on her own.

As usual.

The two bat-men unceremoniously stalked forward, hauling
her with them, and moments later Raphaela was swallowed
by the stygian shadows.

CHAPTER ELEVEN

They rode for an hour, easily keeping the bat-man in sight with the aid of the Nite-Vision device, staying approximately 400 yards back. A deathly stillness permeated the Dead Zone, and except for the plodding of their horses and the creaking of their saddles there were no other sounds.

"This place gives me the heebie-jeebies," Lobo muttered.

"Imagine how Raphaela must feel right about now," Captain Havoc remarked.

"If she's still alive," Sparrow noted.

The captain glanced at the Flathead. "Don't talk like that! She's alive. She's got to be."

"And don't forget about Jag," Doc Madsen said.

"Yeah. Of course," Havoc responded absently, then uttered a rare oath. "Damn those things!"

Riding at the head of the Force, the M60 resting on his stout thighs, Blade shifted and looked over his right shoulder. "Try to keep the noise down to a low uproar."

"Sorry, sir," Havoc said dutifully.

"We're all concerned about Jag and Raphaela," Blade stated. "But we can't let our worry get the better of us or we won't be able to do them any good."

They pressed on for another five minutes.

"I wish Kilrane would catch up with us," Lobo stated.

"Give him time," Blade said.

"What if those things come back before he reaches us?"

"We waste them," Blade answered, watching the mutation he'd gutted wing slowly to the southwest.

"Yeah. Right. Just the five of us takin' on all those hairy farts," Lobo snapped. "Like we'd stand a chance, huh?"

"What would you have us do?" Blade asked. "Give up?"

"No, but waitin' for reinforcements wouldn't be a bad idea."

"You know the reason we came on ahead of the Cavalry," Blade commented. "So do us all a favor and quit griping."

"Okay. But don't say I didn't warn you if we get slaughtered," Lobo declared testily.

The Warrior scanned the monotonously level countryside, then surveyed the heavens for signs of the bat-creatures. He thought of all the Hot Spots scattered about the ravaged remains of America, and wondered if every Dead Zone had its own resident deviate population. He recalled the details of the time his close friend Geronimo had encountered a horde of enormous ants in another Dead Zone, and he resolved to submit a proposal to the Federation Council requesting that every such region within Federation boundaries be checked out. If there were other menaces lurking in the Dead Zones, the Federation should deal with them before they became too powerful or widespread.

Like the bat-men.

He idly scratched his chin, reflecting. If there were bat-men, there must be bat-women somewhere. Sooner or later the thing he'd gutted would lead them to its lair, provided it didn't expire first. Once there, Blade faced the problem of how to rescue Raphaela and possibly Jaguarundi against impossible odds. Rather than dwell on the issue, he decided to cross that bridge when he came to it.

A depression appeared ahead.

Blade stared at the narrow notch running from east to west.

A gully, he reasoned, probably washed out by periodic heavy rains. The gelding came to the northern rim. Blade reined up and scrutinized the oversized ditch, estimating the depth at four feet and the average width at two and a half. The horse would be able to negotiate the fissure with ease.

"Maybe we should go around," Lobo suggested.

"Be serious," Blade said.

"I was."

The Warrior ignored the Clansman and goaded his horse. "Let's go, big fella," he said soothingly.

The gelding's ears pricked up and it shied away from the edge.

"There's nothing down there," Blade said, trying to soothe the animal's nerves. He glanced down at the bottom third of the gully, which lay shrouded in impenetrable shadow, and understood why the horse wouldn't cross the gap. "Come on. You can do it."

"Maybe you should carry it piggyback," Lobo queried.

Blade kneed the gelding, and finally prompted the horse into jumping the obstacle. Shying nervously, the animal nonetheless lowered its haunches and gave a bounding hop, its powerful rear legs propelling it to the opposite rim. Blade smiled and leaned forward to pat the horse on the neck, and the motion accidentally saved his life.

A short, squat form hurtled out of the gully at the Warrior's head and iron jaws snapped shut with a distinct snap within inches of the giant's neck.

"Look out!" Captain Havoc shouted.

Blade needed no urging. He dove from the saddle, the M60 in his left hand, and hit the ground on his right shoulder, rolling as he landed to minimize the pain and present an elusive target in case the thing that attacked him decided to try again. His momentum carried him into a crouch, the machine gun tucked tight against his waist, and he glanced to the right and the left but saw nothing.

"It hopped off," Lobo said.

"To your left," Doc added.

Blade turned on his heels just in the nick of time.

Whatever it was, the animal bounded out of the gloom and leaped straight at the Warrior's face.

Blade glimpsed bulbous eyes and a gaping, toothless maw, and then he threw himself to the right, barely evading the creature. A frog! The thing looked like a frog!

"It's coming at you again!" Sparrow cried.

The Warrior, on his right side, let go of the M60 and flipped onto his back, drawing both Bowies simultaneously. He saw the stocky figure alight six feet away, then vault toward him, and he extended both of his arms and locked his elbows.

The stubby jumping bean couldn't stop.

Blade braced his massive shoulders as the animal arced down onto the tips of the Bowies, and the big knives sank in all the way at the base of the thing's yellowish throat, impaling it to the hilts. A gooey liquid sprayed onto Blade's hands and splattered his forearms.

The animal vented a raspy croak and thrashed wildly, its four legs flapping like wings, its mouth opening and closing convulsively.

Blade held the thing at arm's length, waiting for it to expire. Something heavy thudded onto the ground to his right, and then footsteps sounded.

"Allow me," Sparrow Hawk said. He lanced his spear into the animal's side, wrenched it off the Bowies, and smashed the creature on the reddish earth.

"What is it?" Lobo called out.

Blade rose slowly and leaned down to inspect his assailant. A closer examination revealed his initial impression had been slightly off; the thing was a toad, not a frog. Two feet high and four feet long, the diminutive monster possessed fleshy, webbed feet, rough skin coated with warts, and large eyes containing vertical slits.

"What is it?" Lobo repeated.

"A toad," Blade replied.

"A poisonous toad," Sparrow Hawk amended. "I've seen this variety before, but never one this huge."

"How poisonous?" Blade asked.

"If it had bitten you, if it had broken your skin and its venom entered your bloodstream, you wouldn't have lasted five minutes."

Lobo snorted. "What the hell is a dumb toad doing way out here in the middle of nowhere?" he asked, and motioned at the expanse of arid land. "There's no water within miles of here."

"You're thinking of frogs," Sparrow said. "Most frogs require water to live, to sustain their metabolism. But many toads can exist under very dry conditions. All they need is just a small water hole to survive. Some can burrow down to subterranean springs."

"Do you think there could be more?" Lobo queried nervously.

"Where you find one of a species, it is safe to assume there might be others nearby," Sparrow stated.

"Maybe we should haul ass, dudes," Lobo suggested.

"I agree," Blade said, retrieving the M60.

"You do?" Lobo declared in disbelief. "Do you mean I'm right for once?"

"Everybody gets lucky now and then," Captain Havoc quipped.

The Warrior walked to his horse, took hold of the pommel, and swung up into the saddle. He glanced at his second-in-command. "Thanks for the warning."

Havoc shrugged. "It came automatically. I would have shot the damn thing but you were too close."

"Pardon me," Doc Madsen interjected.

Blade looked at the gunfighter. "What is it?"

"I don't think it's a bright idea to be sitting here jawing when we're the main item on the menu."

"The menu?" Blade repeated quizzically.

Doc pointed at the stretch of gully to the east.

Dreading the worst, Blade twisted in the saddle. The short hairs on his neck seemed to stand on end at the sight of dozens of squat forms, the nearest less than 30 feet away, hopping madly toward the Force.

"I'm out of here!" Lobo exclaimed, and urged his mount over the gully in a surprising display of competent horsemanship.

"Move it!" Blade barked at the others.

Doc and Captain Havoc handily cleared the notch. The gunfighter's body flowed smoothly with his animal's, as if he was part of his horse.

"Ride hard!" Blade directed, and suited his actions to match the command. He glanced over his left shoulder as he raced to the southwest, consternation seizing him when he beheld a wave of bounding toads crest the south rim of the depression and leap in pursuit.

Could those things outrun a horse?

Blade hugged the galloping gelding and gazed at the amphibians. There was no way a normal toad could hope to outpace a full-grown horse, but those mutations, easily 20 times their normal size, could conceivably possess the speed and endurance needed. And if the toads caught up with a horse, all it would take would be one healthy bite and in minutes the larger animal would drop, leaving the rider in the lurch. "Faster!" he bellowed.

The Force members were riding all out. Lobo bounced up and down uncontrollably and held onto the pommel for dear life. Doc Madsen, who could easily outride all of them, even Sparrow, was intentionally holding back, bringing up the rear, the Magnum in his right hand.

Blade could see the toads covering the ground at an astounding rate and he marveled at their prodigious leaps. Fifteen-foot jumps were accomplished effortlessly. The mutations, to his dismay, appeared to be gaining.

One of them came on much faster than the rest and out-distanced the pack. The creature cleared 20 feet at a hurdle. It made a beeline toward the Warrior's steed.

Clasping the M60 securely under his left arm, Blade whipped the reins with his right hand, hoping to impel the gelding to a swifter performance. The flat terrain worked in favor of the Force, enabling their mounts to race unchecked.

But it wasn't fast enough.

The foremost toad narrowed the gap quickly, its legs barely touching the earth between each hop, incredibly fleet for so small a creature.

Blade knew the toad would overtake his animal in the next few seconds. He was about to turn and try nailing it with the machine gun when someone else did him the favor of disposing of the toxic terror.

Doc Madsen's Magnum cracked once.

The toad was in midair when the slug bored into its head and stopped it dead. For a moment the mutation hung motionless, its mouth gaping, and then it sank to the ground with a plop.

"Thanks," Blade said to the gunfighter.

"Anytime."

The Warrior faced forward and concentrated on his riding. He probed the darkness ahead for a change in the landscape, a hill or a ravine they could use to their advantage, somewhere they could make a stand if need be. Far, far off, almost an inky dot on the southern horizon, was—something. A hill? No, not at that distance. A mountain, he reasoned, and he forgot about it for the time being because it was simply too far away to offer them any help.

For minutes the death race continued, with the drumming of heavy hoofs shattering the perpetual stillness of the Dead Zone.

Blade glanced behind him again and was gratified to notice the toads were beginning to fall behind. In short sprints they were greased lightning, but they apparently lacked the stamina for a marathon. Which suited him just fine.

A few more minutes elapsed.

The Warrior straightened and scanned the moonlit land

to their rear, smiling in relief when he failed to find any evidence of the toads.

Good riddance!

Blade held aloft his right hand. "Hold up!" he shouted, and drew slowly to a halt, turning the gelding sideways so he could continue to survey their back trail.

The Force members reined up.

"Do you think we lost those things?" Captain Havoc asked.

"Looks that way," Blade said.

"Oh, Lord!" Lobo declared in a strangled voice. He leaned forward, his hands cupped over his groin. "I'm dyin'!"

Sparrow moved his mount next to the Clansman's. "What's wrong? Did a toad bite you, brother?"

"Forget the damn froggies!" Lobo snapped, his tone high-pitched and squeaky. He gave the pommel a hard smack. "It's this saddle! What moron invented these things anyway? Oh, my poor, poor baby."

Sparrow looked at Doc, who shrugged, then back at Lobo. "Your baby?"

"My rod, dude. My rod. I may never be able to give some fox the thrill of her life ever again."

"Oh," Sparrow said, comprehending. He turned his head aside and started laughing softly.

"What the hell is so funny?" Lobo grunted indignantly. "Some of us weren't born on a horse, you know. My gonads will never be the same again."

"You have my sympathy," Captain Havoc stated.

"Thanks, dude."

"Just be sure to wash that saddle before you give it back to Kilrane."

"Up yours."

Havoc, Doc, and Sparrow all chuckled.

Sitting quietly on the gelding, Blade smiled at their banter. He was pleased to see Doc loosening up. After all they'd been through within the past few hours, they needed the

levity. He cast another glance to the north and tensed.
''Damn!''

The others instantly clammed up and stared in the same
direction.

Perhaps 40 yards off, bounding tirelessly toward the Force,
were scores of toads.

''Ride!'' Blade ordered, and whipped the gelding to the
south. The horse started to gain speed. He gazed at the sky,
at the radiant moon, and abruptly hauled on the reins.

''Look!'' Lobo cried, pointing heavenward. ''Look!''

''I see them,'' Blade responded.

Swooping down out of the blanket of night, their wings
extended as they glided on the wind, their talons ready to
rip and tear, were dozens of bat-men.

CHAPTER TWELVE

Why did his head feel as if an elephant had done a tap dance on his skull?

And when was the last time he'd taken a bath?

Jag slowly regained consciousness, his memory sluggish at first, and kept his eyes closed while he took stock of his condition. From the aches all over his body he surmised someone had used him for a punching bag. Every square inch was aflame with pain, even his toes.

What could have happened?

Where was he?

Where were his friends? Blade? Raphaela!

The remembrance of his battle with the bat-men shot through him like an electric shock and he inadvertently opened his eyes. In his mind's eye he saw them again: all those teeth, hateful eyes, and fists. They'd beaten him, had him at their mercy. Yet he still lived.

Why?

Placing his palms on the dark ground, he pushed up to a sitting posture.

"Jag! You're awake!"

The delightful yell startled him. He blinked, still feeling

dazed, and looked to his right.

"Oh, Jag! You're alive! Thank God!"

Jag saw Raphaela running toward him, her arms outstretched, her face lit by an eager smile. He became vaguely aware of other figures nearby, and he noticed that a pale, whitish glow bathed everything within his range of vision. His mind felt sluggish, and he was slow to rouse himself from a feeling of abject lethargy.

"Speak to me!" Raphaela declared, reaching his side the next moment. She knelt and hugged him firmly, a sigh of relief escaping from her lips. "Oh, God! It's so great to see you again! I was so scared, but not anymore."

"What—?" Jag began, his voice croaking, his throat parched and dry.

"What happened to you?" Raphaela asked, finishing the sentence for him. She leaned back and studied his features. "Don't you remember? You were captured by those bat-things."

"Where—?" Jag said in a grating whisper.

"Where are you? At the bottom of a pit in an enormous cliff. I mean actually *inside* the cliff." She gazed upward. "It's like a huge cavern."

"How—?"

"How did you get here? Why, they brought you, of course. They dumped you in here with the rest of us about thirty minutes ago."

Jag licked his lips and swallowed, biding his time to gather his strength, to recover enough to at least complete a question. He surveyed his surroundings, taking stock, distressed to discover they were at the bottom of a circular pit 40 feet in circumference and an equal distance in height.

"Is this a friend of yours?" a male voice inquired.

Jag glanced to his left, and surprise lined his feline face at the sight of seven humans standing in a cluster a dozen feet away. There were four men and three women. Several of the men sported stubby beards, indicating they normally shaved but hadn't in a while.

"Yes," Raphaela answered, and gave Jag a squeeze. "A dear friend."

"He's a mutant, isn't he?" the same speaker demanded. He wore a brown shirt and jeans and appeared to be in his late forties or early fifties.

"Yep," Raphaela said. She shifted to stare at the man. "What difference does that make? He's in the same boat we are."

The man gazed at Jag. "I was just asking, is all. No offense meant."

"I should hope not, Mr. Norman," Raphaela stated sternly.

One of the other men, a burly specimen attired in tattered clothes, sighed. "Bat-men. Cat-men. I'm so sick and tired of lousy mutations I could puke."

The Molewoman stood, her fists clenched. "That's no way to talk, Mr. Shertzer."

"I can't help how I feel, lady," Shertzer replied. "You'd probably feel the same way if you'd been stuck in this pit for over two weeks."

"Maybe I would. But I won't tolerate having my friends be insulted by you or anyone else!"

Norman interjected a comment. "Calm down, Raphaela. I'm sure Bill didn't mean anything by his crack."

"I meant every word of it," Shertzer snapped. "What's she going to do? Punch me out?" He laughed scornfully.

Jaguarundi had heard enough. His saliva had soothed the torment in his throat and his mental faculties had been restored. He sprang to his feet and took a stride toward the man named Shertzer. "If you want your lights punched out, jerkface, I'll be glad to oblige."

Bill Shertzer's mouth dropped. He extended his right hand, palm outward. "Hey! Take it easy, pal! I didn't mean anything."

"I'm not your pal," Jag hissed. "And if you badmouth me again, getting out of this pit will be the least of your worries."

Shertzer glared but said nothing.

"That's better," Jag said, taunting him. He scrutinized their natural prison and frowned. The sides were sheer and smooth, lacking a handhold anywhere. Barely visible hundreds of feet above the rim of the pit was the roof of the cavern, and framed in an immense, jagged opening in that rock ceiling was the full moon.

Raphaela followed the direction of his gaze. "The top of the cliff and the north face are honeycombed with caves and holes. They all lead into the central cavern in which this pit is located."

"And the bat-men?"

"You can't see them from down here, but they're all over up there. Bat-men, bat-women, even young ones."

"So this is where they breed," Jag said.

"There are hundreds of them," Raphaela informed him.

The man wearing the jeans stepped forward and offered his right hand to Jag. "Hello. I'm Gary Norman. I'm pleased to meet you."

"He's the neighbor of Alan Valesh," Raphaela added.

"I gathered as much," Jag said, and shook.

Norman jerked his head toward the hefty prisoner. "Don't be too hard on Bill. You don't know the whole story. His wife and son were killed by those things."

Jag glanced at Shertzer. "They were?"

Norman nodded. "They were captured about two and a half weeks ago. His wife and son have since been taken out."

"Taken where?"

"Up there," Norman said, craning his neck to peer at the rim.

"That's right," Shertzer interjected acrimoniously. "Some of those freaks flew down here, grabbed them, and carried them up to the cavern floor. First my wife, then my son. Each time I tried to stop the bastards, and each time they knocked me down." He paused. "Every time I close my eyes I can hear my wife and son yelling for help as they were lifted out of this damn pit, and then I hear their screams all over again, their cries as those demons tore them apart limb by limb.'' He shuddered. ''Is it any wonder I haven't slept a wink in days?''

Jaguarundi stared at the man, gauging his sincerity. ''I had no idea. I'm sorry.''

''So am I. I really don't hate you just because you're a mutation.''

''Hybrid. I prefer the word hybrid,'' Jag said. He pointed at the cavern roof. ''Those things are mutations.''

''Whatever, you're in the same boat we are,'' Shertzer stated. ''Those things will eat you too.''

Jag stared at the other men and women. ''Who has been here the longest?''

''I have,'' another man responded. ''Over three weeks. There were twelve people in this pit when I was brought in. I'm the last one from that group.'' He gestured at the rest. ''They were all brought in after me.''

''The bat-men must feed you,'' Jag deduced.

''Yeah, they give us some slop now and then, just enough to stay alive. Mostly it's putrid meat, but when you're hungry enough you'll eat anything.''

''I never will,'' Raphaela declared emphatically.

Jag walked in a small circle, inspecting the pit. ''Since there are hundreds of those things, and they capture so few humans, they must eat more than human flesh.''

''I've heard all kinds of squealing and wild shrieks from time to time,'' the man who had been in the pit the longest disclosed. ''As if animals were being ripped to pieces. Those flying monsters must eat anything they can catch.''

''Do they ever put live animals down here?'' Jag inquired.

''Not that I know of,'' the long-time resident said.

''Just humans,'' Norman stated thoughtfully, then looked quickly at the hybrid. ''Until now, that is.''

''But why did they go to all this trouble for us?'' Raphaela questioned.

''Maybe we're special,'' Jag answered.

''Special?''

"A delicacy."

"Oh."

Jag rotated to the left and a reeking stench assailed his nostrils. He coughed and covered his mouth.

"That's where we go to the bathroom," Shertzer said. "If you don't turn in that direction the odor isn't so bad."

"We've got to escape," Jag asserted, gazing overhead, striving to distinguish details.

"No fooling," Shertzer said sarcastically. "What was your first hint?"

"Do you think we haven't thought about escaping?" a woman in a grimy white blouse demanded. "It's all we *do* think about. But we can't fly like those devils. How are we going to get out of this pit when the walls are as slippery as glass?"

"There must be a way," Jag said.

Shertzer made a snorting noise. "Listen to the hybrid! He's been down here less than an hour and already he thinks he knows a way out."

"I didn't say that."

"Then what did you say? You make us sound like quitters or jackasses. Well, I'm telling you it can't be done! I did everything in my power to try and escape, to save my family. And it did no good! We're as good as dead."

"Speak for yourself," Jag said. "Where there's life, there's hope."

"How corny can you get," Shertzer responded with manifest contempt.

"Please, Bill," Norman said. "You're starting in on him again."

"I don't care. He's implying I let my family down, that I didn't do all I could have."

Jag shook his head. "I never made any such claim."

"Wait!" Raphaela suddenly interrupted, and raised her right arm. "Look!"

A fluttering of heavy wings reached Jag's keen ears and he tilted his head back to behold several bat-men hovering above the pit, partly blocking off the moonlight. The mutations were no more than hairy shadows.

"Oh, God!" Shertzer exclaimed in stark dread.

"What is it?" Norman asked.

"They've come for one of us."

"How do you know?" Raphaela queried anxiously.

"He's right," stated the longtime prisoner. "I know their routine by now."

"We've got to fight them," Jag proposed.

"Are you nuts? What can we hope to do against them?" Shertzer retorted.

The bat-men, five of them, began to slowly descend into the pit, staying huddled near the middle so their wings wouldn't brush the stone walls. One of them, a huge creature, dropped lower than his fellows.

"That's their leader," Raphaela declared.

"How do you know?" Jag inquired.

"I saw him before."

"So did I," Norman said, confirming her statement. "I saw him giving orders to the others."

Jag's eyes narrowed speculatively at the news. What would happen if the leader of the bat-men should die? How organized were the mutations? Could they mount an effective opposition without their head honcho?

"What do we do?" one of the women asked fearfully.

Before Jag could reply, and before anyone else could so much as move, the enormous leader dived straight down, its form a blur, its hands reaching out to grab the man who had been confined in the pit for over three weeks.

"No!" the man wailed.

Jag lunged at the bat-man, but the creature was faster. It shoved off the instant its talons bit into the man's shoulders and shot upwards, conveying the thrashing prisoners effortlessly.

"Help me!"

Raphaela extended her arms in a hopeless gesture. "We've got to help him!"

"There's nothing we can do for him," Gary Norman said.

The creatures flew over the edge of the pit and bore their burden to the left.

"Now you know how I felt when they took my wife and son," Shertzer commented.

For a minute nothing else happened. The vast cavern was quiet. And then a protracted, wavering scream echoed in the gigantic subterranean chamber, profoundly stirring in the sheer, unbridled terror pervading every quaking note.

"No!" Raphela said softly.

"One of us will be next," Norman remarked.

"Not if I can help it," Jag told them. "I have a plan."

"Who cares?" Shertzer responded. "It all boils down to us against them, and we don't stand a prayer."

Jag faced the malcontent. "Would you rather stand around twiddling your thumbs until they come to get you?"

The hefty man scowled, then looked at the spot where their late companion had been standing mere minutes ago. "No, I guess not." He squared his shoulders. "So what's this great plan of yours?"

CHAPTER THIRTEEN

They were trapped!

Blade gazed up at the rapidly descending bat-men, then over his right shoulder at the onrushing toads.

"What do we do?" Lobo queried.

The Warrior glowered in frustrated fury. There was no time for the luxury of indecision. If one horror didn't get them, the other one would. Unless. Unless he had a brilliant brainstorm and turned the tide instantly. A desperate idea flashed through his brain in a burst of inspiration, a death-defying gambit that might save their lives if their timing was flawless.

"They're almost on us!" Lobo belabored the obvious.

"Stick with me!" Blade commanded sharply, reversing direction, pointing the horse directly at the toads.

"What are you doing?" Lobo queried.

"Follow me," Blade directed, and rode to the north at a gallop, his body hunched low on the animal's broad back, the M60 held next to his chest. The success of his strategy depended on the toads. Did the amphibian mutations possess a normal endowment of self-preservation? Would they risk being pounded to a pulp by the drumming hoofs of the horses, or would the toads scatter to save themselves? Everything depended on the instinctual thread of elemental existence.

From the bat-men came a sudden loud chattering and sharp barking noises.

Blade ignored the winged deviates for the moment, hoping he wouldn't feel talons ripping into his back before he broke clear of the amphibians. If he broke clear.

The toads came on swiftly, executing their remarkable leaps, bounding streaks in the night.

"Don't stop for anything!" Blade shouted, and bore down on the middle of the foremost rank of popeyed mutations. He tensed, ready to vault from his animal if the toads should swarm over its legs. At a distance of 25 feet the amphibians were still surging forward without a hint of a break in their strides.

Doc Madsen's Magnum boomed and a bat-man screeched.

The flying abominations must be getting close, Blade realized, and then the gelding was only 15 feet from the first toads and he braced for the impending clash.

But there wasn't one.

At the last second the toads parted like a breaker on a boulder, scattering to the right and the left, jumping out of the way of the five racing horses, out of the path of those 20 driving hoofs, croaking and grunting in a guttural chorus.

The Warrior beamed in elation at their temporary respite. He rode a dozen yards and looked back in anticipation of finding both the bat-men and the toads in hot pursuit, but instead he laid eyes on a spectacle straight out of a madman's nightmare.

None of the toads were after the Force. The amphibians had another problem to deal with.

Incredibly, inexplicably, most of the bat-men had turned aside to chase the toads, swooping and diving every which way as they scooped up amphibian after amphibian. They would each grab a victim by a rear leg and haul the fleshy prize into the air, then immediately go after another one.

Blade straightened, realizing there could only be one

explanation for the surprising behavior. The bat-men must constantly be on the lookout for food, and here was a golden opportunity they weren't about to pass up, the chance to bag scores of plump toads. So the majority of them had been diverted.

Ten bat-men, however, were still in pursuit of the Force.

The Warrior galloped northward for another 30 yards, repeatedly glancing at the flapping creatures, gauging the range, and when the bat-men came within 20 feet he abruptly halted the gelding and spun, the M60 rising to his right shoulder. He sighted on the dark forms and fired, sweeping the barrel from left to right and back again, the machine gun thundering in his ears and causing the black horse to prance skittishly. Compensating for the motion, he drilled the creatures.

Captain Havoc, Doc, Sparrow, and Lobo also opened fire.

Six of the bat-men crashed instantly, their wings fluttering as their lifeless figures plummeted. The other four bravely managed a few more yards before the rain of lead bored through their skulls and chests and brought them smashing down.

"On me!" Blade instructed, and made to the east. He intended to evade the other bat-men by swinging in a loop. Hopefully, the creatures were so involved in snatching toads that they wouldn't pay any attention to the Force for the next few minutes.

Captain Havoc rode up alongside the Warrior. "We lost the one we were following!" he exclaimed.

Blade gazed to the south, anger and frustration flaring within him. Damn! He'd forgotten all about the wounded bat-man in the flurry of activity. There was no sign of the creature. Either it had died, other bat-men had come to its aid, or it was continuing to the southwest all alone. Since the bat-man had stayed on a steady course, Blade felt safe in assuming the thing had been making for its lair. If the Force stayed on the same heading, he was optimistic they would locate where the creatures had their base of operations.

"Look!" Havoc declared, and pointed.

The Warrior spotted them. Five toads were frantically speeding to the southeast, away from the bat-men, fleeing for their lives without a backward glance. He watched them bound into the darkness, then motioned for his men to bear to the south.

To the west, scarcely visible in the faint light, the winged creatures were still gathering toads.

Blade observed the bizarre hunt warily, puzzled that none of the other bat-men broke off the chase to come after the Force. Was food so critical to the creatures that they would rather grab a hundred toads instead of five humans? Or was there a more sinister motive. Did the bat-men feel confident they could capture the Force any time, but desired to catch the toads before the amphibians took refuge in their burrows? The implications bothered him, but there was no turning back.

No matter what.

Blade led his team ever deeper into the Dead Zone, and they covered over a mile in somber silence except for the beating of shod hoofs. He noticed with mounting interest the dot on the horizon, a dot which grew quickly in scope and breadth, acquiring monumental proportions. Initially he surmised the dot might be a hill, then a solitary mountain peak, but when the true width and height became apparent he concluded he was gazing at a towering cliff, an escarpment of staggering dimensions.

"What's that up ahead, dude?" Lobo inquired.

"A cliff," Blade replied.

"I don't like the looks of it."

"Neither do I," the Warrior admitted.

"There is an aura of evil about that place," Sparrow Hawk mentioned gravely. "Even from here I can feel the emanations."

"Aura?" Lobo said, and snickered. "Emanations? Are you for real? It just looks ugly, is all."

"My people believe there are spirits in the forces of

Nature, and that other spirits dwell in animals and objects like trees and rocks. To us, the natural world is alive with a life all its own, both a life we can see with our eyes and a life invisible to our senses," Sparrow explained.

"You don't really believe that garbage, do you?"

The Flathead glanced at the Clansman. "To my people, to our ancestors and the people from many other tribes, such beliefs aren't garbage. We know what we know."

"You don't really expect me to fall for such bull?"

"No, I wouldn't expect a man who hasn't learned to know his own spirit to be aware of others."

"Was that a crack?"

"I'm simply pointing out that certain places are special. Some are good and bring only fortune. Others are wicked and reek of evil." Sparrow nodded toward the escarpment. "I feel much evil emanating from that place."

"You're a few bricks shy of a load," Lobo said. "You know what I mean?"

Sparrow sighed. "White men have never understood the beliefs of my people. Why should you be any different? But I know my words are true. I went through the Sun Dance and I have my own guardian spirit."

"Say what?"

Blade, who had been listening to the exchange while scanning the landscape, looked at the Flathead. "You went through the Sun Dance?"

Sparrow nodded and stared at the giant. "You know what it is?"

"I have an Indian friend by the name of Geronimo. He's a Warrior, like me. Thanks to him, I know more about Indian customs and beliefs than I would otherwise. I know, for instance, the Sun Dance is one of your most sacred ceremonies. It's usually held in the summer, I believe, and the object is for those who take part to dance around a scared pole until they have a vision."

The Flathead nodded, impressed by the giant's knowledge. "Yes. I took part in the Sun Dance four years ago. For four days I danced around the pole of life, four days without food or drink, four days in the blistering heat. I thought I would die.'' He chuckled. ''But I went into a trance and saw my vision.''

''What did you see?'' Blade inquired out of curiosity.

''A supernatural being of light, blue light, with three blue halos above his head and eyes the color of fire.''

Lobo laughed.

''I asked the being if there was a sacred object I should have to make my medicine bundle,'' Sparrow went on, ignoring the Clansman. ''But the being of blue light told me I needed no sacred object. He placed a part of himself, a blue circle of light, inside my head and told me that it was to be my guide and protector. When I'm in trouble, I need only call on the blue light inside my head and I'll be delivered.''

''What a dork!'' Lobo declared. ''Do all Indians believe in such fairy tales?''

''Lobo?'' Blade said.

''Yeah?''

''Shut your face.''

''What did I do?''

''If you want to make fun of Sparrow's beliefs, do it on your own time. There's no reason you should inflict your ignorance on the rest of us.''

Lobo did a double take. ''Ignorance? Are you tellin' me you believe that crap?''

''I've learned to be open to the spiritual experiences of others,'' Blade stated. ''We can't measure reality by the boundaries of our own minds.''

''There you go again. Gettin' weird on me.''

Blade smiled and rode onward, staring at the cliff and searching the heavens for signs of the bat-men. Strangely, the Dead Zone was tranquil. Even the breeze had stopped.

''You know, maybe we should call a halt and wait for Kilrane and the rest of the cowboys to get here,'' Lobo suggested.

"Why?" Blade queried.

Lobo gazed at the escarpment. "You heard Sparrow. He's pickin' up evil vibes."

"I thought you didn't believe in such nonsense."

"I don't," Lobo declared. "But I've got this motto I live by, and my motto has pulled my fat out of the fire more times than I care to remember."

"What motto?"

"Better safe than sorry."

"We keep going."

The Clansman frowned. "What's the big rush, dude?"

"Raphaela, remember? And we still haven't seen any sign of Jag."

"He's probably already saved her butt and both of them are back at the farm, waitin' for us."

"Wishful thinking," Blade commented.

Lobo looked at the stars. "No one ever told me I'd be takin' on man-eating bats when I joined this outfit."

"We take our enemies as they come along," Blade said. "A week from now we could face bloodsucking worms."

"You're kiddin' me, right?"

"You never know," Blade replied, and smiled enigmatically.

For 15 minutes the Force drew ever nearer to the rearing escarpment. Low clouds floated overhead. The stillness became almost palpable, an oppressive, invisible veil smothering the alien wasteland.

"I *really* don't like this," Lobo muttered.

"Do you want me to ride on ahead and scout the cliff?" Captain Havoc inquired.

"No. We'll stick together," Blade answered.

Lobo straightened in his saddle. "Hey, dude. I could ride back and find Kilrane."

"No."

"You're a real grump, you know that?"

The Warrior absently nodded and fingered the reins in his left hand, bothered by the silence. Logic dictated there should be bat-men in the vicinity of the escarpment. As the highest promontory in the Dead Zone—maybe the only promontory in the Dead Zone—the rocky precipice was an ideal site from which to view the region for miles around, the perfect place for a base.

So where were the creatures?

Blade spotted inky openings in the cliff face and his brow knit in perplexity. Caves. There were scores of caves dotting the palisade, and caves were ideally suited as a habitation for bats.

And bat-men.

But why did the caves appear to be deserted? He reached back to rub his neck and relieve a trifling stiffness, and for a second he closed his eyes.

"Blade!" Captain Havoc shouted in alarm.

The Warrior's gray eyes flicked open, and kept opening in consternation as he beheld a seething stream of winged mutations pouring from the escarpment, from every cave in the cliff, angling down in collective might toward the Freedom Force.

CHAPTER FOURTEEN

"**A**re you ready?" Raphaela whispered.

"As ready as I'll ever be," Gary Norman replied.

"This is crazy," Bill Shertzer remarked nervously. "It'll never work."

"Do you have any better ideas?" Raphaela demanded.

"No."

"Then quit griping and do your part."

Shertzer frowned. "Don't worry about me. I'll do my part. I want out of this stinking hole more than you do."

Raphaela stared at the deep shadows on the right side of the pit. Jag and the five other prisoners were well concealed. With a little luck the mutations wouldn't awaken to the deception until too late.

"I wish I had a weapon," Norman mentioned.

"Don't we all," Raphaela said. The three of them were standing in the center of the floor. She gazed up at the rim, took a deep breath, and held her arms out. "Here."

Norman and Shertzer each seized a wrist and pretended to be pulling her in opposite directions.

"Here goes nothing," Raphaela stated, and yelled as stridently as she could. "Take your hands off me!"

"Louder!" Shertzer urged.

"Leave me alone!" Raphaela cried. She screamed until her throat hurt, her eyes on the top of the pit, waiting apprehensively for the bat-men to appear.

"Still nothing," Norman stated irately. "Try again!"

Raphaela nodded and voiced a shriek that would have done justice to a woman being torn apart by ravenous mutates. She shrieked long and hard, until her face turned red, and she had just ran out of breath when one of the creatures fluttered into view.

"Keep going!" Shertzer declared, and tugged on her left wrist with more intensity than he should have properly used. "It's working!"

Opening her mouth wide, Raphaela screamed once more. Now everything hinged on the bat-men. Would the creatures take steps to prevent one of their captives from being harmed, or couldn't the things care less? If Jag was right, if the bat-men wouldn't let one of their precious delicacies be damaged, then something should happen, and soon.

Something did.

Three more creatures materialized at the rim, hovering a few feet in the air and chattering excitedly.

For good measure Raphaela screeched again.

That did the trick.

The four hairy forms sank toward the pit floor, their wings beating slowly, spaced close together in the center just like the last time.

Shertzer voiced an insane cackle. "They're falling for it! The bastards are falling for it!"

"Stay calm," Norman advised.

Raphaela pulled on her arms, feigning a violent struggle while surreptitiously watching the winged quartet drop lower and lower. They were certainly taking their sweet time about coming to her aid.

"Get ready!" Shertzer hissed to Norman.

"Wait for the hybrid's signal," Norman advised sternly.

"Yeah, yeah, yeah," Shertzer said, pulling on the Molewoman's wrist.

Raphaela didn't like the wild gleam in the burly man's brown eyes. Even in the subdued lighting she could tell his features were flushed with excitement, and his palms were sweating profusely where they touched her skin. "Stay calm!" she whispered.

"Yeah, right!" Shertzer declared, openly staring at the bat-men when he should have been ignoring them.

"You'll ruin it for all of us!" Norman exclaimed.

The four creatures were only ten feet above them.

"Now!" Raphaela said, sticking to the plan despite Shertzer's erratic behavior. She sank to her knees.

Shertzer and Norman both leaned over her.

Would the ruse work? Raphaela wondered breathlessly. They were forcing the bat-men to descend as low as possible; the lower, the better. For the plan to succeed, the things must all be within arm's reach. To her supreme joy, the creatures took the bait.

Intent on stopping the presumed fight, their wings swishing back and forth, the quartet alighted in a ring around the two men and woman. One of the bat-men placed its hand on the burly prisoner's shoulder.

"Get them!" Shertzer bellowed prematurely. He foolishly released Raphaela, spun, and lunged at the bat-men, wrapping his arms around its waist.

"Damn him!" Norman snapped, and threw himself at another mutation.

Raphaela felt the same way, but she suppressed her anger at Shertzer's stupidity and made a dive at a third creature, looping her arms about its ankles.

The fourth bat-man began to rise.

"Jag!" Raphaela yelled, knowing the things would break free and escape in seconds, dashing the chance at freedom on the bitter rocks of one man's selfishness. She strained with all of her strength as the creature she held started to flap upward. "Jag!"

And suddenly the hybrid and the five other captives were

there, each clasping a bat-man as the things became airborne.

Jag went after the fourth creature, the one that had risen the highest, at least eight feet from the floor. His sinewy muscles uncoiling like steel springs, Jag vaulted and caught the bat-man just under the left arm. His nails tore into the mutation's chest, digging deep, and he held on as the thing beat him on the head and shoulders in a frenzied effort to dislodge him.

The other captives were doing the same, desperation lending strength to their limbs and resolve to their efforts. They seized hold of the creatures and held fast.

Jag could feel the fourth creature rising. Would the thing take him all the way to the rim in its frantic effort to get away, or would it resist and try to dislodge him? His insane scheme called for the prisoners to break out of the pit and take shelter in the depths of the cavern. After that, slipping out to find the Force and the Cavalry would be the next step provided they lived long enough. He glanced down to see how the others were faring.

Shertzer, two men, and one of the women were all clinging to the same mutation, weighing the bat-man down to the point it could barely get off the ground. Snarling furiously, the thing struck at them and endeavored to shake them off.

Gary Norman and one woman were holding fast to another creature despite its best efforts to beat them into submission.

And Raphaela and the last woman had the third bat-man by the legs. The monstrosity had risen a couple of feet and now hovered while swatting at their heads.

Even as he watched, Jag saw the third bat-man pound the woman's head so hard she went abruptly limp and slumped to the pit floor, which left Raphaela to occupy its bestial attention. He saw the thing hit Raphaela three times in swift succession and she sagged against its legs.

Damn!

Why hadn't they stuck to his plan? No more than three prisoners per mutation, if possible! An even distribution, he'd told them! Enough to subdue each creature but not so many they couldn't fly! Those had been his instructions, but of course Shertzer and some of the others hadn't paid any attention. And now their stupidity threatened to jeopardize their success. Jag simmered.

Raphaela, hit again, was losing her grip.

Jaguarundi wasn't about to leave without her. The creature he held still hovered eight feet from the bottom. His own legs were only six feet from the floor and two feet to the Molewoman's right, and the proximity suggested a mad scheme that could extricate them both. "Raphaela!" he shouted above the din of combat.

Seemingly dazed, Raphaela looked around while clutching the third bat-man's legs.

"Raphaela!" Jag repeated, ignoring the blows delivered to his body.

Her red hair bobbed as the Molewoman glanced upward and spied him.

"When I give the word, let go of that thing and grab my legs!" Jag directed.

Raphaela's eyes narrowed and she shook her head, signifying she hadn't understood.

"When I say the word, let go of him and take hold of my legs!" Jag reiterated, hoping she could understand his words. The other prisoners and creatures were creating a racket as they battled, bellowing and screaming and growling.

Finally Raphaela nodded. She ducked a fist aimed at her cheek, her gaze riveted on the hybrid.

There was no time to lose.

"Now!" Jag cried, and saw her release the third creature. Instantly the thing shot into the air, heading for the rim. As it streaked past him, the breeze from its heaving wings brushing the fur on his face, he let go of the bat-man he was holding and started to fall.

The fourth mutation began to fly upward.

Jag had to execute his move perfectly. He had to allow his legs to drop within Raphaela's reach while simultaneously seizing the departing bat-man's ankles. His hands flicked out, he dug his nails into the creature just above its feet, and as he squeezed with all his strength he felt arms clamp on his own legs. With the next heartbeat he was drawn swiftly upward, and as he went he drew Raphaela along with him.

The fight still raged on the pit floor.

Jag stared at the rim, his body as tense as an iron wall. Could the bat-man support so much additional weight? Would it clear the edge or fall back and doom them to await their horrid fate? He heard the flap-flap-flap as the creature struggled to gain altitude, and for several heart-stopping moments failure seemed certain. They began to sink down again.

"No!" Raphaela shouted.

Down below a woman vented a terrified shriek.

Jaguarundi snarled and gave the bat-man added incentive to reach the top. He dug his nails into the mutation's ankles until he scraped bone.

The creature threw back its head, yelped, and sped for the edge with all the speed it could muster, its wings beating madly.

Raphaela gasped as the movement caused her hands to slip half an inch.

For Jag, the next several seconds seemed to stretch into an eternity. The rim seemed to draw nearer by minute degrees. Raphaela's arms were creeping down his legs, and in another minute or two she would slip off entirely and plummet to the floor almost 40 feet below. They needed to reach a firm footing quickly.

The creature's head rose about the rim.

"Hang on!" Jag yelled.

"I'm trying!"

Its wings beating in a continuous motion, the bat-man rose steadily higher. Its shoulders cleared the pit, then its abdomen.

Jag glanced to his left at a flat stretch of cave floor dimly illuminated by the moonlight streaming in the hole in the roof. He had to reach firm ground before reinforcements swarmed in to knock him off the mutation.

The bat-man's feet ascended out of the pit.

If Jag had been by himself, he would have lunged for the side and clambered to safety. But with Raphaela hanging from his legs he had to wait until just the right moment. In his mind he roared at the bat-man. Keep going! Keep going!

In the pit a man cursed and raved.

Jag's head, shoulders, and chest emerged, dangling from the mutation, less than 18 inches from the rim. His nerves were aflame with impatience. Under him Raphaela continued to lose her hold little by little.

Something moved above the cave floor.

His eyes registered the rhythmic sweep of leathery wings and Jag spotted a bat-man rushing toward him out of the gloom. Its intention was transparent. The thing planned to batter him from his perch and send him back into the pit where he belonged. His knees were now above the edge, but it wasn't enough.

This new menace swept toward the cat-man like an enormous bird of prey.

Jag guessed the thing would try to ram him with its fists. He deliberately held his body out several inches from the bat-man to which he clung, presenting an excellent target, wanting the onrushing creature to believe it couldn't miss. He waited until the very last instant, gazing to one side as if he didn't know the thing was hurling toward him.

The attacking bat-man twisted its body and extended both fists as it closed the final few feet.

His sinews rippling, Jag jerked his body to the right, gritting his teeth against the strain of bearing Raphaela's weight. Knuckles brushed his left temple, and then the attacker had swept past and was arching high for another run. Jag sensed that the mutation supporting both Raphaela and him had intentionally slowed, probably with the intention of giving the attacker a second try. He wasn't about to let that scheme bear fruit. Without evincing any inkling of his aim, he suddenly pressed against the creature's left leg and sank his tapered teeth into its shin.

In a flash the mutation soared another seven feet higher, screeching in torment.

Jag didn't waste a second. He swung his body like a pendulum, back to front, not once but twice, swinging wider on each try, carrying Raphaela with him, and on the third swing he whipped her toward the floor of the cave bordering the pit. He also let go. The cool air in his eyes and the hard ground giving the impression of leaping up to meet them of its own accord brought a knot to his stomach and a lump in his throat.

Raphaela came down first within half a foot of the edge, landing on her knees and sprawling forward.

For a fleeting instant Jag thought he might pitch back into the pit. He dived headfirst for the stone floor and felt Raphaela's arms slide from his legs. Only five feet separated his head from the ground, but it was enough space for him to tuck his chin into his chest, draw his legs up, and flip. His calloused pads smacked down, stinging his feet, but he disregarded the pain in his joy at being free. A short-lived joy.

Raphaela rose awkwardly and swayed near the rim, not in full control of her faculties yet. "Jag!" she cried.

He spun, his feline form a blur, and grabbed her by the shoulders. "I've got you. We're safe."

"Are we?" Raphaela responded, and nodded at the cavern ceiling.

Jag glanced up. After hearing there were hundreds of the creatures, he expected to find the air filled with wings and enraged yowls and barks. To his amazement, there were only two bat-men in sight, circling high above the pit.

The cavern appeared to be deserted otherwise.

"Where are the bat-men?" Rapahela asked in astonishment.

"I have no idea," Jag said, watching the duo overhead.

"I saw them. They were all over the place."

"They're gone now," Jag stated absently.

An injured mutation, its right wing somewhat crumpled, flapped out of the pit and climbed to join its comrades.

"Gary and the others!" Raphaela exclaimed, and dashed to the rim.

Jag warily went along to guard her, his gaze constantly roving to the three bat-men in the air.

Only one creature remained in the pit, and it wouldn't be flying ever again. Two men and one woman were lying on the ground, their faces covered with blood. The rest stood around the dead bat-man, gloating, having overwhelmed their warder by sheer force of numbers and beaten it to death with their bare hands. Bill Shertzer kicked the thing once more for good measure.

Raphaela stared at the two dead captives and recognized one of the casualties. "Oh, not! Not Gary!"

"The fools should have tried to escape instead of taking their revenge," Jag snapped.

"We've got to get them out."

"How? We don't have a rope."

"We've got to try," Raphaela insisted.

Jag pointed at the three bat-men. "We have a bigger problem to worry about."

The creatures were flying near the huge opening in the cavern roof. They unexpectedly angled up and vanished in the night.

"Where are they going?" Raphaela blurted.

"How should I know? Probably to get help."

Raphaela gazed at the gigantic cavern, her nostrils crinkling at the reeking odor of what must be tons of defecation.

"We can't look a gift horse in the mouth," Jag said. "With all the creatures gone, this may be the only chance we'll get to escape."

"But what about *them*?" Raphaela protested, pointing at the pit.

"We'll come back for them," Jag assured her. "First we have to find Blade."

"I don't know," Raphaela said uncertainly, reluctant to leave the captives.

And then they both heard the sounds that made her reservations moot. From somewhere outside, from relatively close at hand, came the sharp retorts of automatic-weapons fire, and mingled in with the lighter chattering of M-16's was the distinctive thundering of a machine gun both Raphaela and Jag had heard in operation many times: the trademark metallic roar of Blade's M60.

CHAPTER FIFTEEN

Kilrane was a man enraged.

He rode at the head of the column of Cavalrymen, his right hand resting on his hip next to the Mitchell Single Action revolver. Behind him were his two lieutenants, Armitage and Treon. Neither spoke a word to him. They knew better than to bother him when he was in one of his infrequent moods. And he was furious.

What a jerk!

How could he have let himself be taken by surprise like that? The statistics ran through his mind again and again. Four dead. Seven wounded. And 26 missing.

Twenty-six!

He fumed, clenching the reins so tightly his knuckles paled. Those flying freaks had gotten in the first lick, but he wasn't through with them by a long shot. Counting the wounded, he still had 70 prime fighting men behind him, 70 men armed with repeating rifles and revolvers, 70 men who were among the best marksmen in the Dakota Territory. He couldn't wait until they tangled with the bat-men again.

Come and get it, you bastards!

Kilrane smiled grimly, surveying the heavens. The first

time those creatures had taken him by surprise. It wouldn't happen again. He didn't care how many bat-men were in the Dead Zone. By the time the Cavalry was done, there wouldn't be a single monstrosity left alive. He glanced over his shoulder at his lieutenants. "Did you pass my instructions along to the men?"

"Of course," Armitage answered. He was the older of the pair, a seasoned gun-hand who had made his living as a rancher before being approached by Kilrane to join the detachment.

"They know what to do," Treon added confidently. He had only served for nine months, but had risen through the ranks swiftly, a testimony to his superior skill and unusual maturity.

"They'd better," Kilrane said flatly. "We were lucky once because those things were trying to take us alive. We might not be so lucky the next time."

"Your plan will work," Treon predicted.

"It better," Kilrane noted.

"I'm surprised we haven't seen hide nor hair of Blade and his people," Armitage commented. "We've been riding pretty hard."

"Maybe the Force was captured," Treon speculated.

"I doubt it," Kilrane said.

"Why's that?" Treon inquired.

"For one thing, Blade isn't the type to get captured easily. You don't know him like I do."

"Is he really as good as they claim he is?" Treon asked.

"He's better."

"Well, I guess when someone is as big as him, with all those muscles, they're just naturally a tough mother."

Kilrane glanced at his youngest lieutenant. "Don't you believe it. Blade got where he is today through hard work and dedication. He spent countless hours exercising to develop that physique of his. He's the toughest hombre on the planet simply because he's Blade."

"He'd make a great Cavalryman," Treon stated.

"Oh, I don't know," Armitage said, grinning. "We wouldn't want a wimp like him in our Territory."

Kilrane smiled for the first time in hours. The smile abruptly faded, though, when he beheld two riders racing toward the column from the southwest. His scouts.

"Here comes Russell and Leonard," Treon said.

"Halt the column," Kilrane directed, and reined up. He watched thin spirals of dust rise into the atmosphere behind the pair of galloping horses, the minute particles opaque in the moonlight. His lieutenants were calling out for the detachment to stop and the word was being passed rapidly down the line.

Within 60 seconds the two scouts drew up. One of them, a lanky, bearded man in buckskins, started right in. "We've found a party of bat-men about a mile ahead. Lots of the critters."

"Did they spot you?"

"Nope. They were too busy."

"Doing what?"

Russell and Leonard exchanged glances.

"You won't believe it," the former said.

"Try me," Kilrane stated impatiently.

"They were beating giant toads to death."

"What?"

"I told you that you wouldn't believe me. We came across about thirty-six of the things gathering big old toads. They'd already caught a whole bunch of the varmints when we spotted them. We crawled as close as we dared and took a look-see. The bat-men were bashing the toads on the ground, splitting the skulls open, then tucking a bunch of the bloody critters under their arms and taking off," Russell detailed.

"I ain't never seen the like," Leonard chimed in. "They had rounded up bunches of those toads before we got there. They'd just hold those toads by the back legs and beat them silly. Some of the toads tried to fight back, but there wasn't much they could do. I saw one of the bat-men get bit, but it didn't faze him none."

"Are some of the bat-men still there?" Kilrane inquired.

"About two dozen, I reckon," Leonard answered.

"Good," Kilrane said grimly. He turned to his lieutenants. "You know the drill. Get hopping."

Armitage and Treon both nodded and went about their business. Both men wheeled their mounts. Treon nodded at the right-hand row, then led them to the east at a 90-degree angle. In due course they had formed a line from west to east, each Cavalryman sitting attentively on his horse.

"Your turn," Kilrane told Armitage.

The older lieutenant gestured at the left-hand row, and in unison they repeated the maneuver performed by Treon's men, cutting to the east and forming a straight line, positioning themselves directly in front of Treon and Company.

Kilrane inspected the disposition of his detachment with satisfaction. Now he had two row of riders extending from east to west, facing the enemy, ready to ride with the wind. He grinned as he rode to a position ten feet in front of the first line, halfway down the row. He turned the palomino toward his men and drew his rifle from its scabbard.

The seventy were waiting expectantly.

"Men of the Cavalry!" Kilrane said to them proudly. "We are about to engage the latest threat to the safety of the Federation. These bat-men made the mistake of taking us on first, and now none of the other Federation factions will have an opportunity to confront them."

Some of the men laughed.

"Seriously, all of us know what's at stake here tonight. Who knows how many innocent lives have been snuffed out by these abominations! Hundreds, at least. *Tonight the killing ends*!"

The riders were all abruptly somber.

"This threat has hit home because it's sprung up within our own borders. We have a responsibility to ensure the horror doesn't spread," Kilrane declared, and looked both ways, eyeing his men affectionately. "The smart thing to do would be to return to Rapid City and send a call out for reinforcements. We're outnumbered. Those things can fly, we can't. They have the advantage because they know this area, we don't." He paused. "But since when has being outnumbered or at a disadvantage stopped the Cavalry? The best of the best. And I say we can teach these scum-sucking genetic misfits what happens to those who attack the Cavalry! I say we pay them back in kind for all the lives they've taken! What do you say?"

For several seconds silence greeted the question, until Armitage raised his right arm aloft and cried out, "Yes! Yes! Yes!" in moments all of the Cavalrymen had adopted the refrain and their shouts rose in a challenging din intended for the ears of the grotesque denizens of the Dead Zone.

Kilrane grinned and nodded. They were as ready as they would ever be. He held up the rifle and the riders promptly quieted. "To victory or death!" he shouted, and spun the palomino. He headed to the southwest, the two scouts falling in alongside him.

"The ones we saw are straight ahead," Russell said.

Nodding, Kilrane adjusted his grip on the Winchester. After so many months of sitting behind a desk at Pierre, dealing with the thousand and one petty administrative problems that governing the Dakota Territory entailed, he savored this chance to be in action again. Gone were the carefree days when he could roam the plains at his leisure. Now thousands of people relied on his judgment and stability to guide them through every crisis, and he had discovered he was tied down to the capital as effectively as if he were a prized steer under lock and key in a barn.

This was a rare treat.

Kilrane thought of Blade. He envied the Warrior, envied Blade's freedom. As the top Warrior and head of the Force, Blade got to travel to any point in the Federation, or outside of it if necessary, to quell problems as they developed. The giant wasn't tied down to one particular spot. He would gladly trade boots with Blade in an instant. Ironically, he knew the Warrior disliked all the travel and would rather spend his time at the Home. Too bad their situations weren't reversed.

"Here they come," Leonard declared.

Surprised by the intrusion into his reverie, Kilrane looked up. He'd lost all track of time. "What?" he said absently.

Leonard pointed at the sky to the south. "They must have heard all that shouting we did. Here they come."

Kilrane saw them. Dozens of bat-men winging in a beeline for his detachment. Now he could test his strategy. "Detachment, halt!" he shouted.

The twin rows of Cavalrymen drew to a stop.

"Rifles, out!" Kilrane commanded as he turned the palomino sideways.

Out came 70 rifles, each held in the at-ready position.

"Chamber and shoulder, now!"

Seventy levers were worked, 70 stocks pressed to waiting shoulders.

Kilrane glanced at the bat-men. During the last battle those things had dropped among the horses, spooking the mounts. Now those creatures were about to learn that Cavalry mounts were the best-trained steeds in the world. Sure, flying mutations might throw a scare into them, but every one of the horses had been trained to take the booming of gunfire in stride. "Detachment, aim!" he bellowed.

Their wings beating powerfully, 36 bat-men swooped out of the night. They were 100 yards from the humans.

"First rank, on my order you will fire!" Kilrane directed, watching the mutations, measuring the distance. The things were so confident in their ability that they weren't even trying to take cover or evasive action.

Good!

Kilrane elevated his left arm. His 26 missing men came to mind and he scowled. Time to even the score. At a range of 70 yards his skin began to tingle. At 40 yards he laughed harshly. And at 20 yards he gave the signal every Cavalryman awaited. "First rank, fire!"

Thirty-five rifles cracked simultaneously.

"Second rank, fire!" Kilrane commanded.

The second row fired on cue, giving the first row time to feed another round in the chamber and take aim on a new target.

"First rank, fire!"

Once more the marksmen cut loose.

Kilrane still wasn't through. "Second rank, fire!"

For the fourth time dozens of rifles rent the air with their crashing discharge.

"Cease firing!" Kilrane yelled, waving his Winchester. He gazed at the barren stretch ahead and nearly whooped for joy.

Not one of the bat-men had managed to get closer than ten yards to the Cavalrymen. Hairy forms littered the ground, many groaning, their wings and limbs twitching or moving feebly. Puddles of blood seeped into the sterile soil.

"Chalk one up for us," Kilrane stated. "Armitage! Take ten men and finish the bastards off!"

The lieutenant promptly obeyed.

"What's next?" Russell inquired.

The Cavalry leader stared to the southwest, his features hardening in remorseless determination. "What do you think is next? It's them or us. No quarter. No mercy. We fight to the death."

Russell looked at the other scout and grinned. "I'm fixing to stuff one of those buggers and mount it in the family room. How about you?"

CHAPTER SIXTEEN

"**T**here's zillions of 'em!" Lobo exclaimed.

Blade scanned the surrounding landscape, seeking cover, a refuge of any kind, and 30 feet off to the west lay a depression of some sort, a bowl-shaped area. "On me!" he shouted, and raced toward it.

Hundreds of bat-creatures had emerged from the caves marking the looming face of the escarpment. They were flying in a packed formation 20 yards wide and 300 feet long. Leading them, several yards in front of the pack, was an enormous bat-man with a 15-foot wingspan. The mutations arced down at the Force, then leveled off at an altitude of 50 feet and circled above the five men in a wide loop, voicing their distinctive cries the whole time.

Lashing the reins, Blade reached the depression first and plunged over the edge. The dimensions of the bowl were barely adequate for defensive purposes. Twenty-five feet in diameter and only four feet deep, the circular bank sloped sharply to the dusty floor. He absorbed the shock as the gelding came down on all fours and goaded the horse to the middle of the bowl. In a flash he dismounted and hastened to the side of the depression as the others imitated his example.

"Why didn't we haul ass?" Lobo asked anxiously, resting his left knee on the bank.

"How far do you think we would have gotten?" Blade responded. He glanced at the horses, huddled in the center, then at his team. "Fan out around the rim. We'll take them as they come."

Havoc nodded and moved to the right. Doc and Sparrow went to the left. Lobo stayed where he was.

"Didn't you hear me?" Blade asked.

"Yeah," the Clansman replied inattentively. He gazed at the circling creatures in awed fascination. "We don't stand a snowball's chance in hell. You know that, don't you?"

"I know nothing of the kind," Blade stated. "We're still alive. We can fight."

Lobo jerked his left thumb toward the mutations. "Fight all of them? Give me a break, dude!"

"When we get back to L.A. we're going to have a long talk about your attitude," Blade said. "Now pick a spot and dig in."

"I'll dig in, all right," Lobo mumbled, walking to the right. "I'll dig all the way to freakin' China."

The leader of the bat-men suddenly whistled shrilly and the creatures stopped and hovered. Hundreds of wings beat the air, creating a subdued swishing effect. They gazed down at the bowl with a collective, malignant intensity.

"I can pick off that big one from here," Captain Havoc offered.

"Not yet," Blade said.

"No, wait for Christmas why don't you?" Lobo muttered.

"Consider yourself on report, Lobo," Blade stated without taking his eyes from the fluttering genetic deviates.

"I should live so long."

"What are those critters waiting for?" Doc Madsen wondered aloud.

"We should be thankful they are," Sparrow said.

Blade scrutinized the assembled mutations, then focused on the apparent leader. Why hadn't it given the order to attack? He saw the thing looking straight at him, and a moment later the bat-man flew slowly down toward the bowl.

"Let me blow it away!" Lobo urged.

"Not yet," Blade reiterated.

The large creature brazenly descended to within 15 feet of the Warrior and paused, its wings flapping in a leisurely fashion, a curious smirk creasing its visage.

Blade pointed the M60 at the leader but there was no reaction. The bat-man boldly stayed in position, not even flinching. It just flapped and smirked. "What do you want?" he demanded, not really anticipating an answer.

Projecting an attitude of smug superiority, the leader pointed at the Warrior, then at the ground underneath its feet.

"Damn! I think the thing is challenging you, sir!" Captain Havoc declared.

"So it would seem," Blade agreed.

"But why?" Havoc wanted to know. "Why not simply overwhelm us and be done with it?"

"I don't know," Blade admitted, studying the leader. He arrived at several conclusions. First, from the rancor reflected in the bat-man's features, he deduced the thing positively loathed all humans, probably hated them with a passion. So part of the leader's motivation was plain and obvious abhorrence. But there was more, an underlying current of condescension, as if the creature held all human beings in complete and abject contempt. The challenge, therefore, ranked as an inconsequential diversion for the mutation, a moment's sport, a way to indulge its self-proclaimed superiority while having a little fun.

"That being radiates evil," Sparrow said from his side of the bowl. "I would advise you to stay away from it."

Blade returned the creature's hostile stare, undecided. He felt an almost irresistible impulse to smash that complacent face to a pulp, to accept the gauntlet, but he suspected the challenge might also serve as a ruse and he held his tongue. Before he could make up his mind, fate intervened.

A lone bat-man streaked out of the north, venting piercing shrieks of alarm, and sped under the ring to approach the leader.

Blade saw an undercurrent of excitement ripple among the mutations. They chattered together in hushed tones and many gazed in the direction the new arrival had come from. Why were they so agitated? What was out there? Kilrane and the Cavalry perhaps?

The messenger and the leader consulted in short barks and grunts, with much gesturing on the part of the harbinger of dire tidings. Several times the huge leader stared grimly to the north. Finally the big one climbed a dozen yards and rotated, staring at all of its subjects.

"What's going down, dude?" Lobo questioned.

"Your guess is as good as mine," Blade said.

"Since when?"

In its guttural tongue, motioning emphatically to stress its points, the leader addressed the mutations. The fiery speech aroused the creatures to a fever pitch and they began snarling and yipping. After a minute of this activity, the leader waved its right arm northward while chittering like a furious squirrel. Immediately two thirds of the monstrosities flew off.

"Where are they going?" Lobo queried.

"After Kilrane would be my guess," Captain Havoc stated.

"Damn! I hope that cowboy knows what he's doing."

Blade kept his eyes on the leader, who remained stationary, watching the horde until they were out of sight. The remaining mutations closed ranks, forming a more compact ring above the bowl.

"There's less of the suckers now," Lobo mentioned. "Maybe we should get while the gettin' is good."

"Not on your life," Blade stated.

"Why not?"

"Because if those creatures did go after the Cavalry, Kilrane will have his hands full as it is. The last thing he'd need would be for us to lead even more of the creatures to him."

"That's nice. But what about us?" Lobo inquired.

"We'll stall."

"Say what?"

"We'll dig in here and keep these others occupied."

"I don't suppose you've noticed that we're outnumbered something pitiful."

"The odds were worse a minute ago," Blade pointed out, and looked at the captain. "I want to make certain these don't leave."

"How can we do that?" Havoc replied.

"I'll engage the leader one on one. You keep me covered. And the instant I win, let those things have it."

"What if you don't win, dude?" Lobo interjected.

"Then kill a few for me," Blade said, and climbed to the top of the bank. He cupped his right hand to his mouth and tilted his head back. "Hey, you! I'm waiting!"

The leader of the bat-men looked down, then went into a dive, its wings outstretched. Gliding swiftly and silently, the mutation came down within ten feet of the Warrior and alighted as gently as a feather.

"I thought you wanted to see which one of us is the best?" Blade taunted. He doubted the thing could understand English, but his tone was unmistakable. For his plan to succeed, if he wanted the head bat-man to forget all about Kilrane for the time being, he needed to anger it, to get the creature too mad to think straight.

Frowning, the gigantic deviate extended its right arm and indicated the M60.

Blade grinned. "No, it wouldn't be very sporting to use this, would it?" He lowered the machine gun to the turf, then straightened. The ammo belts, he decided, stayed on despite their weight. So did the knives. He never took the

Bowies off unless he was in his cabin at the Home, and even then only for certain occasions.

"Go get him, sir," Captain Havoc said.

"Yeah. Waste the chump," Lobo added.

"Stay frosty," Blade instructed them. He took two strides, warily regarding his foe, noting they were about evenly matched in size and stature. How could he hope to overcome the creature's great strength and pantherish reflexes? A frontal assault seemed ludicrous, yet he tried one anyway to test the bat-man's reaction. Whipping his brawny arms up, he lunged.

Displaying consummate skill, pushing into the air with barely a quiver of its leg muscles, the leader arched over the Warrior's head, just out of reach, and performed an acrobatic flip in midair. It landed upright five feet away, turning as it did to fix a mocking stare on its adversary.

Blade spun and smiled. "Neat trick," he said, and stepped to the right, circling. He suspected the mutation intended to play with him for a while, so why not accommodate the deviate and draw out the fight? Again he lunged, but not quite as fast as he could, and once more the bat-man soared overhead and dropped to the ground behind him.

The hovering spectators erupted in yips and high-pitched titters.

It must be nice to have your own cheering gallery! Blade thought, and darted at the bat-man with predictable results. He whirled and pretended to be mulling over his options while the creature watched him with evident disdain.

As if to accentuate its scorn, the leader stretched.

Blade couldn't resist the temptation. He pounced, and this time he grabbed the mutation's ankles and wrenched before it could gain altitude, pulling its abdomen down within reach of his fists. Flicking a one-two combination, he drove his knuckles into the bat-man's stomach and doubled it over. Then, sweeping his right arm down and around, he delivered a powerhouse uppercut to the tip of the leader's chin.

The bat-man was catapulted rearward by the blow, its wings fluttering as it attempted to right itself, and crashed onto its stomach. Hissing like an incensed serpent, the creature stood and glared at the Warrior. Blood trickled from the right corner of its mouth.

"Where's your smug look now?" Blade said, baiting it.

The leader snarled and launched itself in a flying tackle, covering the yards between them incredibly fast. Its rippling arms coiled about the Warrior's waist and they both went down.

Talons tore into Blade's sides, ripping his black leather vest, and he arched his back and drove his right knee into the creature's groin. The action was instinctive, the result rewarding.

Gurgling in agony, the bat-man went airborne, clutching its privates as it rose.

Blade started to stand, wincing at the pain in his sides, feeling a sticky substance caking his skin under the vest. He looked down at himself, mistakenly believing the bat-man was temporarily out of commission.

No such luck.

The creature screeched and dove, feet first, and rammed into the Warrior's head. The impact would have flattened a buffalo.

Blade was knocked onto his back. The universe danced and swirled. The cosmos appeared to have been shaken to its very foundation. He struggled to regain his perception, vigorously shaking his head, and realized he was too late when immensely strong hands clamped onto the front of his vest and he was rudely hauled from the earth. Even in his dazed state the gravity of the situation sparked a flicker of apprehension. The creature was carrying him into the sky!

"Blade!" someone shouted. The voice sounded like Sparrow's.

A rush of cool air brought the Warrior back to reality. He grabbed at the thing's wrists and blinked in amazement at finding them nose to nose.

The bat-man grinned, then let go.

Blade tried to hold on, but the creature's hair was too slick. He fell like a rock, his arms flailing the air, and envisioned his legs being crushed to splinters. The landing jolted his bones and caused his teeth to gnash together, and he pitched forward recognizing that the thing had been toying with him. It had taken him about ten or 15 feet up, not high enough to kill but a sufficient height to rattle him.

There was no respite. Blade surged to his knees, still game, when the creature gripped him from the rear, under the arms, and swept him from the ground once again. He expected to be conveyed to a great altitude. Instead, the mutation took him up 20 feet and released him.

The earth leaped up to make contact.

Blade's legs took the brunt of the fall. He threw himself to the right as his boots thudded into the soil, grimacing at the spasms provoked, and smacked onto his elbows and knees. Apparently the mutation planned to take him higher each time and eventually finish him off. A slow, lingering, terror-filled death.

The Warrior had other ideas.

Blade frantically flipped to the left and continued to turn. A foot or a hand gouged into his right shoulder but couldn't slow him. He turned and turned until he'd traversed a dozen yards, then leaped to his feet, in a crouch, his hands held out from his waist.

Growling deep in its throat, the bat-man knifed out of the darkness.

Not this time! Blade thought, and sidestepped to the right, pivoting and lashing out with his right foot. The kick struck the bat-man on the ribs just as the creature flew past and sent it into a short spiral headfirst into the ground.

Someone cheered.

The Warrior took three paces and leaped, his arms outflung. He slammed into the bat-man as the leader was rising, his arms going around its hips, and they both tumbled.

A bellow of rage burst from the huge bat-man and it twisted in the Warrior's arms.

Suddenly Blade found himself holding a tornado, a slashing, biting, snapping whirlwind intent on tearing his throat wide open. He jabbed his right elbow under its chin to ward off those glistening teeth, then stiffened when the mutation gouged its talons into his exposed arm. His left palm whipped up and across the creature's face, pulverizing its nostrils.

Which produced an unforeseen result.

The bat-man went berserk.

CHAPTER SEVENTEEN

Any shred of self-control the creature possessed evaporated in a twinkling, and venting a roar of primal blood lust, it tried to knee the Warrior in the crotch even as it jerked its head free and sank its teeth into the forearm that had been restraining its chin.

Exquisite agony lanched along Blade's arm as those razor tips sheared deep into his flesh. He attempted to pull his right arm loose, but the mutation held fast, growling all the while, blood spilling over its lips. He felt an arm loop about his waist and he started to rise. The thing was taking him into the air again!

Not this time.

So far Blade had restricted himself to the use of his hands and feet. Not once had he touched his knives, and in the heat of savage combat it was likely that his foe had forgotten all about them. Blade corrected its glaring oversight the next instant when he whipped the left Bowie from its sheath and plunged the steel blade into the bat-man's chest all the way to the hilt.

The creature opened it maw to voice a strangled screech, letting go of the Warrior's arm in the bargain, then shoved as it twisted and sped upward.

The Bowie slid out, and Blade fell a mere four feet to the earth, landing on the balls of his feet, poised for the next attack. He saw the bat-man flap slowly higher, clutching its side, until the mutation reached a height of 100 feet. There it paused, staring down at the Warrior, its features shrouded in shadows.

What was it up to?

Blade glanced at the bowl, 30 feet away, then back at the bat-man. The thing was gazing at the ring of deviates. In a flash of insight he perceived the next act in the tableau, and he whirled and sprinted toward the depression and the M60.

If only they'd give him time to reach it!

They didn't.

At an imperious bark from the leader, the bat-beings swooped down toward the Force.

"Open fire!" Captain Havoc bellowed.

Four M-16's cut loose, raking the creatures, and with the mutations packed so closely together every shot scored. Bat-men and bat-women shrieked and plummeted out of control. Those most eager to reach the Force were the first to die. The main body of mutations broke into two masses, with half veering to the right and half to the left to evade the hail of lethal lead. A few rash individuals speared out of the throng at the bowl and were blasted into oblivion for their effort.

Blade was still 15 feet from from the M60 when a cloud of mutations engulfed him, 11 of the creatures who dropped out of the night after detaching themselves from the main body. They were all around him in the blink of an eye, hissing and snarling and striking, and he retaliated in kind, drawing his right Bowie and wading into them with both big knives slashing in fierce abandon.

Captain Havoc saw the pack descend on the Warrior, and he automatically began to climb from the bowl so he could aid the giant. But a glance skyward showed him the two masses were attacking again, coming in from different directions. He ejected the partly spent magazine in his M-16, then slapped home a new one. "Doc and Sparrow, you take the group on the left. Lobo, you and I will take the formation on the right!" he commanded. "On three!"

The prongs speared toward the Force, diving rapidly lower.

"One," Havoc cried, fingering the trigger. "Two."

Aloof from the other mutations, the leader hovered and observed the battle, still holding its side.

"Three!" Havoc shouted, and fired. He swung the barrel back and forth in a controlled sweep, raking the creatures leading the charge, slowing the swarm as those in front crumpled and those behind collided, creating rampant confusion. The other Force members were likewise pouring it on, exacting a heavy toll among the creatures.

The tide of the conflict hung in the balance.

Blade heard the firing and wanted to help his men, but the press of mutations held him at bay. He cut and whirled and stabbed and spun, always in motion, never pausing for a breath because the slightest hesitancy would spell his doom. The creatures clawed and snatched at him, striving to grab his arms and pin them. He was lacerated again and again. Undaunted, he fought on with the grim ruthlessness of an aroused tiger. The toll he took decimated the creatures. Here he hacked off a hand, there he sliced open a neck, and again he might pierce an eyeball or gut an adversary.

Seven of the 11 littered the soil, and the four who were left suddenly took off.

Go! Blade's mind screamed, and he raced to the edge of the bowl, slipped the Bowies into their sheaths blood and all, and scooped up the M60. As he straightened he heard the strangest sound. From far off in the distance, from the north, came the strident blaring of something that sounded very much like a horn or a trumpet. The exigency of the situation denied him the luxury of indulging in speculation. He jumped into the depression, raised the M60 until the stock was tucked under his left arm, and commenced firing.

Where the M-16's perforated the mutations and left neat holes as entry points and fist-sized exit wounds, the M60 literally ripped them to ribbons. The rounds ruptured torsos and exploded craniums, shattered bones and severed arteries. Creatures fell in droves.

But it wasn't enough.

Even with the M60 and four M-16's in operation, there were too many deviates for only five men to handle. Dead mutations rained from the sky, yet still they came on.

Blade realized the things would reach the bowl, and he knew his men would be easily picked off if they remained isolated from one another. "Close up on me!" he shouted, hoping they could hear him over the bedlam. "Close up on me! Move!"

Captain Havoc and Lobo responded first, firing on the run as they hurried to his side.

"Doc! Sparrow!" Blade yelled. "Close on me!"

The gunfighter and the Flathead dashed around the huddled horses and took up positions near at hand.

"Let them have it!" Blade directed, and did so with renewed vigor. He could still hear the horn, louder now, but he dismissed the oddity from his mind and concentrated on simply staying alive.

The bat-creatures poured down in a close-knit throng.

Blade drilled deviate after deviate, the M60 thundering and bucking in his hands, but despite his blistering firepower and the deadly marksmanship of his team, the mutations reached the air space just above their heads. At such proximity, the things could pounce the moment a weapon went empty.

"Die, suckers!" Lobo cried, discarding his empty M-16 and drawing his NATO. He sank the blade into the stomach of a bat-woman and carved a five-inch incision.

Doc Madsen's M-16 went empty and was grabbed from his grasp. He resorted to his Magnum, the revolver clearing leather and booming at point-blank range into the face of a snarling bat-man.

Sparrow Hawk laid about him with his spear.

Captain Havoc was tackled by a pair of creatures and went down swinging.

All of this Blade took in at a glance, and then the M60 fell silent and he drew his Bowies once again. The blaring horn, which he had generally ignored until now, sounded much louder and a lot nearer. He thrust his left knife into a descending mutation, then rent a throat with his right blade. Talons tore his cheeks and tried to poke out his eyes.

Unexpectedly, gunfire shattered the night, repeated volleys crackling with military precision. The horn added its insistent staccato refrain.

Blade wanted to ascertain the cause of all the noise, but the press of mutations prevented him from doing anything other than preserving his own life. Fists pummeled his body, talons cut his skin, and bat-men endeavored to sink their fangs into his neck. He stabbed and cleaved as fast as targets presented themselves. Heads, hands, arms, and necks were rent asunder or impaled. Blood and gore spattered him from his hair to his combat boots. Dead or dying creatures fell one on top of another on all sides.

The volleys went on and on.

A skinny bat-man clamped its hands on the Warrior's neck from the rear and tried to crush Blade's neck. He snapped forward at the waist and flipped the creature into a bat-woman diving toward him with her arms extended and her fingers shaped into claws.

Another mutation tried to tackle him. It sprang and wrapped both arms around his shins.

Blade reversed his grip on the Bowies, swept down, and planted both knives into the creature's back between the shoulder blades. The thing sagged, its arms going limp, and he stepped clear, bringing his arms up to defend himself.

But there were no mutations to fight.

As swiftly as they had descended, the creatures were fleeing into the darkness, their wings beating frantically as they endeavored to outrun the certain death being dispensed by the two rows of remorseless riders who levered round after round into repeating rifles and fired shot after shot with unerring accuracy.

It was a virtual slaughter.

Blade simply stood there in relieved astonishment and watched Kilrane and the Cavalrymen mow the creatures down. The frontiersmen fired in volleys, first one row, then the other. A bugler inspired them with martial music the whole time.

"Awesome, dude."

The Warrior looked around at the comment. Lobo stood on the left, a ragged tear in his black leather jacket and a gash in his left cheek. Otherwise, he appeared to be unharmed. "Are you okay?"

"I am now."

Blade pivoted, elated to discover all of his men were alive. Sparrow leaned on his spear, which was imbedded in the chest of a mutation. Doc Madsen was standing eight feet off, his normally clean frock coat spattered with crimson splotches that glistened in the bright moonlight. Captain Havoc was rising slowly, his fatigue shirt torn from the shoulder to the waist, a bloody survival knife in his right hand. "Is anyone hurt?" Blade called out.

Each one shook his head wearily.

The volleys came to an abrupt end, as did the blare of the bugle.

Blade turned, scanning the sky. Except for a few scattered, flitting figures heading for parts unknown, the heavens contained only stars. He rotated in a complete revolution, verifying the mutations had indeed fled. From the number of bodies piled on the ground, he estimated very few had managed to escape.

"Blade! Thank God we got here in time!"

The Warrior climbed out of the bowl as Kilrane rode up and dismounted. "Am I glad to see you."

"We came as fast as we could," the Cavalry leader stated. "A big bunch of those monsters tried to stop us. Took eight volleys to drive them off.''

"How many more men have you lost?'' Blade inquired. He gazed at the mounted Cavalrymen.

"Not one,'' Kilrane said, and beamed. "Only a dummy makes the same mistake twice. Once I knew how many of those things there were, once they lost the element of surprise, it was all over but the shooting.'' He scrutinized the Force members. "I see you came through it in one piece.''

"More or less,'' Blade responded. Suddenly he felt very, very tired. He began wiping the Bowies on his pants legs.

Kilrane swung toward the escarpment. "Is that where they came from?''

"Yeah.''

"There might be some left in there.''

"Could be,'' Blade agreed. "Give me five minutes and we'll go on in.''

"It'd be smarter to wait for daylight,'' Kilrane noted.

"Are you forgetting Raphaela, Jag, and your men?''

"I said it'd be smarter. I didn't say it would be the wisest course of action.'' Kilrane peered at the caves. "We'll be ready to go in when you are.''

Blade suddenly had a thought. He tensed and surveyed the sky carefully. "Did you see any sign of a bat-man my size?''

"As big as you? No. I don't remember one your size. But there were so many,'' Kilrane said. "Why?''

"It was the leader.''

"Well, if it's still alive the thing won't be for long. I'm sending riders to Rapid City at daybreak. In two days I'll have three hundred men here. We'll scour every square inch of this Dead Zone, turn over every rock, look behind every clump of dirt, until the last of these bastards has bit the dust. I'm going to make damn sure the Dakota Territory is a safe place to live, to have a family, rear kids, or do anything else without fear of the dark.''

"While you're at it, you should check out every Dead Zone within your borders,'' Blade suggested.

"Maybe I will,'' Kilrane said.

Blade replaced the knives in their sheaths. He reminded himself to clean the sheaths too at the earliest opportunity. "Our first priority is to find our missing people."

"It looks like we've found yours."

"What?" Blade responded, glancing at his friend.

Kilrane nodded at the cliffs. "That guy can really move, can't he?"

The Warrior turned and spied the slim form speeding in their direction, running swifter than any human could ever hope to do even when burdened with someone in his arms. "He can do over fifty miles an hour at times."

"I believe it."

Blade went out to meet them. Behind him came a shout of joy from the Clansman.

"Hey, guys! It's Red and Fur Face!"

The Warrior looked back to see Lobo, Havoc, Sparrow, and Doc clambering from the bowl. He continued running another 20 yards, then halted and placed his hands on his hips. Seconds later the rest of the team pounded up beside him.

"I thought we'd lost her," Captain Havoc commented.

"Both of them," Sparrow said.

"I never figured I'd be happy to see that mutant's hairy puss," Lobo mentioned.

Doc hooked his thumbs in his gun belt and said nothing.

The hybrid and the Molewoman approached to within 15 feet. Raphaela gave a squeal of delight as Jaguarundi stopped and lowered her to the ground.

"Yo, babe!" Lobo declared happily. "Where have you been keepin' yourself?"

"You big dummies!" Raphaela exclaimed. She ran to the giant and gave him a hug, then went to each of the others and did the same.

Blade noticed that she hugged Havoc last, and she seemed to linger in the embrace longer than she had with any of them. Blade glanced at Jag. "We were wondering what happened to you."

"They nabbed me," the hybrid said, walking forward. "Threw me in a pit with Raphaela and other prisoners. One of them was Gary Norman."

"Was?" Blade repeated.

"Yeah. Past tense."

The Warrior gazed at the escarpment. "Where are the prisoners?"

"Still in the pit," Jag replied. "Raphaela and I were lucky to get out as it was." He stared over the Warrior's right shoulder.

Blade twisted and found Kilrane joining them.

"You'll be interested in this next news," Jag informed the Cavalry leader.

"What's that?" Kilrane asked.

The hybrid indicated the cliff with a jerk of his left thumb. "There's a vast cavern inside there. It's incredibly huge. There's a whole series of caves leading to the outside. And when we were working our way out of there, we also discovered a series of pits. We came across nine, but there could be more. Anyway, we were surprised to find a lot of your men had been captured and thrown into those pits."

Kilrane took a stride, his features a study in intensity. "How many did you see?"

Jag glanced at the Molewoman. "How many did you count?"

"Twenty-six," Raphaela said, and looked at the Warrior. "We also found Martha Valesh in one of the pits with three Cavalrymen. She was a little worse for wear, but unharmed."

"My men are alive!" Kilrane stated passionately. "We'll go haul them out of those pits right away." He wheeled and hastened toward the detachment.

"I can't believe we came out of this in one piece," Captain Havoc remarked, his eyes on Raphaela.

"The Everywhere Spirit smiled on us," Sparrow observed.

"We were just plain lucky, Chief," Lobo said. "We came

close to buyin' the farm and you know it.''

"All's well that ends well," Blade commented, starting to turn. His gaze alighted on Raphaela and he saw her head snap up and her eyes widen in alarm. He heard a strange whistling sound and something slammed into him between his shoulder blades, knocking him forward, causing him to lose his balance and begin to fall. But before he could pitch onto his face, even as Rapahela screamed and Doc Madsen tried to bring his Magnum into play, steely hands gripped him from behind, under the arms, and lifted him into the night sky.

CHAPTER EIGHTEEN

A beastly growl sounded in the Warrior's right ear.

Stunned by the blow, Blade hung limply in his captor's arms, while the earth receded rapidly below them. Enough sentience remained to enable him to comprehend what had happened and to determine the identity of the creature holding him.

The leader of the bat-men was getting revenge.

Blade realized the mutation must have dived from a great altitude after lurking high in the clouds until the right moment presented itself. He had no doubt as to the bat-man's intention. The thing would carry him aloft and let go. It would be as simple as that.

The rhythmic beating of the creature's wings and heavy, raspy breathing attested to its exertion. The air grew cooler as the bat-man climbed steadily.

Blade's faculties returned to normal. Invigorated by the chill, he stared at the ground, at the diminishing figures of his friends, and racked his brains for a way to extricate himself alive. At any moment the bat-man could release him. He had to do something—anything—and do it quickly or his wife and son would never lay eyes on him again.

But what could he do?

Already they were 150 feet up and sweeping higher. He had to fight back, even though he ran the risk of falling to his death. His arms were dangling at his sides. Slowly, exercising the utmost caution, he inched his right arm upward. Once his elbow brushed the furry chest behind him and he froze, anticipating a violent reaction.

Nothing happened.

Blade eased his hand over the sheath to his right Bowie and grasped the hilt. Now came the hard part. How could he draw the knife without alerting the mutation? His forearm would need to lift almost to his shoulder and the creature was bound to notice.

Suddenly, unexpectedly, the bat-man broke into a fit of rough coughing. Its entire body shook and its grip slackened somewhat.

Blade knew the thing was suffering from the stab wound he'd administered. By all rights it should be dead. Only a being endowed with extrordinary vitality and stamina could survive a Bowie knife in the chest. Even so, he guessed the creature was bleeding internally, which explained the coughing. He took advantage of the fit to slip the blade free and lower his arm again.

Now he was ready.

The bat-man's hacking subsided and it seemed to gain strength.

Blade couldn't wait any longer. Every second of delay meant another foot gained in altitude. He was hanging with the back of his head pressed against the mutation's sternum, and he took a moment to mentally calculate the proper angle before he whipped his right arm up and back and rammed the Bowie into the creature's rib cage. The blade struck bone, glanced off, and sank all the way in.

A protracted gasp issued from the bat-man as its body stiffened and its wings ceased beating.

For a heart-stopping moment they hung motionless in the air. Blade gazed at the murky stretch of landscape below and gulped, thinking of how he would be smashed to a pulp if they dropped.

They did.

The mutation hissed and plummeted like a boulder, its fingers slipping from under the Warrior's arms.

Blade's mind raced. His only hope of survival lay in forcing the bat-man to break their fall, provided the thing still lived, and to do so he had to stay next to the creature. With that as his goal, he spun and reached out, locking his arms around the mutation's legs. They gained momentum, the wind rushing by their heads.

The bat-man kicked its legs feebly, attempting to dislodge the Warrior.

Blade held on, peering downward in consternation. If the leader wouldn't use its wings, he was finished. He had to goad the thing into flying, to provoke it, to get its adrenaline flowing. And the best catalyst for creating a surge of adrenaline was sheer, undiluted rage. He balled his left fist, drew his arm back, and slugged the mutation in the stomach.

Suddenly the creature came alive, snarling and thrashing, its wings flapping feebly.

Still they continued to pick up speed. The rush of cold air brought tears to Blade's eyes. He blotted the image of crashing into the earth from his mind and punched the bat-man again.

The mutation bucked and clawed at the Warrior's head and shoulders. Its leathery wings flapped harder, but they weren't beating fast enough to act as a brake on their descent.

Flap, damn you! Blade thought, and delivered two more blows, holding back, though, afraid he would render his adversary unconscious if he employed all of his strength.

Apparently he'd used just enough.

Growling and wrenching from side to side, the bat-man went into a paroxysm of fury in a supreme effort to tear itself loose from the Warrior. And the harder it struggled, the harder its wings beat.

Blade felt them begin to slow down, felt those powerful wings begin to arrest their fall, but the effort seemed to be too little, too late. They were dropping too fast. Less than 50 feet remained. In a final act of desperation he turned his face to the creature's right leg and bit, tearing his teeth into the fur and the flesh.

The mutation became insane, kicking and kicking and digging its talons into the Warrior while its wings beat like those of the mammal it resembled.

They slowed even more.

Not enough! Blade realized. He had mere seconds in which to save his life, and he reached overhead, dug his fingers into the creature's skin, and pulled himself higher, drawing up his legs at the same time.

The bat-man, oblivious to the peril, pummeled the Warrior savagely.

They were going to hit! Blade shoved against the creature's chest with all of his might and succeeded in swinging the mutation under him as a makeshift cushion.

None too soon.

With a pronounced thud they plowed into the ground, raising a cloud of dust from the concussion.

The sensations were almost too swift for Blade to register. He felt the shock of the abrupt stop, as if he had run into a brick wall at full speed, and a sticky liquid spattered all over his face. His hands sank into a pulpy substance. And a millisecond later everything blanked out.

Someone was whistling.

Blade opened his eyes and instinctively attempted to sit up. A wave of vertigo washed over him and he groaned, sagging onto his elbows, feeling confused and weak.

"Whoa there, mister! Don't be rash!"

Blinking his eyes, squinting in the bright light streaming

in a nearby window, Blade swallowed and looked around.

An elderly man attired in an old brown suit, the jacket open and revealing a considerable paunch, came over to the cot on which the Warrior reclined. "You're not going anywhere so settle back down."

"Who are you?" Blade croaked, his lips and throat both parched. His face felt slightly swollen.

"I'm Doctor Mills. I've been tending you for the past two days."

"Two days!" Blade exclaimed, and the exertion produced pain in his temples. He inadvertently winced.

"I'll explain everything," Dr. Mills said. "But first I must make it clear that you're not to get excited in the least. You must take it easy. Don't strain. Your system sustained a massive shock."

Blade nodded his understanding.

"You've been on this cot, under my care, ever since Armitage brought you in. I don't mind telling you it was nip and tuck for a while. You were fortunate to pull through," Dr. Mills stated, and regarded the giant appreciatively. "You must have the constitution of an ox."

"Where am I?" Blade asked.

"In my office in Rapid City."

"Rapid City!"

"There you go again," Dr. Mills admonished sternly. "I warned you to stay calm. If you don't cooperate, you run the risk of a relapse."

"I was that bad?"

The physician nodded grimly. "They told me that you fell something like one hundred and fifty feet. From what I've gathered, you would have died if that thing you were fighting hadn't absorbed the brunt of the impact."

"I nearly died," Blade said softly, the reality staggering him. He'd survived so many battles in recent years, come through dozens of conflicts with only a few scratches, that he'd begun to discount the possibility of his own death. Now, thinking of Jenny and Gabe, he shuddered. "You say Armitage brought me to Rapid City?" he commented absently to change the train of his thought.

"Yes. Kilrane would have come himself, but he's been busy exterminating those vile creatures responsible for slaying so many of our people. A rider was sent to Pierre for reinforcements at the same time they brought you in. Boone and the rest of Kilrane's personal guard should arrive at any minute."

"I'd like to see Boone again," Blade said, gazing at the spartan accommodations in the office. "Where's my unit?"

"They came into town with Armitage. Apparently they wouldn't leave your side no matter what. They hovered over you like mother hens when you were carried inside, and I had to chase them out to get any privacy to work," Dr. Mills related, grinning wryly. "I wouldn't permit them to remain in here and be underfoot, so they camped out in my anteroom. Except to grab a bite to eat, they haven't left. And I donn't mind telling you it's scared off a few of my regular patients."

"I don't understand."

"The threat of violence, I mean, No one wants to visit my office when there's a chance they might be caught in a cross fire. One of your men is Doc Madsen, I believe."

"He's a good man," Blade said.

"As well he may be," Dr. Mills commented. "But everyone in the Dakota Territory knows about his reputation as a gunfighter. And three men, three disreputable gentlemen named Kiernan, Millnick, and Lockaby, have been frequenting the vicinity of my office waiting for Madsen to show his face outside. They've publicly called him out."

"And Doc hasn't gone out to face them?"

"Not yet. Everyone in Rapid City is wondering why. He's the talk of the town, right up there with those bat-things. Some folks are claiming Madsen has lost his nerve, but that's ridiculous. The man is braver than most ten people put together.''

Blade shifted and stared at a closed door on the wall opposite the bed. "I'm surprised he hasn't gunned them down by now."

The physician leaned forward conspiratorially. "Just between you and me, I suspect he's been waiting for you to come around. Yesterday I heard your Captain Havoc and Madsen arguing quite loudly. Evidently the captain informed Madsen he couldn't go out to confront those three under any circumstances, that Madsen is part of the Force and has an image to uphold."

"And how did Doc react?"

"He sort of snickered, which ticked off your captain no end. Madsen told Havoc he'd tend to those vermin, to use his own words, when the time was right. Do you have any idea what he meant?"

"Maybe," Blade said. "I'd like to see them now."

"I don't know," Dr. Mills remarked. "You sustained a concussion. Strict rest is called for."

"Now, Doctor," Blade stressed gently.

Mills expelled his breath. "Very well," he stated in a huff. "But I won't be held accountable if you have a relapse." He pivoted and walked toward the door. "I must say that you Force types certainy are—forceful."

Blade smiled and watched the physician open the door and step into a smaller room beyond. A distinctly female shout of pure joy precipitated a rush into the office with Raphaela in the lead.

"Blade! You're back in the land of the living!" the Molewoman declared ecstatically as she came over to the side of the bed.

"You didn't think you'd get out of your daily calisthenics that easily, did you?" Blade quipped, noting the concern on all of their faces. Genuinely touched, he coughed to clear an obstruction in his throat.

"I will give thanks to the Everywhere Spirit for your

deliverance,'' Sparrow Hawk said.

"You celebrate your way, I'll celebrate mine, dude,'' Lobo stated.

"How will you celebrate?'' Sparrow inquired.

"I'll find me a fox and show her why I've got such a heavy rep as a lean, mean lovin' machine.''

Captain Havoc stepped forward and smiled at the Warrior. "It's great you've recovered, sir. I've held off sending a message to General Gallagher until we knew one way or the other. I didn't want word to prematurely get back to your family.''

"Thanks, Captain,'' Blade said, and looked toward the doorway. Doc Madsen stood to the left of the door, his thumbs hooked in his gun belt as usual, his wide brimmed hat low over his eyes. "Doc.''

The gunfighter simply nodded.

"Thanks for waiting,'' Blade mentioned.

"The least I could do.''

"You can take care of it now if you want.''

"Thanks,'' Doc said, and turned toward the anteroom.

"Wait a minute, sir,'' Captain Havoc interjected. "Do you know what he's going to do?''

"Yes,'' Blade said.

"And you're going to let him?''

"I have no right to stop him.''

"How can you say that? You're in charge of this unit. If you let him go outside, he'll either get himself killed or add to his tally as a gunman. How can you allow that to happen?''

Blade sighed. "I'm allowing him to be a man.''

"Sir?''

"Think about it,'' Blade directed, and glanced at the gunfighter. "Get going.''

Doc nodded and departed.

"I'll go with him,'' Lobo offered. He took several paces toward the door.

"No,'' Blade stated.

The Clansman halted and cast a peeved expression at the Warrior. "You can't let him go up against those three chumps alone. Aren't you the one who's always tellin' us we're a team? We should back his play."

"No one leaves this room."

"But he might need our help," Raphaela noted.

"No."

"I could cover him from the roof," Sparrow suggested.

"No."

Captain Havoc pointed at the window. "We can see the street from here. I could provide cover fire if he needs it."

"No."

Lobo slapped his right hand against his thigh in frustration. "Boy, you can be a prime hard-ass when you want to. Anybody ever tell you that?"

"Practically everyone," Blade acknowledged.

"So we just stand here and do nothing?" Lobo snapped.

"That's the general idea."

"Damn if I will." Lobo marched to the window and leaned on the waist-high sill. "At least I'll watch what goes down." He looked over his right shoulder. "What about the rest of you?"

Raphaela shook her head. "I don't think I can watch. What if he loses?"

"Sparrow? Mike?" Lobo asked.

Neither man moved.

"What a bunch of wimps," Lobo muttered, and gazed through the glass pane. "Hey! I can see those three scuzzies across the street They're standin' next to a hitchin' post, just talkin'." He suddenly straightened. "And there goes Doc out to meet them."

Sparrow Hawk stepped to the window.

"They've seen him!" Lobo continued, his tone tinged with excitement.

"What are they doing?" Raphaela inquired anxiously.

"They're lookin' at him like they can't believe their eyes.

Now they're spreadin' out," Lobo detailed. "Doc is still walkin' toward them. He's about twenty feet away. Fifteen. Now he's stopped and he's movin' the flap of his coat aside."

"And? And?" Raphaela prompted.

"They're talkin'. That bastard called Kiernan must be bad-mouthin' Doc," Lobo said, and laughed lightly. "You should see all the people in the street. They're haulin' ass to get out of the line of fire. There's a broad draggin' her kid by the arm." He chuckled.

"What about Doc?" Raphaela asked, taking a tentative pace nearer the window.

"He's just standin' there listening to Kiernan flap his gums. Those other two, Millnick and Lockaby, are ready to draw if Doc so much as bats an eye."

"We should help him," Raphaela said.

"Too late for that," Lobo stated. "Kiernan must be callin' Doc every dirty name in the book. I don't think Doc has spoken one word, but I can't really tell because I can only see him from the side." He paused. "Wait a minute. Doc just said something. Just three words, I think. Kiernan is madder than hell. His face is as red as a whore's lips. It won't be—"

They all heard the blasting of the three shots, *bam-bam-bam*, sounding almost as one.

For five seconds no one uttered a word.

Finally Lobo swung away from the window, amazement etching his visage. He took a few strides and shook his head in disbelief.

"What about Doc?" Raphaela practically shouted.

"Doc? He's fine," Lobo said softly. His eyes strayed to the Warrior. "I didn't see his hand move," he whispered in awe.

"What?" Raphaela asked. "What did you say?"

"I never saw the dude's hand move," Lobo related emphatically. "I mean, one moment his hand was hanging by his holster, and the next those lowlifes were lying in the street with holes in their foreheads.'' He glanced at the Mole-woman. ''Would you do me a favor?''

''Sure,'' Raphela replied. ''Anything. What do you need?''

''The next time I start to make fun of Doc, remind me to have my head examined.''

EPILOGUE

There was no excuse for putting it off any longer than necessary.

The Force had been back from the Dakota Territory for almost a week. In an hour he'd be leaving for two and a half weeks at the Home, precious time he could spend with those he loved most in all the world, his darling wife and precocious son. The army doctors had given him a clean bill of health and marveled at his recuperative powers. Just to play it safe, he decided to let himself be checked by the Family Healers.

When he returned to California he'd need to be in perfect condition if he intended to embark on his personal quest.

But what choice did he have?

Blade sat in his chair behind the desk in his office and gazed thoughtfully at the stack of paperwork in front of him. That would all have to wait. The training would have to wait. Even missions, unless they were extremely critical, would have to wait. It was bad enough he would be spending two and a half weeks at the Home before launching his investigation.

Still, a year had already elapsed.

What difference could two and a half more weeks make?

He stood and walked outdoors. If his deduction proved

to be correct, there would be hell to pay. There could be no justification for such a deception, not when it had caused such profound sorrow. Someone would be held accountable. He guaranteed it.

Blade halted and stretched, enjoying the warmth of the sun on his body. He wondered if, perhaps, he should leave well enough alone, if he should let the matter drop.

No.

He had to discover the truth, no matter what the cost.

The thought made the Warrior smile.

Lobo wasn't the only one who should have his head examined.

 **DAVID ROBBINS**

A $7.00 VALUE FOR ONLY $4.50!

Pirate Strike. Thriving in the waters off the Pacific coast are vicious buccaneers more barbarous and savage than the pirates of legend. And the sea wolves will continue to rule the waves—unless Blade and the Force can drive them to a watery grave.

And in the same action-packed volume....

Crusher Strike. From the human cesspool called Shantytown, Crusher Payne and the most ruthless degenerates alive lead an attack to annihilate the civilized zones. And they'll succeed unless Blade can single-handedly penetrate Crusher's operation and wipe Shantytown off the face of the planet.

__3371-2 $4.50

L.A. Strike. When Los Angeles falls victim to an incursion of mindless savages, it is up to the Force to lift the siege. Matching violence with superviolence and death with megadeath, Blade and his comrades blow into the City of Angels like devils out of hell.

And in the same red-hot volume....

Dead Zone Strike. When deadly mutants start terrorizing the Dakota Territory, Blade and the Force track them to the heart of the Dead Zone. There the Force must destroy the marauders—or die in the infernal depths that have spawned them.

__3446-8 $4.50

LEISURE BOOKS
ATTN: Order Department
276 5th Avenue, New York, NY 10001

Please add $1.50 for shipping and handling for the first book and $.35 for each book thereafter. PA., N.Y.S. and N.Y.C. residents, please add appropriate sales tax. No cash, stamps, or C.O.D.s. All orders shipped within 6 weeks via postal service book rate. Canadian orders require $2.00 extra postage and must be paid in U.S. dollars through a U.S. banking facility.

Name _____

Address _____

City _____ State _____ Zip _____

I have enclosed $_____in payment for the checked book(s). Payment <u>must</u> accompany all orders.☐ Please send a free catalog.

SPEND YOUR LEISURE MOMENTS WITH US.

Hundreds of exciting titles to choose from—something for everyone's taste in fine books: breathtaking historical romance, chilling horror, spine-tingling suspense, taut medical thrillers, involving mysteries, action-packed men's adventure and wild Westerns.

SEND FOR A FREE CATALOGUE TODAY!